Sam's Pro.

This Thanksgiving comes with all the fixings...and something extra hot.

Sam Jennings promised his father he'd always take care of the woman who yanked him and his four brothers out of foster care. When his adoptive mom has a near-fatal heart attack, Sam knows it's past time to live up to his word.

As he sets out to put the Blackwater Diner back on its feet, he runs into his first snag. Waitress Julie Rose's sweet curves and long legs are driving Sam to distraction. Even his brothers aren't immune to her kind heart. But Sam is determined to be the only man in her bed.

Julie doesn't regret the years she lost caring for her grandmom, but now, between business classes and her job, she's left with very little time and energy for dating. Then there's her policy about never getting mixed up with the boss's son. But Sam's hard body and wicked ideas have Julie forgetting all about annoying things like rules, and she accepts his invitation to show her all she's been missing.

Sam is more than willing to take things slow as he teaches her all about the pleasures of the flesh. Luckily for him, Julie is a darned good student...

Warning: Contains explicit language, a sexy carpenter, and extra helpings of naughty fun under the stars. Heat and increased heart rate may help burn off extra holiday calories.

Vance's Rules

His tools, his rules...

Looking at Vance Jennings now, no one would guess that the tough-as-nails building contractor once suffered a broken heart. Twelve years has blunted the pain of the breakup with his high school sweetheart, but not the memory. Until she shows up on his doorstep asking for a second chance.

One look at the sexy redhead, and Vance adds a foot or two to his rock-solid emotional barriers. No way is he letting her back into his life. But he'll be happy to let her close enough to sample her delectable body.

Shayla Riggs is no longer the vulnerable teenager who was forced to give up her first and only love. She's older, wiser, and determined to make things right. Except the changes in Vance throw her for a loop. He's definitely not the sweet boy she remembers. In fact, the grown-up version lights her up hotter than a firecracker.

It takes only a kiss, a caress, to bring back the explosive passion they once shared. But if Shayla can't find a way to break through the bitter walls around his heart, it just might destroy them both. Again.

Warning: This story contains a stubborn woman intent on seduction and an alpha male with some naughty ideas of payback. Let the fireworks begin!

Breaking Brodix

She wants to get all up in his business? She'll have to get real personal.

Brodix Jennings has a head for business, but his skills are put to the test when his brothers call on him to bring the family restaurant back into the black. With the grand reopening only days away, it'll damn near take a miracle to keep the doors from closing for good.

Reporter Sarah Greer knows exactly what Brodix needs—free publicity on the front page of the town's only newspaper. All she wants in exchange is the Jennings brothers' rags-to-riches story. Except none of them are talking. And Brodix, who cuts a blazing path through her body with just a smile, is the most tight-lipped of the lot.

Brodix wouldn't think twice about seducing prissy, buttoned-up Sarah into his bed, if her lousy profession didn't leave him cold to the bone. A second look at the bar's books, though, makes him think twice about saying no. But if he's going to open the floodgates, it'll be on *his* terms.

When Brodix asks her out, Sarah agrees, confident she can keep personal at arm's length from professional. Until physical attraction melts their emotional barriers...and Sarah gets way more than she bargained for.

Warning: Expect an annoying ex-husband, a slightly pushy reporter, a fiercely protective hero, and some meddling family members. Of course there's also a whole lot of naughty sex, and in numerous positions too. Possible overheating of various electronic devices could occur.

Look for these titles by
Anne Rainey

Now Available:

Haley's Cabin
Burn
Turbulent Passions
A Little Bit Naughty
Rider's Kiss

Vaughn
Touching Lace
Tasting Candy
Taking Chloe
Tempting Grace

Cape May
What She Wants
What She Craves
What She Needs

Blackwater
Sam's Promise
Vance's Rules
Breaking Brodix
Reilly's Wildcard
River's Redemption

Man-Maid
No Turning Back
No Letting Go
No Regrets

Print Anthologies
Seduce Me
Dare Me
Tahoe Nights
Desired

Hard to Handle, Volume 1

Anne Rainey

SAMHAIN
PUBLISHING

Samhain Publishing, Ltd.
11821 Mason Montgomery Road, 4B
Cincinnati, OH 45249
www.samhainpublishing.com

Hard to Handle, Volume 1
Print ISBN: 978-1-61922-336-3
Sam's Promise Copyright © 2015 by Anne Rainey
Vance's Rules Copyright © 2015 by Anne Rainey
Breaking Brodix Copyright © 2015 by Anne Rainey

Editing by Linda Ingmanson
Cover by Angela Waters

This book is a work of fiction. The names, characters, places, and incidents are products of the writer's imagination or have been used fictitiously and are not to be construed as real. Any resemblance to persons, living or dead, actual events, locale or organizations is entirely coincidental.

All Rights Are Reserved. No part of this book may be used or reproduced in any manner whatsoever without written permission, except in the case of brief quotations embodied in critical articles and reviews.

Sam's Promise, ISBN 978-1-60928-778-8
First Samhain Publishing, Ltd. electronic publication: December 2011
Vance's Rules, ISBN 978-1-61921-089-9
First Samhain Publishing, Ltd. electronic publication: May 2012
Breaking Brodix, ISBN 978-1-61921-186-5
First Samhain Publishing, Ltd. electronic publication: July 2012
First Samhain Publishing, Ltd. print publication: January 2015

Contents

Sam's Promise
~11~

Vance's Rules
~103~

Breaking Brodix
~199~

Sam's Promise

Dedication

For my mom and dad.
This last year is proof that with a bit of courage and a lot of love anything is possible.
I'm proud to be your daughter!

Chapter One

Sam rolled his eyes. "You better be on your way, damn it. You promised Mom." As he shut off the engine, Sam stared out the driver's side window at the large, two-story brick house. It'd been the first real home he and his four brothers had ever known. Guilt washed over him as he realized how long it'd been since his last visit. Nearly a month. Nice.

"Christ, relax," Brodix muttered on the other end of the cell phone. "I'm on my way. Besides, have I ever missed Thanksgiving?"

His brother was right. Shit. "Sorry for snapping. I'm sort of on edge is all."

There was silence on the other end of the line. "Because of Mom's phone call?" Brodix finally asked.

Sam started to get out of his SUV, but Brodix's words stopped him. "She called you too?"

Brodix sighed. "Yeah. Sounds like there might be trouble in paradise, huh?"

"The Blackwater Diner has always done a good business, but Mom sounded worried. If she's worried, then I'm worried," Sam said. "I wonder if she called the others."

"I haven't talked to them about it, but I imagine she did." He paused, then added, "She told me the restaurant is our legacy, Sam. That Dad wanted it to stay in the family. She sounded heartbroken, like she'd let him down or something."

Sam didn't want to think of their mother as anything other than happy. She'd been his guardian angel since the first day he'd met her. She'd walked into the social worker's office and smiled at him as if he were someone worthy. Someone other than the nobody he'd been. Someone other than a kid who'd never even known his father and had a drug addict for a mother. And like any belligerent twelve-year-old boy who'd been dragged through the system kicking and screaming, Sam had cursed at her. He'd known what would come, and he'd braced himself, waiting for the slap, or worse. Wanda had only patted him on the back. The kind gesture had sucked all the anger right out of him. It hadn't taken him long to know she was different from all the rest. She was special.

"I'm going to get some answers after dinner." Sam stepped out and headed toward the front porch. "Since I'm the one with the most job flexibility around here, I plan to go over to the restaurant tomorrow and check out the books, and I'm not leaving until things are back on track." One of the perks to being an all-around handyman/carpenter was that he could set his own hours. "Which is part of why I'm calling. Between you and me, you're the one with the head for business, so maybe you can give me a hand."

"I can stay for a few days, but my condo is a two-hour drive, and I can't exactly take an impromptu extended leave from work."

"Do you have any vacation time coming?"

Brodix went silent, and Sam let a grin slip. While most people had to look at their calendar to see what was on their agenda for the following day, Brodix could figure out within seconds what the next four weeks looked like, right down to the hour, simply by concentrating.

"Yeah," his brainiac brother finally replied. "Actually I could probably take a few weeks off."

"Let's wait and see what's going on before we make any plans. It might not be necessary." Even as he said it, Sam knew he was lying to them both. When he'd called his mom to confirm the time for dinner, she'd seemed stressed, and Sam's gut had been bothering him ever since.

"Whatever it takes, man."

"Good. Now get your ass here."

"God, you're worse than an old woman. I'm less than fifteen minutes out. Chill."

Sam heard the distinctive sound of a diesel engine from behind. He turned in time to see Vance pulling into the driveway in his black pickup truck. Behind him was a new, shiny, silver BMW. "Vance just arrived. River and Reilly are right behind him."

He heard Brodix curse. "Great. I'm the last one. Why am I always the last one?"

Sam laughed. "Because you suck more than the rest of us."

"Thanks for clearing that up, bro."

"That's what big brothers are for." Brodix offered up a few anatomically impossible ideas, then hung up. Sam shoved his cell back into the holster on his belt and watched as his brothers parked and got out. One by one, they made their way toward him. Sam hadn't seen them since early summer. They'd all been busy. Too damn busy to visit? He grimaced when he thought of what his father would've said about that were he still alive. *Family*, his father had always said, *is all that really matters in this world.* Sam gave in to the instinct to look each of them over now. He needed to see for himself they were well.

Vance looked good, bigger and meaner than ever, but good all the same. As usual, he wore black work boots, a pair of faded jeans and the brown leather coat their mom had gotten him four or five Christmases ago. Hell, he looked more muscular, if it were at all possible. Owning his own construction company suited him, apparently. Reilly and River were mirror images of each other with their pale green eyes, shaggy black hair and lean six-foot-four build. The only difference between the twins was River's constant scowl. Sam's gut clenched. He could count on one hand the amount of times his youngest brother had cracked a smile in the last decade.

"Brodix is on his way," Sam said by way of greeting.

Vance snorted. "Late, what else is new."

Sam laughed. "In his defense, he does live farther away than the rest of us."

Reilly smiled and held up a bag. "Picked up some fresh bread from that bakery on Fifth. River's been salivating the entire way here."

River glared at his twin and slammed a fist into his shoulder. "I still don't see why I couldn't have a piece, damn it."

Reilly rolled his eyes. "Mom would've skinned us both, and you know it."

Sam shook his head. "You're a bottomless pit, River."

"Are you boys going to stand out here in the cold all day or what?"

The soft, feminine voice had them all turning. Their mom stood in the doorway with a dish towel in one hand and a wide smile curving her lips. She looked flushed, Sam thought, and her normally neat-as-a-pin gray hair was messy, as if she'd been running her fingers through it. Sam's worries went up another notch. None of them spoke as they closed the distance. She ushered them in and quickly shut the door behind them. "You boys always could stand the cold easier than me."

"That's because our hides are tougher than yours," Vance said as he leaned down for a hug.

Sam unzipped his black Carhartt and tossed it over a chair. "Happy Thanksgiving, Mom," he said when she wrapped her arms around his shoulders. Her rounded figure and the scent of honeysuckle always gave him a feeling of peace. Of home.

"Happy Thanksgiving, Sammy."

"Brodix is on his way." Sam answered the unspoken question in his mother's blue eyes as he stepped back to let Reilly and River have their turn. "Should be here any minute."

"I'm here."

Sam turned. Brodix stood in the doorway, wearing a dark gray wool coat and carrying a glass pie pan.

"If that's your pumpkin pie, I just might kiss you, Brodix," River said as he crossed the room to take the dish.

Brodix unbuttoned his coat. "It makes absolutely no logical sense how you stay so lean, River."

"Leave your brother alone and give your mom a hug."

Brodix chuckled and opened his arms. "Yes, ma'am." Sam watched on as their mom stepped into his brother's embrace. The only thing missing was their dad. It would be their second

Sam's Promise

Thanksgiving without him. Pain hit Sam square in the chest when he thought of how much he missed the man who'd raised him. By example, Chet Jennings had shown them how to be men worthy of respect. Sam still missed hearing his booming voice and feeling his rib-crushing bear hugs. He looked over at his brothers and saw the same unhappy expressions.

"I know what you're all thinking, and you might as well stop it right now," their mom chastised. "We always had laughter and love filling this house when your father was alive. Do you think he'd want that to change just because the good Lord chose to bring him home?" As one they all shook their heads, and she smiled. "Good, then. Let's get this dinner on the table so you boys can fill me in on what you've been up to."

Vance laughed. "You just want to know if any of us have found our *one true love* yet."

She tsked. "Well, I'm not getting any younger, and I'd like to have grandkids while I'm still able to feed myself."

"Speaking of age," Sam said as he noticed his mother perspiring. "It might be time to think about slowing down a little, Mom."

Her brows drew together. "You mean retiring, don't you?"

Sam started to answer, but the doorbell rang. He frowned. "Are you expecting anyone else, Mom?" Their Thanksgiving dinners had always been for immediate family only. It'd been that way since Sam could remember, and he wasn't real fond of change.

His mom's eyes lit up, and she turned and headed for the door. "I nearly forgot Julie!"

"Julie?" River asked as he looked over at Reilly. "Is that the waitress you were telling me about the other day? The one from the restaurant?"

Julie? Sam mouthed as he looked over at his brothers. They all shrugged and stared at the door as if equally curious. Sam watched and waited. Considering they'd never asked an outsider to Thanksgiving dinner before, he figured Julie must be pretty special or his mom never would've extended an invitation to their private gathering.

17

As she pulled the door open, Sam got his first look at the mysterious woman. Long, dark hair was about all he could make out. There was a hell of a lot of it. The big blue tote she carried blocked part of his view, and the heavy black parka covered everything else. "Julie, dear, I'm so glad you could make it."

"I'm sorry I'm late, Wanda" she said, a little breathless. "I would've been here sooner, but I had to make a second batch of sweet potatoes. The first batch burned. I'm afraid I got a bit distracted studying."

"No, no, you're right on time," his mom said as she took the bag out of the woman's hands. "The boys just arrived, and the turkey is just about ready to come out of the oven."

Vance stepped forward and took the bag from his mom, while Brodix helped the woman with her oversized coat. Sam was too busy staring to be of any real use. Curves. He could see them now that her coat wasn't hindering his view. She had sweet, luscious curves and a smile that kicked his heart into a sprint. She wore a tight red sweater that stretched over breasts he desperately wanted to touch. More than a mouthful, he thought. A hell of a lot more. The long black skirt wouldn't be anything overly sexy on the average woman, but on her it looked hot as hell. She had wide hips and some damn long legs. His mind went straight into the gutter as he imagined them wrapped tight around him while she rode him into oblivion.

"Julie Rose, I'd like you to meet my sons. The tallest there is Sam. He's the oldest and is sort of a jack of all trades."

Sam stayed where he was, safely several feet across the room. "Pleased to meet you, Julie."

She smiled but didn't speak as she tucked a lock of hair behind her ear. He had the crazy notion to untuck it. "And the one grinning from ear to ear there is Vance," his mom went on.

Julie's gaze went to his brother. "You're the one with the construction business?"

Vance grinned. "Yep," he said as he stepped forward and shook her hand. "Nice meeting you, Julie."

"And Brodix there," his mom pointed out, "is the executive

of the bunch."

Brodix didn't smile. He simply nudged Vance out of the way and took possession of Julie's hand. "Happy Thanksgiving, Julie," he murmured in that annoyingly charming way he had.

Julie blushed. "Thank you. Same to you." For some unknown reason, Sam had the urge to toss Brodix on his ass.

"You're quite welcome," Brodix said. "Such a pretty face is a refreshing change around here."

Sam noticed Brodix still hadn't bothered to let go of Julie's hand.

"Brodix, behave," his mother admonished as she slapped his forearm. Brodix let go and moved to the side of Julie, then glanced over at him. Sam glared at his younger sibling, willing him to back off. Brodix, the letch, only wagged his eyebrows.

"You've met Reilly, but I don't think you've met his twin River yet."

Reilly winked. "Nice to see you again, Julie."

"Hi, Reilly." She looked over at River. "Reilly's told me quite a bit about you."

River squinted at his twin before glaring at Julie. "In case he wasn't clear, I'm the sexy, smart twin."

Julie laughed, and Sam went rigid. Damn, she was gorgeous when she did that. And unless he missed his guess, his brothers thought the same thing. None of them seemed capable of speech all of a sudden.

"Modest too, I see," Julie responded, her eyes twinkling with mischief.

His normally brooding brother actually cracked a smile. "At last, a woman who gets me."

Sam noticed the way Julie bit her lip and looked down at the floor. "Okay," his mother intervened. "Now that we have the introductions out of the way, how about we get dinner on the table?"

"Thank God," River said. "I'm starved."

Everyone laughed and filed into the kitchen. Sam held back, waiting for Julie to go through the doorway first. She smiled shyly as she stepped in front of him. As he took up position behind her, his gaze inexorably went to her ass. Ah hell, he never should've looked. Sam had a thing for that particular body part on a woman, and Julie had nicely rounded globes that he eagerly wanted to reach out and squeeze. He felt a hair guilty for mentally undressing the woman, but as he glanced up and caught Brodix's gaze, he knew he wasn't the only one thinking dirty thoughts. The knowledge sent his good mood into the crapper.

Chapter Two

"So, you work at the restaurant?"

The question had come from the man seated next to her. Sam, the oldest. Oh, Julie knew all about the Jennings brothers from Wanda's many stories. Although, Julie had to admit, she hadn't expected them to be so overwhelmingly masculine. Especially Sam. For some odd reason, she was having a terrible time keeping her gaze off him. He was big and strong. Her body had immediately come to life when she'd been introduced to him. His long-sleeved black T-shirt shouldn't seem nearly so yummy, but Julie had a feeling Sam could stop traffic in just about anything he chose to wear. The dark chocolate shade of his hair had just enough length to drag her fingers through, and she had a wild urge to do exactly that.

Julie thought about his question and dreaded answering. A twenty-nine-year-old waitress who was still in college. It was downright pathetic. As she swallowed a mouthful of cranberries, she said, "Whenever my classes allow, yeah."

Sam arched a brow at her. "You're in college?"

She nodded as embarrassment swamped her. "I'm a year away from getting my BA. I...sort of started late."

"Better late than never," Vance replied, smiling down the length of the table at her. "What do you plan to do once you graduate?"

"I've been thinking of something along the lines of business management, but to be honest, I'm not sure." As she looked around the table, she noticed everyone had stopped eating. They were riveted, clearly curious about the newcomer in their midst. Julie sighed. "It's a long story, but the short version is that after high school, my grandmother fell ill with stage-four colon cancer. She was the only family I've ever known, because my parents both died in a car accident when I was two years old."

"So caring for your grandmother fell to you," Sam said.

The softly spoken words sent shivers up and down her spine. "Yeah," she replied, "and before she died, Grandmom made me promise to sell the house and use the money to get out and live my life. I think she felt guilty. As if it were somehow her fault that she'd gotten sick." She shook her head. "Anyway, after she passed away, I honored her request. Sold the old two-story I grew up in and bought a small condo. Then I enrolled in college."

"And I told her that since she didn't have a fella to spend the holidays with that she should come and spend it with my fellas." Wanda grinned, and a few of the guys laughed and shook their heads. Julie thought it adorable how the guys seemed to hang on Wanda's every word.

When Wanda stood and brought an empty dish to the sink, Julie noticed how slowly she was moving. At the restaurant, Wanda always moved with efficiency, but as she came back to the table, there was a light sheen of sweat on her forehead. Wasn't she well?

"Can I help with anything, Wanda?" Julie offered as Wanda sat back down.

"No, thank you, dear."

"Mom, are you feeling okay?" Sam asked as he watched his mother with obvious concern.

She smiled, but Julie noticed it didn't quite meet her eyes. "I'm fine, Sammy. Really."

Julie could feel the mounting worry in the room and decided to inject some levity to lighten the mood. "Uh, anyway, I think your mom might have had the idea to play matchmaker," Julie said, with no small amount of embarrassment. "But like I already told her, I'm not in the market for a relationship right now. So none of you have to worry that I'm here for anything other than the good food and company."

"I say we draw straws," River quietly replied as he winked

Sam's Promise

at her. "Short straw gets a date with the pretty brunette."

Several deep, male voices sent up energetic agreements, but there was one male who didn't say anything at all. Julie gave in to temptation and looked at Sam. Her gaze clashed with his sexy hazel eyes. He stared at her with such intensity, Julie actually began to fidget. She hadn't done that since her grandmom had caught her in the cookie jar when she was ten. As he narrowed his gaze and looked away, Julie had the distinct impression he wanted her gone. Like yesterday. It was not a comfy-cozy feeling.

Suddenly there was a loud gasp, and Julie looked to the head of the table. She noticed Wanda clutching at her chest now. Julie dropped her fork. "Wanda?"

Sam quickly leaped into action. "Mom, what is it?"

"H-heart," Wanda cried.

"Sam, she might be having a heart attack," Julie said, attempting to stay calm. "Call 911."

"I'm on it," Vance said as he pulled out his cell phone.

"Good, then can someone help me get her to the couch?"

"I've got her," Sam replied as he bent and picked Wanda up as if she weighed no more than a child and carried her to the other room. He placed her gently on top of the worn, brown plaid cushions. Wanda clenched her eyes shut. "It's going to be okay, Mom. Help is on the way."

"Is there a pillow or something? We want her head elevated or in a semi-seated position."

River appeared with a large hunter-green throw pillow. "This do?"

"Perfect," Julie said, keeping her voice soft, calming. She took it and handed it over to Sam. Once he had her propped up, she heard him murmuring to her that everything was going to be okay. Wanda responded with a shaky nod. Julie quickly leaned down and placed her cheek close to the older woman's mouth to ensure her breathing wasn't labored. Satisfied when she felt warm air, Julie started to stand. Someone cursed. Julie swiveled around and glared at the two men closest to her. River

23

and Reilly both glared right back, but she knew they got the message. They all needed to stay calm for Wanda's sake. Getting upset would only make the situation worse. She thought she heard sirens, and she looked down the length of the couch to where Brodix stood, hands fisted at his sides, looking grim.

"Can you go out front and watch for the paramedics?" she asked. He nodded and took off at a sprint, obviously grateful to have something to do. Being helpless was the worst; Julie knew that only too well.

When Wanda looked as if she wanted to sit up, Sam was there, soothing her with his big palm against her forehead. "Shh, be still now." Julie was struck by how gentle he was. As his head came up and their gazes connected, Julie saw the anguish he was clearly trying to hide from his mother. *I know CPR*, she mouthed.

Sam nodded and slowly smoothed his hand over Wanda's hair. The sirens grew louder. "They're almost here, Mom."

When two men in EMT uniforms burst through the front door, Brodix bringing up the rear, Julie stepped back and allowed them to do their job. She heard Sam explaining the situation. Within minutes, all the brothers were watching from the driveway as Wanda was loaded into the emergency vehicle. Vance ended up riding along with them. After they were on their way, sirens blaring, River, Reilly and Brodix came up to her.

"Are you okay?" River asked as Reilly placed his hand on her shoulder.

Julie frowned. "Me?"

"You're shaking, sweets," River said as he took hold of both her hands and rubbed them between his warmer ones.

She looked down, shocked to see he was right. "I didn't even notice."

Reilly patted her on the shoulder. "Come on, you can ride to the hospital with us."

"Or me," Brodix offered. "You shouldn't be driving."

"Oh, thank you all, really, but I'm fine." The twins gave her

Sam's Promise

a "yeah right" look. She smiled to reassure them. "Seriously."

"She'll come with me."

The deep, hard voice came from directly behind her, and she knew without a doubt that it belonged to the eldest of the Jennings brothers. Julie didn't have to turn around to know that, because only Sam Jennings seemed to possess the power to send shivers of awareness down her spine without even trying. Julie swiveled around, ready to give him the same answer she'd given his brothers, but stopped. The worry she saw stamped into the lines on Sam's forehead and the stiff way he held himself kept her from speaking the words aloud. Instead, she nodded.

He looked over her head. "We'll meet you there."

"Careful, Sammy," Reilly said before he took out a set of keys and strode off, River at his side.

Julie supposed Reilly was cautioning Sam about the drive to the hospital, considering Sam's emotional state, but judging by the look he'd sent her just before turning away, she had to wonder if there was something she was missing. Her mind stuttered to a halt when Sam placed his hand against her lower back and nudged. "Come on, you can grab your coat while I lock up."

Julie bit her lip and tried not to respond to the heat of his touch so close to her bottom. "I appreciate the concern, but truly I can drive."

"I know."

That was all he said before he urged her to toward the front door. Julie told herself that she was letting him have his way because he was upset. His mom had just had a heart attack, after all. Picking a fight with him at this particular moment would be unkind. Deep down, where she often feared to tread, she knew that was only part of it, though.

Something about Sam Jennings made her want to give him everything.

Anything.

She wanted to surrender to him. She wanted to please him.

25

And damn if that didn't scare the bejesus right out of her.

Sam paced the waiting room. "What the hell is taking so long?"

"Relax, damn it," Vance demanded. "You're making me nuts."

"She's in good hands, Sam. I know it's tough, but you need to be patient."

Sam turned at the feminine voice. Once again, she was the calm in the face of chaos. He admired her, but it pissed him off that he couldn't be as cool and collected. "Why are you so calm?"

Julie crossed her arms in front of her and looked down at the floor. "My grandmother had a rough go of it. I learned the hard way that panic only brought on more trouble."

Sam knew there was more to that story, but now wasn't the time to hammer her with questions that could upset her. For some inexplicable reason, the thought of Julie upset, or worse, in tears because of him, tugged at every one of his protective instincts. "That how you learned CPR?" he asked, curious about the woman who was fast becoming a fascination for him.

"Yeah. I didn't know any sort of first aid in the beginning, but after Grandmom had to be rushed to the hospital once and I felt so helpless"—she shrugged—"I don't know, I guess I knew I needed to learn a few things."

"You stayed cool and kept us from freaking," River said from the chair beside her as he patted her thigh. "I think I speak for all of us when I say you're pretty damn awesome."

Vance nodded his agreement. "I can see why Mom invited you to Thanksgiving when she's never done that before."

Julie's head shot up. "What do you mean?"

Sam stopped pacing and answered, "You're the first person to ever get an invite to the Jennings' Thanksgiving dinner."

"Oh," she said, clearly stunned by the news. "I didn't know."

"Mom always did have good taste," Reilly murmured from the other side of her.

Sam wanted to snarl at the way the twins had Julie boxed in. What was it with the two of them? They never acted territorial over a woman. When River's head came up, his sly expression said it all. Sam took a step toward him, ready to get rid of some of his pent-up frustration on his youngest brother, when the sound of his name being called stopped him.

A nurse approached. "Are you Sam Jennings?"

All of them stood. "Yes," Sam answered, steeling himself against whatever news he was about to receive. "Is my mom okay?"

The woman smiled. "She's doing just fine, Mr. Jennings. She's had a mild heart attack, but she's doing quite well. You can see her now." She looked at his four brothers, and then Julie. "Uh, it might be best to visit a couple at a time. We don't want to stress her right now."

"Of course." Sam turned to the group and said, "How about Vance and I go in first? Sound good?"

"Yeah," Brodix said, tucking his hands into the front pockets of his slacks. "Tell her..."

That Brodix, of all people, was suddenly speechless said more than anything about his emotional state. Sam clapped him on the shoulder and squeezed. "You can tell her yourself in a few minutes, bro."

He nodded, and Sam watched as Julie stepped up and patted Brodix on the shoulder. She appeared perfectly at ease around his brothers. Sam was equal amounts pleased and perturbed by that fact, considering she'd been anything but at ease around *him*. Hell, during the car ride over, she'd said all of two words to him. In fact, she appeared rather adept at completely dismissing him. Sam wasn't sure what to make of it, or her.

The nurse led them down a hallway, then went through a set of double doors that brought them to a large room with several beds. Each bed was walled off by curtains to give the patient privacy. The memories of coming through the very same room when they'd rushed his dad to the hospital after the stroke swamped Sam until he thought he'd be sick. His dad hadn't made it home. Sam was determined to see his mom sitting in the front porch swing, reading and hatching new and devious ways to marry her sons off, even if it killed him.

As they approached her section, the nurse pushed a curtain aside. "Your big, handsome sons are here to see you, Wanda."

Within seconds, Sam took in his mother's pale face. She looked tired, too tired. "Mom?"

She smiled and held out her arms for a hug. Vance moved to the other side of the bed and leaned down. Her hands shook as they came around his shoulders. "I'm going to be fine, honey. Don't look so worried."

Sam looked at the nurse for confirmation of his mother's statement. "The doctor will be in to see you soon," she replied.

Sam didn't like the fact that the nurse didn't rush to reassure him. "Is surgery required?" he asked, not bothering to dance around the issue.

"I don't want to give you false information, Mr. Jennings. I really think it would be best if we let the doctor explain your mother's condition, as well as the treatment options."

"Sammy, don't badger the girl," his mother reprimanded.

Sam smiled, despite the gravity of the situation. "Even from a hospital bed, you're scolding me." After the nurse left, Sam moved next to the bed to receive his hug. As he pulled back, he grumbled, "You scared the daylights out of us."

"I'm sorry, honey." She patted his cheek, but her hand shook a little. "I'm going to be okay, though, you'll see."

"Yeah, you will be," he confirmed. "The first step is getting you to slow down." Sam could see the pallor in her mother's cheeks, and there were dark circles under her eyes. Retirement was definitely on the horizon. When he looked over at Vance, he could tell his thoughts were running along the same lines.

"I'm with Sammy," Vance said, his voice leaving no room for argument.

Wanda laughed. "How'd I raise such bossy men? Must be your father's influence."

"Ha!" Sam exclaimed. "We all know that when push came to shove, Dad always surrendered to your stubborn will."

"It was my sweet smile that always had him melting." She paused, then said, "Speaking of sweet smiles, did Julie go home?"

"No," Vance quickly answered. "She's in the waiting room."

"She should be a nurse," Sam admitted. "Didn't lose her head one time through all this."

"Yeah," Vance agreed in a soft, faraway voice. "She's something else."

"Pretty too," Wanda said. "Don't you think, Sammy?"

Sam narrowed his eyes as comprehension dawned. "You wouldn't be trying to fix me up with her, would you?"

She shrugged. "All I did was invite her to dinner. Would you rather she spend the holiday alone with a microwaveable meal instead?"

Sam rolled his eyes at his mother's description. "A bit dramatic, don't you think?"

"I'm only speaking the truth. She has no one, Sam."

An image of Julie sitting in some dimly lit room, alone and sad, clouded his vision. He didn't like it and swiftly shoved it away. "And it didn't once enter your mind that one of us might find her sexy? That one of us might not be able to resist her pretty smiles and infectious laugh?"

"I don't care if you did invite her with the intention of fixing one of us up with her," Vance said with total sincerity. "I'm just glad you did."

He glanced over at Vance and wondered at the sideways grin he sent his way. "Because she was there to help when mom had the attack?" Sam asked, even though he was damn sure that wasn't what Vance meant.

Vance shook his head. "Because she's a yummy addition to dinner."

"Jesus, she's a person, not a slice of cake." Deep down,

Sam knew Vance had it right, though. Yummy, yeah, that described her to a T. The hell if he wanted anyone else to think of Julie in that light, though.

"Both of you need to clean up your language."

"I—" Sam never got to finish his statement because the doctor walked in. Their discussion of the delectable Julie Rose took a backseat.

Chapter Three

By the time Sam left the hospital, his mother had been moved to a private room, and she'd been sleeping soundly under River's watchful eye. It turned out surgery wasn't necessary. Medication and a heart-healthy diet was all she needed in order to get better. For that, Sam was eternally thankful.

As he walked across the hospital parking lot, a gust of cold air hit him in the face. Sam pulled his collar up around his neck to ward off the cold and noticed a few other people doing the same thing. Hell, the early morning sun didn't stand a chance at warming things up. It might be November and technically still fall, but winter sure as hell didn't feel far away. As Sam approached his SUV, his cell phone rang. He looked at the caller ID. Reilly.

He hit the answer button as he opened his car door. "Hey."

"I just dropped Julie at her car. How's Mom?"

Sam thought of Julie and Reilly alone together and wondered if she'd given his brother the same quiet, dispassionate routine she'd given him during the drive to the hospital. Somehow, he doubted it. "Mom was still sleeping when I left. River's still there. He won't leave."

Sam heard Reilly sigh. "Yeah, I figured as much."

"He's as protective as a mama bear when it comes to her. Kept giving the nurses the evil eye whenever they came in to check her vitals and write in her chart."

"She saved him that morning she walked into the social worker's office," Sam said as he recalled that day all over again. "That shithole of a foster home he was in before Mom came along still haunts River, doesn't it?"

"Yeah, it does," Reilly replied in his usual quiet way. "Mom saved all of us."

Sam would never forget the place River had been living before Wanda Jennings had taken them all in and raised them as if she'd given birth to them herself. River had had it worse than any of them. It still made Sam angry that he hadn't protected River all those years ago.

"Sam?"

Sam had to swallow several times before he could speak. "Yeah?"

"You couldn't have stopped it, you know," he said, his voice a little rougher than usual. "You were just a kid yourself."

His mind knew Reilly was right; his heart didn't much care. His youngest brother had suffered, and he hadn't been able to stop it. "What's done is done," Sam said as he got in behind the wheel. For the thousandth time, he wished they could simply bury the past. "I'm going home to get some shuteye, then I plan to head back up to see Mom in the morning."

He heard some shuffling, and then, "What time? I could meet you there."

"Actually, I think I'm going to stop off at the restaurant first. I want to check out a few things. I'll be at the hospital around ten, probably."

Reilly was quiet for a few seconds. "You think the heart attack is related to the stress of the restaurant?" he asked.

"It's a good possibility." Sam paused, and then Reilly's words registered. "Mom mentioned the Blackwater Diner troubles to you too?"

"She told me about it on Wednesday. I planned to talk to you after Thanksgiving."

He shoved the key in the ignition and cranked the heater to full blast. "I need to get an idea as to where things stand."

"You want to assess whether it's a matter of making a few changes or if it's it time to declare bankruptcy, you mean?"

Sam bit back a curse. "Yeah, something like that."

"You're not going to bring it up at the hospital, are you?"

"Of course not." He rubbed his frozen hands together as he waited for the engine to warm up. "Beyond telling her I'm going to take over until things are in the black, that is. I don't want her unnecessarily upset."

"FYI, Julie might have some information for you about the restaurant. Mom confides in her quite a bit."

Sam stopped rubbing and scowled at the mention of Julie. "She's a waitress. Why would Mom talk to her about the restaurant's finances?"

"From what I've seen, Julie has become more than a mere employee to Mom. I think they're fairly close."

The news bothered him, but he couldn't put a finger on why exactly. "As in, the daughter Mom never had but always wanted?"

"Hell, I'm not sure," Reilly replied. "Just talk to Julie. I'll meet you at the hospital."

"If you get there before me, try and make River go home. He's going to be tired as hell, if he's not already."

"I doubt he'll listen."

"I'm just glad one of us will be there round the clock to keep Mom company. You know how she is about sitting in bed when there are things to be done." A sudden image of their Thanksgiving dinner sitting cold on his mom's kitchen table shot through his mind. "Shit, I forgot about the turkey."

"Julie took care of it."

"Huh?"

"She mentioned that Mom wouldn't want to come home to see all that food ruined and the kitchen a mess, and offered to clean it up. I told her we'd take care of it, but she insisted. She's a persistent little thing."

Sam smiled. He owed Julie for everything she'd done for them. "She has a key to the house?"

"I loaned her mine. Said she'd leave it at the restaurant for me to pick up later. Speaking of the restaurant, did you know that Julie has also been opening in the mornings?"

"No, I didn't. I thought Mom took care of all that. She

always refused to hire a manager, so it didn't occur to me." Sam shoved a hand through his hair. "Is there anything Julie can't do?"

Reilly snorted. "Smart, efficient, sweet as sunshine and easy on the eyes. I can't figure why she's still unattached."

Sam's gut clenched when he thought of Julie with some faceless stranger. "She more or less said she hasn't had time to think about dating."

"For a woman like her, I'd be more than willing to work around her schedule."

Sam cursed. "What's with you guys? You'd think you'd never seen a pretty woman before. Christ."

"Jealous?" Reilly asked in his usual no-nonsense way.

"Why the hell would I be?"

Reilly chuckled. "Good question."

"I'm going home," Sam muttered. He knew damn good and well Reilly had him pegged, and it pissed him off. "See you later."

He hit the End button and tossed his phone onto the middle console. It wasn't until after he was on his way that he let himself think of Julie again. She'd been an angel. The least she deserved was a thank-you. All he'd given her so far were a bunch of frowns. Maybe he could take her out to dinner to make up for it. A friendly, no-pressure evening as a way to pay her back for all she'd done for them.

But even as the thought entered his mind, Sam knew he was lying to himself. He didn't want to be friends with the woman. He wanted to get her into his bed. To sink himself into her sweet heat until they both had a good, long taste of heaven. His cock hardened as image after image bombarded his mind. Damn, what was it about her that he couldn't stop thinking of getting her naked? He'd never let his libido rule, but hell if he could keep his mind out of the gutter whenever her name popped up.

One thing was certain—Julie Rose had crawled right under his skin, and for the sake of his sanity, he needed to do something about it.

"We've had this talk before, Bryan. The Blackwater Diner only serves food."

Julie tried not to let her irritation show, but it wasn't easy. Bryan Delaney was a handsome man, in a polished suit-wearing sort of way, and he'd been coming into the diner at least once a week for months. Unfortunately he never failed to ask her out on a date. He also never seemed to understand that *no thanks* was code for *never in a million years*. His attention had been sweet—for about the first five minutes.

"Is there a problem?"

The deep, rough voice coming from behind had her turning on her heels. The big, strong body encased in a black T-shirt and jeans sent her blood pressure into the dangerous range.

"Sam?" Julie asked. She was surprised to see him at the diner. Although with Wanda in the hospital, Julie should've expected one of the Jennings men to take over. When Sam didn't so much as glance her way and all his attention seemed focused on Bryan, she remembered his question. "Uh, there's no problem."

His gaze flashed ice as he balled his hands into fists at his sides. "Planning to order anytime soon, Delaney?"

To her utter shock, Bryan paled. The man had always appeared so confident, a little too confident in her mind, but there was no mistaking the fear in his eyes as he looked at Sam now. "Sam Jennings," Bryan said. "I didn't know you were working at the diner."

"If you're looking for a date, find it somewhere else, Delaney," Sam advised. "The waitresses are off limits."

Bryan turned a rather ugly shade of green. "Of course. My apologies."

Julie glanced over at Sam and noticed his expression hadn't changed. He still looked ready to commit murder. She smiled and did her best to diffuse the volatile situation. "How about I get you a slice of that apple pie you like so much, Bryan?"

"Sure. Thanks, Julie."

She turned to go but realized Sam didn't budge. She got all the way to the counter before her curiosity got the better of her. When she looked back over her shoulder, she saw Sam leaning close to Bryan, their faces mere inches apart. After a few seconds, Sam straightened, and Bryan slid out of the booth and practically ran for the door. All Julie could see was the money Bryan would've spent all but vanishing into thin air.

She glared and waited for Sam to reach her before blasting him. "I hope you realize that you just cost the diner a regular customer."

His eyebrows shot up. "You want that asshole around?"

"That's not the point. The point is, the diner can't afford to lose even one customer. No matter how annoying he might be." She paused a moment, then added, "And don't curse."

"I've known Delaney since high school, and he's nothing but trouble. Always has been. He chases every woman under the age of fifty. Trust me, we'll get by without him just fine." He leaned close and whispered, "Unless you enjoyed him staring at your chest."

She rolled her eyes. "Don't be crude. He was a pain in my backside, but he was still a paying customer. And one with a really big mouth too. You could've cost us a lot more than just one customer." Curious, she asked, "What'd you say to him anyway?"

"I told him that you were *especially* off limits."

Julie's stomach did a little somersault at the way his voice dropped to a more intimate, sexy tone. "Why would you tell him that?"

Sam cupped her chin in his palm. "Mom is fond of you, so that makes you one of us. And the Jenningses tend to be damned protective over those we care about."

She jerked away from him. "Wanda is not the one who chased Bryan off just now." Julie realized she hadn't asked how his mom was doing and said, "Speaking of your mom, how is she?"

"She's better. I'm heading over there later to talk to her doctor. And she might not be the one to get rid of Delaney, but for damn sure she wouldn't have been too happy if she'd seen the way he was salivating all over you."

Julie didn't believe for a second that his motives were so innocent. She stepped closer and squinted up at him. "So you're looking out for me for Wanda's sake?"

He ran a hand through his hair before stepping back a few feet. As if needing the distance to think clearly? Julie wondered. "Look, I owe you for everything you did for her. For us. I thought maybe you and I could have dinner together."

The fact that she had the big bad Sam Jennings on the run sent a little thrill up Julie's spine. "A simple thank-you would suffice. No need to suffer through another meal with me."

"Suffer?"

"I got the distinct impression you didn't want me at your Thanksgiving celebration. In fact, I sort of thought you didn't want me anywhere near you or your family."

He shook his head. "Why on earth would you say that?"

"Oh, gee, I don't know. Maybe it was because of all the nasty looks you sent my way?"

"You misunderstood."

"Really?"

"Really." He held his hands out to his sides as if in surrender. "It's only dinner, Julie. Let me make it up to you."

Julie bit her lip and looked down. She hadn't dated much since her grandmother's death. And never someone as potent as Sam Jennings. *You are way out of your depth, sister.*

Sam closed the space separating them, then nudged her chin with his index finger until their gazes locked. "Please have dinner with me?"

God, like she was strong enough to say no to that! "Yes."

"I'll pick you up tomorrow night. Seven okay?"

"That's fine."

Julie jotted down her address and phone number on her order pad, then ripped the sheet off and handed it to him. "Here, this might be helpful."

He took it, then looked her over. Like, really looked. Finally he said, "I was thinking a step up from casual. That work for you?"

She crossed her arms over her chest and glared at him. "I actually clean up pretty good. You'd be amazed."

He crowded closer and whispered, "I never doubted it."

Julie watched as Sam walked into the office and closed the door behind him. It might be the biggest mistake in the world, and no doubt she had absolutely zero skills when it came to men, but that didn't stop her heart from racing with excitement at the prospect of getting Sam Jennings all to herself for an entire evening.

Mentally, she ran through her wardrobe and came back with absolutely nothing to wear. Great. She wanted to look good for her date, and all she owned were jeans and a few boring skirts. Nothing that made much of an impression. She'd need to go shopping. When Eddie, the cook, yelled, "Order up," Julie forced herself to concentrate on waiting tables. There'd be time later to think about dark-haired hunks with brooding good looks.

Chapter Four

Julie let the emerald green fabric glide down her body, then checked herself in the mirror. The deep V neckline was hot. The crisscross back made her feel sexy without being too overt. Heck, she wanted to get the message across that she could look good. That she owned something other than her waitress uniform. The plain black skirt she'd worn to Thanksgiving dinner didn't exactly scream hottie either. More like schoolteacher of the year. Yippie. Still, she didn't want to appear as if she were trying to impress Sam, even if that was exactly what she was doing.

As she pulled up the side zipper, she inspected the skirt of the dress once more. Normally she didn't go for pleats; they made her feel poufy, and she already had a little too much around the hips as it was. She didn't need to bring more attention to that particular area than necessary. But when she'd seen the dress on the rack, it'd been the accordion-style pleating that had tugged at her. The satin ribbon trim around the waist added just the right touch. Opting to go with black hose and heels seemed to pull the whole look together nicely.

Julie grabbed the metal comb off the counter and did a little upsweep with her hair before starting on her makeup. She never wore much, just a little lipstick and mascara. Tonight was a special night, or so she hoped it would be, so she applied a light dusting of blush and some smoky gray eye shadow to bring out the green in her eyes. Satisfied with the results, Julie left the bathroom, but as she stepped into her bedroom, she stopped abruptly and looked around the spacious room. As always, she half expected to see the old puke green carpeting that had once covered her grandmother's floors. She'd hated that carpet, but now she missed it terribly. The house and her grandmom were gone, though. Julie's stomach clenched; she wished she could see the smile. The one her grandmom gave her just before hugging the stuffing out of her.

"I'll always live in your heart, Julie dear."

It'd been something her grandmother had said several times during her final days. Remembering the words gave her comfort. As she looked at the small window on the far wall, she smiled. The curtains were one of the few things from the old house that she'd kept. Not because they were gorgeous. Definitely not. The huge yellow and pink flowers all over them had always seemed a bit psychotic to Julie. She'd kept them because her grandmom had made them by hand. The sunny yellow could nearly blind a person if they stared too long, but they still made Julie smile every time she saw them.

The rest of her bedroom had been paid for with the money she'd received from the sale of her grandmother's house. There weren't fond memories attached to the furniture, but she aimed to change that. Sooner rather than later. The bed had been an indulgence, and an expensive one at that. The king-size cherrywood four-poster could comfortably sleep three adults—or one large man. A man like Sam Jennings, maybe? Julie would bet a week's worth of tips that Sam liked lots of room when he slept. Did he like plenty of space when he made love to a woman? Did he like to take his time or was he the rush-to-the-finish type? With any luck at all, she'd find out. Damn, it was way too easy to picture the delicious man lying against the white down-filled comforter, naked, of course.

Then again, what did she know about sex? Very damn little, that's what. Her introduction had been a quickie in the back of Clint Radley's Buick. She'd been a junior in high school at the time. It'd been over with before she could let out a single *ahhh*. After that, all her time had been spent taking care of her grandmother. Crap, maybe saying yes to dinner wasn't such a great idea.

Julie plopped down on the edge of the bed and contemplated canceling. Then the doorbell rang. Sam. Her stomach suddenly filled with butterflies. As she stood, her legs shook a little. "Get ahold of yourself. You're a grown woman, you can do this," she muttered.

Julie took a deep breath, then let it out and left the bedroom, turning off the light as she went. As she walked down the hall, her heart seemed to beat faster with each step closer to the front door. She reached the living room, and the doorbell chimed again. She had the insane urge to run in the opposite direction, but the part of her that wanted to move on with her life, the part that didn't act like a scared cat in a room full of Dobermans, kept her feet moving toward the door. Maybe if she'd had more than a handful of dates, let a guy show her the ropes, so to speak, she wouldn't be so nervous now. Although Julie had a feeling a big part of her anxiety had to do with whom she was going out with. Sam Jennings simply made her insides turn all mushy and warm.

When she reached the door, she double-checked her appearance in the mirror that hung next to it. Not a hair out of place. If not for the petrified stare, she wouldn't look half bad. Julie groaned, straightened her spine, and pasted a smile on her face. When she opened the door, she about swallowed her tongue.

He was wearing black trousers, a three-quarter-length black wool coat, and a black V-neck T-shirt peeked out from beneath the open collar. It appeared he'd even attempted to tame his dark, messy hair. Hot, yeah, that word fit Sam nicely. Hot as hell fit even better.

"Hi," she said, realizing too late she'd been standing with her mouth open.

He smiled and looked at her from head to toe. "You look fantastic."

Julie stepped back to let him enter. "Thanks. Let me grab my coat and we can go."

He nodded and stepped over the threshold, shutting the door behind him. Julie now had Sam Jennings in her condo. All to herself. If only she were bold enough to do something about it. She sighed and headed to the couch where she'd left the new black knee-length coat she'd purchased to go with the dress. It draped open in the front and looked classy, but the wool material and long sleeves would still keep her from freezing her tush off, she hoped.

"I hope you like steak. I made reservations at Kane's."

Deciding to tweak him a bit, Julie let her eyes grow big as quarters. "Uh, I'm a vegetarian."

His gaze narrowed. "You came to our Thanksgiving dinner."

"But did you see me actually eat any meat?"

He rubbed his chin. "Well, now that you mention it—"

"I'm teasing you." She laughed. "I love a good steak."

He shook his head, and a small smile kicked up one corner of his mouth. The left corner, to be exact. Well, heck, wasn't that just adorable in an ornery sort of way?

"Had me worried there for a minute. Not that I have a problem with vegetarians, but I had to do some serious sweet talking to get those reservations."

She pulled her coat on and grabbed her purse. As they headed out the door, his words registered. "You know, now that you mention it, Kane's is a bit upscale. How'd you get reservations on such short notice?"

He placed his hand at the small of her back, and Julie's heart skipped a beat. "I know the owner's daughter. We belong to the same church."

The church thing wasn't a surprise. Wanda was always trying to get Julie to go to church with her. So far Julie had managed to hold the woman off with one excuse or another. The truth of it was, she couldn't get the sight of her grandmom lying in a casket out of her head. That'd been the last time Julie had been inside a church.

After she locked the door, Sam escorted her to his waiting SUV. Once they were both inside, Julie turned to him and asked, "So, what sort of sweet talking did you do with the owner's daughter?"

His wink before turning away and starting the engine sent a surge of lust through her apparently sex-starved system. "In exchange for a table for two, I've agreed to take a look at her car for her. She's having some trouble with it stalling out."

An image of Sam wearing a pair of well-worn jeans and covered in grease came to mind. Suddenly her coat felt a little too warm. "You know your way around an engine?"

He turned on the heater and checked his rearview mirror before pulling out of the parking space. "Dad taught all of us how to work on cars. He used to say there was no sense in paying someone to do a job that you could do yourself. It's how Vance learned construction and how I learned carpentry work. Dad was all hands-on."

So, the indomitable Sam Jennings was good with his hands. No surprise there. *Geez, he just gets more perfect with each passing minute.* At this rate, Julie estimated that she'd be salivating over him by the time dessert arrived. "Is that what you do for a living? Carpentry?"

"I do a little bit of everything. Remodeling and roofing for the most part. Some building but not a lot. That's Vance's gig."

"And you live in the area?"

He nodded. "About twenty minutes to the south, near Amanda."

"I'm surprised I never ran into you at the restaurant, then."

A muscle in his jaw twitched. "That's because I've been too wrapped up in my own life. I should've been checking on things."

"I don't know, your mom seems pretty independent. I'm not sure she would've welcomed a lot of interference, even coming from her own son."

"And yet she's confided in you," he stated in a quiet voice as he took his gaze off the road for a second. "Let you help her."

"Ah, I'm sneaky, though." She bobbed her eyebrows. "I have ways of getting around her."

"I'll bet you do." His somber expression lightened a bit, and he went back to watching the road.

"So, how's your mom doing?" She'd seen Wanda the night before. After Julie's shift at the diner had ended, she'd headed up to the hospital. She'd been feeling better, but it'd been a chaotic visit with all the brothers there, so Julie hadn't caught any details about Wanda's condition beyond the obvious fact she'd been feeling better.

Sam let out a deep breath, and she noticed his hands clenching the steering wheel in a tight grip. "The doctor ran about a million different tests. Don't ask me the names of them—that shit confuses me to no end—but they've determined that the blockage can be taken care of with a better diet and medication. No surgery. She should be released in the next couple of days."

"That's great news! She'll be glad to get home, I bet. Hospitals have a way of making you feel worse than you are."

He snorted. "You're being kind. She's driving everyone crazy up there, and we both know it."

Julie attempted to stifle a laugh when she remembered Wanda all but lecturing one of the nurses the previous night about the merits of healthy food that didn't taste like dust. "The nurse on duty last night did seem a bit harried. River looked ready to bang some heads together."

"That's because Mom keeps insisting she be released. We told her not to worry, that we're all taking turns handling the diner, but the woman never was good at sitting around doing nothing. Even on our family vacations, Mom was always cleaning or cooking something." He paused, then in a quieter tone, he said, "And River has a hard time seeing Mom upset or in any kind of distress. Always has."

"I don't mean to pry, but Wanda told me once that she and your dad adopted the five of you when you were very young. That must have been tough."

He turned a corner, and Julie looked out the windshield. She could see the restaurant up the road on the right. Food was forgotten at the moment, though. All she really cared about was hearing more about the man who was quickly becoming an obsession to her.

"Yeah. We'd been split up, put into different foster homes until she and Dad came into the picture."

"But I thought social services usually kept siblings

together? And what about your biological parents? Where were they?"

"I never knew who my real father was, and I only have a few memories of my real mom. She was a druggy." He paused, then added, "And normally, yes, they do try and keep siblings together, but there were five of us, and we weren't the easiest bunch of boys to take care of either."

Julie's stomach ached for Sam, as well as his brothers. "Then Wanda came along..." she said in the hopes he'd fill in the blanks.

Sam nodded. "She seemed too good to be true at first. Took all of us a long time to realize she was the real deal."

Julie frowned, uncertain what he meant. "The real deal? As opposed to what?"

"The do-gooders." Sam shook his head. "The ones who set out to do something charitable, something that will make *them* feel good, but then when reality sets in and they realize that we're people, that there's some actual work involved in raising a kid, they cut and run."

"That's awful." Julie wanted to reach out to Sam, to comfort him somehow, but they weren't a couple, and she didn't have that right.

"Some people can be damned awful, Julie. Especially to a defenseless kid."

She tried to picture Sam as a scrawny boy, but it didn't quite mesh with the man sitting across the seat from her. He was simply so big and unyielding, able to leap tall buildings and all that jazz. "I have a hard time seeing you as vulnerable."

"Not me. River. He was a skinny bag of bones. He and Reilly were yanked apart and placed with different foster families for a time. It was hard on them, being twins and all." He shook his head. "Let's just say that River didn't end up with June Cleaver as a foster parent."

Julie thought of River and the fun teasing he'd done at Thanksgiving. His smiling eyes had revealed a hint of mischief. Pain shot through her chest when she realized what River must have gone through. All of them, for that matter."

"Anyone who could hurt a child is scum in my book."

"Couldn't agree more. Anyway, it all worked out. We ended up with two loving parents."

"And River's no longer a scrawny little boy unable to defend himself."

"No, he's not." He pulled into a parking lot, then found a space close to the front and parked. "And we're here."

Julie forced down the urge to learn more about Sam. She had a feeling he was merely brushing the surface about his days in foster care, and she vowed that before long, she'd learn all there was to know about him. Until then she simply wanted to enjoy an evening out with a man who made her go all gooey inside.

"Good, because I'm starving," she said with a smile. "Let's eat."

Sam grinned and opened his door. "I love a woman with an appetite."

Julie snorted as she opened her own door. "And I have the thighs and rear to prove it."

"Julie," Sam said, his voice deeper than before, effectively halting her progress out of the vehicle. When Julie turned, Sam pinned her with a look hot enough to scorch. "There isn't a damn thing wrong with your curves, sweetheart."

It was several seconds before Julie could breathe again.

Chapter Five

"Thank you for a wonderful evening."

Julie's soft voice floated down his spine like a gentle kiss. As they stood at her front door, her big eyes staring up at him, Sam knew he had no right to be perturbed by the fact that she wasn't inviting him in. He was left wondering if he should kiss her or simply play it off. Like the date was nothing more than a thank-you, as he'd said it would be. He felt awkward, damn it. Hell, he wasn't a damn teenager anymore.

"You're welcome." Not what he wanted to say, but he wasn't sure of Julie. She had a sharp wit, and she was kind—to everyone. Even their waiter had been enraptured by her. It made Sam wonder if she saw him any differently than a casual acquaintance. Somewhere along the line, he'd decided he wanted to be anything *but* casual with Julie.

"I hope it was worth the work you'll have to do on your friend's car."

"Well worth it." Shit, they'd been reduced to small talk.

She sighed and turned around, then pressed her key into the lock. After Julie had the door open, she turned to him. "Look, I don't know what to do here. My dating days have been pretty limited. I don't want you to think I'm a prude for not inviting you in, but I don't want to appear too…easy if I asked you in for a nightcap. And to top it all off, I have no idea if this is still just a thank-you date. So basically I'm a fish out of water here."

Her rushed speech and the fact she was nervous made Sam feel a shitload better. They were both thrown for a loop, it seemed. "This whole thing is new ground for you, huh?"

"Very new. Like brand-spanking new. So new it's still

sealed in cellophane."

He chuckled. "How about we leave the decision up to me, then?"

She bit her lip. "What do you mean?"

He planted his fist against the doorjamb and asked, "May I come in for a cup of coffee, Miss Rose?"

Her gaze narrowed. "First, Miss Rose makes me sound like a sad, old woman with thirty cats to keep her company. Second, just coffee?"

"Unless you have lemon merengue pie to go with it." He tapped her on the nose. "Do you?"

He watched as all the nervousness seemed to evaporate. "No pie, but I do have some chocolate chip cookies."

"Sounds good to me." She nodded and smiled finally, much to Sam's relief, then opened the door. Sam followed her into the condo and shut the door behind him.

After their dinner, which Sam had found to be an exercise in self-control, they'd shared a slow dance on the restaurant's small dance floor. He'd enjoyed holding her close. Her curves fit him as if made for him. Together they'd walked out to his SUV, hand in hand, without speaking to each other.

The drive back to her place had been quiet. For some reason, Sam hadn't wanted to say anything to screw it up, like he usually did. Christ, it wasn't as if he hadn't dated. He'd dated plenty of pretty women, but none of them had ever had him on his toes quite the way Julie did. The whole night seemed special somehow.

"Not to sound corny, but I am *so* slipping into something slightly more comfy." She took off her coat and tossed it onto the couch. "This dress is adorable and these shoes were definitely worth every penny, but I'm in need of something that doesn't itch and pinch."

Sam frowned as he watched her finger one of the straps of the dress. "Please tell me you weren't miserable all night."

"Not until the end of the evening," she replied. "I think this dress has a time limit. Wear it too long and it turns into an itchy burlap sack."

"Well, let me be the first to say that you look great in burlap." A light blush filled her cheeks, and Sam found it cute as hell.

"Uh, I'll be right back."

"Take your time."

As she left the room, Sam took a moment to shed his coat and take in his surroundings. When he'd picked her up for their date, he'd been too busy taking *her* in; her furniture could've been made out of cardboard for all he'd noticed.

Julie had a nice place, not too girly but definitely warm and inviting. The tan suede couch and recliner were nice, and they went well with the white oak end table and coffee table. None of it appeared particularly lived-in. When she'd said she'd started fresh after her grandmother's death, she hadn't been kidding.

Sam spied a framed photo on the coffee table and crossed the room to get a better look. It was a picture of a teenage version of Julie with an older woman. Her grandmother, no doubt. They resembled each other. And it was easy to see the love in her grandmother's eyes. Then again, who wouldn't love Julie? She simply had a way of getting under a person's skin. He started to sit on the couch when he spied a CD on the end table. Curious about her taste in music, Sam picked it up, then grinned as he read the name of the band.

"If you laugh at my Styx, I'm kicking you out."

He turned around and came to an abrupt halt. She stood on the other side of the room in a pair of black sweats and a gray hoodie big enough to fit three average-sized adults. "Lady," Sam began singing, doing his best to imitate Styx's lead singer, Dennis DeYoung, "when you're with me, I'm smiling."

She covered her mouth in an attempt to stifle a laugh. "Wow," she finally managed, "that was...awesome."

"Yeah, I can't sing for crap, and we both know it." He looked her over and winked. "I have to say, you dress up real nice, sweetheart, but this does feel more like the real you."

She shrugged. "That's because it is. I only bought the dress and heels tonight."

"You went shopping for our date?" The notion pleased the shit out of him, and he wasn't sure why.

She started toward the kitchen. "You implied I couldn't do classy," she tossed over her shoulder. "I had to prove you wrong, didn't I?"

He put the CD back down on the table; then her words hit him. "Wait, when in hell did I say that?"

She headed straight for the coffee pot. "At the diner," she answered with her back to him. "It was in the way you looked at me in the waitress uniform. Felt like a challenge, that's all."

"Julie, look at me." When she turned around, Sam strode toward her and cupped her cheeks in his palms. "I looked at you then the same way I looked at you the first time I saw you. Like I wanted to know you. Inside and out. You took me by surprise is all, and I don't do well with surprises."

She frowned and pulled away. "Should I apologize?"

"No." He shoved his hands in the front pockets of his pants to keep himself from reaching out and tugging her into his arms. "Just know that I like you in the waitress getup. I like you in the sexy-ass dress and heels too. And I really like you in the oversized sweats. The fact is, I just like *you*."

"Oh." She teased the hem of her sweatshirt and said, "Well, that works out nicely, then."

"Why is that?"

"Because as it turns out, I like you too."

He chuckled. "Do you like me enough to share a few of those cookies you mentioned?"

"I made two dozen. More than enough for a decent sugargasm."

He rubbed his chin, pretending to contemplate the merits of a sugargasm. "Not sure I've ever had a sugargasm before. Could prove interesting."

She dropped the hem, then turned and grabbed the empty glass carafe. "You've been terribly deprived, then."

Sam let his gaze travel over her lush curves. Jesus, even in the oversized sweatpants, her ass made him hard. "Very deprived," he growled, wishing he could close the distance and grab a handful of her.

As she filled the pot with water, she said, "How about I get the coffee and cookies while you get the fire started?"

Baffled and momentarily dragged out of his sexual musings, Sam peered over his shoulder and looked into the living room beyond. "You have a fireplace?"

"It's one of those cast-iron fire pits. It's out on the back patio." She pointed to a pair of sliding-glass doors. "The wood is already out there." After she poured the water in the well of the coffeemaker, she replaced the pot and hit the power button. "This is the perfect night for a fire." She opened a drawer and took out a box of matches. "Here." She handed them over. "You'll find the rest of the things you need in a metal cabinet near the door."

Sam liked the idea of holding Julie tight next to a warm fire, but the temperature had dropped as the evening had worn on. "It's probably in the high thirties. Sure you won't get too chilly?"

She looked down at herself, then held her arms out to her sides. "Have you seen this hoodie? It's ginormous!"

He tucked the matches in his front shirt pocket and murmured, "If it's a fire under the stars you want, then that's what you'll get."

She wrinkled her nose. "You don't think it's silly?"

Damn, hadn't a man ever taken the time to romance the woman? "Not at all. I'm looking forward to keeping you warm."

"You've been doing that all night long."

Sam's eyebrows shot up at the bold confession. Julie slammed a hand over her mouth, and her face turned bright red. "Didn't intend to say that aloud, did you?" She vehemently shook her head. His chest swelled a little. "If it helps, the feeling is mutual," he admitted before bending forward and placing a light kiss to her soft lips. Julie went utterly still beneath him. When he angled his head, fitting his mouth to hers, he felt her

51

relax and lean in the slightest bit. Sam kept it quick, managing to barely get a taste of her sweet flavor before he lifted his head. When he walked out to the patio, he looked back and saw her touching her lips with her fingertips. Leaving her standing there sure as hell wasn't easy.

A few minutes later, Sam had the beginnings of a fire. When he heard the patio door slide open, he stood. "Here, let me." Sam took the tray laden with their cookies and coffee and placed it on the little glass table in front of the swing.

She laughed. "Sam, I'm a waitress, remember?"

"Doesn't mean I can't be a gentleman." He poured them both a cup of coffee. "Cream or sugar?"

"Neither for me, thanks." She took the mug and wrapped her delicate fingers around it. Sam imagined her wrapping them around his cock instead.

As they sat down on the cushioned porch swing, Sam took a cautious sip from his own steaming cup. "Mmm, tastes good."

"Thanks," she said, settling in next to him. Sam wished like hell he had the right to pull her in closer. "The cookies aren't too bad either," Julie admitted. "If I do say so myself."

"You baked them?" When she nodded, Sam picked one up and took a large bite. "Delicious. Maybe we should fire Eddie and hire you as our cook at the diner."

"No way. Cooking is for fun, not work. Besides, Eddie does a great job."

"Speaking of the diner, I hear you've been opening for Mom. And Reilly tells me you might have some insight about the financial state of things there."

"I don't mind opening. I'm an early riser. When I noticed Wanda was always there, every morning without fail, I offered to do the early shift a few times a week."

"It doesn't interfere with your classes?"

She shook her head. "It hasn't yet."

When he thought of her going to college, it reminded him of the way she'd been raised. "You said at Thanksgiving that you helped take care of your grandmother. That couldn't have been easy. Especially at such a young age."

She pushed a lock of hair behind her ear and said, "No, it wasn't easy, but she and I were close, and I was glad to do it. She was my best friend."

Sam heard a hint of sadness in her tone, and it bothered him. He wanted to make it all better for her. "Did she go through chemotherapy?"

She took a sip of her coffee, then placed the half-empty cup on the table. "Grandmom never liked to go to the doctors, hated it. Swore they were all quacks."

"So, by the time they caught the cancer, it was too late," he surmised.

"Yeah," she said, her voice soft and far away.

"You miss her, huh?"

"Sometimes, but she was in a lot of pain in the end." Her voice trembled as she murmured, "I hated seeing her that way."

He patted her thigh, needing to take away her sadness in some small way. "Well, I don't know if it helps to hear this, but I think my mom considers you the daughter she never had."

"Aw, I care about her too." She shrugged. "I think she needs to hire a full time manager at the diner, though. Of course, I'm not sure she can afford it right now." Her gaze landed on his, and he could see her worry. "Sam, I'm afraid if something isn't done, she'll lose the restaurant."

He took one last swig of his coffee, then sat his cup next to hers before saying, "I won't let that happen."

"Short of declaring bankruptcy, I don't see how you have a choice," she muttered.

"I spent a good part of the morning looking everything over, and at first I had the same depressing thought. But I have an idea. I just need to talk to the others first."

Her eyes widened. "What sort of plan?"

"A remodel. I want to turn the restaurant into a bar and grill."

"It sounds great, but how will you get the funding? I'm not sure the bank will find that the restaurant is a sound investment."

"We might not need a lot. I've got a little money saved back. Besides, with Vance and me doing the work and the five of us pooling our resources, I think it might be the best way to turn the diner around."

"Our very own version of Applebees right here in Blackwater?"

"Something like that." Sam reached out and cupped Julie's chin, urging her to look at him. "How about we worry about the diner tomorrow?"

"Okay." She crossed her legs and glanced over at the fire. "I love this time of year."

Sam couldn't pass up the chanced to learn a little more about her. "Is it the chillier weather or the holiday season you like?"

"Both." She plucked at her sweatshirt and admitted, "I do get cold easily, but I love sitting by a warm fire. It reminds me of going to church camp when I was little."

Sam imagined her as a young girl in pigtails and smiled. "I can see you roasting marshmallows and eating s'mores."

She rubbed her belly. "Mm, there's nothing better than s'mores."

Sam tipped her chin up until he could see her eyes. "Nothing?" he murmured. "Not even gooey chocolate chip cookies with me?"

Julie clenched her eyes tight and let out a heavy breath. "I have a confession to make, Sam."

"Yeah?"

She opened her eyes and said, "Uh, I'm nervous. It's been a long time since I've been on a date, but you could probably tell that already."

"It's okay. No pressures or expectations tonight, Julie." He leaned back into the swing and put his arm around her shoulders. "All you have to do is enjoy the night."

She leaned her head on his shoulder and looked up at him. "Are you enjoying the evening?"

Sam's Promise

"I have a pretty woman snuggled up close under the stars. It doesn't get much better in my book."

"Maybe we should make a wish. You never know, it might come true."

He smiled down at her. "I haven't done that since I was a kid."

Her eyes twinkled in the firelight as she whispered, "I will if you will."

"Deal."

"Close your eyes. It won't work unless you close your eyes, Sam."

Sam did as she asked. After he made his wish, he opened them again to see Julie watching him. "Did you make a wish?"

She nodded. "Did you?" she asked in a faraway voice.

"Hmm, yeah. We'll just have to wait and see if it comes true or not, won't we?" he said cryptically.

She offered him a sexy grin, one clearly designed to fell a lesser man. "I don't suppose I can convince you to tell me what you wished for, huh?"

"Nice try, sweetheart." Julie pouted, and Sam knew he was putty in her hands. God, she was captivating. Sam was desperate to lean down and kiss her. He wanted to undress her and touch every inch of her body with his lips and tongue. "You know that if I told you, then it wouldn't come true anyway, remember?"

"Yes, I suppose you're right. Will you let me know if you get your wish at least?"

"I will if you will," he murmured.

Satisfied, Julie nodded. "Deal."

Sam stroked the silky length of her dark brown hair. "We could shake on it," he suggested.

Her eyes lit with mischief. "We could. Sounds a little boring, if you ask me."

"Or..." He dipped his head and pressed his lips to her soft, warm mouth.

Julie sighed and wrapped her arms around his neck. She

55

moved closer, as if she wanted to spend a good long time sampling him. Damn good plan, Sam thought. He nudged the seam of her lips with his tongue, and her lips parted beneath his. Tongues met in a wild mating dance. She tasted of sweet, warm chocolate, and Sam knew he could easily become a glutton.

He pulled back a few inches. "Earlier you said that I made you hot and bothered."

"Blurted it out, you mean," she grumbled as she turned away, presenting him with the perfect view of her neck. Sam kissed her there, just behind her ear. Julie shivered.

Sam's voice dropped an octave as he admitted, "Either way, I'm glad you said it."

"Yes, well, I think you've managed to turn the heat up a notch." She cleared her throat. "In case you were curious or anything."

"Still feels a little chilly to me," he said as he coasted his lips over her earlobe and nibbled.

"W-we can't have that," she whispered, tilting her head to the side and giving him better access to her neck.

Sam caved in to temptation and licked the smooth line of her neck. He could feel the rapid rise and fall of her chest as she pressed her body closer to his. Sam's cock pulsed with the need to be buried inside her soft pussy. Damn, he hadn't even taken off Julie's clothes and already he ached for release. Sam was desperate to tear off her sweats, to see the full curves she kept hidden, but he didn't want to rush her. She'd admitted her inexperience earlier, and Sam knew it would be better if he took the time to coax Julie's passion to the surface, not demand it.

"I'm out of my element here, Sam," she softly confessed, confirming his conviction that he needed to take it slow.

Nervous tension creased her brow, but the fingers tugging at his hair spoke of how turned on she was. The very last thing he wanted was for Julie to be shy and reserved. He wanted her to let go of her shyness, to feel free to explore him a little, because he sure as shit planned to explore her.

Sam nudged her face toward his. "Sweetheart?"

"Hmm?" she asked as her pleasure-filled gaze snared his.

"Kiss me," he urged.

"Good idea." She leaned into him and barely touched her lips with his.

Unlike the mating of lips before, this kiss was light and fleeting but enough to have Sam's blood pounding hot. He dipped his head and tasted the V-shaped bit of skin exposed at the front of the hoodie. He licked the warmth he discovered there, enjoying the beat of her pulse pounding out a staccato rhythm beneath his tongue.

Lifting a little, Sam asked, "More?"

He watched her swallow hard, and even that seemed sexy. "It'd be oh so wrong to stop now," she said, her voice not quite as steady as before.

"Christ, you're turning me on here."

She mumbled something unintelligible, but it was her responsiveness that sent a wave of primitive satisfaction through him. He wanted to be the only man with the privilege to hear that particular husky tone of voice from Julie. He brushed his lips across her throat one more time before placing a hand on the back of the swing next to her, caging her in.

Sam ran a hand down her arm, then let his fingers drift over one cotton-covered breast. Through her bra and the thick material of the hoodie, he couldn't tell if her nipples were hard little points or not, but if her breathing was any indication, she definitely liked his ministrations. As he cupped one full, round breast, shaping and kneading, he heard her beg his name. Sam stopped and looked her over. With her hair all around her shoulders, eyes half-closed with desire and her lips swollen from his kisses, she looked like an offering.

Sam reached down with one hand and cupped her pussy through the sweats. "You want to come, sweets?"

"So very badly." She moaned. "I just might implode if I don't."

Sam tsked. "We certainly can't have that." He kissed her

cheek and breathed in her delicate scent. Sam took her hand in his and pressed it against his cock. "Feel what you do to me, Julie," he gently ordered.

"Oh, God. You're so big, so hard." When she wrapped her fingers around him and squeezed, Sam had to bite back a curse.

He left her fingers to play, then journeyed beneath the hem of her sweatshirt. As he nudged the bra upward and encountered the pillowy softness of her tits, Sam knew he'd never touched anything softer in his life. He pinched one turgid peak, relishing the sounds she made with each of his teasing caresses. As Julie pumped his cock through his slacks, all rational thought scattered. She was a powerful mix of inexperience and aroused woman.

As Sam glided his palm down her ribcage to her belly, he felt her tremble.

"More?" he asked, giving her a chance to call a halt. It would kill him to stop now, but he wouldn't push her.

"Please, you feel so good," she breathed out. "So right." She spread her legs wider in obvious invitation.

"Jesus," he growled as he reached beneath the elastic of her sweatpants and came into contact with the satin material of her panties. He was curious what color they were, but not curious enough to stop and look. He didn't want to risk breaking the sensual spell around them.

At last Sam touched her damp curls, and the head of his cock swelled. "Lean back a little for me, sweetheart."

She hesitated, and Sam could feel her stiffening a little. "Wait, what if someone sees?"

"Our clothes are staying put, I promise." He flicked her clit. "And you do have a privacy fence."

She glanced around, then bit her lip and slowly surrendered. She leaned back in the swing and gave him better access to her pretty body.

"Mm, yeah, that's it," he praised her. When Sam caressed her tiny bud, Julie moaned his name and released his cock. She

Sam's Promise

gripped on to his forearms instead, as if needing the support.

Sam watched her toss her head backward, her fingernails digging into his shirtsleeves. "Don't stop," she begged.

"Not a chance," he murmured as his fingers continued to stroke and play. When he delved his middle finger into her wet opening, letting his thumb slide over her swollen clitoris, her moans turned to cries. "Damn, you're wet. I want a taste of some of that cream, Julie." He swallowed the lump in his throat. "Soon, sweetheart."

Every whimper and shudder drove him higher and higher. Her pussy tightened around his finger, and he closed his eyes, reveling in the delicious torture.

"So fucking hot and tight," he said, as he pushed two fingers deep. "God, I want my cock here." He curled his fingers upward, hitting a particularly sensitive spot, emphasizing his point.

"Sam," she cried as her hips lifted off the seat. His mind went blank, and all his blood traveled to his dick as Julie began bucking wildly beneath him.

"Yeah, fuck my fingers," Sam urged as he pushed in and out of her. He moved slow at first, then faster.

"More," she ground out. "Harder."

"Anything," he whispered as he increased the rhythm. When he flicked her clit once more, Julie stiffened. Sam slammed his mouth over her hers and drank in her cries as she came all around his fingers. When her spasms subsided, Sam pulled his fingers free. He touched her lips with his fingers wet with her come. "Taste yourself for me."

Sam couldn't take his gaze off Julie as she wrapped a hand around his wrist and sucked both his fingers into her mouth, licking them clean. "Ah, damn," he groaned, "you're making it so hard to do the right thing here."

Her green gaze traveled down his body and stopped for a few seconds on his cock. Desire burned bright in her eyes when she looked back up at him. "We could—"

Sam cut her off with a hard kiss. He slid his tongue into

her mouth, tasting the tang of her pussy juices. When he pulled back, they were both breathing hard. "No, this is just a sample. The appetizer," he explained. "You'll have to let me see you again if you want the main entrée."

Her smile, when it came, was every bit as sexy as the woman herself. "Oh, I *so* want."

Chapter Six

After Sam had left Julie the night before, all flushed and looking hot as hell from her orgasm, he'd sent his brothers text messages asking them to meet him at the diner the following morning. Now that he had a plan to turn the restaurant around, he didn't want to waste another second.

Since it was Sunday morning, the diner was closed. Now, as he looked at the four of them sitting in stools across the counter from him, Sam knew a sense of rightness about the proposal he was about to make. The diner belonged to all of them; it was only right that they all took part in bringing it back into the black. Still, as he looked around the room, taking in the long, white countertop scarred from years of use and the red cushioned booths with little tears at the corners, Sam felt a jolt of pain go through his chest.

He could still remember his dad making them all strawberry shakes on the occasional Saturday afternoon. Sam recalled the girl he'd made out with in the far booth, after hours, during his senior year of high school. The place held a lot of memories, for all of them, but it was time to make some new ones. Time to move on.

"I have a plan," he said, "but it's a big one, and it'll take all of us to make it work."

"Make it quick, Sammy," River grumbled. "Mom is due to get out of the hospital today, and I don't want her to be alone when they release her."

"Julie is with her." He'd called her the minute he woke up, partly because he'd wanted to hear her sweet voice and partly because he couldn't get the image of her coming for him out of his head. "Mom's in good hands." Sam looked closer at River and noticed the dark circles under his eyes. "When was the last time you slept?"

River sat back in his stool and crossed his arms over his chest. "I'll sleep when Mom is home. Away from those damn tubes and nurses poking her with needles all night long."

Reilly glared at his twin but stayed silent. Brodix yawned. "Why couldn't we meet at the house? And where the hell is the coffee?"

"Because this is about the diner, not the house." Sam rolled his eyes at Brodix's pissy mood. He'd always been the worst morning person on the planet. It took him three cups before he was even remotely civil. "You want coffee make it yourself, I'm not your maid."

"If you were, I'd fire your useless ass."

"If you'll shut up and let me talk, maybe we could get through this within the next century too."

"So talk," he bit out.

Sam started right in, no sense dancing around it. "I've had a chance to look over the books. Things are bad."

"Bankruptcy bad?" Vance asked, speaking for the first time since arriving.

He nodded. Several curses filled the air. Sam held up a hand. "However, we're not without options here. I've been looking at the property. We own it outright, thanks to Dad's financial skills, and it's large enough that we could expand the diner."

"Customers aren't clamoring to eat here as it is, and you want to make the place bigger?" Reilly asked. "How does that make sense?"

"Not bigger, necessarily, but a remodel. I think we should turn the diner into a bar and grill."

Suddenly alert, Brodix sat up and placed his elbows on the counter. "How? I don't see a bank loaning us the amount of cash that sort of remodel would entail."

"I have some money in savings," Sam offered.

"Me too," River added as he looked at the clock on the wall for the tenth time. "We might not need the bank."

"Hell, if you both have money in savings, then why don't the five of us just put in equal shares to pay the bills around here?" Reilly said as he waved a hand in the air. "Problem solved."

"Because Sammy is thinking of a long-term solution," Brodix said as his quick mind caught on. "Paying the bills is only a bandage."

"In my opinion," Sam began, "a bar and grill would gain us a damn sight more customers than a diner ever could. I don't want to end up right back here six months down the road, few customers and too much overhead. We need to make some changes."

"Vance's Construction has the remodel covered," Vance stated. He rubbed his hands together and looked around the room before saying, "It's about time this place got a facelift."

"I agree with everything you guys are saying here, but," River said, still looking unconvinced, "what do you think Mom will want? The diner was always her thing."

For a moment, they all fell silent as they glanced around the room. Sam knew his brothers were recalling all the times they'd spent there growing up. They'd each taken turns waiting tables and washing dishes. Sam hadn't minded the work, though, because the diner was *theirs*. And for a motley bunch like they'd been before Wanda and Chet Jennings came into their lives, having a place to call their own had been worth a little sweat.

"I think she'll be thrilled, River," Sam said. "That we're all taking an interest in the family business is what she always wanted anyway. Her and Dad both. Besides, if she decides she wants to keep things as they are, then we'll go with what Reilly said." He made a circle in the air to indicate the five of them. "We'll put our money together and pay the bills. Do our best to help out."

"The heart attack was a wake-up call for all of us," River muttered. "Mom needs to slow down. She needs help."

"No doubt, bro." Sam was ashamed that he hadn't noticed until it'd been almost too late. "We're going to see that she gets it."

"If we do this, then we're going to need new menus, a bigger staff. New uniforms. More than Eddie to cook." Brodix shoved a hand through his hair. "This is big, Sammy."

"No joke there, it's a huge undertaking. But I have some ideas how we can get some help with some of it."

"You're thinking about Julie," Reilly surmised.

Vance quirked an eyebrow. "What's she got to do with this?"

"She's majoring in business, and I think she'd be a real asset through all this. In fact, I'm thinking of asking her to be the manager of the Blackwater Bar and Grill."

"Makes sense." Brodix grinned. "The Blackwater Bar and Grill... Has a nice ring to it, doesn't it?"

"Damn straight," Sam growled.

"Speaking of Julie," Brodix said as his gaze met his and held, "what's this about you two going out to dinner last night?"

It wasn't the abrupt change in topic that had Sam on alert so much as the tone. Brodix sounded jealous. Had he been into Julie? Sam had assumed Brodix had just been doing what he usually did when he was around a pretty woman—flirting.

Sam glared at Reilly. "Big mouth."

Reilly stood and held up his hands. "Hey, don't get all angry with me. He's the one who asked if I knew her phone number. I told him that I didn't, but you might."

Sam turned his attention back to Brodix. "You were planning to call Julie?"

Brodix sat back and tapped his fingers against the countertop. "I thought about it. Is it a problem?"

"Yeah, it's a problem," he gritted out as he recalled the sight of her during her climax. "Julie is off limits."

"Seriously? You just met her on Thursday! Jesus, you've gone out all of one time."

Sam didn't say anything, only stared. To his way of thinking, there wasn't anything left to say.

Vance laughed. "Mom is going to have a heyday with this."

"Whoa." Sam's gut clenched up. "I'm interested in Julie, yeah, but I didn't say we were picking out matching robes." He paused, then thought to add, "And if any one of you says a word to Mom, I'll beat you to a bloody pulp."

"Might not have to," River said, smiling for the first time since their mother's heart attack.

"What do you mean?"

"Julie's at the hospital now, remember? Mom's probably already gotten all the information she needs." He chuckled. "The woman is better than a CIA operative when it comes to gaining intel on her *boys*."

Sam groaned. "Christ, I never even thought of that." Hell, he'd be lucky if his mother hadn't already set a wedding date.

"If I were you," Reilly said, "I'd get my ass down there before Mom gets carried away."

"Like that time Vance brought home Shayla Riggs. Remember her?" River asked, punching Vance on the arm. "Mom was ready to break out the horse-drawn carriage and champagne flutes for the two of you."

Vance stayed silent, but Sam saw the flicker of pain all the same. Sam remembered Shayla. She'd broken his brother's heart. The others weren't aware of how serious Vance had been for the girl. But Sam had known, and it still pissed him off to know how easily Shayla had found it to kick Vance to the curb.

"Before we end this meeting," Sam said, changing the subject for Vance's sake, "I need to know if we're all onboard with the remodel."

They all sent up their agreements. Reilly, River and Brodix high-fived one another. Vance sent Sam a look of thanks before he stood. "I'll start working on the plans."

"Good deal. I'll talk to Mom, and we'll go from there. Agreed?"

"Agreed," his brothers said in unison.

When Sam arrived at the hospital, Julie was sitting next to

his mom's bed. They were laughing and carrying on as if they'd known each other their entire lives. He liked seeing his mom happy. He hadn't seen her laughing much, not since their dad had passed. And it was good that Julie was so at ease around his family, but some part of him wondered if he held any importance in her world. The thought turned his good mood sour.

Sam cleared his throat. Both women glanced over at him. "Am I interrupting?"

"Sammy dear," his mother said in her usual cheery voice as she held her arms out for a hug. "We were just talking about you."

"That's never good," Sam muttered.

Julie smiled, and unless he was seeing things, Sam thought he saw the hint of a blush filling her cheeks. He wanted to go to her, to pull her out of the chair and give her a proper hello, but he didn't have that right. She didn't belong to him. One date, one hot as hell date—that was all they'd shared. When she gave him a puzzled look, Sam frowned, and he wasn't even sure why.

"Sammy, stop glaring and come over here and give me a hug."

Sam strode across the room and leaned down to kiss his mother on the cheek. "How are you feeling?"

"Much better now that I'm to be released from this prison."

"The doctor just came in and gave the okay," Julie said. "Your timing couldn't be better."

"Good," he said, not taking his eyes off his mom as he lifted away and took the seat at the bottom of the bed. "You do know that this doesn't mean you're going right back to your old diet and routine, right? It's time to start eating healthier. You need to think of *you* for a change."

"Yes, yes, so I keep hearing." She pointed a finger at him. "You and your brothers have turned into a bunch of mother hens."

Sam winked. "What can I say, we learned from the best."

Sam's Promise

Julie stood, and Sam was able to get a better look at her. She wore a pair of tight, dark blue jeans and a white blouse. Her hair was pulled up into a ponytail, and Sam thought she looked cute as a button. His cock went semi-hard as he remembered how good her pussy had felt in his palm, how sweet she'd tasted. Sam started to get up, then realized what he was doing and stopped. His mom had plans, he reminded himself. The marriage-and-white-picket-fence type. He was sure of it. Sam didn't even know if Julie still wanted a second date.

Sam watched as Julie took her purse off the back of the chair and flung it over one shoulder. When she leaned down to hug his mother, Sam got a glimpse of Julie's ass in the denim. Jesus, the woman was built.

"You're leaving?" he asked.

She nodded. "Unless you wanted me to stay?"

Her gaze darted down his body and when she looked back up at him, Sam saw the way she bit at her lower lip, and her breathing had increased. Unless he was way off, Julie appeared turned on. It wasn't anything obvious, but after their little make-out session on her back patio, Sam recognized the small telltale signs. He desperately wanted to take her in his arms and press her for a day and time when he could see her again, but as he glanced over at his mom, he saw the twinkle in her eyes. The one that said she'd already decided where they should register for gifts. He stayed firmly planted in the chair.

Sam remembered she'd asked him a question. "There's no need to hang around, but I appreciate you coming by."

"Okay," she said in a quiet voice before quickly turning her attention to his mom. "Hanging with Wanda is always my pleasure." The two women said their good-byes, and without another glance his way, Julie left.

"Sammy, if you were looking for an opportunity to stake a claim, that was it."

"What do you mean?"

"The heart attack didn't affect my mind, dear. I can see the way you two look at each other. And I know you took her out to dinner."

Same raked his fingers through his hair. "Does everyone know my business these days?"

She ignored him as only a mother on a mission could. "So, what gives?"

"A date, that's all we've shared, Mom. One date."

"Was it horrible? Did she get drunk and pass out?"

Despite his irritation at being grilled like a schoolboy, Sam chuckled. "No, she didn't get wasted. We had a great time."

She waved her hand impatiently back and forth between them. "Okay, and...?"

"And that's all you're getting out of me on the subject of Julie Rose."

"If you insist. May I at least give you one small piece of advice? I promise I'll let it drop."

Sam snorted. "I don't believe that for a second, but I'm listening."

"Love is a risk, dear. No one knows that better than you do. The thing is, some people are worth it."

An orderly came in and saved Sam from replying. He didn't know what he would've said anyway except the truth, that Julie was worth the risk. Of that, Sam had no doubt. But would she feel the same way about him? One way or another, he needed an answer to that nagging question.

Chapter Seven

Since leaving Wanda in Sam's capable hands, Julie had been parked on the couch attempting to catch up on all her television shows. Her usual Sunday ritual had always been homework and vegging in front of the TV. After rewinding the same scene for the third time, however, she had to admit defeat. It was no use, because her mind was on Sam. He'd been so sweet and oh-so-romantic on their date. Wishing on stars, who would have thought? And then he'd taken her clear to heaven with his skillful touches. God, she still burned from the feel of his fingers buried inside of her pussy. She knew he'd enjoyed every second of it too. His sensual words on the phone that morning had been proof of that. So was the hard-on she'd seen him sporting at the hospital.

When he'd called and woken her up, he'd explained that he'd wanted to hear her sleepy voice first thing in the morning. He'd said he hadn't been able to sleep for thinking of her in his arms. He'd reminded her that she'd promised him another date. She'd ended up stammering, too excited to speak with any degree of intelligence.

Unfortunately, when he'd shown up at the hospital, he'd been back to frowning. She wasn't sure what had changed. At one point she could've sworn he was going to cross the room and pull her into his arms, but he hadn't. Julie wondered now if maybe she'd been imagining things. He hadn't acted at all like the same man who'd called her that morning simply because he couldn't get her off his mind. A knock on the door pulled Julie out of her gloomy thoughts.

"Saved!" Much more of that and she would've driven herself senseless.

Julie jumped up and went to the door. When she flung it

open, she came face to...Carhartt. Ah, she'd know that black coat anywhere. Julie looked up. "Sam? What are you doing here?" Right about then she realized she hadn't bothered to change out of her ankle-length red plaid flannel nightgown. And her hair was in rollers. Good God Almighty.

His gaze traveled down her body, then back up. His grin sent her blood rushing. "You like to be warm and cozy, huh?"

Embarrassment swamped her. "In my defense, it *is* five thirty on a Sunday and I wasn't expecting company."

He fingered one of her rollers and murmured, "I can see that. May I come in anyway?"

"Of course, sorry." She quickly stepped back, but before she could take her next breath, Sam was pulling her into a tight embrace and kissing her silly. He kicked the door shut behind him and pushed her up against it, then coasted his soft lips over hers. His tongue probed, demanding entrance. Julie wrapped her arms around his neck, then opened up and let him inside. He tasted good. Spicy and warm and so darn yummy. Julie knew she'd crave the taste of him.

When he pulled back an inch, he whispered, "I missed you."

"Uh-huh," she mumbled. Reality intruded when she remembered his odd behavior at the hospital. Julie pushed out of his arms and planted her hands on her hips. "Now wait a darn minute, Sam Jennings, if you missed me so much, then how come you were rude to me at the hospital?"

"Rude?"

She poked his chest. "Don't dare deny it. You were frowning at me. Again. Heck, you barely acknowledged my presence."

To her surprise, he looked shamefaced. "You're right, and I'm sorry."

"Thank you, but I still want an explanation," she demanded.

He unzipped his coat and pulled it off, then slung it over the recliner. "It's complicated."

"I'm a real whiz with complicated issues."

He looked pointedly at the couch. "Can we sit down?"

Julie didn't say a word as she strode toward the couch and sat. He followed and took the cushion to her left. "Brodix wanted to call you."

"He did? Why?"

"I assume to ask you out. I told him you were off limits."

"Don't try and tell me it's because you were protecting me. Not this time. I won't buy it."

"No, my motives were totally selfish."

"They were?"

"Yes. I don't want to share you."

"Why?"

He quirked a brow. "You're just chockfull of questions today, huh?"

"Yes."

"Stubborn," he whispered. "No wonder Mom likes you so much."

"Sam, I'm losing my patience."

Without warning, Sam reached out and took hold of her waist, then hauled her across the couch and plopped her onto his lap. He cupped her chin. "I don't want to share you because I want the right to call you my woman. Get the picture now?"

"And I'd like the right to call you my man, but that doesn't explain why you were pouting today when I saw you at the hospital."

His face went hard as granite. "I was not pouting."

She reached out and flicked a piece of lint off his collar. "Call it what you like, but I still want to know why."

"It threw me for a loop."

"What?"

"Seeing you next to Mom's bed, the two of you smiling together. She cares about you, and you care about her. I remembered at Thanksgiving how Brodix flirted with you. River was even a little taken with you, and that's a big deal for River. He's usually so closed up, barely lets anyone in. With you, he was at ease." He wrapped a hand around her nape and pulled her closer. "Everyone has a part of you, except me."

"Oh." Julie didn't know what to say. Sam had completely undone her with his stark confession. "Any thoughts on how to fix this little problem?"

"Give me a part of you, Julie. Give me the most intimate, sweetest part of you."

"Yes," she answered, her body suddenly ablaze with sensation. Caving in to his erotic demand was the easiest thing she'd ever done.

Sam's lips drifted back and forth over hers before he gently pulled back. He was aroused. His fierce gaze and the hard length beneath her bottom testified to the fact. Her pussy throbbed as she imagined his thick cock stretching and filling her. Julie started to bring him back to her mouth, anxious for more, but he stopped her.

"What is it?" Had she done something wrong to ruin the moment?

"You haven't been with many men have you, sweetheart?"

His question wasn't critical, but Julie still felt like a lumbering giant in a china shop. "How could you possibly tell that from only a few kisses?"

His smile was gentle as he said, "It's in the way you look at me. As if you want me in sixty different ways, but you aren't sure how to go about it."

Her gaze shot to his chest, unwilling to watch if he laughed at her. "I haven't had a lot of opportunities to experiment."

Sam tugged on one of her curlers. "Look at me, Julie." She squared her shoulders and met his gaze. "How about you experiment with me?"

Oh, now she was starting to get the drift. She let a small smile slip as she asked, "You want to be my canvas, is that it?"

He chuckled. "Sort of. That's what foreplay is for, to tease and play."

"And if I do something you don't like?"

"I'll like it. As long as it's you, I'll like it."

"And here I thought guys went for women who knew their

way around a man's belt."

His hands smoothed their way down her back to her bottom. He cupped and squeezed her through her flannel gown. "I don't know what other men want, nor do I much care. All I know is what I want, and I want you comfortable. For now, just let all your worries go, Julie."

"That doesn't sound too difficult."

He pulled her closer until his cock was pressed into the seam of her buttocks. Julie moved her hips back and forth, teasing them both.

"Sweetheart?"

"Hmm?"

"How much is not much?"

Her stomach sank. "Oh, lord."

"I need to know, are you a virgin?"

"No, it's not like that. But I can count on one hand the amount of lovers I've had and still have a finger or two left over."

His eyes shot wide. "Seriously?"

"Yes, seriously." She pushed against him, not willing to be humiliated by her lack of experience no matter how badly she wanted him. But he was about as movable as a cement wall. He wasn't budging. "Let me go."

His brows drew together. "What the hell for?"

"Because I don't need you staring at me as if I'm some sort of loser."

"I don't think you're a loser," he quietly explained. "I'm surprised, that's all. I mean, a woman as smoking hot as you should have men lined up on her front porch." He shook his head. "I'm glad they aren't, because I seriously don't share well with others."

She squinted, still leery. "You don't think I'm hopeless, then?"

He licked his lips and looked at her chest, as if mentally picturing her naked breasts. "You're the furthest thing from hopeless, sweetheart. Sexy, delicious and overdressed, but not hopeless."

Sexy and delicious, yeah, that works. She swallowed hard as his hands began to massage her backside. Sam had somehow managed to wiggle her nightgown higher, exposing her thighs in the process. His rough fingers there, teasing, nearly had her moaning, and he hadn't even gotten to the softer parts.

"Jesus, Julie, we need to lose the clothes. And the rollers."

Her hands flew to her head. "Wow, I actually forgot I had them in."

"Here, let me," he offered. It took him a few tries to figure out the catch on the side of the foam curler, but once he had it, Sam made quick work removing them.

"I'm a little bit impressed with your skills, you know," she admitted.

He chuckled. "You haven't seen anything yet." Soon, his fingers were sifting through her hair, massaging her scalp.

Julie moaned. "God, that feels good."

"You have beautiful hair, sweetheart."

"Thank you."

"But I'd really like to see the rest of you now."

Julie's eyelids popped open. "And I'd like to see you."

He picked her up and stood her in front of him, between his widespread thighs. "First, take off your clothes for me so I can see all of you."

Julie froze and looked around. "Uh, shouldn't we move this little party to the bedroom?"

Sam shook his head. "No, I want to see you now. Here." When she took hold of the hem of her gown and pulled it upward, exposing her legs, Sam hummed his approval. "Mmm, yeah, that's the way."

Sam sat back, watching her every move. His messy, dark hair curled up around his collar, and his jeans pulled tight over his straining erection. Julie licked her lips and tugged the gown higher, high enough that her white panties and belly were on display for him.

"So damn pretty," he whispered.

Julie's entire body hummed with excitement, and her pussy was wet with arousal. Her fingers shook as she slipped the nightgown over her head and tossed it to the floor.

"Ah, damn, I've died and gone to heaven," Sam declared, then he reached down and popped the button of his jeans, and Julie could only stare in anticipation of the big unveiling.

Chapter Eight

Julie's gaze roamed over his body, stopping and staring for several seconds at his cock before finally meeting his face. "You're magnificent," she replied, her voice a little husky. "And, uh, big."

Sam hadn't taken it nearly as slow when he'd shed his clothes. The way he saw it, the faster he was naked, the faster he could get back to drooling over her. "Hell, I want to go easy with you, sweetheart, to be gentle."

"A little speed never hurt anyone," she murmured as she licked her lips and stared at his cock once again.

He plucked her off her feet and sat her back down on his lap so that she straddled him, his dick a heavy weight between them. Every damned inch of her was perfect. "I went to bed last night thinking about your soft pussy beneath my hand. I couldn't get the look of you as you climaxed out of my head," he admitted. "I thought of how good it'd be to have you all spread out naked for me or bent over while I took you from behind."

She wrapped her arms around his neck and asked, "You did?"

He nodded. "But having you stand before me and strip in the stark light of day was by far the hottest thing I've ever witnessed."

She laughed. "Hotter than the rollers and flannel? I'm shocked."

"I don't mind the flannel or the rollers, but they were in the way of my goal." He'd liked her hair in the ponytail earlier too, but seeing the dark waves all around her shoulders, brushing her nipples, was damned sexy.

"I wouldn't want anything to get in the way of your goal,

Sam."

"When you were perched on my lap and that flimsy nightgown and panties were the only thing keeping me from paradise, I had the urge to shove it up and bury my cock inside you. I could've been balls-deep inside your sweet heat so fast, sweetheart."

"Why didn't you?" she asked, her voice not quite as steady as before. When she moved from side to side, Sam felt her wet pussy.

"Because that's not the way I want our first time together to be," he murmured. "No quick fuck on the couch, Julie."

She toyed with his hair, sifting her fingers in and out of the strands. He wondered if she even realized she was doing it. "What do you want?"

"I want to have a little playtime." Sam's mind stuttered to a stop when his gaze settled on her breasts. Lush and round, with large, mauve nipples. He wanted to taste her, to suck on her for hours. As he reached out with both hands and cupped her breasts and squeezed, Julie shivered.

"Cold or turned on?"

"I'm not sure it's possible to be cold with you sitting naked on my couch."

He grinned and continued to plump and knead the creamy swells. "So, turned on, then. Good."

He looked into her pale green eyes and declared, "You're mine now, Julie, and I'm going to make you feel so damned good." She nodded; then his lips were covering hers in a rough show of possession.

Sam licked and bit at her, hungry to take all that he could for fear she'd disappear in a puff of smoke at any second. Julie tugged him forward, and he was forced to tilt her head back. "Look at me," he ordered. As her eyes opened, he covered her mouth with his. She let out a little whimper, and the sound drove him higher. His cock was rock hard.

Sam kissed his way over her chin and neck. When his lips encountered her jumpy pulse, he gave in to temptation and suckled.

"Oh, God," Julie moaned as her fingers tightened and pulled at his hair.

Sam lifted an inch and whispered, "I need more of you."

"Anything," she promised. "Just please don't stop."

"No way in hell is that happening." He scooped her up and laid her out on the cushions beside him, then stood. When her eyes opened, her gaze wandered down his body in a heated journey that left Sam singed. Her curious eyes stopped on his cock, and he watched her lick her lips.

"Yes, taste it," he softly ordered. He wrapped his fist around the length and stepped to the couch until he was directly in front of her face. "Lick it, Julie."

Her sweet excitement thrilled Sam. It was all he could do to keep from grabbing her silky head and thrusting her onto his throbbing, aching cock. Knowing how little experience she had stirred his blood and squeezed his heart at the same time.

Her tongue darted out and licked every hard inch. "Jesus," Sam groaned. She teased the sensitive, bulbous head. When her hands came up to his balls, fondling and kneading, Sam's blood pounded hot and fast through his body. He took hold of her face and guided his cock into her mouth. "Fuck yeah. That's good. So damn good."

Julie started to suck him deeper, and Sam had to flex his legs to keep from falling to his knees. Her mouth was a hot, wet suction taking him to paradise. Julie moaned and began drawing him in and out. She went up and down on his pulsing erection, making love to him with her mouth. Sam reached down and pinched one nipple before wrapping his hand around the creamy weight of her tit and squeezing. When his thumb grazed her erect nipple, Julie nearly shot off the couch.

She pulled her mouth off him and moaned his name before running her tongue back and forth over the slit in the tip. A bead of precome appeared, and she lapped it up. Sam's gaze narrowed, and his jaw clenched tight as he pushed between her lips the tiniest bit. "Clamp down on me with your lips, sweets," he demanded.

When she tightened around him, he just about came. Sam pulled out instantly. "Mmm, that feels a little too good."

"I was enjoying myself," she said with a pout.

Julie's dark, shiny hair was spread out all around her and curling around one nipple, and her lips were swollen. Unable to resist, Sam leaned down and kissed her. Tasting himself on her mouth sent a shot of possessiveness through him.

"I gathered," he murmured. "But it's your turn now."

Julie's slow smile was all the encouragement he needed. Sam crouched low in front of her, slipped one arm behind her knees and the other beneath her neck, then lifted her into his arms, cradling her against his chest. Damn, she felt right there. She felt good. "Bedroom," he explained. "I'm going to need plenty of room for what I have in mind for you tonight."

Julie smiled and curled against him. "As it turns out, I have a king-size mattress."

"Handy," he said, unaccountably charmed by her. Seeing her in his arms and knowing she was giving him a part of herself that few had ever seen warmed Sam clear to his core. By the time their night was through, she wouldn't just be giving him a piece of her, but she'd be taking a piece of his heart. A mighty big piece.

Entering the bedroom, Sam went straight to her king-size bed and laid her gently down on top of it. Street light filtered in through the window, and he glanced over to make sure the curtains were pulled. Unfortunately they were. "Wow, those are...bright."

"They're horrendous and a little psychotic, but my grandmom made them."

He grinned. "I have a throw blanket on my couch that Mom crocheted. It's the ugliest damn thing I've ever laid eyes on."

"The sacrifices we make for love," she murmured, smiling up at him.

"Yeah," he replied as realization dawned. He was falling for Julie. Like knock-it-out-of-the-park in love. He should be a little freaked, but it felt too natural, too real. When he looked at her, sprawled out on the bed, her skin the gentlest shade of ivory, he pushed heartfelt-confession time to somewhere in the near future in favor of feasting on the beauty instead.

Her rounded hips tapered to a slim waist, then flared out again to full, womanly breasts. She had a voluptuous, hourglass figure that a man could sink right into and get lost in pleasurable bliss. Her nipples were dark, hard points, and he couldn't deny himself a good long suck.

Sam dipped his head and licked at the sweet treat, savoring the warmth of her satiny flesh. This moment would be etched in his brain forever. As he continued suckling and teasing, he flicked his tongue back and forth, creating a maelstrom of need with each stroke. His cock throbbed, and as Julie arched upward, thrusting her flesh into his voracious mouth even farther, he caved and gently bit down.

"Sam," Julie moaned.

He had to wrap an arm around her to keep her still as he kissed the little sting away. She whimpered, and Sam did it all over again to her other breast, taking his time, savoring the delicious flavor of his precious rose.

When he lifted away, releasing Julie's slim body, her eyes were closed and her mouth was open on a sigh. His cock swelled another inch when he saw her nipples glistening wet from his ministrations.

"Julie, open your eyes for me, sweetheart." Slowly, her lashes fluttered open, and he witnessed the heat in her green eyes. "You're hot and ready for me?" She nodded as if unable to speak. Sam stayed beside the bed and softly urged, "Then open your thighs. Nice and wide. Invite me in."

At first, Sam was afraid she was too modest to expose her pretty pussy for him so openly. She surprised him when she hesitated for only a few seconds before moving her legs apart, spreading herself for his view.

"Better?"

"Oh yeah," he growled. Sam saw the softness of her pussy lips and clit. She was wet, a testament to how aroused she was, to how badly she wanted him. Son of a bitch, he'd never wanted a woman the way he wanted Julie. She made him feel things with her trusting smile and loving nature.

Sam got onto the bed, between her smooth, shapely thighs, and looked his fill. She had a neatly trimmed bikini line. Her clitoris was swollen and totally exposed to his view. He licked his lips. "I need a taste of that. A good long taste, Julie." He lowered his head and licked her from her clit to her dewy lips before dipping in between. Her legs started to close, as if she were embarrassed, but Sam was faster, stronger. He clutched her thighs and held her firm. "Do you want me to stop?"

"No, it's just..."

"What is it, sweets?" Sam urged.

She slapped a hand over her eyes. "I get a little antsy sometimes. Nervous."

Sam tasted her tangy flavor on his tongue and knew he'd never sampled anything sweeter. "Does it help to know I don't bite?" he teased. "I might nibble a little, but no biting, I swear."

He inhaled her womanly scent, sucked her clit in between his teeth and nibbled. Julie's hand came away from her eyes and instead wrapped around his head. She clutched on to him as if she were on a runaway train.

He lifted an inch and whispered, "Easy, sweetheart."

When his tongue thrust between her folds, her head flung back, and she began to press against his face. Sam tongue-fucked her, licking and savoring. He sucked the little bud into his greedy mouth, and his balls drew up tight. God, he needed to fill her with his cock. He wanted to feel her inner muscles stretching and clasping his dick. She'd squeeze him like a vise, and he could die a happy man.

His tongue moved in and out of her, and his hands gripped on to her bottom, bringing her closer, delving deeper. A few more licks to her clit and she burst wide, screaming and straining against the unyielding hold his hands had on her. Sam stayed in place and watched as she collapsed, all but boneless, a languorous expression on her face.

He waited her out, keeping his tongue and lips against her

wet mound while she gained control. When he lifted to his knees and dipped a finger into her slippery heat, her eyes flew open. "Just making sure you're still among the living," he softly explained before sliding it back out and bringing it to her lips. He rubbed her juices against them, then leaned down and kissed it off. Julie whimpered and wrapped her arms around his neck, pulling him down on top of her. Just as her breasts came into contact with his chest, he caught himself and stopped. Rising up, Sam asked, "Condoms?"

"Top drawer."

He reached over and pulled it open, then found a box sitting on top of what appeared to be journal. He plucked it out and held it up. "You journal?" he asked as he quirked a brow at her.

"Yes, and it's private." She yanked it out of his hands and tossed it back into the drawer. "Mitts off my journal, buddy."

He chuckled. "Got it." Leaning back on his heels, Sam checked the date on the box to make sure they hadn't expired. Satisfied, he opened it and took out a condom. As he ripped it open and rolled it on, his gaze came back to hers and held. Sam saw a touch of that nervousness again, and he didn't like it. "I thought we already established that I don't bite."

She bit her lip and looked away. "It's been a few months."

Sam took hold of her chin and brought her back around to face him. "How many is a few?"

She frowned. "You're obsessed with details, do you know that?"

"Julie," he warned.

She rolled her eyes. "Fine. Right around thirteen, give or take."

Sam cupped her cheek and whispered, "That's a bit more than a few, but I'd never do anything to hurt you, sweetheart."

Julie took a deep breath, her chest rising and falling slowly, before she whispered, "Of course, I know that, silly. But you're not exactly Tiny Tim."

He burst out laughing at her description. "Tiny Tim?

Really?"

She giggled. "Well, it was the first thing that popped into my head."

Sam moved over on top of her and planted his hands on either side of her head. "I'm not tiny, that's true, but I am very focused when I set out to do something. And right now, my goal is to bring you pleasure. A thousand times more than you've ever had before." He smoothed a lock of hair off her forehead and kissed her before saying, "So, hush and let me focus, woman."

She smacked him on the shoulder. "You aren't supposed to tell a woman to hush when making love. It's rude."

Sam didn't respond but merely hooked her legs over his arms and glided his cock slowly into her. The skin over her cheeks tautened, and her breathing increased. He'd only gone an inch, but it was enough to have her clenching up on him. Sam watched closely as Julie chewed at her lower lip and closed her eyes tight.

"Relax, sweets," he urged as he slowly began rocking his hips back and forth.

Sam carefully controlled every motion, waiting for her tight opening to accommodate his intimate invasion. He wanted her to feel nothing but pure pleasure. He ached to hear her sexy sigh of repletion again.

"S-so good," she moaned. "Oh, God, Sam."

"Hell, yeah," he bit out between clenched teeth. "So fucking tight."

He kissed his way over her face and to her neck where he found that same jumpy pulse that he'd tasted earlier. He nibbled on her, creating a little purplish bruise against her alabaster skin. His gut tightened at the knowledge that he'd marked her. Julie's hand came up and covered the spot. When her eyes opened, he could see the desire building inside her.

Julie started moving her hips, a gentle thrust against his lower body. Sam placed his palm against her lower belly to hold her still. "Pleasure, not pain. Remember?"

"Sam, I need more," she explained in a breathless voice. "I need all of you."

"And you'll get it, I swear," Sam murmured. He feasted on her gorgeous tits, intent on building her passion so that when he was imbedded deep inside her pussy, she would feel nothing but white-hot satisfaction.

Sam thrilled when her inner muscles relaxed for him, and he moved into her a little more. Her legs came around his hips and held him close. The move caused his cock to slip in a little farther. It felt so damn good, and all he wanted to do was thrust deep.

"Mmm, that's the way," he whispered when she began moving her hips slowly up and down beneath him. "Let it all go."

Soon, they were moving in unison. Sam braced himself on his elbows beside her head and watched as Julie's desire mounted; then he pushed in, deep and hard.

"Yes!" she shouted as she clutched on to his forearms.

"Damn, you're something else," he said, worshiping her with kisses to her lips and cheeks. "Come again, Julie, with my dick inside this hot little pussy."

As if he had touched a button, her body stiffened, and she screamed as an orgasm overtook her.

"That's my girl," Sam growled, then he slammed his cock deep, driving into her, hard and fast. His hips flexed as he pounded against her. Julie grasped handfuls of his hair, and with one last stroke Sam came, filling the condom.

"You're mine now," he ground out seconds before he covered her mouth in a bruising, claiming kiss. "I'm not letting you go."

"That sounds somewhat sexist," she said, her voice hoarse from screaming out her climax. "But I don't really have it in me to argue."

Sam smiled and nipped her bottom lip with his teeth, which got him a light slap on the back of the head. "You said you didn't bite," she muttered, glaring up at him.

Sam's Promise

"That was a nibble, not a bite," he explained. When she still looked unconvinced, he leaned close and licked the little sting away. "Better?"

"Yes," she said, smiling.

He shook his head. "Good. Now, stay put. I'll be right back."

Sam slid out of her boneless body and went to the master bath to dispose of the condom. He grabbed a washcloth, ran warm water over it, and brought it to Julie. Her eyes were closed, and she had a dreamy smile on her lips. His body burned all over again at the sight. As he bent down and pressed the cloth to the juncture of her thighs, her eyes flew open. "What are you doing?"

"Soothing you so you won't be sore." He massaged her pussy with the warm, wet cloth and asked, "Does it feel good?"

"Very," she breathed out. "I could get used to this."

He remembered how she'd moaned when he'd taken out her curlers and massaged her scalp. "You like to be pampered, don't you?"

She laughed. "There isn't a woman alive who doesn't."

"True," he conceded. Sam removed the washcloth and took it back to the bathroom. As he came back out and slipped into bed beside her, she immediately snuggled up against him. He reached down and dragged the blanket over on top of them.

"Sam?"

"Yeah, sweetheart?"

"That was beyond amazing," she said as her fingers sifted through his chest hair. "Just thought I'd point that out."

He kissed the top of her head. "I couldn't agree more."

As she slipped off to sleep, Sam was left lying awake and contemplating his next move. Hell, he'd always heard it was the woman who got clingy and needy after sex. Here Julie slept in blissful contentment while he wondered if she would even want to be exclusive or not. An open relationship? No way in hell. They belonged together; he knew it in his gut. He just needed to prove it to her.

Chapter Nine

After several hours of sleep, Julie had woken to the feel of Sam's arms wrapped around her and his big, muscular leg slung over hers. He'd had her completely surrounded, and it'd been the best half-night's sleep she'd had in years. When he'd told her he was hungry, she'd offered to make peanut butter and jelly sandwiches. It was the middle of the night and it was silly, but she'd had fun carrying on with Sam in the kitchen. She'd ended up with strawberry jelly on her lips and chin, which Sam had seemed only too pleased to lick off.

At some point, she'd lost control over the remote, and he'd spent several minutes channel surfing before she'd managed to distract him with a kiss.

"You have the softest lips," Sam whispered as he dropped the remote on the coffee table and cupped her chin in the palm of his hand. He pressed his mouth to hers, and Julie surrendered. She whimpered, and Sam murmured something unintelligible against her mouth, then licked her plump lower lip. As his kisses drifted downward, his large hand wrapped around her breast through the T-shirt she'd slipped on earlier. He pinched her nipple, and Julie shuddered.

"Sam," she breathed out, edgy and restless all of a sudden. It was as if he wanted to devour her, and she was loath to stop him.

"I want to hear you scream out your pleasure again. It's so fucking beautiful when you come for me, sweetheart."

His tongue delved into her mouth and played with hers, teasing and tempting, driving her mad. She flung her arms around his neck and pulled him closer, pushing against him in a desperate bid for more. For all of him. One taste, one touch, and she was on fire. Julie pulled back, breathless, her chest heaving. "I-I can't get enough of you. Why is it never enough?"

"Because we were made for each other," he explained in a rough voice. "It's that simple." As he tugged her toward him once more, Julie felt him nip at her bottom lip with his teeth. "Stay with me next weekend," he growled. "At my place."

At his quiet demand, Julie's heart did a little somersault. She ached to say yes, but it felt too fast, and fear welled up. She pushed at his chest, and he got the hint and moved back with a frown. "I can't," she said.

"Why the hell not?"

"Just because, and don't curse."

"I'm sorry." He shoved a hand through his hair and let out a long breath. "Just because is not a good enough reason, though."

She straightened her spine and did her best to ignore how tempting he looked sitting on her couch in nothing but his black boxers. Holy heck, the man had an amazing body. All muscular and tanned. And big, she thought as she looked at his cock tenting the fabric of his underwear. She licked her lips and firmed up her resolve not to cave to the glorious man. "Yes, well, it'll have to do."

Sam quirked a brow at her. "I'm not dropping this until you give me a decent reason."

She got up off the couch and started to walk past him, but he was quicker. His hands snaked out and grabbed her right off her feet. Julie yelped as he flipped her upside down over his knees. She was now facing the floor.

"Sam Jennings, you let me up this instant!"

He snorted. "With your sweet ass all but in my face? I don't think so."

Her face burned with outrage as she stared at her beige carpet. "Damn it, Sam."

He tsked. "Now who's doing the cursing?" She felt his hand stroke her butt through the pink sweats he'd dressed her in earlier. "You know, a little tug on the waistband and I could have your flesh in my hands, considering you aren't wearing any panties."

She shivered at the notion, but her inner vixen aside, Julie wasn't about to give in to his dominance. "Let me up!"

"Nope," he murmured, "I sort of like you this way."

Julie began to wiggle around in an attempt to get away, but he easily held her down with a palm against her lower back. "You have such a pretty little ass, sweetheart."

His pleasure-filled words had Julie going perfectly still. "I do?"

Julie felt his fingers gripping onto the elastic waist of her sweats and tug. Cool air coasted over her bare skin. "These heart-shaped globes make me want to reach out and squeeze. I love your ass."

When he massaged one buttock and slid a finger between her ass cheeks, her pussy swelled and dampened. "Oh, God, what are you doing to me?"

"Playing," he answered in a voice barely above a whisper. She wouldn't have even heard him had she not been so tuned in to him in that moment.

"I've n-never played like this before," she felt compelled to admit.

"Hmm," he said, "that must be why you didn't know that bad girls get spankings, then."

Julie's clit throbbed at his erotic words. "Have I been bad, Sam?"

"Very naughty, Julie."

She was equal amounts turned on and outraged as she realized what he was about to do. Her squirming recommenced. "Don't you dare!" she shouted, slapping his leg.

He smoothed his palm over her bottom. "Will you tell me why you won't stay the weekend with me or not?"

"No," she bit out, knowing full well what he was about to do and excited by the taboo prospect.

"Too bad," he murmured seconds before swatting her left butt cheek.

Julie jerked, then froze. "You did not." Her skin stung a

little, but it wasn't painful as much as it was stimulating.

"I did." Sam sounded a little surprised himself. "I've never spanked a woman before, but I can see the appeal now."

"Well, I can't. Let me up!" she cried out, needing to be angry with him. The idea of playing the naughty girl to this dominant man was too tempting an opportunity, though. Besides, hadn't she been the good girl long enough?

He rubbed his hand over her bottom, effectively soothing the spot he'd swatted. Then he dipped his fingers between her thighs, and she knew he would encounter wetness. "You're turned on," he growled. "Admit it."

When she didn't answer, Julie knew Sam had his answer. "Why won't you stay the weekend with me?" he asked again. "Tell me, and I'll let you up."

Julie's skin tingled in anticipation of what would come if she denied him. There was only one word she wanted to say. "No," she moaned.

Sam swatted her twice more. First one cheek, then the other. Julie dropped her head against his leg and whimpered at the stinging pleasure. "This is so wrong," she breathed out.

"You like this as much as I do, don't you?" She offered nothing but silence and heard him groan. "So damn stubborn."

The observation didn't sit well, and she attempted to kick him but missed. "I'm not stubborn," she ground out.

"Sweetheart, you're as stubborn as a mule." He paused then added, "And if you don't tell me what I want to know, I'm liable to come in my boxers."

Julie reached beneath her hips and cupped his hard length in her palm. "Oh, God, I love your cock."

"Christ, you're killing me, woman," he muttered as he thrust his cock into her palm. Julie squeezed, relishing the way he thickened even more. "With your ass facing me, tempting me, I'm ready to self-combust here." His palm coasted over her stinging skin. "And knowing how close you are is making me want to fuck you. Hard." His hand left her and came down once more, harder than before.

She moaned his name, and her pussy dripped with her need to come. When Sam pulled her ass cheeks apart and pushed his index and middle finger inside her pussy, Julie cried out, widening her thighs. "Yes, Sam. More, please."

"Ah, that's my sweet girl." He pumped her pussy, slow at first, then faster. When she squirmed, rubbing her clit against his thigh, she nearly flew over the edge. Sam used his other hand to swat her buttocks. "Be still," he gently ordered.

"Please, let me come," she begged, beyond caring about her own pride in that instant.

"You will, I promise, sweetheart," he whispered as he finger-fucked her. "I could never deny you."

Little by little, Sam's fingers penetrated her until they were buried deep inside her hot pussy. She shuddered and pushed against him as she fondled his cock through the cotton material of his boxers.

"That's good," Sam groaned as he danced his thumb over her clit. He used one hand to hold her in place while he caressed and squeezed with the other. He seemed to have all the time in the world, teasing her body and bringing her higher with each stroke.

"My sweet little rose," Sam murmured, his fingers moving in and out.

His boxers dampened with his pre-come, and Julie desperately wanted to pull the material away and feel the silky hardness of his cock in her palm. When he alternated between slow and fast thrusts, her mind splintered. All rational thought fled as her need for release rushed in and took over.

As Sam held on to her, he flicked and toyed with her clitoris. Julie screamed as her climax surged through her, sending her skyward. It was fast and unexpected, and Julie lost all sense of time and place for several seconds.

Once her body collapsed, Sam gently pulled his fingers out of her and lifted her until she was perched sideways on his lap. She snuggled against his chest, her juices coating the insides of her thighs. Her butt stung a little as she nestled it against Sam's hard dick. Her lungs burned as if she'd run a marathon.

She felt him brush the top of her head with his lips before he wrapped one had around her nape, urging her to look at him. When their gazes caught and held, he whispered, "All I want is to sink my dick inside your wet pussy right now, sweetheart, but first tell me why you won't you spend the weekend with me. Pretty please?"

Julie kissed his chin, enjoying the feel of his stubble beneath her lips. She felt his arms tighten around her. "Talk to me," he said, his voice hoarse.

"Because I'm afraid," she said, giving him nothing more than the brutal truth.

His entire body stiffened. "Afraid?" It was clear that had been about the last thing Sam had expected from her. "Of me?"

"Of the way I feel about you," she rushed to explain. "Things are moving too fast."

"Ah, now I'm beginning to get the picture." He tapped her on the end of the nose and said, "Would it make any difference in your decision-making process if you knew I was falling for you?"

He seemed to be holding his breath. Was he afraid she'd reject him? Julie's chest tightened as she realized how easy it would be to give Sam everything. But the cautious side of her forced her to ask, "How do you know it's not just lust you feel?"

He didn't speak for a few seconds, but to Julie it felt like an eternity. "I know because I've felt lust. This isn't the same thing. Not by a long shot."

She started to answer, but when she felt his cock against her, she groaned and moved off his lap. As she stood, her legs wobbled a little. Sam reached out and grabbed her arms. "Thanks," she mumbled as she reached down and yanked up her sweatpants. She glared at him when the soft material rubbed against her bottom. "My butt hurts."

All at once, he appeared contrite. "Aw, baby, I'm sorry." Then he wrapped both arms around her middle and hugged her to him. "Want me to kiss it and make it all better?" he asked with an innocent smile on his handsome face.

An image of Sam on his knees kissing her behind invaded her mind, and Julie had to push it away in order to think clearly. He had her coming and going. She swatted his shoulder. "Stop distracting me." He released her, and Julie put several feet between them. "I want to have a rational discussion here."

One side of his mouth tipped upward in a delicious grin. "I thought that's what we were doing. No?"

"No." Julie eyed the cushion next to him and gingerly sat. "Look, I think I'm falling in love with you too, but Sam, this is fast. Like light-speed fast."

He leaned back, and Julie could see the wicked length of his cock beneath the boxers. Her mouth watered for a lick. "You're afraid you'll wake up and realize *you* were the one madly in lust, is that it?"

Julie winced and looked down at her lap. "Maybe. Yes." She clenched her eyes closed tight. "Oh geez, I don't know. I only know I've never felt this way before. It's a little scary." She opened them again and looked at him. "Aren't you afraid?"

Sam snorted. "Are you kidding? I'm scared out of my mind here, sweets, but I'm not about to let that stop me from exploring this."

"I don't want to stop either. I just don't know if we should start thinking of weekends together—yet."

He frowned. "I don't like it, but I'll take what I can get of you." He paused, then added, "And we're exclusive."

Every muscle in Julie's body went taut at the thought of Sam kissing another woman. "The only one in your bed had better be me," she warned.

His frown turned into a traffic-stopping smile. "Feeling territorial, little rose?"

She narrowed her eyes and poked him in the chest. "This particular rose has thorns, buster."

Sam suddenly stood and grabbed her hands, pulling her to her feet. "And the only man spanking that sweet ass of yours is me."

She tried to bat his hands away, but he wasn't budging. "You're perverted, and you're never touching my butt again." Okay, that was the biggest lie in the world, but she had to say something.

"Bullshit," he grumbled seconds before crouching low and flinging her over his shoulder. "I'll touch every part of you, Julie. Every sexy inch."

All the air rushed out of her, and the world turned upside down. "Dang it, Sam, I'm not a sack of potatoes." She smacked his back and shouted, "Put me down!"

He didn't bother to respond, merely strode right out of the room and into her bedroom. Once there, he flipped on the light and placed her back on her feet. Julie swayed, but before she could get her bearings, he swiveled her around until she was standing and facing the bed. "I want you," he murmured in that totally deep, sexy voice of his. "Tell me you want me too."

Like she was stupid enough to say no. "Yes," she breathed out.

From his position behind her, Julie felt him tug at her bottoms until they were down around her knees. He stopped a second, and she heard him curse. "This red ass has my dick so fucking hard." Julie's breathing was out of control, and her pussy ached to be filled by him. When he used his foot to nudge her feet apart, Julie looked over her shoulder in time to see him pushing his boxers down his thighs.

"You're so beautiful," she whispered.

He shook his head. "I'll accept hot, handsome, even delicious, but not beautiful."

She shrugged, not willing to argue the point when he stood there, his cock rock-hard and pulsing with vitality. As he reached for the box of condoms they'd left sitting on the end table and rolled one on, Julie turned back around and succumbed. It took only seconds before she was bent over the bed with his cock stretching and filling her hot pussy.

"It's too much, Sam," she said, feeling completely overwhelmed by him.

He stilled instantly. "Did I hurt you?"

"No, it's just...it feels s-so full," she confessed in a breathless voice. "I feel like you're everywhere."

He clutched on to her hips and began a gentle rhythm inside her. "You want it slow and easy, sweetheart?"

Did she? She couldn't think straight. "I-I don't know."

Sam pulled all the way out, then pushed back in, holding her in place as he rotated his hips. Julie felt the full extent of his arousal, and it fueled her own. "You like it when I get wild, though, huh?" he asked, leaning down and licking the shell of her ear.

"Yes, damn you!" Julie cried as she pushed backward, needing more. Needing everything he could possibly give her.

Sam placed his hand between her shoulder blades and gently pushed until her breasts were smashed against the mattress. "Tell me what it feels like when I fuck you hard."

"It feels like I'm going to break into a million pieces and I can't catch my breath."

Sam's hand moved to her buttocks, and she could feel him massaging away the slight tenderness from his spanking. "Trust me, Julie," he softly urged. "I'll never truly hurt you. I'd rather die than hurt you."

Her heart melted at his loving words. "God, when you say things like that..."

"Shh," he soothed. "Just feel me. Feel how good we are together."

He began moving, slow, easy, giving her a sweet tempo that had her pussy wet with pleasure. When her inner muscles gripped his cock like a lover's fist, Julie pushed her ass backward and pleaded, "More."

"Fuck," Sam gritted out as he wrapped his hands around her hips and began thrusting in and out.

Julie's legs shook, and her pussy throbbed.

"Damn, your little pussy is sucking my dick so good."

"Yes. God, Sam, come inside me." Julie's passion spun out of control as tremors shook her body.

Sam leaned over her and placed a line of kisses up her spine. When he reached the back of her neck, she felt his fist in her hair as he clutched a handful and turned her face to the side. He suckled the tender skin of her throat, and Julie whimpered. Her pussy clenched around him. Julie was on the very edge when Sam lost it and shoved into her once, twice. She screamed as her climax swept over her.

"Son of a bitch." Sam's arms wrapped around her, holding her tight as he came, shouting her name.

Julie collapsed. It was only after she caught her breath that she realized how late it was. "We are going to be so freaking tired tomorrow."

Sam chuckled and kissed the back of her head. "Today, you mean."

Julie groaned and buried her face into the mattress. When Sam lifted off her and pulled out, she instantly missed the deeper connection. She turned over and watched him pull his boxers up.

He held out a hand. "Come on, we need a shower."

Julie placed her palm in his, content to let him lead her into the bathroom. The water was cold by the time they were through. Sam had thoroughly washed every inch of her body, praising her as he went. She felt completely cherished by the time they were under the covers, the early morning light filtering through the curtains.

"I am falling for you, Sam Jennings," she confessed, unable to contain the sense of rightness she felt in his arms.

He brought her hand to his lips and placed a kiss to her palm. "That's going to make what I'm about to say easier all the way around, then," he whispered.

She lifted her head. Even in the darkness, Julie could see the smile on his sexy face. "Oh?"

"Mm," he mumbled as he placed little kisses to each of her fingers. "I was thinking maybe you'd like to help with the diner's remodel."

Julie's heartbeat sped up at his words. "You want my

help?"

He placed her hand back on his chest and smoothed a palm down her hair. "You have a head for business, and you said yourself you're a year away from graduating. This could be good experience for you. Besides we could really use your knowledge through all this. And I'd like to hire you on as manager once it's all said and done too."

Julie couldn't be more thrilled. She loved working at the diner. Becoming a bigger part of it was too exciting for words. Still, she erred on the side of caution. "Have you discussed all this with your mom and the others?"

"The guys are onboard, but I need to go over everything with Mom still. I didn't want to hit her with it the first day out of the hospital."

She scooted higher up on the bed until her face was aligned with his and said, "If she agrees, then you have yourself a manager."

Sam winked. "How about a kiss to seal the deal?"

She placed little butterfly kisses along his jaw and chin before finally taking his mouth. His lips were too tempting, though, and she soon became distracted. Sam's arms closed around her, holding her tight as he deepened the kiss.

"God, I'm addicted to you." He groaned as he licked her bottom lip. Julie arched against him, but it was Sam who came back to the present and gently pulled her away. "You need a break," he explained.

When Julie cuddled up next to him, she could feel his heart beating beneath her cheek. "I want more of this—ending the day in your arms," she whispered. "It's nice."

"Me too," he admitted.

Julie laughed as she thought of Wanda. "Your mom, the matchmaker, is going to be thrilled. You do realize that, right?"

Sam snorted. "No doubt there are times when the woman knows me better than I know myself."

Chapter Ten

It was Friday night, and Julie had spent all her spare time with Sam. They'd gone to the movies, to dinner, even bowling, and they'd made love more times than she could count. Now, as Julie looked around the room, she realized how similar the scene was to Thanksgiving. She was right back where she started, sitting at Wanda's large oak table with every eye on her. She knew now what the fireflies must feel like in the glass jar. The one exception was the man sitting to her right. Sam was staring at her as if she hung the moon, and with his support, she knew she could do anything.

"So, you've agreed to this, Julie?" Wanda asked, the first to speak.

Julie tamped down on her mounting nervousness and said, "Yes. I know I haven't graduated yet, but I think I would do a good job as manager. If you'll have me, of course."

Wanda nodded. "I'd be crazy not to hire you as the manager." She looked around the room. "And all you boys think that turning the diner into a bar and grill is the best solution?"

Several of them nodded, except River. Wanda frowned. "River?"

"The diner is yours, Mom, always has been. I want whatever makes you happy."

Wanda smiled as she reached across the table and patted River's hand. "The diner is ours, son. And it pleases me no end to see all of you taking such an interest." She looked down at the table and said, "But I do have an apology to make." When her head came back up, her eyes looked troubled. "To all of you."

"Mom?" Sam asked, concern etched into the hard lines of

his face.

"It's my fault it's come to this." Several disagreements filled the air, but Wanda merely held up a hand, effectively halting the stream of remarks. "I've never been good with money. That was your dad's thing, and I'm afraid I was too proud to ask you boys for help. If I had, then you wouldn't all be forced to take time out of your lives to fix this mess."

"Wrong," Sam shot right back.

"What?" Wanda said, surprise in her expression.

"You said yourself the diner is ours," Sam explained.

Wanda nodded. "It is. Your father and I both wanted it that way."

"Then we're the ones who should be apologizing for not stepping in to do our part."

Vance spoke up, adding his two cents. "We left it all on you, and we should've known better. It's too much for one person to handle."

"Not that it matters now," Reilly inserted. "Sammy has come up with a way to make things right."

"It'll be a lot of work," Brodix said as he flipped open a pad of paper that looked as if it had numbers scrawled on it. "I've been running some numbers, and we'll all need to pitch in, but Sam's plan can work."

"Mom, is this what you want?" River asked, still looking worried.

Wanda grinned. "I can't think of anything I'd want more."

Sam smiled. "The Blackwater Bar and Grill it is, then."

A fresh start, Julie thought, and she was a part of it all. She couldn't stop the joy from spreading through her chest as she looked at the Jennings bunch and realized she was fast becoming a part of them as well. They were loud and unorganized, even a little dented in spots, but she adored them. They spent the rest of the afternoon making plans. Several times Sam had turned to Julie and asked for her opinion, and she'd fallen for him a little more each time. When they got ready to leave, Sam wrapped his hand around her nape and kissed her, right there in front of everyone. She heard a few wolf whistles, but for the most part, all she heard was the sound of her own heart beating out of control.

Sam tended to have that effect on her.

When they got in his SUV, he turned to her. "You've started to slip inside my heart, Julie Rose." And before she could get her mind wrapped around what he'd declared and possibly respond, his mouth was on hers in a bruising kiss, and Julie didn't have it in her to resist. She wrapped her arms around his neck and pulled him in as close as the middle console would allow and let him feel every ounce of what she felt for him. He angled his head and sucked her lower lip into his mouth, then bit down lightly. Julie inhaled the clean, masculine scent of him. When he lifted his head, they were both breathing hard. "Sweet and tangy, that's what you are. I'm fucking addicted to you, sweetheart."

She cupped his cheek in her palm. "Sam?"

He absently fingered the top button on her blouse and murmured, "Yeah?"

"You already know that I'm falling for you, but I need to take this one step at a time, okay?"

His gaze came back to hers and stayed there. "As long as we're in the same ballpark here, then we'll go at a snail's pace if you want," he confirmed before descending on her once again. It was several seconds before they parted, her body on fire with liquid need.

"I'm desperate for you, sweets, and your place is too damn far away."

She laughed, knowing full well that he was hinting they should go to his place. He still wanted that weekend with her. "You just had me this morning, remember?"

"I remember, but I'm a greedy son of a bitch. I'm going to want you several times a day. In and out of bed. Be warned."

"Bossy," she whispered before kissing him sweetly on the mouth. Then he took control, and the sweet caress of lips turned into hot searing desire. She was thrown off balance completely. She should be used to that by now, she thought wryly. This time when they broke apart, Julie said, "You win."

He quirked a brow at her. "I do?"

"Yes," she moaned. "I'll spend the weekend with you."

"Thank God," he exclaimed. He flicked the top button of her blouse open and bent his head to her neck, feasting on her as if she were his last meal.

She tried to stop him by leaning as far back in her seat as she could. He stopped and frowned at her. "What?"

Julie pointed a finger at him. "Stop that, we're in public, and there are laws."

He winked. "Just a taste, I promise." He wrapped his hand around the back of her head and nudged her forward. "Come here," he growled.

Julie relaxed and let him drag her closer. "Resisting is apparently futile," she mumbled, and he rewarded her with a soft, gentle kiss. She melted under the onslaught.

Sam licked the seam of her lips, then delved inside. Julie reached out and gripped his shoulders, then lower to his strong biceps and forearms. Sam had the most delicious arms, so firm and sculpted. She couldn't prevent a moan of pleasure from escaping as his tongue skated inside her mouth and played with hers. Sam's mouth slowly left hers and made a trail downward. His lips teased her chin and cheek; then her neck received a little suckle. Her breasts swelled, and her nipples hardened, as if desperate for his touch. When his lips found the opening of her blouse, he placed a loving kiss to the cleavage there and pulled back.

"I don't think I've ever enjoyed kissing a woman as much as I do you. Your mouth is made for mine. So sweet and soft." He bobbed his eyebrows. "It reminds me of something else I've had my mouth on recently."

At the reminder of their early morning lovemaking, Julie's cheeks heated. "You're very bad."

"Ah, there it is, that pretty blush." He stroked one too-warm cheek with his calloused thumb.

Sam started to say something when someone banged on the driver's side window. She looked over his shoulder and saw Brodix standing on the other side. She quickly did up her top button as her blush turned into a full-on fire.

Sam cursed and rolled down the window. "What?"

Brodix laughed. "Am I interrupting?"

"Yes," Sam bit out, "now go away."

Brodix leaned closer and in a quieter voice said, "Just thought you might like to know that Edna has been watching you two for the last five minutes or so."

Sam looked out her side window and frowned. "That woman is a nuisance."

Curious, Julie asked, "Who is Edna?"

"Mom's neighbor. Always sticking her nose in other people's business. Drives everyone on the street batty."

Sam's gaze went back to Brodix. "Thanks, man."

Brodix gave him a nod. "No problem. You kids be good now," he said as he headed toward his car.

After Sam rolled up the window, his attention came back to her. His grin was pure sin when he tapped her nose. "The entire weekend, sweetheart. Hmm, what to do..."

"We could always play Monopoly," she offered with a grin.

Sam started the engine and put the truck in gear. "If it's strip Monopoly, then you've got a deal."

"Like, you land on one of my hotels and you have to take off an item of clothing and vice versa?"

"Yep," he answered.

Julie crossed her arms over her chest. "I have to warn you, I always win."

He entwined their fingers and brought her hand to his mouth for a kiss. "It'll be my pleasure to lose to you, sweet rose," he murmured against her skin.

"This is bound to be some weekend," she replied as butterflies took flight in her stomach.

He chuckled. "Damn straight."

As he took off down the street, Julie sat back in her seat,

content to enjoy the ride with the sexy man who'd so sweetly stolen her heart.

Vance's Rules

Dedication

To my awesome family. Without your love, support, and endless supply of hugs I would've thrown in the towel ages ago. Thanks for always being in my corner!

Chapter One

Shayla stood on the porch of Vance's home, shaking with nerves. She hadn't seen him for twelve years. Each day away from him had caused her heart to ache. Stomach in knots, Shayla thought again about how much time she'd wasted, and all because of one man's hatred. Her father had done everything in his power to keep her away from Vance Jennings, but those days were over, and Shayla aimed to set things right. If Vance slammed the door in her face, so be it, but at least she had to try.

She took a deep breath and rang the bell. After a few seconds, the door swung wide. A shiver ran the length of her spine at the sight of Vance standing in front of her in a heather-gray T-shirt and well-worn jeans. She'd always had that reaction to seeing him. Why should the years apart change anything? Vance Jennings had the looks of a charmer, only with a rougher edge, as if he'd had more than his fair share of hard knocks and had come away with more than a scratch or two. She took a moment and looked him over, all but breathing in the perfection of him.

His hair was as dark as the night itself, shiny and thick and long enough to be irresistible, even if it did need a good comb-through. The glow from the light behind him cast iridescent colors throughout the thick mass. Her gaze traveled over the angles of his face, noting every taut plane, the stubble covering his chin, and especially the generous line of his mouth. God, not even an artist could draw a mouth as soft and inviting as Vance's. The man was just so damn kissable. Always had been. Shayla sighed as she realized how much harder this meeting was going to be than she'd originally thought.

She noticed the way he watched her. Like an angry

panther, his eyes were always so intense, and they seemed to see right into her soul. When he looked her over from head to toe, Shayla stiffened. Sure, the years had been kind to Vance, but what would he think of her after all this time? She'd filled out, pretty much all over. Gone was the skinny young girl with stars in her eyes.

Enough, she chastised herself. She wasn't here to visually devour the man. She was supposed to explain why she'd dumped him like so much garbage and walked out of his life over a decade ago. Should be a ton of fun.

"Shayla," Vance gritted out. He blinked a few times, and Shayla wondered if he was as baffled as she was by her presence. And the way he said her name, as if it left a bad taste in his mouth, didn't give Shayla much confidence either.

"Hi," she said, smiling in an effort to hide her anxiety.

Vance frowned. "It's been a long time, Shay."

Don't I know it? A gust of cold January wind hit her in the face, and Shayla stiffened. "May I come in?"

He hesitated, but Shayla couldn't blame him. After what she'd done to him, he had every right to slam the door in her face. When he stepped back and let her into the foyer, Shayla counted it as a small victory. "I hope I wasn't interrupting," she said, then cringed at the sound of her own voice. She was talking to him as if he were a perfect stranger. As if they hadn't once been in love.

Vance shut the door and tucked his hands into the front pockets of his jeans. "Nope."

"Oh, well, that's good," she said as she looked down at the floor and hitched her purse up her arm. Where was she supposed to begin? Even though she'd rehearsed this a million times, Shayla was suddenly at a loss for words.

"You might as well get to it."

At the sound of Vance's deep voice, Shayla looked up. Their gazes connected, and she opened her mouth to speak, but nothing came out. Her throat closed up and her heart rate sped. When her face felt as if it were on fire, Shayla groaned. *Oh please, not now.* She simply could not have a panic attack now. When her lips began to tingle and her eyes felt as if they were bulging out of her head, Shayla knew that was exactly what was happening.

Vance stepped forward and took hold of her shoulders, his expression filled with concern. "Hey, you okay?"

Shayla couldn't get her mouth to work properly, so she shook her head instead. Her hand went to the front of her turtleneck sweater and yanked in an attempt to get air into her starving lungs. It didn't help; nothing would. She felt Vance tugging her coat off, and within seconds, he had her sitting on the couch.

Vance crouched in front of her. "Easy now," he murmured. "Just relax and take a few deep breaths."

She did as he instructed, and when her face started to cool down, she knew the anxiety was beginning to pass. A large palm pressed to the back of her neck and rubbed. For a moment, Shayla let herself sink into the warmth of having Vance's gentle palm against her skin. After so many years without his touch, she wanted to soak in every second. Too soon, he was moving away. He sat in the chair across from her, his expression unreadable.

"Thanks," she said. "I'm not sure what happened there."

He cleared his throat and sat back. "Now that you can breathe, care to explain why you've decided to show up on my doorstep after all this time?"

Here goes nothing. "I wanted to clear the air," she blurted out.

Vance's gaze shot wide. "Are you for real?"

Oh yeah, there's that Vance Jennings temper. "I know I don't deserve it," she said, "but please listen to me."

Vance shrugged. "Why would you think I'd even care? It's been twelve years, Shay. A lot of time has passed."

She held up her hands, palms out. "You're right, there's no reason you should give a fig, but aren't you a little bit curious? Didn't you wonder why I wrote that letter telling you we needed some time apart?"

"No," he bit out, "because I already knew why."

Her own temper flared. He was so sure he had all the answers, but Shayla knew better this time. "Oh really?"

Vance leaned forward, so close she could smell his intoxicating male scent. "You were Daddy's good little girl, and you got tired of playing with the bad boy of Blackwater." He looked her over, lingering for a heart-pounding few seconds on her chest before meeting her gaze again. "I was good enough to fuck but not good enough to keep."

Shayla paled. Was that what he'd thought? That she hadn't loved him? That he hadn't been her whole world? Good Lord, Vance hadn't just been her first boyfriend; he'd been the first guy she'd ever let get to second base. And on one warm summer evening, Shayla had even given him her virginity. It'd been a magical night for her, despite the fact that they'd made love in the front seat of his truck. Afterward, they hadn't been able to keep their hands off each other. She'd loved him with her whole heart. Although he didn't know it, to this day Vance still held the distinct honor of being the only guy who had ever managed to send her to the moon with a single touch, and yet he thought she'd only been in it for the kicks? "You cannot be serious."

"Don't look so dumbfounded, honey." His cold grin sent a shiver down Shayla's spine. "I knew then that I had no business coming within a hundred feet of you. Trust me, when you dumped me, you did us both a favor."

Confused, Shayla asked, "How's that?"

He leaned back in his seat and crossed one ankle over the other. "It made me realize that some little rich girl could never satisfy me for the long haul."

Her ears were playing tricks on her; that had to be it. Shayla counted to ten in an attempt to regain control. It didn't work for crap. "Is that how you saw me? Like some bubble-headed daddy's girl?"

Vance stood as if to end the conversation. "Like I said, we dated for two years a long time ago. None of it matters now."

Shayla stood too, but not to leave. Oh no, he was going to listen to her if it was the last thing she did. "Look, I came here to clear the air, and that's what I'm going to do." Vance started to argue, but she barreled right on, consequences be damned. "Sit down, shut up and let me talk, Vance Jennings."

A muscle in his jaw jumped, giving away just how much anger he was holding in check. "Look, I—" The phone interrupted him, and Shayla felt as if she'd been given a reprieve. When it rang again, Vance cursed. "Stay put, damn it."

As he strode from the room, Shayla let out a long breath. Well, she'd accomplished the first step in her plan, at least. Keep Vance from kicking her to the curb, which was nothing short of a miracle. The question was, could she get him to listen? The really bigger question, the one she hadn't let herself think too long on, was could she get him to give her another chance? Because in addition to clearing the air, Shayla desperately wanted one more shot at a relationship with Vance.

The man had haunted her dreams. She'd tried to forget him, but even dating other men hadn't helped. Shayla always ended up comparing them to Vance. No man could hold a candle to him.

It was a nightmare, nothing more. Sure as shit he'd wake up from it any time now, because no way in hell was Shayla Riggs—high school sweetheart and the woman who'd torn out his heart—really sitting in his living room. As the house phone rang a third time, Vance grabbed it off the counter and hit Send.

"Hello?"

"Hi, sweetie, did I wake you?"

His mom's cheerful voice on the other end of the line was pretty much the only thing that could bring his temper down to a low roar. "No, Mom, I'm awake. What's up?"

"I was curious if you were coming into the diner today. You mentioned some changes to the plans you drew up for the remodel."

Damn, with Shayla sitting in the other room, he'd be late to the diner. When he and his brothers had decided to remodel the family restaurant and turn it into a bar and grill, Vance had volunteered his construction company for the job. The diner had been struggling, and in order to keep from seeing it go under, they'd all decided to pitch in and help out. Vance would do anything for his family, and he'd especially do anything for his mom. She and his adoptive father had taken him and his four brothers from foster care and given them something they'd never had before: love. Two years ago, a massive stroke had taken his dad away, and Vance still missed hearing his deep voice and feeling his rib-crushing hugs.

"I'll be there," he said, then thought of the woman sitting on his couch. "It'll be later, though. I have something to take care of first." Like getting rid of a ghost from his past.

"That's fine, dear. Julie and I are going to go to the mall to do some shopping anyway. Call me when you get there, okay? I want to see the changes you've worked on."

At the mention of his brother's new girlfriend, Vance smiled. "I'm surprised Sammy's letting Julie leave his bed on a Sunday morning to go shopping. How'd you manage that?"

Instead of sounding scandalized, his mom laughed. "That son of mine does have a hard time sharing, but I have ways of getting around him."

Vance chuckled. "I'll just bet you do." No one knew better than he did how sneaky his mom could be. When Wanda Jennings wanted something, she moved heaven and earth to get it. As Vance realized what his mom had said about going shopping, he frowned.

"Wait, shouldn't you be staying home and resting?" he asked, worried that she was overdoing it. "After all, it was less than two months ago when you were laid up in the hospital."

A heavy sigh filled his ear. "It was a mild heart attack, not a triple bypass, Vance. Besides, Julie has me taking yoga classes with her now and eating healthier too." She tsked. "I swear she's worse than you boys when it comes to my health."

"And we're all plenty grateful," Vance said, meaning it, "but the doctor ordered you to take it easy, remember?"

"And that's what I'm doing," she replied, speaking more slowly, as if he were an idiot, "taking it easy and going shopping." Vance shook his head at the woman's screwed-up logic, but before he could get a word in edgewise, she plowed right on. "Oh, and before I forget, I got a phone call today from Shayla Riggs. Do you remember her?"

Vance stiffened and peeked around the corner and saw the woman in question sitting on his couch chewing at her lower lip. "Uh, yeah."

"Well, she called asking about you."

Vance was beginning to smell a rat. His mom was notorious for playing matchmaker, and he suddenly felt as if she'd set her sights on him. It would make sense, considering Sammy was all but headed to the altar with Julie. Vance would be the next in line, to his mom's way of thinking. "And what'd you tell her?" he asked, already knowing the answer.

"Oh, we had a nice chat. She was always such a sweet girl. I'm not sure whatever happened to you two."

Vance snorted. So sweet she'd dumped him via a letter. She'd left town quickly after, and he hadn't even gotten a chance to talk to her. To beg her to take his worthless ass back. He hadn't heard a word from her since, until now.

"Vance? You still there?"

"I'm here," he grumbled.

"Anyway, like I was saying, Shayla mentioned that she was back in town and wanted to get in touch with you. I told her where you lived." There was a slight pause before his mom added, "I hope you don't mind."

And bull's-eye, Vance thought, a direct hit from Wanda the Cupid. "Mom." He said her name in warning, knowing it was futile.

"Sorry, dear, Julie's here. I need to go. Love you!"

Vance barely had time to bite back a curse before he heard the dial tone in his ear. He couldn't really blame his mom, though. She didn't know what Shayla had meant to him back then. How much he'd loved her. How he'd imagined marrying her. He'd been good at playing it off, acting as if it was all just good fun. And for sure, Vance hadn't let on how much Shayla's betrayal had cut him. He'd hidden the hurt well.

Her unexpected return brought all those feelings out of hiding, the good and the bad. He'd loved her so much, but when she'd dumped him, Vance had grown to almost despise her. Now she was back and looking better than ever with her cute shoulder-length red hair and hourglass figure. The grown-up Shayla had a body that didn't quit. The girl he'd once known with the modest curves had developed into quite a woman. His cock flexed in his jeans as Vance gave in to his imagination and thought of how good she'd feel tucked up close to him. Then again, how long would she be around? Was she in Blackwater to visit or to stay?

Vance took a moment to regroup before heading back into the other room. What did Shayla possibly hope to accomplish after all these years by showing up on his doorstep? Too damn many questions, and the only way he was going to get any answers was if he stopped dicking around in the kitchen. He'd let her say whatever it was she had to say. She had something to get off her chest? Fine and dandy by him. After she was finished, he'd show her the door. He planned to make it crystal clear that she wasn't welcome back through it too, because no way was he getting involved with the woman again. Once was enough. He'd learned his lesson the painful way.

Chapter Two

Shayla watched Vance stride back into the room, anger turning his hazel eyes cold and distant. The firm set of his powerful shoulders brought Shayla to her feet in an attempt to feel less vulnerable, not that it helped. Vance's six-foot-plus frame dwarfed her, sitting or standing.

"If you have something to say, then you best get to it," he ordered in an irritated voice. "I have somewhere to be."

"The diner, I know," Shayla replied, recalling the lovely talk she'd had with Mrs. Jennings earlier. She'd always liked the woman with the gentle smile and kind eyes. Shayla had been surprised Mrs. Jennings hadn't hung up on her when she'd given her name, considering how she'd treated Vance.

"That's right, you spoke to my mom." He crossed his arms over his chest and quirked a brow at her. "Have a nice talk, did you?"

"Yes, actually, I did. Your mom is really kind."

"She's also not up to par, considering she had a heart attack in November."

Shayla sucked in a breath. "Oh, Vance, I had no idea. She's okay now? And how's your dad doing?"

"Dad passed away a few years back. A stroke."

She flinched at the pain she heard in Vance's voice. "I'm sorry. I didn't know."

He nodded stiffly. "Yeah. And to answer your other question, Mom thinks she's just peachy, but the doctor doesn't want her stressed."

Ah, now she saw where he was going. "And my being back in Blackwater is stressful. Is that what you're saying?"

"I'm saying you should say whatever it is you came here to

say, then leave."

"First of all, I'm not going anywhere. I'm back in Ohio for good."

For the first time that Shayla could remember, Vance Jennings seemed truly speechless. "Huh?"

"I've been back for a month now. And I've moved my business here." She smiled. "So you see? I'm pretty much here to stay, whether you like it or not."

"Jesus, I can't deal with this right now." He strode across the room and grabbed a pair of black work boots from the front door. "Just say what you wanted to say and go."

Shayla's heart sank at the finality of Vance's tone. "No, not like this," she said, frustrated at herself for believing the visit would go better. For believing they could be civil. More than anything, Shayla was mad that even though Vance was sending her the "go away" vibes, she still felt something for the man. "I'll come back when you aren't so busy."

"I'm always busy," he gritted out.

Shayla merely stared at him, unwilling to be browbeaten into giving him a clipped version of why she'd dumped him. Of why she'd come back after all this time. "I'm not about to try and condense it into a few short, easy-to-swallow sentences just so you don't have to deal with me," she said, feeling bolder than she should. "You're just going to have to make time."

"Fine." He sat on the edge of the couch and started to pull on his boots. "But don't expect me to stop whatever I'm doing just to accommodate your newfound conscience. I did that once. Never again."

Oh, now that was going way too far. "You sure as hell weren't the only amenable one back then, Vance."

He stopped lacing up and glared at her. "What's that supposed to mean?"

"I did whatever you wanted, and you know it. I never said no to you. Never." Of course, she hadn't really wanted to say no, but that was beside the point.

Vance laughed, but the sound was far from joyful. "Is that

why you broke up with me in a letter? Because you knew if you faced me, you wouldn't be able to go through with it?"

She slumped at the bitterness in Vance's voice. "No, that's not the reason."

He shot to his feet. "Then why, damn it? Spit it out, Shayla!"

Shayla lost it. "I was trying to protect you!"

"Bullshit," he ground out as he pointed a finger at her. "You were protecting yourself. You never gave a damn about me."

"Forget it." She threw up her hands and headed for the front door. "I should've known better than to come here."

A pair of strong hands took hold of her shoulders from behind, halting her exit. "You aren't getting off that easily, Shay," Vance said as his warm breath caressed her neck. "Not this time. You came here to tell me something, and you're damn well going to follow through this time."

She took a few deep breaths to calm her racing heart, then turned in his arms so she faced him once again. Vance's hard body brushed against her, and Shayla's knees threatened to buckle. Good Lord, he was so lean and powerful, as if fat didn't dare come near him. Electricity raced through her bloodstream at his nearness. When his intoxicating woodsy scent hit her senses, Shayla had to force herself to stay cool. "You don't want me here, and I get that. In fact, you have every right to be angry. It was a mistake to expect anything different from you. I'm sorry."

"I—" His cell phone started to beep, forcing Vance to let go of her in order to grab it out of the clip on his belt. He frowned when he looked at the screen. "Damn, I need to go," he said as he hit a button.

She nodded. "The diner, I know."

"But this isn't finished," he said, calmer now. "Come back tonight. Seven o'clock."

Was he really extending an invite to her? Shayla wanted to hope, but she, better than anyone, knew hope could lead to a big heaping pile of disappointment. She bit her lip and looked down, uncertain what to do. Would she be setting herself up for another fight? For more disappointment? "I don't know," she admitted, closing her eyes tight to hold back the tears.

"You coming here took a lot of guts, and you wouldn't have bothered if you didn't have something important to get off your chest. You caught me off guard showing up so suddenly, Shay, that's all."

She looked into his eyes and saw the anger was gone. Maybe he really would listen to her. Maybe he'd even believe her. "Seven?"

He nodded and smiled a little, although it seemed forced. "I should be finished up by then. I can give you my undivided attention."

"I can't ask for more than that." Shayla picked up her coat and pulled it on. "I'll see you tonight."

Vance only nodded. As Shayla opened the front door, the blistering cold took her breath away. It was abundantly clear that January in Ohio was nothing like the weather she'd grown used to in Florida, and she wasn't at all prepared for it. Her coat was too thin, and the frigid air went right through her. At least that was what she wanted to think was causing cold shivers to travel the length of her spine. When she got in her car, she dared to look back. Vance stood tall and proud in the doorway, watching her. Even from the distance, Shayla could make out the annoyed scowl.

Oh yeah, tonight was bound to be a big old bowl of cherries.

Chapter Three

"Goddamn it, Brodix, I told you that wall cannot be removed," Vance gritted out. "It's a load-bearing wall."

Brodix held up both hands. "Fine, whatever. Christ, what's your problem? Someone piss in your Wheaties?"

True to form, Brodix appeared as fresh as a freaking daisy even though he'd already put in a few hours of work. His long-sleeved, navy-blue shirt looked as crisp as when he'd walked in that morning, and there wasn't a hair out of place. How the man could stay so damn clean even as sawdust coated the floor was a mystery.

Vance tossed his hammer aside and moved closer to his brother, angry when he saw him pecking at the small device in his hand. "I'd be in a fantastic mood if I didn't have to constantly repeat myself." He pointed to the black-and-silver piece of electronics in Brodix's hand. "Hell, if you'd listen instead of playing with your damn calculator, maybe I wouldn't have to."

"I'm trying to figure out how to pay for this, remember?" He looked down and punched a few more keys, then shook his head. "The material for this remodel is going to cost us a friggin' bundle."

"Vance."

When he turned around to find Sammy standing a few feet away, frowning, Vance knew he was in for it. He could practically feel his oldest brother's disapproval. "What?" he shot right back.

"You and I need to talk." Sammy pointed toward the kitchen, then turned and started walking, as if Vance would simply follow.

Of course, that was exactly what he did. He always had a hard time saying no to Sammy. They all did. It wasn't that Vance was afraid of him. They'd butted heads and left bruises on each other plenty over the years. It was more about respect. Before Wanda and Chet had come along and adopted them, they'd all looked to Sammy for guidance. Even though he'd only been a kid himself, Sammy had done what he could to watch out for the rest of them at a time when no one else had wanted to take on the lousy job.

When they reached the kitchen and the swinging doors closed behind him, Vance felt boxed in. Immediately, he wanted to turn and leave. He hadn't felt that way since his father's death, helpless and at a complete loss as to what to do. No doubt, Shayla's sudden reappearance in his life was doing a number on his calm, well-ordered world.

"You've been snapping at everyone since you got here," Sammy said, leaning his large, six-foot-plus frame against the stove. His work boot started to tap out a rhythm against the tile floor, and Vance immediately recognized it as a sign that Sammy was settling in to give one of his lectures. "What's going on?"

"Nothing," Vance bit out. "I'm just tired of constantly repeating myself."

"Vance, we all know you have the biggest part to play here since your construction company is doing the work, but Brodix has been working day and night trying to crunch the numbers to keep this thing within budget. No easy task."

Vance immediately felt like shit. He shoved a hand through his hair and admitted, "I know. I'm being a pain in the ass."

Sammy shrugged. "Yeah, you are, but why?"

Vance knew there was no way around it. If he didn't tell Sammy about Shayla, their mom would. "You'll find out sooner or later. Might as well be sooner."

Sam stiffened. "I seriously hate surprises, Vance."

"Shayla's back in town," Vance bit out. Saying her name brought her image to his mind. She was older, but the years had been good to her. She'd lost some of the sweet innocence that he remembered, but she'd gained a good amount of backbone to replace it. Her thin frame had filled out in all the right places too, he'd noticed. God, how was it possible to be attracted to someone who'd torn out his heart? Was he just that pathetic?

"Shayla Riggs?"

"You know any other woman with that name?" he asked, wishing he could start the day over again. "Yes, Shayla Riggs."

"Damn," Sammy muttered. "And she's been by to see you?"

"This morning. She stopped in as if she hasn't been gone for the last twelve damn years. Can you believe that shit?"

His brother shook his head. "Fuck, no wonder you've been acting like you wrestled with a porcupine."

Vance rolled his eyes. "Gee, thanks for the sympathy, bro. Appreciate it."

He waved a hand in the air. "Yeah, yeah. So, what did she want?"

"To clear the air, she said. As if that's even possible." He grunted. "I mean, why would she think I'd care after all this time? We've both moved on. What we had is over."

He quirked a brow. "You sure about that?"

"Yes," he replied, knowing it was a lie. Seeing Shayla again had brought it all back, as if the last twelve years hadn't existed. No, God damn it, he'd gotten over her. She'd just surprised him with her sudden reappearance. There wasn't any more to it than that. And maybe unicorns really did exist. "She can confess all her sins, but it won't change the fact that whatever we had is in the past." Vance thought of how well he'd handled the situation and groaned.

"What?"

He looked down at the floor. "I, uh, didn't exactly welcome her with open arms."

Sam was silent a moment, then in a low tone, he asked, "You still carrying a torch for her? And be honest."

He thought about lying, to himself and Sammy both. Unfortunately, Sammy would see right through it the way he always did. "I don't know," Vance admitted. "Maybe."

Sammy shook his head. "Did you at least find out if she's married?"

Ah hell. "Christ, I didn't even think to ask. I was too busy trying to figure out if I was having a really fucked-up nightmare or something."

"You'd better find out, if you plan to go any further with her."

Vance stiffened. "The only thing I have planned is to find out the truth. I figure she owes me that much."

"True, but I don't want to see you hurt." Sammy closed the distance between them, clapped a hand on his shoulder and squeezed. "She cut you pretty bad once, Vance. I know you don't want to hear this, but you nearly dropped out of school when she dumped you. You were pretty friggin' raw over Shayla, and it took you a long time to get over her. Don't let her do that to you again."

He knew Sammy was right and that he had the best of intentions, but it still stuck in his craw that his brother had to issue the reminder. As if he was too dense to look after himself. Then again, Vance did have a tendency to forget common sense whenever that woman was anywhere near. "She's coming over tonight," he replied. "I figure we'll have a calm, polite discussion; then she can leave. She'll have a clear conscience, and I'll know the real reason why she left. A win for both of us."

"I hope you're right, bro."

When they heard a curse in the other room, they headed back into the dining area in time to see his youngest brothers, the twins Reilly and River, striding through the door. Reilly wore the heavy black parka their mom had bought him for Christmas and carried a couple of bags from the hardware store. River had his brown leather coat zipped clear to the chin. The dark sunglasses he sported gave Vance a pretty good idea why Reilly was glaring at his twin. Another late night? Probably. When Reilly punched River on the arm and River punched back, Vance knew the answer was yes. He checked the clock on the wall and frowned. "Where have you two been all morning?"

Reilly scowled at River. "Well, I've been busy picking up supplies from that list you gave me yesterday, but sleepyhead's been in bed getting his beauty rest."

Vance laughed for the first time that day. "Out too late again, River?"

He yawned, then took off his shades and stuck them in his coat pocket as he headed toward the coffeepot. "Nope, just up too late."

About three weeks ago, River had started taking out a different woman every night, as if he was on a damn quest to bed every available woman in Blackwater. "What's her name this time?" he asked, curiosity getting the better of him.

"Christy," River answered. The coffeepot paused halfway to his cup, and Vance watched as he frowned. "Or maybe it was Crystal."

Vance chuckled, but Sammy wasn't nearly as amused. "You seriously need to chill with the one-night stands or you're going to catch something. Christ, River."

River waved the warning away and continued pouring the coffee. "I'm not an idiot, Sammy. I do take the necessary precautions." He held the pot out for Reilly, but he shook his head. River replaced the carafe on the warmer, while Reilly continued to frown at his twin. After River took a cautious sip, he looked over at Vance. "So, where's your crew? I figured they'd be pounding the shit out of this place by now. We're removing the counter today and installing the bar, right?" He paused, then added, "And where's Mom? I thought she wanted to see the changes you drew up."

Vance headed around the bar and sat on a stool at the counter. "Mom and Julie are out shopping; should be along any minute. And we are installing the bar, but I gave the crew the day off. They've been working their asses off on this place and needed the break."

Brodix took the seat next to him and glared. "Hey, why didn't you bitch at him the way you did me?"

Confused, Vance asked, "Huh?"

"You told all of us yesterday that the crew had today off," he reminded him with a kick to the side of Vance's shin. "You hate to repeat yourself, remember?"

Vance scratched his chin. "Yeah, sorry about the attitude earlier. My day didn't quite start out the way I planned."

"Why?" Brodix asked. "What happened?"

"Shayla Riggs happened," Vance replied, knowing there was no use trying to keep his private life private.

"Shayla? Like, Shayla from a decade ago?" Brodix asked. When Vance nodded, Brodix let out a low whistle. "Whoa. And I see it didn't take her long to get your boxers in a twist," Brodix helpfully supplied. "See? This is why I don't bother with long-term relationships. Too many cute fish in the sea to start getting all tangled up with just one little piranha, if you ask me."

"Vance, you still hung up on that girl?" River asked with a cocky grin on his face, as he picked up on only part of the conversation.

Vance flipped him the bird and turned his attention back to Brodix. "You know, one of these days a woman is going to come along and knock you on your neatly pressed ass. Like the supportive brother that I am, I'll gladly help you up while I laugh myself fucking silly."

Brodix chuckled. "Not going to happen, but you keep dreaming, sugar."

Annoyed that he hadn't managed to ruffle his brother's feathers in the slightest, Vance tried to come up with a witty response, but River's cell phone started to chirp, interrupting them. He took it out of the front pocket of his coat and looked at the screen. The wide, toothy grin River suddenly sported had the room going quiet, all of them curious if the woman on the other end was the same one River had spent the night with.

When River hit the Answer button and shouted, "Sunshine!" Vance instantly knew that the person on the other end was none other than Jeanette Munroe. She happened to have the distinct role in River's life of being his one and only friend. Jeanette was a sweet, tomboyish type and a few years younger than River. She also happened to be the only person River ever allowed to sleep in his bed. Not even the women River dated stayed all night. Vance figured it was a remnant from his brother's nightmarish childhood. Being a foster kid had sucked for the lot of them, but River had had it worst. Abuse seemed like a tame word when Vance thought of what River's foster father had put him through.

"God, he'll be on the phone an hour at least," Reilly grumbled as he watched his brother and drummed his fingers on the counter. "Now that I think about it, I remember River saying something about Jeanette coming home from college for a few days."

Vance nodded. "Looks like we're down one, then, because sure as shit River will be spending the rest of the day with her."

When River set his cup down and went into the other room to talk in private, Sammy cursed.

Sammy's entire body seemed to go rigid, and Vance frowned. "What's wrong?"

He took a pack of gum out of his shirt pocket, ripped open a piece and popped it into his mouth before he asked, "Do you think that boy will ever figure out that Jeanette's feelings run deeper than friendship?"

Reilly snorted. "Hell no. I asked him once why they don't date. She's good for him, makes him happy. He's always more relaxed around her too."

They all three nodded in agreement. "What'd he say?" Vance asked.

Sadness seemed to drain some of the life from Reilly in that moment. "That Jeanette deserved better than damaged goods."

"Fuck," Sammy replied.

"Pretty much," Reilly said. He moved away from the counter and headed for the front door. "I'm going to start unloading the truck."

Brodix grabbed his wool coat from a booth near the door and offered, "I'll help."

"Good deal," Vance said. "We have spackling to do and a

counter to rip out. Might as well get started." After the brothers nodded and headed out, Vance looked over at Sammy. Neither of them said a word. They wanted River whole again, but they both feared that was one dream that may never come true. Hell, Vance knew too well how quickly a dream could disappear. He'd had plenty of dreams once upon a time, and several of them had included Shayla.

Chapter Four

Shayla watched Vance dish up the penne pasta and alfredo sauce he'd made for their dinner into a couple of cream-colored bowls. He placed one in front of her and smiled. "I hope you like it. The alfredo sauce is Mom's recipe."

Vance definitely had the "Doctor Jekyll and Mister Hyde" routine down pat. When she'd arrived, tension had filled the air as Vance took his time looking her over. Shayla's body had responded to the heated journey his gaze took with a trickle of moisture between her thighs. Of course, she had taken an extra few seconds to admire Vance's long, muscular legs in the snug-fitting jeans. What woman wouldn't? When she'd finally managed to tear her gaze away, she'd gotten stuck on the way the white T-shirt stretched across his wide chest. Unfortunately, the frown he sent her way effectively chased away any remnants of desire.

"When I arrived earlier, you looked about as happy as a kid with a toothache, and now you're cooking for me and smiling." She squinted suspiciously at him. "What gives?"

"It's dinnertime, and I'm hungry." Vance shrugged. "Don't eat if you don't want it."

She considered it a moment, then caved. No sense in looking a gift horse in the mouth. "I'm sure I'll love it," she offered. As she inhaled the aroma of parmesan cheese and fresh garlic, her stomach rumbled. "It smells heavenly. When did you learn to cook?"

Vance smiled as he took a seat across from her. "Mom taught all of us. She's always held strong to the belief that whatever a woman can do, a man can do—and vice versa."

"She's a pretty special lady." Shayla smiled as a memory surfaced. "I'll never forget that time she brought that care package to the hospital for me when I had my tonsils removed. Remember that?"

"Yeah, she insisted on buying you that little red-and-white teddy bear. Swore it'd make you feel better." He shook his head, a small smile playing at the corners of his mouth. "I didn't have the heart to tell her that you were a senior in high school and probably didn't sleep with teddy bears anymore."

Shayla bobbed her eyebrows. "Ah, but you'd be wrong there. In fact, I still have George. He sleeps next to me every night."

Vance's eyes rounded in surprise. "Get out! Seriously?"

She laughed. "Yep."

Vance went quiet, and she wondered where his mind had gone. She took a bite of her food and realized it tasted better than she'd imagined. It wasn't at all fair that the man cooked as wonderful as he looked. How was a woman supposed to keep from drooling when she had a tanned, hazel-eyed hottie sitting so close? Shayla let out a sigh and dug into her food, wishing she had the right to do more than admire Vance from afar. For a while, they both ate in silence. Soon, Vance pushed his bowl away and sat back.

"I don't see a ring," he stated as he stared at her hand.

Shayla swallowed the last bite of her dinner and dabbed her mouth with a napkin. "Uh, that's because I'm not married. Not dating either." A horrible thought struck, and she asked, "You?"

"No. I've been too busy getting Vance's Construction off the ground to even consider marriage."

"Starting your own business isn't a walk in the park. Lots of late hours."

"You sound like you speak from experience."

She stood, then brought her bowl to the sink and ran water in it. "I do. I started my own digital-first publishing company a few years ago. It's just now making me enough money that I was able to quit the dreaded day job."

He cocked his head to the side. "Digital? Like those books

you can download to your phone and laptop?"

She smiled and propped herself against the counter. "Yep. And I've moved the company here, which was nothing short of a nightmare, let me tell you. I mean, I have a terrific staff, but there are always problems." She shrugged. "First there was an issue with the Internet in the building we're leasing, which took forever to fix. Then some new software we purchased recently didn't want to cooperate with the old computers, so we were forced to upgrade. We managed to get things all worked out, but we were all pulling our hair out."

"It sounds like a nightmare," Vance said. He paused before adding, "So, you were serious when you said you were here to stay."

"Very serious. I never wanted to move away in the first place. That was Dad's idea. I didn't have a choice in the matter. Now I do. And even though there are some bad memories associated with Blackwater, it still feels more like home to me than anywhere else."

He watched her with suspicion. It was clear to see in his gorgeous eyes, and Shayla wished she could ignore it, pretend it wasn't there. "You're in Blackwater for another reason too," he said.

Shayla sat back down and picked up her napkin. She crumpled it in her hand, unfolded it, then crumpled it again. Okay, so she was nervous, but who wouldn't be? Taking a deep breath, she slowly released it before saying, "It's way past time you learned the truth, Vance."

"I agree," he replied in a tone that gave no hint to his mood.

"Before we go down this road, though, you need to understand a few things."

He propped his elbows on the table and crossed his arms on the tabletop. "I'm all ears."

"You remember my parents?" she asked, jumping right in.

"Who could ever forget them? Your dad was the richest man around. A big-shot lawyer. Your mom was a stay-at-home mom. Nice lady."

Shayla nodded. "Dad was a district attorney and a very good one. Never lost a case. Mom basically took care of everything else."

"All really interesting, but what does that have to do with you and me?"

"My dad is the reason we broke up, Vance."

Vance stiffened. "Come again?"

"He wasn't just hell in the courtroom. Dad was hell at home too." Shayla looked down at the table, scared all of a sudden. It was as if that by telling Vance her family's dirty secrets, her father would come back from the grave and punish her all over again. Even dead he intimidated her.

She heard Vance shifting around, and she looked up to see a dark scowl marring his handsome face. "What are you saying, Shay?"

"Dad's motto was a little different than your mom's. He believed that if you spared the rod, then you spoiled the child. Or in Dad's case, it was the belt he rarely spared."

Vance fisted his hands on the table. "Are you saying he beat you?" His gaze narrowed. "If so, how come I never saw any marks on you?"

She crossed her legs, then uncrossed them. Her heart raced and her palms grew damp. It'd always been very clear she was never to speak of what went on inside the Riggs home. Her father had drilled it into her head on numerous occasions. "Oh, not just me. My mom too. He thrived on pain, but he was always careful not to hit so hard that he left any permanent marks. A few welts that would go away in a day or two, but that's it."

Vance stood and began pacing the room. He was silent for several minutes before he turned and glared at her. "You talk about him in past tense. Does that mean he's dead?"

She nodded. "He passed away five years ago. A brain embolism. He died sitting in his study going over a court case."

"Good, saves me the trouble of hunting him down."

Shayla didn't know what to say to Vance's protective

Vance's Rules

attitude. He was an honorable man and would view any sort of domestic abuse as unforgivable. Instead, she stuck to the words she'd rehearsed. "Anyway, Dad's the one who forced me to break it off with you. He's the reason I wrote that letter."

Vance snorted. She watched him go to the refrigerator and take out a beer. After popping the top and taking several swigs, he said, "The prick never liked me. Never liked any of the Jenningses." He placed the beer on the counter and looked over at her. "Still, you could've told me in person. None of what you've said so far explains why you chose to take the coward's way out and send me a letter." He stepped closer and pointed a finger at her. "A letter, Shay! Do you know what I went through when I realized you were already gone by the time I read that damn scrap of paper?"

Tears stung the backs of her eyes, and she had to work hard to keep them in check. "I'm sorry, but it was the only way I could keep you safe."

Vance stood there and stared at her for several seconds. Once he was calm, he sat in the chair he'd vacated earlier. "You said before you were trying to protect me. From what?"

"Do you remember that day Dad caught us kissing outside the school?"

"Yeah. He was pretty damn worked up about it." His jaw went rigid. "Did he hurt you that day?"

Shayla looked down at the table. "No, but he threatened to destroy you. He was in a rage and swore he'd ruin the Blackwater Diner if I didn't stop seeing you."

"Bullshit," Vance shot back. "He was just spouting off."

Shayla's eyebrows shot up. "What?"

"Think about it. What could he possibly do to me? I wasn't a juvenile delinquent, and my parents ran a good, honest business. He wouldn't have had anything on us."

She quirked a brow, completely flabbergasted by Vance's uninformed opinion of her father. "You have no idea what you're talking about," she muttered. "My dad never made threats. If he said he would destroy you and your family, then he would've done whatever it took to make that a reality. When I said he never lost a case, I wasn't trying to imply he won them by honorable means. You're measuring his values as if they were the same as yours. Believe me, they weren't."

"Okay, I'll concede that your dad was a crooked son of a bitch. I never liked him, not from the start. And after what he did to you, I'd beat him to death if he were still alive. But that doesn't explain why you didn't get word to me *after* you moved away. You could've gotten in touch with me somehow. Through Mom and Dad, if nothing else."

Shayla slumped in her seat. This was the part she'd dreaded. The part she couldn't forgive herself for. "I-I was scared. That's my only excuse, Vance."

"Of your dad?" he asked, his voice softer than before.

She bit her lip and looked down at the napkin in her hand. God, she'd all but shredded the poor thing. She dropped the pieces on the table and said, "Yes. I hate to admit this, but he still scares the hell out of me."

She felt a strong hand covering hers, and she glanced across the table to see understanding in Vance's expression. "It's okay to be afraid. It doesn't make you weak, Shay."

She couldn't handle the kindness she witnessed in Vance at that moment. It made her want too much. It made her wish they hadn't lost the last twelve years. Instead, she focused on her confession. "When he moved us to Florida, I thought Dad would be happy. After all, he'd gotten what he wanted, a dutiful daughter and a promotion. But things only got worse for my mom and me."

Vance released her hand and sat back. "Christ, how could it be any worse?"

"Dad turned into a tyrant. One of us was always on the receiving end of his violent temper. It didn't stop until Mom got sick."

"Sick?"

She nodded. "Breast cancer. When Mom was diagnosed, Dad grew distant. Stayed late at the office. Meetings out of town, that sort of thing. We rarely saw him. Then he died. God help me, but it felt like a blessing for both of us. We no longer had to walk around on eggshells, no more late-night rants. Best of all, no more belt. Still, that left me to care for Mom, which I didn't mind doing, but it did sort of cause me to put my own life on hold for a little while."

He nodded. "How is your mom now?"

"Oh, I'm happy to report that she totally kicked cancer's butt. And it gave her a sense of self-respect that I'd never seen in my mom before." She grinned. "She's living it up in Florida as we speak. Even has a new man in her life. Fred is a really sweet guy and nothing at all like Dad, thank goodness."

"So, let me get this straight. Your piece-of-shit dad threatened you, beat you and your mom, threatened me and my family, and then you took care of your sick mom, and still somehow found the strength to start your own business."

"That's the short version, I suppose, yes."

He stood and walked toward the sink, then turned and looked out the window for a time. Shayla couldn't gauge his mood now. Would he call her a liar and send her on her way, or would he give them a chance to make up for lost time? She waited. Waited and hoped.

Chapter Five

Vance couldn't look at Shayla. Not after everything he'd just learned. He felt like a total shit for the things he'd thought about her over the years. She'd lived in fear of her own father, and Vance had been totally oblivious. "I've spent the last twelve years resenting the hell out of you, Shay," he said, unable to turn around and face her. "The entire time you were living a nightmare, and I was feeling sorry for myself." He rubbed a hand over his face and muttered, "Jesus."

"No, don't do this. After Dad passed away, I could've contacted you. I could've gotten in touch after Mom's cancer went into remission. I didn't because...because I wasn't sure you'd want to hear from me. And you would've had every right."

He turned around and looked into her eyes. "You could've, yes, but I could've gotten in touch with you too."

"You didn't even know where I was." She cocked her head to the side. "Give yourself a break, okay?"

He closed the distance between them and tugged her out of the chair. "It wouldn't have been that hard to find you," he murmured. "All I would've had to do was ask my mom. She'd have tracked you down faster than a bounty hunter."

She smiled. "You do have a point there."

"It doesn't matter, not anymore. All that matters is what happens next."

"What does happen next, Vance?"

He grinned. "Stick around and find out."

Shayla's heart sped up at his deep, sexy tone and the wicked gleam in his eyes. When Vance smiled, Shayla's insides turned to pudding. "Your mom said you built this house."

His lips twitched. "Are you changing the subject, honey?"

"Yes," she answered, totally wishing she had the nerve to pull him in for a kiss instead.

"Okay," he said as he released her. "Want me to give you the penny tour?"

"I'd love that."

"Then again, you already saw the downstairs."

She looked around the kitchen. "Yeah, but I've barely paid attention. I was a bit distracted." She turned in a circle and took in the spacious room. Beautiful tile floors and a rectangular, dark mahogany wood table. The ceiling fan wasn't anything fancy, but it suited the room. "I love all the dark wood and the tan walls. Very warm and inviting." She wondered what the rest of the house looked like. Like his bedroom, for instance. Pretty darn spectacular, no doubt.

"I can't take all the credit. My mom played a big part with the colors and furniture." He motioned to her with a wave of his hand.

She followed him into the other room. "Dad brought in a professional decorator when we moved to Florida. By the time the woman was done, I felt like we were living in a museum. It was about as warm as an iceberg."

He stopped and moved to the side so she could precede him into the living area. "Didn't your mom have any say?"

"Mom learned early on not to speak her mind." Shayla stepped into the spacious room, immediately impressed with its sheer size. It was big but comfortable, with large bookshelves lining one wall and a warm fire burning in the fireplace. How had she missed the fire? God, she really had been stressed about tonight's visit.

The furnishings weren't anything extravagant. A beige couch and matching loveseat faced the hearth, and a cozy pair of recliners in the far corner appeared perfect for reading. Shayla about drooled when she looked at some of the titles of the books. "You have great taste in reading material," she admitted as she turned her attention back to Vance. "Your home is beautiful."

He smiled, one of those sexy half-smiles that made her knees weak, and murmured, "I get the feeling you expected a lot of steel and black leather."

"Steel, yeah, that about sums it up." She walked to the bookshelf and grabbed a leather-bound copy of *The Scarlet Letter* off the shelf and held it up. "Hawthorne? I so didn't expect that."

He crossed the room and snatched the book out of her hands, then placed it back on the shelf with the utmost care. "Is it a crime to like quality writing?"

Vance's nearness kicked Shayla's hormones out of whack, and her body suddenly felt entirely too warm. "Nope. I just didn't figure you for much of a reader."

Vance tsked. "You shouldn't assume, especially when it comes to me."

The deep timbre of his voice caressed her senses. "You're a constant surprise," she said, feeling a little light-headed, "that's for sure."

Vance started for the kitchen again. "Enough with the tour. How about a nightcap instead?"

Shayla's gaze went straight to Vance's butt as he turned and headed toward the doorway. He wore a pair of low-slung jeans, tight and sexy, much like the white T-shirt that stretched over a drool-worthy, muscular back. No matter what the man wore, Vance Jennings simply had the finest ass she'd ever laid eyes on. Oh yes, she would dearly love to reach out and grab a handful, but when his words registered, she frowned. "I thought you'd show me the upstairs."

"That's for another night."

"I can't wait," she mumbled, unable to pull her gaze away from the man's oh-so-squeezable butt. He was the picture of perfection and always had been. Shayla recalled the way he used to encourage her to play with him. They'd spend hours touching and teasing each other. Shayla swore she could feel Vance's rough palms coasting over her skin even now. An inferno of need had burned inside her whenever Vance's hands were on her body. That was before she'd broken his heart and destroyed the trust he'd had in her, though. What would it be like to make love to Vance now with so much resentment and hurt between them?

Vance glanced over his shoulder, and Shayla held her breath, afraid she'd spoken the words too loud. When he shook his head and said something incoherent, Shayla released her breath.

Oh, yeah, she definitely had it bad for the man. The years hadn't changed that at least. But she couldn't tell what he wanted. Was he even remotely attracted to her? A few times during dinner it seemed like she'd seen desire in his eyes, but maybe that was just wishful thinking.

Watching the emotions flit across Shayla's expressive face brought Vance back to the first moment he'd seen her. It was in Biology II, and Shayla had been wearing a demure white blouse and a pair of loose jeans. Her hair had been pulled back into a ponytail, little strands hanging around her face. At first, he'd thought her mousy and sort of forgettable. It hadn't taken him long to start imagining what her slight curves would feel like pressed up against his body.

He'd flirted with her, and she'd blushed. It'd turned him on. He'd spent too many classroom hours staring at her ass. She'd caused a riot within his hormones, then and now. More than once, he'd imagined taking hold of the little elastic band holding her hair back and yanking it free so he could watch as all her rich, red hair cascaded down her back.

When they'd started dating, Shayla had spoiled him with her sweet, giving nature, Vance admitted to himself. He hadn't been forced to do much chasing because she'd been so enamored of him. The first time they'd made love, in the front seat of his pickup truck, no less, Vance had been thrown for a loop by the fact she'd been a virgin. Guilt had assailed him. Hell, she'd been innocent until he'd gotten hold of her. The next morning in class, she'd looked at him and smiled. The combination of sweet innocence and naughty vixen had done him in. He'd been toast after that. Vance hadn't been able to keep his hands off Shayla. If he remembered correctly, she'd been every bit as greedy for him.

Vance knew now what they'd had was puppy love. Shayla was more confident now. He had a feeling she wasn't going to be quite so malleable this time around. She'd all but tossed a wrench into his well-ordered world with her sudden appearance as it was. He grinned in spite of himself. If she had any clue how intent he could be when he wanted something, she never would've stepped foot into his house.

When she sat on the couch in front of the fire and smiled up at him, Vance wasn't sure whether he wanted to lick her from head to toe or push her out the door.

With resignation, Vance went to the kitchen cupboard and took out a bottle of wine. "Merlot, okay?" he called out.

"Perfect, thank you. So," she said, "have you always lived here alone?"

It didn't surprise him she would fish around to see if he'd ever had a woman living with him. Shayla was curious by nature. As he headed back into the living room, Vance hid a grin and decided to tease her a little.

"Actually, Elizabeth lives here with me."

Shayla squinted. "Elizabeth? But you said you weren't seeing anyone."

"Elizabeth isn't just anyone. She's upstairs," he said as he poured them each a glass of wine, "sprawled out on my bed."

The look she shot him was downright lethal. "I see. Well, I hope I didn't interrupt...anything."

Yep, the woman was definitely jealous. Vance sat down next to her and took a sip of his wine. "Eh, Elizabeth doesn't mind, but don't expect her to come down and visit. She's shy."

Shayla tucked a wayward strand of hair behind her ear, then started drumming her fingers on her thigh. Vance knew Shayla well. The twelve years she'd been gone hadn't changed the fact that she only performed that little ritual whenever she was agitated—and without a doubt, right now she was agitated. "How long have you two been together?"

He swirled the wine around in his glass. "Ten years, give or take." When her eyes grew wide, Vance added, "Shayla, Elizabeth is a cat."

Her gaze narrowed. "A cat?"

Vance winked. "Yep. A pretty, slightly obese, gray-and-black-striped cat that I found at the animal shelter."

She placed her glass on the coffee table and crossed her arms over her chest. "You were putting me on."

Vance's gaze zeroed in on Shayla's breasts. She wore a high-necked, peach-colored blouse, and he could just barely make out the outline of her bra. God, how he wanted to see her strip. He imagined licking her nipples, and his cock stiffened. When an image of her naked and beneath him sprang to mind, he quickly pushed it away. "Yeah," he said as he cleared his throat, "I was. Sorry."

She chuckled. "You really don't sound sorry."

Vance had to tamp down the need to reach over and simply take what he so badly wanted. He needed to do something and quick, or Shayla was going to find herself sprawled out on the couch. To hell with crazy things like logic and good sense. "I'm really not."

Vance put his wine next to hers on the coffee table in front of them, then scooted closer. When he took her in his arms, he noticed the shock registering in her eyes. "W-What are you doing?"

"When you came here, did you want more than a clear conscience, Shay?"

She closed her eyes tight and nodded. "Yes."

Vance's blood heated. "Do you still have feelings for me?" he asked, all but holding his breath.

Her green eyes opened and held his captive. "I don't know, but I'd be lying if I said I haven't thought about you over the years."

It wasn't a lot to go on, but it was enough that he wanted to shout in triumph. "Maybe we should get reacquainted, then. See where things go."

"Yes, I'd like that."

Vance cupped her face in his hand and drew her close until she was nestled against him. "Let's start this off right, shall we?" he murmured as he dipped his head and tasted her for the first time in what seemed like forever. Oh, hell, yeah. The woman was made for him. God, he'd missed her taste. Her scent. Her sweet, bow-shaped mouth. No woman had ever gotten to him the way she did. It was as if with a single kiss the years melted away. His sweet Shay. It pissed him off that she got to him so fast, so easily.

Vance locked his thoughts away and devoured Shayla's plump lips. He licked, torturing them both with ideas of more. Then he teased his tongue back and forth over the seam, thrilled when she parted them for him. Only him. It was a small sign of surrender, but Vance would take whatever he could get. She twined her arms around his neck, and her curves melted against him. He ached to sink into her hot pussy. To bury his dick deep and feel her shudder all around him as they loved each other.

He moved until she was lying back over the cushion, his body covering hers. He accidentally kicked the leg of the coffee table, and the wineglasses shook. Shayla stiffened. She began to push him away, and Vance let her, but only so he could taste the delicate skin on her throat. His hand wrapped around the slim column. He licked a spot behind her ear, and she moaned his name. His cock grew hard as stone, and he let loose a low groan of need.

"Wait," she murmured. "Please."

Vance pulled back and looked into her eyes. Her need tore him up, but there was a good amount of apprehension there as well. "What's wrong, honey?"

"It's too fast. Just this morning, you were ordering me to leave."

Vance smoothed his palm down the side of her body until he was clutching her hip. He squeezed and felt her tremble.

"Don't you think we've waited long enough?" He held himself in check, giving her the ultimate decision.

Her answer was pure Shayla. "I want you like crazy right now, but it can't be merely sex. There has to be more between us."

He frowned down at her. "It's not just a quick fuck I'm looking for here."

"Are you so sure?" she asked, her voice unsteady.

"Yes," he growled as he leaned in to kiss her neck. He felt her hands against his chest and wondered if she would push him away or tug him closer. "God, you have the sexiest curves," he murmured.

"And you're so hot I could catch fire just looking at you, Vance, but that's lust. Nothing more."

The uncertainty in her words cooled him down enough to release her and move to the other end of the couch. He took in her disheveled blouse and kiss-swollen lips. Fucking delicious, but she was right. This was way too damn fast. "How about I take you out tomorrow night? Do you still like action movies?"

She smiled, and his heart sped up. God, she was so pretty when she did that. "Yes, I love them," she replied as she sat up and adjusted her clothes. Her face was flushed and her chest rose and fell in rapid succession. She might be trying to feign nonchalance, but Vance knew the signs of arousal when he saw them. He'd gotten to her.

"I'll take you to see that new one that's playing."

She scooted off the couch and smoothed a hand down her blouse. "I'd never turn down a chance to watch Vin Diesel."

Vance stood and shifted from foot to foot, willing his cock to chill. "Where do you live? I can pick you up."

She looked down at herself, then quickly crossed her arms over her chest. "I can come here. It's no trouble."

Vance knew she was trying to hide the evidence of her arousal, but it was useless. He'd already noticed her pert nipples poking the flimsy blouse and bra. "If we're going to do this, then we do it right. I'll pick you up and I'll pay."

Her lips quirked up. "The times have changed, Vance. Men no longer have to pay."

"The times might have changed, but I haven't."

Her chin went up in the air. "You were always too bossy."

"No, I just like things to be a certain way." He took hold of her arms and tugged her closer. "If you want to be with me, then I'll pick you up and I'll pay."

"Vance's rules or no date, is that it?"

He brushed her lips with his own and murmured, "You want more of that, don't you?"

She sighed. "You know I do."

"Then let me have this one thing, honey."

"Fine, but I'm getting the biggest tub of popcorn they have."

He chuckled. "And malted milk balls, if I recall."

"Yes, those too."

"Deal," he promised, kissing her once more. He kept it brief, and when they separated, they were both more than ready for second base.

He tapped her on the nose and said, "Go, before I change my mind and carry your cute ass up the stairs."

Shayla didn't say another word but simply nodded and walked over to the chair where she'd left her coat. He helped her into it, and by the time she left, he was kicking himself for letting her leave. Would she still be around tomorrow? Old fears resurfaced, and he wondered if he'd made a mistake by asking her out. She was back for good, she'd said. Her explanation of why she'd dumped him was plenty plausible. Still, doubts lingered.

He lay awake way into the night thinking over everything that had transpired. He was taking a big chance by letting Shayla back into his life. Regardless of the reason she's given him for breaking it off, losing her had turned Vance off from trusting any other woman. Jesus, it'd been difficult enough for him to rely on someone outside his immediately family. As a foster kid, he'd learned early on that people could and would be despicable creatures. Shayla's betrayal had only added to his already suspicious nature. Since she'd left, Vance had managed to keep a tight leash on his personal life. The women he dated now liked to keep things light and easy. No strings attached, which was just freaking dandy with him.

One thing for certain, Vance had given up on meaningful relationships with women when Shayla left Blackwater twelve years ago. If that was the case, though, why was he entertaining the idea of getting Shayla into his bed? He knew good and well sex with her would open up a whole slew of old feelings. He had a full plate right now with the renovations on the diner. He didn't need the kind of trouble one sexy redhead could bring him.

Chapter Six

"Oh, God, I'm so sorry. This is horribly embarrassing," Shayla grumbled as she hugged her toilet after another bout of throwing up the dinner they'd had earlier.

"Shh, it's okay, honey. You'll feel better as soon as your stomach gets rid of the food," Vance promised. "It's partly my fault for suggesting seafood anyway."

Her stomach burned, and every muscle in her body ached. "It's no one's fault. Just some bad fish, I guess."

He cursed. "I hate to see you in pain. Are you sure there's nothing I can do?"

She shook her head. "Like you said, I'll feel better once it's all out of my stomach." God, Vance was being so sweet, so attentive. She couldn't remember a time when a man had stayed by her side while she vomited up her dinner. It made her fall in love with him a little bit more. Oh, God, the thought of falling for Vance all over again caused her stomach to twist with nerves.

"I should've gone with your idea and gotten pizza, but I wanted to impress you, take you to a nice restaurant." He groaned. "Real freaking impressive."

Shayla tried to smile, but it seemed to take all her energy, so she gave up and rested her head against the wall next to the toilet. Vance had taken her to the movie, which had been better than she'd anticipated. Then they'd gone to Hook, Line and Sinker. The food had been wonderful, right up until they were halfway back to her apartment and she'd started to feel the first rumblings in her stomach. She'd raced to the bathroom the instant she had her front door unlocked.

She felt Vance's hand against the top of her head, and her

gaze shot to his. "You really don't have to stay, Vance. I'll be fine."

"I'm sorry, honey, but you're stuck with me."

Somewhere in Shayla's haze of pain, she saw the honest worry in Vance's hazel eyes. "I—" Another pain caused her stomach to seize up, and Shayla bent her head over the ivory rim and heaved some more. Finally, there just wasn't anything left to throw up, but the heck if her stomach was through torturing her.

Suddenly, she was thrown back in time to another stomach-clenching episode. Shayla had gotten a flu bug that had been going around at school, and it'd been her mom who had held her hair back. She'd been in the seventh grade, but she could still hear her mother's calm voice, feel her mother's soft touch as she stroked a cool washcloth over her forehead.

Vance's hand smoothing her hair away from her face brought her back to the present. When she was sure her body was finished heaving, she lifted her head. Vance was there with a damp paper towel. She took it and swiped it over her mouth. Her stomach suddenly settled, and she knew she was on the downhill slide.

As she started to stand, Vance's strong hands closed around her arms, lifting her to her feet. "Want to take a shower?" he asked. "Might help you feel better."

"Oh man, a hot shower sounds great." She looked up at him and cringed. "I bet this isn't quite how you pictured the night going, huh?"

He winked. "We'll have plenty of time for a do-over once you feel better."

Her heart promptly turned to mush. She placed her hand on his chest and said, "Thank you," then realized she probably had awful breath and quickly covered her mouth.

He pried her hand away from her mouth and held it tight. "Relax, Shay. I'm not going to bolt out the door just because you tossed your cookies." He let go of her and stepped toward the door. "You have any green tea?"

She shifted from one foot to the other, embarrassed that he'd seen her like this. God, she could just imagine what she must look like. "There's some tea in the cupboard next to the refrigerator."

"I'll make you a cup while you shower."

"Oh, no, that's really not necessary. In fact, if you'd rather head home—"

"Hush, woman. I'm not going anywhere until I see you settled."

To hell with it. Shayla didn't really want him to leave anyway. Maybe it was selfish of her, but it'd been so long since she'd had Vance all to herself, she wanted to soak in every minute. She smiled her consent, and he left the room, closing the door behind him.

Shayla went to the sink and looked into the mirror hanging above it. "Have mercy," she grumbled when she saw her reflection. Her hair was sweaty and sticking to her head, and she was so pale she could've been mistaken for a corpse. Her stomach twisted a little, but not so much that she needed to hug the commode, thank God. A shower would help her look less like something the cat dragged in, at least.

Shayla stripped out of her clothes and turned toward the tub. After she had the water temperature right, she stepped in and let the massaging jets work their magic. As the water cascaded down her body, she heard what sounded like pans clinking together. Vance was in the other room, she realized. Making her a pot of tea and caring for her.

In all her wildest dreams, never once did she imagine a moment like this. She'd hoped and prayed she'd have a second chance with him, but never had she let herself believe it might actually happen. Her heart soared, and a burst of adrenaline flooded her system. She felt instantly better. "Figures Vance Jennings would be the cure," she mused aloud, suddenly in a hurry to finish.

As Vance rifled around in Shayla's cabinet to find the tea, he thought back over the evening they'd shared. He'd enjoyed himself. Shayla was different than she used to be in a lot of ways, and tonight had felt like a real first date to him. Not like they were picking up where they'd left off, but more like they were two people getting to know each for the first time. When he found a box of green tea, he searched through another cupboard for honey. He found it sitting next to the toaster, took a teakettle off the stove and ran water in it. By the time the water was boiling, Shayla was walking into the room, a towel wrapped around her head. Vance looked her over, checking for signs that she should still be hugging the porcelain god. He noticed her pale face and the slow, careful way she moved, but since her skin no longer had a nasty greenish tint, he figured things were looking up for her.

She wore a pair of loose-fitting, hunter-green sweatpants and a baggy sweatshirt that sported a picture of a bull and boldly stated University of South Florida. "You went to USF?" he asked, curious about her life. He'd heard the bad stuff, but he wanted to hear that she'd had some happy times too.

"Yeah. I loved it there. Even though Dad wouldn't let me live on campus, the classes still got me away from the house, away from him. It was the only time I could let my guard down." She went to the cupboard and took out a couple of mugs, then placed them on the counter next to the stove. "What about you? Did you go to college?"

"Yep. Ohio State University. Partied a little, studied a little, no great scholar or anything like that." He looked at the pair of mugs and smiled. "I don't do tea, Shay."

"Oh." She blushed. "I could make coffee or something. I don't have any alcohol, though, sorry."

He placed his hand on her back and nudged her. "Go sit down. I've got this."

She laughed, and Vance thought it sounded way better than hearing her retch. "You always were too bossy for your own good, but this time, I don't really mind."

He grinned as he poured hot water over a tea bag. "I'm not going to lie; I do tend to give orders a lot. It annoys the crap out of my brothers."

He held the mug out to her. After she took it, she said, "Speaking of your brothers, how are the renovations going at the diner?"

He sat in the seat next to her, worried when the thin wooden legs wobbled a little. "Everything is on schedule so far, but there's a crap ton of work to go."

He watched her blow on her tea to cool it down. The action had the opposite effect on his cock. Her full lips sans the peach lip gloss she'd worn earlier in the evening were even sexier than he once remembered. Her cute, oval-shaped face and the delicate line of her neck made him want to brush his lips against her satiny skin just to taste the warmth of her. At one time, it'd been her sweet innocence that had tugged at Vance, but Shayla was older now, and every curvy inch of her was all woman. "What are you doing exactly? Wanda didn't really elaborate."

Vance cleared his throat and said, "We aim to turn the diner into a bar and grill. It'll be bigger, and there will be live music, a few big-screen televisions on the walls, and happy hour. The works."

She took a sip of the warm liquid and hummed her approval. "That's a huge project, Vance. Expensive too, I'd imagine."

He nodded. "We're trying to keep costs down as much as possible. My company is doing the bulk of the labor, and Brodix has a few ideas on how to pull in more business once we reopen."

"Did you have to get a loan?" she asked. "And when will the reopening be?"

He tapped his foot on the floor in a lame effort to keep himself in check. She wasn't up for what he had in mind, at least not tonight. "The grand opening will be April first. That gives us a month and a half. Not a lot of time for such a big job, I know, but there are a lot of us working on it."

She sat up straighter and offered, "I'd like to pitch in, if I can."

The idea of Shayla covered in sawdust and driving nails

had his lips kicking upward. "Can you swing a hammer?"

"I don't have any real experience, but I'm a quick study."

He was unaccountably charmed by the notion that she was offering to help out his family. "Do you have the time? I mean, with your publishing business and all."

She took another sip of her tea. The towel covering her head started to come unwound, and Vance had the urge to yank it off her and toss it to the floor, along with her clothes. "I'm sure I can work it in," she said as she placed the mug back on the table. "A few hours here and there are better than nothing, right?"

He gave that some thought and knew she had it right. Besides, if she was at the diner helping him, then he'd have her close. Not a bad deal, all things considered. "What are you doing tomorrow afternoon?" he asked. "We can head over there, and I can show you around, if you want."

Her eyes brightened. "I'd love that. Thank you."

"Don't thank me yet. Wait until you've seen the mess you're about to walk into."

She reached up, grasped the towel and pulled. It fell away from her head, and a tangled mass of wet red hair fell down around her shoulders. Vance reached out and fingered a lock. "I've always loved your hair, Shay. So soft and baby fine."

"Thank you." She yawned. "Oops, sorry."

"You're exhausted. Come on," Vance said as he stood and reached out a hand. She took it willingly and smiled up at him. "How's your stomach?"

He watched her swallow. "Better. Much better."

"Good, but you need a good night's sleep."

"You're leaving?"

She sounded disappointed. Hell, Vance knew that feeling well. He cupped her face in his palms and whispered, "Only because you aren't one hundred percent right now. Tomorrow, when you're feeling better, I plan to make up for it."

Her gaze turned drowsy as her small hand came up to cover his. "I'm looking forward to it."

Vance groaned and lowered his head. When their lips touched, the fire inside him built to an inferno of need. Her lips were the sweetest temptation. For a moment, he allowed himself free rein. He forgot that he was supposed to leave. Everything went up in smoke as the flavor of her fresh mint toothpaste and warm tea hit his tongue. Vance licked her bottom lip and sucked it into his mouth, nibbling and enjoying the eager sounds she made. She arched against him and whimpered, as if ready to plead for him to fuck her. He wanted to. God, how he wanted to. He would take her hard and fast. Slow and easy. He wanted her in so damn many ways it made his head spin.

When Vance reached out and massaged her left breast through the heavy sweatshirt with the palm of his hand, Shayla shuddered. He skated his lips over her cheek to her neck. He licked a spot just above the neckline of the sweatshirt, and Shayla let out a greedy sound. As he cupped the back of her head, her wet hair against his hand brought Vance back to reality. She wasn't up for this, he reminded himself. Not an hour ago, she'd been hugging the porcelain. Christ, he was a royal ass.

With the last remnants of his willpower, Vance pulled away from her. "Sleep, honey," he whispered. "You need it."

"Uh, I'd rather do other things right now," she said as she reached out for him. He took her hands in his and kissed the backs of her knuckles before dropping them away.

"Think of this as the end of chapter one," he said. "Tomorrow we'll get to chapter two, I promise."

Shayla wrinkled her nose and plopped into the chair. "In that case, chapter two better be fantastic, because I'm not happy how this one ended."

He chuckled and crouched in front of her. "Chapter two is going to be explosive. Just you wait and see." He kissed her one last time, needing another taste of her, then said, "Two o'clock sound good to you?"

She thought for a moment. "That should work. And I can fix us lunch."

He nodded and touched her lower lip with his thumb. The

soft, plump lip brought a carnal image to his mind. Her mouth wrapped tight around his cock, suckling and licking. "I'll see you then," he said in a rough voice. "Sleep tight, Shay."

Without another word, he strode to the front door. If he didn't get out fast, he was never going to leave. A man had only so much control, damn it.

Chapter Seven

It was a little before two in the afternoon, and Vance would be showing up any minute. In fact, if Shayla remembered correctly, the man would be early. Being late had always been a pet peeve of his. She grabbed the pepper grinder and sprinkled some over the salad before turning to the stove. She'd decided on grilled chicken, oven-roasted russet potatoes and a garden salad. Unless he'd changed drastically in the years they'd been apart, Vance was a meat-and-potatoes man. Shayla had wanted him good and satisfied. Part of her also wanted to show him that he wasn't the only one who could cook.

As she placed the plate of chicken and potatoes on the table, the phone rang. Shayla froze. Was he cancelling? God, she hoped not. When it rang again, Shayla dragged herself to the other side of the room and picked up the cordless phone attached to the wall next to the fridge. "Hello?"

"Hi, sweetie, are you busy?"

Oh, thank you, God. "Hi, Mom, not at all." She looked at the lunch she'd prepared and smiled. "How are things at home?"

"Everything's fine. I just called to see how it was going with the new apartment and everything."

Her mom was her best friend. They'd been through thick and thin together, which was why Shayla knew that the "everything" her mom referred to was Vance. "Um, great. The cold weather is taking some getting used to, but other than that, I'm good."

There was a beat of silence, and Shayla thought maybe they'd gotten disconnected. "Have you talked to him yet?" her mom asked in a quieter tone.

Shayla heard the worry in her mom's voice, and that was the last thing she wanted. Evelyn Riggs had had enough to deal with in her life, having been married to a monster like Peter Riggs, not to mention the breast cancer. She certainly didn't need to waste time fretting about her daughter's love life, or lack thereof.

"We've cleared the air, Mom, so you don't need to be concerned," Shayla said. "In fact, he's coming over for lunch in a few minutes."

"It's been a long time since you two were an item," she prodded. "I imagine a lot has changed. I'm sure he's changed."

"True," Shayla said, unsure where her mom was going with the conversation. "But don't read a lot into it. It's just lunch."

She tsked. "Ha! You've cared about that boy for as long as I can remember, young lady. Moving to Florida didn't change a darn thing, much to your father's dismay."

Why had she thought she could fool the woman? "You're right, but if I start overthinking it, I'll make myself crazy. Today we're going to have lunch together, nothing more." *If I hope it'll lead to more, well, that's my business.*

"How'd he react to seeing you again?"

"At first he was angry, but we talked, and I think he understands why I did what I did."

"You told him about your father?" she asked, her voice a little unsteady.

"Yeah. I think if Dad were still alive, Vance would've..."

"Of course he would've. He's an honorable man. Nothing like the man I married."

Sympathy for her mother prompted her to say, "Vance is a good man, that's true, but so is Fred."

Her mother sighed. "He's so good to me that sometimes I can't believe he's real."

Tears sprang to her eyes, and Shayla said, "But he is real, and you deserve someone like Fred."

"We both do, sweetie." She paused, then added, "I love you."

"I love you too, Mom," Shayla replied. After they hung up, Shayla's nerve endings were firing like pistons in a racecar engine. Was she doing the right thing? She'd gotten frustrated with Vance for wanting only a physical relationship, but she couldn't deny her body ached for his just as much. All he had to do was glance her way, and her clit swelled and throbbed. When she imagined him stripping out of his jeans, his engorged cock within her reach, Shayla's panties grew damp. All they'd done so far was some hot and heavy kissing, and already she was spiraling out of control. Her emotions were all over the place when it came to Vance. If she wasn't careful, Shayla could end up on the losing side. When she heard her doorbell chime, her pulse quickened. Vance. She checked the clock. Right on time, of course.

Shayla tucked a lock of hair behind her ear and smoothed her beige sweater down. Her jeans were a bit tighter than what she was used to, but they showed off her rear better than any of her others. When the doorbell blared again, Shayla sprinted from the room. She yanked the door open before a third ring.

Vance stood in the hallway to her apartment building and boldly eyeballed her. Slowly. As if afraid he'd miss something if he went too fast. Her pussy throbbed when his gaze stopped for a few seconds too long on her lower half.

"You look hot," he murmured.

Her face heated. Oh my God, it wasn't as if she'd never heard a compliment before. What was wrong with her? "Thanks," she said as she let him in and watched him remove his heavy leather coat to reveal a black pocket T-shirt and a pair of snug-fitting jeans. "So do you," she told him, appreciating the sight before her. Appreciating that for now, for today, she had him all to her greedy little self.

He sniffed the air. "Mm, something smells good."

She smiled and led the way to the kitchen. "I hope you like grilled chicken."

"Love it." He leaned over the platter sitting on the table. "Are those potatoes oven-roasted?"

Worried he hated it, she answered, "Yeah, is that okay?"

"More than okay. I love those things." He glanced over at her as he took his seat. "So you're feeling better?"

"Yep. A twinge here and there is all." She opened the fridge and peered inside. "What do you want to drink? I have sweet tea, water, and a few cans of soda in here somewhere."

"Iced tea sounds great."

She took the pitcher out and poured them each a glass. As she handed his over, she said, "I just made it this morning. I hope its sweet enough."

Vance took the glass from her and drank a third of it down. "It's perfect," he said when he came up for air. "Damn, I was thirsty."

"I gathered." She laughed and sat down, acutely aware of their knees touching beneath the table.

He picked up the platter and served them each a chicken breast and potatoes. "We've been at the diner all morning beating the crap out of four-by-fours and tearing out the old wiring. I've worked up an appetite."

She started on her salad first but noticed he didn't follow suit. "It sounds like you have quite a job ahead of you."

"We do. Not sure any of us knew how big a job until today." He cut a large chunk from his chicken and brought it to his mouth. Shayla held her breath, wondering if he would love it or hate. When he cut another and stabbed it with a fork, she started to breathe easier. "You're a hell of a cook, Shay," he said as he cut yet another. "Want to come work at the diner?"

"As a cook?" She rolled her eyes. "Yeah, right."

He swallowed a few more bites of his chicken and took a long drink. "Woman, if you didn't already have your own business, and clearly a successful one, I'd try and talk you into coming to work for us."

That he was serious surprised Shayla. "But you have a cook, don't you?"

He shrugged. "Eddie is great. He's been with us for years, but if the restaurant gets as many customers as we're anticipating, then he'll need help."

When he started on the potatoes, Shayla's heart melted at the notion that he was so enthusiastically eating the lunch she'd cooked for them. How wonderful would it have been to have this every afternoon with Vance? And each morning, sitting across the table from each other before they headed off to work.

All too easily, Shayla pictured Vance coming home after a long, hard job at some construction site, taking her into his arms and kissing her senseless. They would've talked about their days over dinner. God, so many years lost, and all because she'd let her father dictate the way she should live her life. All because she'd been too much the coward to stand up to the tyrant and take control of her life.

After her salad was finished, she dug into her own meal. Soon Vance was wiping a napkin over his mouth and sitting back, a look of utter satisfaction on his gorgeously rugged face. When she noticed he had yet to touch his salad, Shayla frowned. "You didn't eat your veggies."

He picked up a cucumber slice and popped it into his mouth. "Tastes good, but I'm full."

She pushed the bowl closer to him. "You were supposed to eat your salad first, though."

He pushed it right back where it was. "Says who?"

She started to pick up her drink, but his question stopped her. "It's just something you do. In our house, Dad had a very specific way of doing everything, and that included dinner."

Vance laughed and leaned one elbow on the table. "You need to come to a Jennings gathering, then. It's total chaos there. Every man and woman for themselves."

Shayla couldn't comprehend a meal like that. "When Dad was alive, we would dress in our Sunday best every night for dinner. No one spoke, and you were to eat every last bite or you didn't leave the table."

"That doesn't sound like much fun," he said in a tender voice.

Her brows scrunched together, and she looked down at her

barely touched meal. She was full, but she'd been prepared to eat all of it. God, even now her father had her obeying his every command. It was ridiculous. She was a grown woman, for Lord's sake.

"Shay?"

She glanced up to find Vance staring at her with sympathy and understanding. Too late she realized she'd been sitting there staring at her plate, not speaking. "Sorry, I got lost there for a second."

He reached out and took her hand in his. When he twined their fingers together, Shayla knew that nothing had ever felt more right. "When you're with me, you eat what you want. Dessert first, if that's your preference. Got it?"

His words thrust Shayla back to the first time they'd met, and she smiled. "Do you remember that time you came up to me at lunch? You asked to sit with me."

"How could I forget?" Vance bobbed his eyebrows. "I'd been looking for an excuse to talk to you ever since I first saw you in Biology."

Even now Shayla's cheeks heated as she recalled how shy she'd been around Vance. "I'd been secretly crushing on you, you know."

He cocked his head to one side. "You were, huh?"

Shayla nodded "Yeah, but I couldn't bring myself to actually talk to you. I kept losing my voice whenever you came within ten feet of me."

He squeezed her hand. "If I recall, I offered you my dessert."

"Apple crisp," she said, as if it were yesterday. "I ate every bite too."

"Hmm, yeah," he murmured. "I liked watching you eat. It kind of turned me on."

Shayla's entire body warmed at Vance's admission, but as she thought again about her father and his strict rules, she cringed. "Sometimes it's like I can hear my dad's condemning voice in my head. I forget that I don't have to do what he says any longer." She paused and added, "Thanks for not thinking

I'm certifiable."

He brought her hand to his mouth and caressed the back of it with his lips. "You're beautiful and delicious, and I can't stop thinking about you, but I don't think you're crazy."

Her heart stuttered. "Do you have to be back at the diner right away?"

His grin was pure wickedness. "Nope."

Shayla couldn't think straight when Vance looked at her like that. "Oh, uh, that's good. Would you like dessert, then? I-I made some chocolate chip cookies."

"Definitely dessert," he replied in a deeper tone, "but I'm not really in the mood for cookies."

She watched him stand, and her body revved to life. "You aren't?"

He shook his head as he tugged her out of the chair. "The only thing I want to taste is you, honey."

"Oh, God," she moaned, her legs turning to rubber as he brought her up against his body. The solid wall of his chest snagged all her attention, and she was loath to look away. No one would blame her if she stared, though, considering Vance had a body that would surely make women of all ages pant. Why should she be an exception?

"Take off your clothes for me," he murmured. "I need to see you."

Shayla's face heated. "Here?" *In the bright light of day?*

"Yes, here." He paused, then, a little softer, he added, "You aren't bashful, are you?"

She clenched her eyes closed tight. "It's been so long. A lot has changed. I've changed."

She felt a fist beneath her chin, and she opened her eyes to see Vance staring down at her with such a gentle expression it made her heart ache. "You think I won't like what I see," he murmured. "Is that it?"

"I might have been brave enough to seek you out after twelve years apart, and I won't deny I've gained a great deal of confidence in myself in recent years, but stripping in my kitchen in the middle of the afternoon is a bit much. I...I just can't."

He kissed the tip of her nose. "You have a soft inner core that makes me feel fiercely protective of you, do you know that? It's always been that way with you."

That surprised her. "I do? It has?"

"Mm, and it's just me, honey. There isn't a single inch of you that could possibly disappoint me."

"But—"

"I promise," he reiterated.

Shayla took a deep breath and grabbed hold of the hem of her sweater. As she dragged it up her body, Vance stepped back and watched her every move. It turned her on, made her feel bolder. Her stomach clenched, and her nipples hardened to stiff peaks as Shayla became acutely aware of Vance's gaze on her. When she removed the soft cashmere and placed it over the back of a nearby chair, she heard Vance let loose a low growl.

"Fuck, you're pretty as a picture."

A sense of pride took hold at Vance's roughly spoken words. She removed her white, satin bra next. Her pussy throbbed as she noticed the way Vance kept his hands balled into fists at his side, as if he had to work extra hard to keep from reaching for her. Shayla slid her hands up and cupped her breasts in her palms, then squeezed. God, she wanted Vance's hands on her, his mouth suckling her. She looked down the length of his body and noticed the bulge in his jeans had grown bigger. Her mouth watered for a taste of him. She ached to run her tongue up and down his shaft. Her mouth all but craved the taste of his precome.

When she plucked the hard tips with her fingertips, Vance groaned. "You're killing me here. Strip, honey, show me the rest before I die."

Shayla had no intention of denying him. Within seconds, she stood before her soon-to-be lover totally nude. She trembled when Vance descended on her.

Chapter Eight

"All I want is you," Vance murmured as he pressed his mouth to hers. He pried her lips open with his tongue, too eager to wait a minute longer to taste her sweet flavor. He needed her, ached for her like no other. She opened willingly, her body pliant under his seeking hands. Her slender arms wrapped around his neck, and his strong hands clutched on to her waist. He lifted her easily, cradling her against his chest while his tongue dueled with hers, sucking and savoring her sweetness. He pulled back long enough to ask, "Where's your bedroom?"

"Stairs," she breathlessly replied. "First door on the left."

Vance strode out of the room, carrying her in his arms. When he reached the stairs, she wiggled. "Be still, honey," he gently ordered.

"I can walk," she said as she pushed against his chest.

Vance wasn't about to let her go. "I'm aware."

Damn it, he wished they were in his house. He wanted her in his bed. Later for that. For now, he just needed Shayla. Vance took the steps two at a time. When he reached the upstairs landing, he took her to the room she'd indicated.

"You know," she said, "if I were at all coherent, I'd be awed at how strong you are."

The mischief in her voice had him looking down. The prettiest woman in all of Blackwater stared up at him. Her smooth curves tucked up against his body had his cock feeling strangled in his jeans.

"You'll have plenty of time later to think," he whispered as he spied a large bed covered in a red satin comforter. "For now, the only thing I want you to do is feel."

Vance's Rules

Vance had driven himself crazy all day picturing them together in just this way. From the moment she'd shown up on his doorstep, he'd wanted her with a desperation that scared him. His sweet Shayla.

When he set her back on her feet, she stared at him with a mixture of passion and nervous tension. "Relax, honey," he softly urged.

"It's been so long, Vance."

He quirked a brow at that small confession. "Since you've been with a man, you mean?"

She shrugged. "Well, yes, but that's not what has me worried."

"Then what is it?" he asked as he attempted to keep himself from throwing her onto the bed and shoving his cock deep. The thought of other men touching any part of Shayla's body made him angry enough to bit back an ugly curse. No way in hell. Her tantalizing body was for him alone. Jesus, Vance had never felt such a powerful need to stake a claim as he did with her.

Shayla crossed her arms over her chest as if to cover the bountiful swells. "It's been a long time since I've been with *you*."

Good answer, he thought, as a ridiculous amount of possessiveness sped through his bloodstream. While their gazes locked, Vance drifted his finger over the smooth column of her neck, tracing the few freckles that ran in a tempting line down to her collarbone, and lower to the smooth V between her breasts. "I've missed your freckles, Shay."

She shuddered. "It feels so good when you touch me."

"Are you turned on, honey?"

She covered her eyes with one hand. "Yes. Oh, God, yes."

"Look at me," he gently ordered. When her gaze once again connected with his, he whispered, "I'm eager as hell to feel your hot, little pussy wrapped snug around my cock right now, but first things first." His gaze never left hers when his finger skated along her skin. When he flicked a nipple with his index finger, she jolted. "I bet you taste like sweet cream, huh?" He didn't wait for a response as his head descended, taking one turgid bit of flesh into his mouth and sucking.

Shayla grabbed on to his head and moaned his name. Never in Vance's life had anything tasted so good or felt so right. She pleaded, and his cock hardened further. When her fingers delved into his hair, clutching on to him as if he'd disappear into a puff of smoke, Vance knew she was as far gone as he was.

He rose back up and looked at her half-closed eyes, her face flushed with arousal. "Pretty as a picture and every bit as sweet," he praised her as he took hold of her waist and walked her backward until they reached the edge of the bed. He pushed her gently down, then let her watch as he quickly did away with his clothes.

"You're so strong." Her gaze took in his entire body from head to toe. She eyed his cock, and he watched her lick her lips. Damn, as if he needed more provocation. "And so wonderfully hard all over," she said, not taking her gaze away from his dick.

He smiled. "Glad you approve."

She lifted to a sitting position and reached out. She smoothed her hand down over his chest to his abs. Her fingers followed the trail of hair, but when she reached his cock, she pulled back.

"Shy?"

She bit her lip. "A little."

"Are you wet for me, Shay?"

Her head bobbed. "Oh yes," she murmured.

He reached out and took hold of her wrist. "Touch me, honey," he said as he brought Shayla's hand to his swollen cock. "Feel how much I want you. I'm dying for you."

Her small fingers wrapped around his length and squeezed. "Hell, yeah, like that."

She brought her other hand up and cupped his balls, squeezing and testing their weight and size. When her soft palm stroked him in a slow, torturous rhythm, Vance groaned. "No more. I'm only human, honey."

Her naughty smile as she stroked him once more nearly

brought him to his knees.

He brought her hand to his lips and kissed the palm. "Little tease," he growled as he pushed her backward until she was sprawled out on the bed. He lowered his body on top of hers, bracing himself on his elbows beside her body. Vance took in the sight of her beneath him. "This is what I've missed, Shayla." He cupped one large breast in his hand and licked the tip. One more swipe of his tongue, then he gave in and sucked on her. With deep pulls of his mouth, Vance laved and nibbled on her satiny flesh.

She squirmed under him. "Please, yes. Lick me, Vance."

"Like this?" he moved to the other breast and continued his assault, licking and suckling as if she were his last meal.

She moaned and arched her back. The action mashed her breasts against his face. Vance cupped both her tits and nuzzled his face into her cleavage. Her legs came around his waist and held him tight, and her fingers dug into his back. Vance groaned.

He released her breasts and went on an exploration of her ribs and stomach. "Your skin is like satin," he whispered as he wrapped his hands around her hips and held her firm, then dipped his tongue into her belly button. When he skimmed his fingers over her hips and touched the springy curls between her thighs, Vance felt Shayla freeze up.

"Vance," she said, her voice a barely there thread of sound in the room.

Her soft voice was the only thing that could stop him in that instant. "We've been here before, honey. You trust me, remember?"

"But where will we go from here? What happens tomorrow?"

"I told you before, I'm not looking for a quickie here." He danced his fingers over her pussy lips and asked, "Do you like my touch?" When she nodded and relaxed, he continued his erotic discovery. Vance rubbed his thumb across her swollen clitoris, enjoying the way her eyes slowly drifted closed and her breaths began to come in short gasps.

As he thrust his middle finger into her tight opening, her mouth opened, but no sound came out. Vance began sliding his finger in and out, slow at first, then faster, deeper. The feel of her inner muscles clenching and unclenching around the single digit was a sweet kind of torture to him.

She was warm and wet and inviting. He slipped a second finger in and felt her body stretching to accommodate. Shayla began to thrust upward, and the action forced his fingers deeper. When he glided his thumb over her little nub, rubbing back and forth and pumping her tight passage with his fingers at the same time, Shayla moaned his name. Caught up in the fire building inside her body, Shayla undulated against his hand and threw her head from side to side, pleading and begging as her body flew out of control. Her screams as she orgasmed around his fingers sent his control scattering.

He slowly pulled his fingers free, relishing the way her body clasped around them, and levered himself on top of her. Vance positioned his cock at her opening and waited. "Are you protected?"

Shayla blinked a few times, then seemed to grasp what he said and nodded. "I'm on birth control, and I've had a clean bill of health."

"Same here, but if you'd rather I used a condom, it's no problem."

She shook her head and wrapped her arms around his neck. "No. I only want to feel you, Van," she murmured.

He stiffened. "You called me Van. No one has ever done that but you."

She cringed. "Do you hate it?"

"No, I don't hate it." He bent his head and crushed her mouth beneath his. The kiss was rough and demanding, but he was beyond being easy. When he lifted, they were both panting. One slow torturous inch at a time, Vance slid his dick deep. She cried his name as her body molded around him. While he moved in and out, Vance trailed little kisses on her cheeks and temples. He spied a few freckles on the delicate slope of her chin and kissed each one with tender care. He tucked his hand between their bodies and began stoking her passion to new heights. Vance watched her expressive face as desire turned to red-hot passion. Shayla's quickened breathing amplified his need a thousand times. Her arms tightened around his neck, and her legs quivered as they clutched on to his waist.

With her entire body draped around him, enfolding him in her little web of sensuality, Vance felt something inside him give way, as if a barricade had been torn down. He emitted a low growl of possession and pushed harder, faster, into her inviting wetness, continually toying with her swollen clit. She arched upward, mashing her breasts against his chest as she soared over the precipice once more.

His hunger took over when she screamed out his name. Vance pumped harder, driving her body into the mattress, oblivious to anything but the soft, inviting woman beneath him. He grabbed hold of her wrists and brought her arms above her head, extending her body so that she was an erotically submissive offering. He trapped both her small wrists beneath one of his hands and held her firm.

Vance continued to plunge into her, over and over, claiming her until he thought he'd die from the sheer ecstasy of it. He came in a frenzy of thrusts, splintering into a hundred pieces. Shayla's arms went limp, and her legs fell away from his body. She let out a long sigh and whispered, "Vance," and then she was out. Ah hell, had he been too rough? Taken her too hard? He lifted off her and lay down beside her, content to watch her sleep. Red marks marred her breasts and her neck where he'd kissed her. Even her waist and wrists bore the marks of his rough fingers.

He recalled what she'd said about her father ruling with an iron fist, and anger suffused Vance. The thought of any man putting his hands on Shayla in anger fired up his protective side. A father was supposed to be loving. The bastard should've been offering her security and kindness. Instead, Shayla had known only fear and pain at her father's hands. It still bothered Vance that she'd kept that side of her life hidden from him. Even if she hadn't told him, he should've known. Christ, the fact he hadn't seen the signs was a testament to what a lousy boyfriend he'd been toward her.

"You're staring," she murmured with her eyes still closed.

He pushed the maudlin thoughts away, and his lips kicked up to one side. "Thought you were passed out cold there for a second."

"Nope, just basking," she said, still not looking at him. "A woman is allowed to bask."

He took hold of her chin and nudged her to look at him. When her eyelids lifted, Vance asked, "I wasn't too rough?"

A gentle smile teased the corners of her mouth. "You could never be too rough."

He snorted. "You've got marks all over you, honey." He massaged her breasts in an attempt to soothe her, but all it did was get him started again.

"I love that you wanted me so desperately. It makes me aware that I'm not the only one."

"Good," he said in a rough voice. "Because after you rest up a bit, I'm going to be desperate all over again."

She cupped his cheek with her palm ad smoothed her thumb back and forth over his lower lip. "I thought you needed to be at the diner. You were going to take me with you, remember?"

He wrapped his hand around her wrist and held her still while he sucked on her thumb. "Plenty of time for that." He released her and stood. "Come on," he urged as he tugged on her arm.

"Where are we going?" She began to scoot off the bed.

When she got to her feet, Vance moved behind her and cupped her ass. God, she had a lovely shaped ass. "To the shower," he replied. "It's not just for cleanliness anymore, you know?"

She laughed. "You're impossible."

"Yep," he said as he watched her walk. Jesus, she was sexy. He'd always been half-crazed for Shayla. Apparently, some things didn't change.

Chapter Nine

When Vance got out of the truck and jogged around to her side, Shayla held back. He frowned and opened her door. "What?"

"Are you sure about this? I mean, they might not be so keen on seeing me after all this time."

He leaned down, placed a tender kiss to her lips and whispered, "It's going to be fine. You'll see."

Shayla let out a long breath and unsnapped her seat belt. Vance helped her to the ground. "They're not going to bite, honey," he said as he slammed the truck door shut behind her.

"Why not? You did."

He chuckled and took possession of her hand. "I'm allowed."

With him so close, Shayla felt better, until they stepped into the diner and she came face-to-face with Sam Jennings. It was abundantly clear he and Vance were related because they had the same messy dark hair and hazel eyes. But Vance was bigger, more muscular. Unfortunately, Sam looked about as welcoming as a cougar. The cold look he gave her rivaled the frigid temperatures outside.

Vance nudged her forward and said, "You remember Sammy, don't you?"

She didn't know whether to hold out her hand for him to shake or not. His expression said not, so she merely stood there. "Hi, Sam, it's good to see you again." She smiled in an attempt to break the ice. It didn't work.

"Vance said you were back in town. Here to stay this time?"

All work seemed to grind to a halt, and everyone in the room stared at her as if anticipating her answer. Now she understood what fireflies must feel like when little kids trapped them in jars so they could watch them helplessly flit around.

"Yes," she said firmly as she stood a little straighter. She needed to make herself perfectly clear. She needed Vance's family to know she wasn't the coward she once was. If nothing else, her father's strict upbringing had taught her to stand her ground. "I've moved my business here permanently. I have absolutely no intention of leaving."

Sam's gaze narrowed a second. She held her breath. When he gave her a sideways grin, Shayla about fainted dead away. One down, three more to go.

As another man stepped forward, a flirty grin on his face, Shayla thought maybe it was Brodix. He'd changed over the years, the way they all had. Brodix had gotten taller and broader than she'd remembered. His dark hair was neatly trimmed, and although he'd been working in dust, he looked freshly showered. His grin was every bit as wicked as always, she noticed too. That, at least, hadn't changed.

"Brodix," she said. "It's nice to see you again."

"Looking good, Shayla," he said, as he opened his arms for a hug. Shayla was only too happy to step into them, relieved that at least he wasn't shooting daggers at her.

When he released her, she said, "Thanks, you too."

"You ever get tired of this lug"—he pointed a thumb in Vance's direction—"just yell."

"Lay off, Brodix," Vance gritted out as he moved up next to Shayla and slung an arm around her neck. "Find your own redhead."

Out of the corner of her eye, Shayla saw someone punch Brodix on the arm. When he moved to the side, she saw the twins, River and Reilly. They had shaggy black hair and the palest green eyes Shayla had ever seen. Sexy didn't even begin to cover it. Boy, they'd sure grown up since she'd last seen them. Twelve years ago, the twins had been rather gangly, all long limbs and not a lot of meat. They'd definitely filled out since then. One of them smiled at her, but the other only stared, no expression at all to give away his feelings toward her.

It was almost more disconcerting than Sam's scowl. Was the animosity directed at her because of the way she'd broken up with Vance? Oh, man, probably. Shayla's stomach did a free-fall when she realized that Vance's family had every right to hate her for what she'd put Vance through.

Vance pointed to each of them in turn and said, "Reilly and River. And if you're ever confused which is which, just know that River is a bit like Eeyore, walks around pouting all the time."

"Not true," he grumbled. "I smile plenty."

"It's like pulling teeth, and you know it," a feminine voice from behind River said. When he stepped to the left, Shayla saw a tall, thin woman with dark hair up in a ponytail and white dust all over her face and clothes. She wore a mask over her mouth and nose, and Shayla wondered if she was sick or something.

She yanked the mask off and stepped forward. "Hi, I'm Jeannette," she said as she held her hand out.

Shayla took her hand, surprised by the strength in the young, petite woman. "Shayla," she said.

"Pleased to meet you, Shayla." She brushed a hand over her face, and dust fell to the floor. "Don't mind the mess. River's been teaching me how to sand drywall."

River chuckled and yanked on the woman's ponytail. "I tried to tell you it was a messy job, but you wouldn't listen."

"Hey, men aren't the only ones allowed to get a little dirty," she said, bobbing her eyebrows.

Shayla heard Reilly snort. "I think you have more dust on you than the floor, sweets."

As the three of them bantered back and forth, Vance leaned close and said, "Jeanette is a friend of the family. She and River have been pals for years."

Shayla turned toward him and smiled. "You have a terrific family. You're very lucky." She heard the door open behind her, and she turned to see a slightly plump, grey-haired woman. Wanda, Shayla realized, and another woman who she didn't recognize. Wanda's companion was beautiful. She had long dark hair and the kind of curvy body Shayla only dreamed of having. In comparison, Shayla felt short and fat.

"Here comes the best of the lot," Sam said as he closed the distance and pulled the dark-haired beauty in for a big bear hug. Soon the pair were kissing, and Shayla heard a few catcalls from Vance's brothers. As they pulled apart, it was clear to Shayla they were deeply in love. She envied them right off. Would Vance ever look at her that way?

Earlier it'd been abundantly clear that Vance hadn't been able to get enough of her body, but that was merely sexual desire and a seriously poor substitute for love. Would he ever see past the exterior? She wanted more than simple lust from Vance? Shayla's heart sank at the idea he might not ever give it though.

Wanda spotted her, and her eyes rounded. "Shayla, dear, I had no idea you would be here."

Shayla crossed the room and let Wanda pull her into her arms. "It's wonderful to see you again, Wanda," she said, meaning every word. She'd always considered Wanda a second mom when she and Vance had dated. Shayla had missed her nearly as much as Vance when her father had moved them away.

"You too, dear." Shayla helped the older woman off with her coat. "Has Vance been treating you well?"

"Oh, yes." Her face heated when she thought just how well Vance had treated her.

Vance tugged her into the crook of his arm. "We've been getting caught up. Haven't we, Shay?"

His look was so devilish it was a wonder he wasn't sporting horns. "Yes. We've had lots to catch up on."

Wanda smiled from ear to ear. "Oh, that's just lovely. I'm so happy you're back in Blackwater."

Shayla looked up at Vance with her heart firmly planted on her sleeve and said, "Me too."

To her shock, Vance leaned down and kissed her. It was

brief, but it was enough to make it clear that she was very thoroughly claimed. Her pulse quickened, and she looked over to see Sam staring at her, a mixture of surprise and worry on his face. Before Shayla had time to ponder it, the woman in Sam's arms came forward and held out her hand. "Sam didn't get around to introducing us, so I figure I might as well do the honors." The woman's smile was warm, and Shayla found herself grinning right back. "I'm Julie. Sort of a newbie to the group."

She liked her immediately. "Shayla. I used to live in Blackwater. I've only recently moved back. For the last twelve years, I've lived in Florida."

"Florida sounds like heaven right about now." She cocked her head to the side and asked, "What made you decide to move back to this frigid cold state?"

She felt Vance stiffen beside her. "Well, this was always more my home than Florida." She glanced up at Vance to find him staring down at her, his expression unreadable. "I missed it," she said, hoping he understood that she was talking about him and not the state. When he smiled, Shayla's legs shook a little.

Vance cupped her chin and asked, "Ready to get to work?"

Shayla took off her coat and placed it on top of Wanda's. She rubbed her hands together and grinned up at him. "Just point me in the right direction."

He chuckled. "How about I show you around first?" Vance took her by the hand and led her away from the group. As she looked around the room, she was thrown back in time to when the diner had been in its prime. She remembered the shiny stainless-steel barstools with the red padded seats and Wanda standing behind the counter with a smile as she poured Shayla a soda. Shayla's gaze darted to the far corner, and her heart sank when she realized the booth she and Vance shared once upon a time had been ripped out. There were good memories tied to this place for both of them. It was a little sad to see it changing.

When they reached the long, wooden bar, he said, "I'm not

sure you remember, but there used to be a scarred countertop here."

Shayla took in the beautiful, dark wood finish and the pretty swirl design down the sides of the bar. "This is gorgeous," she said as she smoothed her palm over the shiny top. "Did you build it?" she asked, suitably impressed with the workmanship.

"Yep. I'm happy with the way it turned out, but it was hard to see the old counter go. A lot of memories there," he said, his voice a little gruff.

Shayla squeezed his hand and knew he was thinking of his father. "You'll all make new memories. I'm sure your dad would be proud."

He nodded. "Remember when we used to come here after school?"

She smiled. "Your mom would get me a soda, and we'd sit in the back of the room, kissing, the soda usually forgotten." Butterflies took flight when she said, "You asked me to be your girlfriend in that booth."

"Mm, and you said, yes. Happiest day of my life," he whispered as he leaned in to kiss her cheek.

Shayla's heart overflowed with love in that moment. The best times of her life were when she lived in Blackwater, and every good memory she coveted were all tied to this one man.

Vance cleared his throat and pointed to a far wall. Shayla promptly yanked her head out of the clouds and turned to see the section Jeanette must have been working on, because there was drywall dust all over the floor. "We're redoing all the walls. We want a more rustic look. The old plain white had to go."

She noticed one wall had a bright red X on it and asked, "What's happening there?"

He took her there and flatted his palm against the surface. "We plan to take this wall out completely, but it'll have to wait for the weather to warm up. We want to expand on the dining area to add a dance floor. We're thinking of maybe hiring a local band to play live music on the weekends."

"Oh, how fun!" She could easily picture herself in Vance's

strong arms as they danced to a soft, slow love song. *Focus, girlfriend.* She mentally squashed the image and cleared her throat. When her gaze travelled upward, taking in the loose wires hanging willy-nilly from the ceiling, she asked, "Um, why does it appear that someone has a grudge against the electric company?"

Vance snorted and tugged a lock of her hair. Shayla's nerve-endings buzzed to life. "The lighting is way outdated," he explained. "We're working on installing recessed lighting. Don't forget, woman, it's still a work in progress."

Shayla grinned. "With you leading this project, I'm sure it'll be terrific."

He bent and picked up a piece of broken drywall. "Let's hope so, otherwise we're all going to be living out of cardboard boxes. This thing is sucking away all our savings."

"By the time it's finished, the people of Blackwater won't know what hit them." She waved a hand around the room and asked, "So, where do I begin?"

He winked. "You might regret asking me that question after a few hours of sanding. Your muscles will be crying uncle, trust me."

"Try me," she said, anxious to prove to him that she wasn't the delicate flower he seemed to think she was.

He leaned down and placed a quick kiss to her lips. "Oh, I intend to, believe me."

Shayla's heart sputtered at the sensual promise. The wicked gleam in Vance's eyes sent all the blood in her body traveling south. Oh, God, the man was too yummy. Entirely too yummy.

After a few hours of sanding and spackling, Vance drove them back to his house. They'd eaten pizza with the rest of the bunch, and Shayla had felt like she was a part of their group. Sam had stopped scowling, and Brodix had flirted enough that Vance had threatened bodily harm if he didn't cut it out. Shayla's head was still reeling. They were an overwhelming bunch in comparison to her own family. She'd never been allowed to tease and play the way the Jennings brothers did. It was without a doubt a day to remember.

Shayla's pulse quickened as they reached Vance's house in his truck. She glanced over at him, wondering at his quiet mood. The green light from the dashboard cast an odd glow over the angles of his face. She could see a muscle in his jaw jump, and her pulse quickened. When he pulled into his driveway and killed the engine, Shayla held her breath, unsure what to expect next. Without a word, he grabbed the keys from the ignition and got out. She clutched her purse in a tight fist as she watched him jog around to her side. Suddenly, her door opened, and Vance stood there, a large barrier between her and the rest of the world. He leaned in, pressed his mouth to hers, and Shayla promptly surrendered. She wrapped her arms around his neck and gave in to the need to taste him. There were hints of the peppermint candy he'd sucked on after dinner, but mostly it was Vance's unique flavor she craved. When he ended the kiss, they were both breathing heavily.

"Ready?" Vance asked, his voice low and rough as he held a hand out to her.

She didn't have to ask ready for what, because she knew he meant to make love to her. It was there in the firm set of his shoulders and the dark look in his eyes. Shayla put her hand in his and nodded. By the time they were in Vance's bedroom, Shayla couldn't seem to catch her breath.

"You worked your butt off at the diner today," he murmured against her lips. "Are you sure you aren't too beat?"

"I'm never too tired for you. Never," she said, meaning it. Vance was better than caffeine: one touch and she was alert and raring to go. She placed her hand on his cheek and felt little flecks of sawdust and his five o'clock shadow beneath her fingers. The smell of paint lingered in the air between them. It permeated their clothes. Shayla knew they should shower first, but she didn't want to wait another second. She wanted Vance naked. Every, smooth, solid inch of him on display for her to stroke and kiss.

"I've wanted to do this all damn day, honey," he whispered as he pulled her over to the bed.

Shayla's hands had a mind of their own, it seemed, skating over the hard, muscular length of Vance's shoulders and back. Their clothes somehow disappeared, and Vance's strong hands clutched her tightly against him. Vance's hard cock against her belly had her mind going utterly blank. When her legs quivered, she felt her body being lifted as Vance cradled her in his arms and pressed his lips to hers. Her bones melted. He never removed his mouth from hers as he placed her in the center of the bed. He angled his head as if attempting to get a better taste of her, before pulling back a mere inch.

She felt bereft without his touch. It scared her to think he'd gotten under her skin so fast. Shayla hadn't anticipated how fulfilling it would be to have Vance back in her life. Today, she'd been surrounded by his family, and it'd seemed like a piece of her life had fallen into place. After so many years without Vance, it was almost too much to take in, but God, how she'd missed his playfulness.

When Vance had included her in the fun as they'd worked side by side, Shayla had felt right at home. The Jennings family could be an overwhelming bunch to a woman who'd grown up veritably alone the way she had, but Shayla adored every second spent in their company. And having Vance's full attention now sent a zing of pleasure through her.

With a swiftness that surprised her, Vance came down on the bed and lay down next to her. A pair of large, calloused hands grasped her around the waist, pulling her up and sitting her down on top of him in one smooth motion. At once, Shayla felt totally exposed.

He seemed to sense her nervous jitters. "You're beautiful, Shayla," he murmured. "I want to watch you this time." She started to say something, anything, but Vance hushed her with a finger to her kiss-swollen lips. "You can be the one to run the show when we're in this position. Wouldn't you like that?"

To be in control of the powerful Vance Jennings? Yeah, Shayla liked the idea a lot. When his arousal pushed at the cleft of her bottom, a little thrill ran through her. He was hard for her. She wanted to think that no other woman could do that to Vance, but she knew she'd be kidding herself. Still, she could pretend.

Shayla wiggled her hips, and the sound of her name came from somewhere deep inside of Vance. The sight of him beneath her held her spellbound. A sexy dusting of dark curly hair sprinkled his muscular chest, and his six-pack abs made her anxious to dance her fingers across every hard inch of him. As her gaze wandered lower, she took in the enticing trail of hair that brought her to his cock, which stood out from his body, a long, thick length of steel that had Shayla's mouth watering. When she glanced into his hazel eyes, they darkened with the fire burning bright inside him. She watched his lips thin as if he wasn't too sure about letting her be in charge all of a sudden.

"Are you certain you wouldn't rather be on top?" she offered. "I don't mind." He was such a sexual man, meeting his needs suddenly seemed like a major undertaking. She didn't know if she had it in her to please him.

"I'm sure," he said in a rough voice. "I like seeing your pretty body perched on top of me. I'm free to explore this way."

When Vance's hands closed over her breasts and massaged, Shayla became lost to the sensation of his work-scarred palms teasing her sensitive nipples. She closed her eyes and began to move her hips back and forth, slowly at first, enjoying the feel of his hard cock nestled between her buttocks. Bracing herself on his chest, she rolled her hips back and forth, clenching her thighs around him. Vance growled low in his throat and moved his hands to her ass cheeks. He squeezed and tore a moan from deep within Shayla. She opened her eyes again and bent down far enough that her nipples grazed his chest hair. The dark curls rasped them to taut peaks.

"Kiss me, honey," Vance urged.

Unable to deny him a single thing, Shayla brought her mouth to his and licked at his full lower lip. God, no man should have a mouth so beautiful. Her teeth nibbled at the satiny skin, and his arms came around her and crushed her to him. She felt herself spiraling out of control, felt Vance's instinctive need to dominate boiling to the surface. He was more demanding, and definitely rougher than before. The grown-up Vance had a wild side, and it turned Shayla on something fierce. Her passion burned hotter as she gave herself freedom to do the things she'd dreamed of for so many years.

Shayla rose up a fraction and gazed into his heavy-lidded eyes. "I want to taste more of you," she said. "Please."

As if not trusting himself to speak, Vance nodded. She lowered her head to his chest and tasted his salty skin. He was so deliciously male, Shayla knew she'd never get enough. Her tongue darted out and laved his nipple. Her fingers curled in his chest hair, and she tugged a little. He groaned, and Shayla smiled. She slid down his body, oblivious to her own nudity now, and kissed his flat, rock-hard abs. She ran her hands over his steely chest and his thick biceps. Shayla had a need to touch him everywhere at once, to memorize every line and angle.

When she reached his cock, Shayla looked up the length of him and saw the raw need in his gaze as he watched her, his entire body still and tense. She swept her hair out of the way and lowered her head. Without breaking eye contact, Shayla grasped him in her hand and squeezed.

"Fuck yeah," he growled.

Her tongue darted out to taste his dripping wet tip. A sense of feminine excitement ran through her when she saw the look of pure pleasure on Vance's face.

His hands came up and burrowed in her hair, pulling her head onto his cock a little more. Soon, Shayla had half his length inside her mouth. She sucked, hollowing her cheeks, and Vance cursed. Without warning, he pulled her upward until she was once again seated on top of him.

Curious if she'd done something wrong, Shayla asked, "Didn't you like it?"

Vance tapped her nose. "Another few seconds and I would've been fucking that hot mouth of yours."

As his words registered, Shayla decided to tease him a

little. "So on a scale of one to ten, I'm a ten. Is that what you're saying?"

He chuckled. "You're a twenty, beautiful, believe me," he murmured. "But I want to be inside you. Deep. You going to make me beg?"

She smiled, enjoying her role as master a little too much. "Vance Jennings would never beg, but it might be fun to try."

He closed his eyes as if in torment. "You're a witch. An evil one too."

She laughed. "If I were a witch, I'd totally use my powers for good."

His gaze landed on her again, and he took hold of her hips and lifted her into the air as if she weighed nothing. "In that case, use them to guide my cock inside that pretty pussy."

When Shayla took his hard, thick length in her hand and guided him to her entrance, all teasing fled. She'd managed only an inch before he stopped her.

"Are you sore from earlier?" He frowned. "I was pretty rough with you."

It touched her heart that he was willing to see to her comfort, but her body hungered for him. She ached to feel the delicious width of his cock stretching her pussy as he drove himself deep. A rush of heat swept through her and her voice was unsteady when she said, "I'll only be sore if you stop. I need you, Vance. So badly."

He appeared to consider that a minute. Finally, he whispered, "At the slightest twinge of discomfort, we stop."

She nodded, then moved her hips until her pussy clasped every inch of his hard length. "You fill me up." She moaned. "As if we were made for each other."

"Christ, you're tight," he growled. "Fuck me, Shay."

Shayla could tell that Vance wanted to change their positions. Wanted to be the one in control. But he was determined to allow her to have her way. He stayed put, and Shayla loved him all the more for his restraint.

She moaned and placed her hands on his chest for

support, then pushed herself onto his cock.

"God damn," Vance groaned.

Shayla whimpered and began moving up and down, fucking him, driving his cock deep, then back out again. "Ah, Van," she breathed out.

"You want my come filling this beautiful pussy, honey?" Vance said as he reached between them and toyed with her clit.

"Oh yes. Now, Vance," Shayla said, knowing she only had seconds before she flew right over the edge.

Shayla arched her back, and the action forced his cock deeper. Vance pinched her clitoris, then flicked it back and forth with his finger. "Let go, beautiful, I've got you," he softly ordered.

Shayla lifted, then thrust against him once more. Her inner muscles clamped on to his cock, and her passion rose to new heights. As Vance plucked at her little nub, her breaths quickened, and she moved faster. Skin slapped against skin as their movements became frenzied. When Vance glided his thumb over her clit once more, Shayla flew apart. Her orgasm sent her rocketing into outer space.

After the last throb of her release began to ebb, Shayla collapsed on top of him. Vance clutched her hips in his strong grasp and whispered against her ear, "You're mine, Shay. Only I get to see you like this."

The declaration had Shayla lifting her head and staring into his dark eyes. He pushed his hips upward, taking over their lovemaking. He thrust into her, fast and hard. All too quickly, he exploded inside her and filled her up with hot jets of his come.

They were both breathing heavily and their bodies were slick with sweat, but as Vance wrapped his arms around her rib cage and held her against him, Shayla knew there was no place she'd rather be.

Oh, God, she was in so deep. She loved Vance. Truly, madly and forever. He'd always been her one and only. Why hadn't she seen that until now? Sure, she'd come back to

Blackwater to take back what her father had ripped away from her, but she'd also come back for Vance. She'd desperately wanted a fresh start. Things were happening too fast, though; they'd only just begun to mend their fractured relationship.

Fear rose up at the knowledge that Vance might never be able to give her what she truly craved—his whole self. As she rested her head against his chest and heard the rapid beating of his heart, she knew she'd given him her heart years ago. It was too late to take it back now.

They were quiet awhile, both of them simply soaking in the moment. "Shay?" Vance said, his voice low and rough.

"Yeah?" she replied without lifting her head.

"What I said, about you belonging to me… I meant it."

Shayla decided if she was ever going to have the strength to say the three little words, now was the time. Vance might not want to hear them, and it was way too soon for such deep feelings, but the heart wants what the heart wants. There was no going back now.

She lifted her head and stared into his eyes, then murmured, "I love you."

He stared at her as if she'd lost her mind. "Love?"

Oops. The incredulous tone didn't bode well. "Yes," she said, even though she suspected Vance was about to break her heart.

"It's too early to know if what you're feeling is love, honey," he said in a tender voice. "We care about each other, and the chemistry is definitely there, but is that really love?"

Tears stung her eyes. She'd known. Deep down Shayla had known Vance would buck at the notion of having something deeper with her. She'd hurt him too deeply when she'd dumped him. It didn't matter that she'd had a good reason or that she'd been forced by her father; Vance had still been left bleeding. Shayla feared he might never let down the walls he'd erected around his heart.

"I know what I feel, and it isn't chemistry. This isn't about having a good time together either. I've always loved you, Vance.

The years apart didn't change a thing." To heck with it. He might want to backpedal, but Shayla knew her own heart, and tiptoeing around it wasn't going to change how she felt.

Vance shifted them until they lay spoon-fashion. He pulled her in close, and she cozied her bottom against his groin, content for now to lie next to him. He placed a possessive arm over her stomach and said, "You might know what you feel, honey, but I need a little time to process." He paused, then added, "And since you're back in Blackwater for good, there's no reason to rush, right?"

"It seems to me like you're dodging the subject," she said as she caressed his arm.

"No, I'm resting up for round two. There's a difference."

Good heavens, round two? "You couldn't possibly..."

"Oh, I can," he whispered against the top of her head. "Do you remember that time we went to the drive-in movies? I believe there was a round two and three that night."

"I remember." Shayla was thrown back in time as she recalled the night Vance had taken her to the drive-in for the first time. "I had to lie to my dad."

"You did?"

"Uh-huh. I told him I was with a friend. Otherwise he never would've let me go."

"Naughty, naughty," he said as he caressed her belly with his work-roughened hand. "Did he ever find out?"

"Nope, and I'm not sorry I lied."

His fingers drifted lower until he was within an inch of her pussy. "Hmm, why is that, beautiful?"

"Because that night turned out to be one of the most magical nights of my life," she said in an unsteady voice. Vance played havoc with her senses. Between his passionate touches and the walk down memory lane, Shayla wasn't sure if she was coming or going.

Vance's hand stilled. "For me too, honey," he told her in a low voice.

His words sent Shayla's heart into a tailspin. "Really?" she asked, holding her breath for his answer.

"Really," he replied. "I don't even remember the movie we went to see. All I remember is you. How pretty you looked with the moonlight shinning through the windows. The way you sort of breathed out my name when I finally managed to get beneath your pretty jean skirt."

Tears stung her eyes. "I can't believe you remember what I wore."

"I could never forget that night, Shay," he said as his hand slid a little farther south. When his palm covered her mound, Shayla could hardly breathe without panting. "Especially since I managed to coax three orgasms from you."

His cocky words had her grinning. "Of course, you were much younger then."

He stiffened. "Are you saying I'm too old to get it up, woman?"

She turned her head to look into his eyes. "If the shoe fits..."

He took hold of her chin and pressed a kiss to her lips. When she felt a hard length pressing against her bottom, she moaned. "Does that thing ever rest?" she whispered against his mouth. "Not that I'm complaining, mind you."

His hand coasted upward and covered one breast and squeezed. "Not where you're concerned." He turned her to her back and moved on top of her. With his arms at either side of her body, caging her in, he murmured, "And I'm not dodging what you said. I just need time to think it through, okay?"

She nodded. "Just promise me you will think about it."

He licked her bottom lip. "I will. Later," he said as he proceeded to take her to heaven once more.

Chapter Ten

As Vance sat at his kitchen table the next morning going over a bid for a small strip mall, Shayla's words ran through his head. She loved him, she'd said. Just like that, as if it were that simple.

"Damn it," he muttered as he realized the figures he'd written were wrong. He'd been sitting there for an hour trying to get the damn thing right, but he was distracted. Shayla's voice kept playing over and over in his head like a broken record.

He wadded the paper up and tossed it in the vicinity of the trash can. He needed to finish the freaking thing already. More coffee; that was what he needed. Maybe it'd help him get his head out of his ass so he could focus for five damn minutes. When he stood and started for the coffeepot, a loud knock on his front door stopped him. Not Shayla—she'd said she had a phone conference with an online vendor and email to catch up on. Apparently, she'd been away from work too long and shit was piling up. Suited him fine. The day away from each other was supposed to do him good. Give him time to think straight. But the only thing he'd done so far was think about Shayla's little bombshell.

Well, that and the way she'd come undone in his arms. His cock thickened in his jeans at the reminder.

Another knock on his door, louder this time, tore Vance out of his lusty musings. When he reached it and yanked it open, Sammy stood on his porch, frowning.

"It's cold as hell out here," he groused. "Mind letting me in?"

Vance stepped back. "Sorry, I was going over a bid."

Sammy stepped inside and slammed the door shut. He

looked around the room before asking, "Shayla here?"

"No, she had some things to do today. We're meeting later tonight." And already he missed her. Christ, this wasn't good.

Sammy unfastened his coat and tossed it over the recliner, then rubbed his hands together to warm them. "How's it going between you two anyway? You seemed awfully chummy at the diner."

"She told me she loves me," Vance blurted out as he headed to the kitchen.

"Already?" Sammy took a chair out at the table and straddled it.

"My thoughts exactly." Vance grabbed the coffeepot and held it up. Sammy nodded. As he went about pouring them each a cup, he said, "I didn't return the sentiment."

"I don't imagine you did. It's too soon." He took the cup from his outstretched hand and blew on the hot liquid. "What did you say?"

"That I needed to think about it." He shrugged and leaned against the counter. "I don't think I handled it well, but she blindsided me." He shook his head. "What was I supposed to say?"

"Women have a tendency to do that," Sammy replied with a grin. "Julie sure as hell managed to throw me for a loop."

"A good loop, though. With Shayla, I just don't know. Sometimes it's like we're just getting to know each other, but other times it feels like I've known her my whole life. Like the years we were separated didn't even exist."

"About that. What was her reason for dumping you, if you don't mind me asking?"

Vance related the story about Shayla's tyrant father. "Damn," Sammy said. He took a careful sip of his coffee. "I can't believe that bastard had the nerve to threaten you. To threaten the Jennings."

"Well, according to Shayla, she broke it off because she was trying to protect me." He shifted from foot to foot, suddenly uncomfortable with the discussion. Uncomfortable with the knowledge that Shayla had tried to shield him when he hadn't even known what she was going through. Oh yeah, he was a real friggin' catch.

Sammy rubbed his chin. "I remember her dad. I ran into him a few times at the diner. Both times, he tried to get out of paying his bill."

Vance snorted. "And how'd that work out for him?"

Sammy chuckled and took another sip of his coffee. "Oh, you know Dad. All he had to do was glare and grown men scattered. Riggs was no different."

Vance sighed. "I still can't believe Shayla went through all that shit. I should've known, God damn it. I should've protected her."

Sammy took one last drink and stood. "She's a strong woman, Vance. I could see it in her eyes at the diner yesterday."

"You were giving her the evil eye," Vance grumbled as he stared at his oldest brother. "What was that, a test?"

He brought his cup to the sink and ran water in it. "I needed to know if she was good enough to date my little brother." He turned and said, "I haven't forgotten what it did to you when she left. You were a fucking mess for a long time, bro."

He couldn't deny it, so instead, Vance asked, "And did she pass?"

"I like her," he said with a grin. "So, don't screw it up by being an idiot."

Vance shook his head. "Gee, thanks for the words of wisdom, Sammy."

He chuckled. "Any time, buddy." He checked the clock. "I need to head to the diner. Will you be there later?"

"Maybe, but I need to see Shayla first." He wondered if she'd even want to see him, considering how he'd reacted to her declaration.

Sammy hit him on the back, nearly breaking a rib. "I've got faith in you, bro."

After his brother left, Vance stood in the kitchen and

thought back over the last few days. His stomach clenched as he imagined how different things would've been if Shayla hadn't walked back into his calm little world and turned it upside down. He would've lived the rest of his life thinking she'd dumped him all those years ago because she'd gotten bored. The truth was a much harder pill to swallow because it forced him to face up to the fact he'd been wrong about her. She'd tried to keep him safe from her father's wrath.

Sammy was right, Shayla was a strong, confident woman now, and Vance could easily imagine spending the next fifty years with her. Did he dare risk it? Yeah, she'd confessed her love for him, but what if she woke up tomorrow or next week or next month thinking she'd made a mistake? He couldn't lose her again. Once had been hard enough.

By the time Vance arrived at Shayla's apartment, his hands were shaking. They'd talked on the phone, and she'd said the "L" word again. Once more, Vance had managed to evade her. Her ensuing silence had scared him more than he cared admit.

As she opened the door and their gazes connected, Vance saw her stiffen. "You're here," she said. Okay, that didn't sound too damn inviting.

He frowned at her. "We decided on five o'clock, right?"

"Of course," she said, not letting him in. "It's just...I have more work to do tonight. I really should—"

Vance planted his hand on the doorframe and leaned closer to her. "Are you blowing me off, Shay?"

"No," she quickly replied. She looked down at the floor. "Maybe. Gees, I-I don't mean—"

Vance leaned close and swallowed her ramblings with a kiss. He wrapped his arms around her middle and pulled her against him, aching to feel her curves and valleys up close. Vance had a need to taste her. To flood his system with her floral scent and tangy flavor. To forget all the past hurts and start anew. He licked her lips, and they parted for him. Vance thrust his tongue in and teased the inner recesses. She moaned and wrapped her arms around his neck. Vance nudged her backward, into the apartment, then kicked the door shut behind him. He reached back and flipped the lock.

When her soft body molded to his, he went a little wild. In that moment, Vance knew he would do anything, say anything to keep her close. The idea that she had so much control over him bothered him to no end.

Vance lifted his head and stared down at her. Her eyes were closed, and her face was flushed. He stared at the soft, black sweater covering her heaving breasts and the snug-fitting jeans that emphasized her gorgeous curves and knew he would never be able to walk away from her. She fucking owned him. When she shook her head and opened her eyes, Vance could see the worry in the pretty green depths.

"What's wrong?" he asked, all but holding his breath.

"You know the answer to that. I want more from you, Vance. I want some indication that you feel something other than chemistry here."

"I do," he bit out.

She rolled her eyes. "I've told you I love you twice now. You never said a word either time."

She was pushing for a commitment, but Vance's heart rebelled. She'd burned him once. Even if it wasn't her idea and she'd had no say in the matter, it still had him erring on the side of caution now. "We're good together, honey," he offered. "Can't that be enough for now?"

Vance didn't give Shayla time to respond as he bent his knees and lifted her into his arms. He took her to her bedroom and flipped on the light. Her eyes shot wide, and he saw realization dawn.

"Vance, please," she pleaded, "we need to talk."

"We will," he promised as he bent his head and covered her mouth with his. It lasted only a few seconds before Shayla pulled back and moaned, "I can't do this."

"Yes," he growled, "you can, dammit." He let her pull away, but only because he had other plans. Vance enjoyed kissing Shayla, but there were other, more exciting things he wanted to do with her—like drive her wild with pleasure. Anything but think about love and commitment, two things he'd managed to successfully avoid for the last twelve years.

Vance placed her on the bed, then moved on top of her. When she turned her head away, he took her face in his hands and forced her to look at him. "Do I stay or go, Shay?" he asked her in a gentle voice. "I won't touch you unless it's what you want. I swear it."

She brought her hand to his face and caressed his jaw. "I always want you, Vance."

He touched a freckle next to her lip and asked, "Even when I make you angry?"

A smile played at her mouth, and Vance let out a long breath. "I might want to strangle you, but that doesn't seem to dampen my desire one iota."

Vance moved between her legs and unbuttoned her jeans. "I think about you twenty-four hours a day. When I'm brushing my teeth, I imagine your pretty smile. When I'm going over a bid, your soft voice in my head breaks my concentration." Vance saw fire spark in Shayla's green eyes. "It's been over twelve hours since I last tasted you, honey. I'm going crazy."

Her cheeks bloomed pink at his erotic words. So sweet and yet so full of passion, that was his Shay. Vance took his time removing her clothes. Her jeans went first, then her sweater and bra. Her distended, mauve nipples beckoned him to suck. The soft red curls covering her mound were still hidden from his view by a pair of black silk panties. "That won't do," he said as he took hold of them in both hands and yanked, effortlessly tearing the flimsy material. He tossed them aside, pleased now that her glistening curls were visible.

"Those weren't cheap, Vance Jennings," she muttered.

"I'll replace them," he vowed. "Black. Red. White. Any color you want, honey." Staring at the beauty of her pussy, Vance murmured, "Fuck, you are one sexy woman. Wet and so damn lickable."

"Oh, Vance," she moaned.

"Put your legs over my shoulders," he instructed her. She did as he bid, and the position put the apex of her thighs directly in line with his mouth. Vance's cock hardened at the luscious sight. He grasped her hips, then pulled her closer and placed a soft kiss against her pussy. "Mm, that's the flavor I've been craving," he whispered as he used his thumbs to spread her pussy lips open, exposing her clitoris. He sucked it into his greedy mouth. Fuck, he was starving for some of her sweet cream.

Emotions tore at him as his tongue moved inside her succulent channel. His hands clasped her bottom, bringing her more fully against his mouth before he delved deeper. Vance groaned as Shayla raked her fingers through his hair and clutched on to him as if for dear life. When he flicked his tongue over and around her clit, she breathed out his name. It was the sweetest sound he'd ever heard. Over and over, Vance played with her puffy, sensitive lips and extended clit.

All too quickly, her thighs began to quiver, and her body arched upward. Shayla screamed as her sweet honey flowed into his hungry mouth. Her legs fell to the mattress, and Vance relished the sight of her totally replete and at his mercy. He couldn't take his eyes off her. She was so open and trusting in that moment. He'd never seen a more beautiful sight. He kissed her mound and lifted to his knees. When her drowsy gaze landed on him, he wondered for a second what it would be like to see her this way every morning. It'd be a hell of a way to start the day.

"You're rotten," she muttered, pouting. "A dirty rotten scoundrel."

The words were unexpected, and Vance laughed aloud. "You didn't like it, huh?"

When her eyes began to twinkle with mischief, Vance knew he was in big trouble. Shayla sat up and pushed against his chest. "Lie down," she ordered.

Vance was no dummy. He did as he was told. Her hands went to the fly of his jeans, and his cock flexed in expectation. When she had them open, Vance took over, pushing them down his hips and legs until they pooled at his feet. He kicked, and they fell to the end of the bed.

"I'm all yours, Shay," he growled.

When her lips kissed the head of his cock, Vance groaned. All reason fled, and his blood rushed south. Tender little touches of her tongue drew a primitive response in him. He placed his hands on either side of her head and showed her the way he liked it. Soon she took over, and Vance was putty in her hands.

"That's it, suck it, Shay," Vance murmured.

Her eyelids drifted downward, and with one hand, Shayla guided him between her lips. A few inches of his dick was all she could manage, but it was enough to have precome dripping from the bulbous tip. She licked and teased, and his balls drew up tight. Vance clutched a fistful of her hair and pulled her mouth onto him a little more. She arched her neck and took him to the back of her throat. She moaned, and the sound vibrated clear down the length of his cock.

"Jesus," he gritted out, hanging on to his control by a thin thread.

She sucked hard, and her hand moved to his balls, squeezing and fondling. When Shayla pulled his rigid length all the way out and placed a gentle kiss to the slit in the head, Vance cursed. She swept her soft tongue down the underside of his cock, as if she had all night to lick and play.

Vance groaned her name. It seemed to spark something wild in Shayla, and she began moving faster, sucking harder. It was as if she was hungry for his climax. The idea sent Vance over the edge.

He pumped her mouth, once, twice, and then he was shooting his come onto her waiting tongue and down her throat.

A few seconds passed before Shayla released him and sat up. Her lips were red and swollen. With her curvy body on display and her heart in her eyes, Vance knew it was a sight that would surely be etched into his brain forever.

"Now are you ready to talk?" Shayla asked as she planted her hands on her hips.

"Honey, I can't even think straight much less hold a conversation after that."

She swatted his thigh and got off the bed. "I knew you'd say that." She pointed to the door and said, "You need to leave. Now."

Vance stiffened. "Whoa, you're throwing me out?"

"Yes," she gritted out. "I don't want to be a convenient plaything to you, Vance. I want more than that."

Her words had him alert and angry in an instant. He shot off the bed and moved toward her. "Is that what you really think of me? That I'm that much of a bastard?"

She threw her hands in the air. "I don't know what to think," she tossed back. "All I know for sure is that you won't talk to me. For whatever reason, you refuse to open up to me. I need more than that. I need a man who will want me for more than sex."

In a heartbeat, he took hold of her arms and yanked her against him. "The only man you need is me."

She wiggled her shoulders, and he let her go. "Yes, I know," she said. "I love you and only you." He watched her walk to her closet, his eyes drawn to the delectable sight of her ass. She pulled out an oversize pink terrycloth robe. After she had it belted, she said, "The problem is, you don't need me. See how this is all one-sided?"

Vance felt cornered, and he wasn't even sure why. He didn't know what to say to make it right. She was right about one thing. She did deserve a man who could give her 100 percent. Could he do that? "I care about you," he blurted out. "More than any woman I've ever known."

Shayla sighed and stepped toward him. She placed her palm against his cheek and murmured, "I'm rushing you, and that's not fair. I've only been back in your life a few days, I know, but I've imagined this moment for so long. I've thought about it over and over. Blackwater is my home. I want a family of my own. I want to raise kids here. My whole life I've let someone else tell me who I should be and what I should do. Those days are over. I came back because I wanted another chance with you. You're the man I think of when I imagine my future. Only you." She closed her eyes tight and groaned. "Oh, God, I'm sorry. This is too much too soon."

He took her hand and kissed the palm. "Don't ever be sorry for coming back to me. For loving me. There have been a lot of screwed-up things in my life, but you wanting me isn't one of them, honey."

She nodded. "Still, I do think we need a few days apart. To think straight. I don't want you regretting anything."

He started to protest because the idea of being away from her sent cold chills down his spine, but he knew she had a valid point. Besides, the strength of his emotions was beginning to scare the shit out of him. In a matter of days she'd wiggled her way back into his life, and, he was afraid to admit, his heart. "Maybe a few days to clear my head would do us both some good," he hedged, still unsure. She started to move away from him, but he held her firm. "Only a few days, though."

She smiled up at him. "I told you before, I'm here to stay. I'm not going anywhere. Not ever again."

He knew she meant every word, but Vance still felt as if he'd screwed up. As if he'd lost something precious.

Chapter Eleven

A week. It'd been exactly seven days since he'd seen Shayla last. Oh, they talked day and night and even sent text messages back and forth, but it wasn't the same. He missed her. Missed touching her. Missed looking into her beautiful eyes.

But even Vance had to admit that the time apart had been the very thing to force him to evaluate his feelings for Shayla. Still, when they'd talked that morning, Shayla hadn't said "I love you" at the end of the conversation, and he hadn't been able to say it yet either. Vance felt her slipping away, and he needed advice. Preferably from someone who had been there and done that.

When he stepped into his mom's house, the only true home he'd ever known, Vance called out, "Mom?"

"In here," she called back.

The first thing that hit him when he walked into the kitchen was the smell of his mom's cinnamon rolls. "Something smells awesome."

"You're just in time, dear." She scooped up a couple of the warm, sweet treats and placed them on a small plate, then set them in the center of the table. "Have a seat while I get the milk."

His stomach growled. "You won't get any arguments from me," he said as he pulled out a chair.

After she poured them each a glass, she sat down. "So, besides your sweet tooth, what brings you by? I thought you'd be hard at work at the diner."

"I need some advice," he mumbled around a mouthful of pastry.

Her eyes brightened. "I love giving advice. Shoot."

"It's Shayla," he blurted out. "I think I'm in love with her."

His mom's eyes lit with amusement. "You think?"

He bit into the roll, and the taste of cinnamon and icing hit his tongue. Damn, his mom sure could cook. "See, that's the thing. How do you know it's the real deal? How did you know Dad was the one for you?"

She took a sip of her milk before she replied. "Because he drove me crazy."

Confused, Vance asked, "Come again?"

She swiped a finger in the icing, brought it to her mouth and licked it off. "My emotions were all over the place whenever your dad was near. No man had ever managed to make me lose my temper one minute and laugh the next."

He understood now. "Shayla is beautiful and strong and intelligent, and she makes me laugh," he said as he took another bite. "I can't stop thinking about her."

She quirked a brow. "And how does she feel about you?"

Vance cringed, suddenly not real interested in the dessert. "Well, right now she probably wishes I'd jump off a bridge."

She chuckled, then tore off a piece of the roll and popped it into her mouth. After she swallowed, she said, "If the look in her eyes when you brought her to the diner the other night was any indication, then I highly doubt it, Vance."

His mom's words gave him hope. "She told me she loved me, and I sort of froze."

"Well, it is awfully soon. Especially for you."

Vance stiffened. "What's that supposed to mean?"

"You aren't the impulsive one that your brother Reilly is, dear. You always think a thing through. You have to look at it from several different angles before you make a decision. It's what makes you good at your job."

Vance knew his mom had it right. "It might be a good trait to have in business, but I'm afraid it might've caused me to lose the only woman I've ever really cared about."

"So, go to her," she urged him as she placed her hand on his. "Be impulsive, just this once. What could it hurt?"

"And if she decides later on that I'm not worth sticking around for?" he asked, voicing his worst fear. "What then?"

"Is that what's bothering you?" she asked as her eyes widened. "That she'll leave again?"

"Yes. No. I don't know," he admitted. "Why me?"

"I'm not following you," she replied, clearly confused.

"Shayla could have any man she wants, Mom. Why would she want me? Hell, I don't even know who my biological father is, and my biological mother wanted drugs more than she wanted me. How am I a catch?"

"Well, let's see." She held up a hand. "You're honest," she said as she began ticking off his attributes with her fingers. "Intelligent. Kind. You have your own successful business, and it doesn't hurt that you're gorgeous. She's lucky to have you, if you ask me."

Vance shook his head at his mother's description of him. "You know, a few weeks ago I would've laughed if someone said I'd be getting love-life advice from my mom. Yet, here I sit."

She sat up straighter and stuck her nose in the air. "What can I say, you came to the best."

He laughed and sat back in his chair. "Okay, love guru, any advice on how I should proceed?"

"Tell her how you feel. Don't hold back," she offered in a stronger tone. "There's no room for pride and ego between a man and a woman, Vance."

She was right, and he knew it. A plan started to form in his mind, and Vance felt better than he had in days. "Thanks, Mom," he said as he leaned across the table and kissed her cheek.

"Any time, son," she said with a smile. "Now, finish your roll."

He chuckled. "Yes, ma'am."

Butterflies took flight in Shayla's stomach as she watched Vance pace her living room. He'd called her earlier and asked if he could come over. He'd said he needed to talk about their relationship. Shayla hadn't been able to figure out his mood over the phone, but watching him now scared her to no end.

"Vance, is something wrong? You're beginning to worry me."

He stopped and looked at her. "I reacted like an ass when you told me you loved me," he explained as he crossed the room. When only a few feet of tan carpet separated them, he said, "It scared me because I'm afraid...I'm afraid of losing you again." He frowned and looked down at the floor. "The thing is, Shay, you make me feel...needy. The Jennings men do not like to feel out of control." He shrugged, and his gaze met hers once more. "It goes against our grain." He closed the gap between them and stroked her cheek with his thumb and murmured, "You send me out of control every time you're near, honey."

Oh boy, did she understand that feeling all too well. "This may come as a shock, but the Jennings bunch aren't the only people who hate that feeling."

Vance's eyes held hers captive as he wrapped his hand around the nape of her neck and drew her close. "Yeah, I'm beginning to see that," he murmured as he kissed her. It was so quick and gentle, Shayla barely had time to take in his clean, masculine scent before he pulled away.

"I've laid awake nights thinking of you," Vance admitted. "Thinking of your cries of passion, your laughter, your pretty little freckles."

Shayla didn't have time to digest his words. Suddenly, his hands were everywhere. He stripped her out of her clothes so fast her head started to spin. She nearly forgot her own name when his warm fingers skimmed over her breasts. She moaned, aching for him. The last seven days had been nothing but torture without him.

"I love you, Shay," he whispered. "Hell, I think I've always loved you."

As he finished divesting them both of their clothes, his words hit her like a semi-truck. "Wait, what did you say?"

Vance wrapped his arms around her and said, "I love you."

He loved her? Had she heard him correctly "Y-You do?"

His grin was slow and sexy. "It might have taken me a few days to figure it out, but yeah."

Shayla's heart soared to the clouds and beyond. "Oh, Vance, I love you too, so much," she said, needing him to hear her this time. Really hear her.

"I know, and I'm one lucky bastard," he said in a low voice. "Now will you let me make you feel good, honey?"

Shayla noticed he hadn't gone beyond touching her. He was waiting for her consent. "Yes," she answered, grinning at him. Vance gave her a sexy hum of approval.

Within seconds, Shayla found herself sprawled out on the floor on her back. "Here?" she said. She felt strangely exposed, making love in the living room.

"Yeah, here," he replied, his voice rough and low. "And every other room in this apartment. Then we'll head to my place and make love in all those rooms too."

He went to his coat and took something out of the inside pocket, then came back to her. As Vance moved between her knees, she watched him hold up a tube of lubricant. He took off the cap and squirted a little onto his finger. It excited her to know he'd come to her prepared to seduce her. A trickle of moisture ran down her thigh at the knowledge that he'd been thinking about loving her.

When he stroked the seam between her buttocks with his index finger, Shayla's breath caught in her throat. A moan erupted from deep within as he let the digit drift back and forth over her puckered opening.

He leaned over her and kissed the side of her neck. "I want to fill this sweet ass, Shay. Will you let me?"

Her face flamed hot as a carnal image sprang to her mind. She'd had anal sex before, but it hadn't been all that pleasurable. Of course, it hadn't been with Vance. "Oh, God, I don't know."

"Come on, honey, let me make you feel good," Vance urged as his finger penetrate her a little at a time until soon it was buried deep inside the tight opening. Shalya shuddered and pushed against him. "Yeah, that's it, fuck it, Shay," he said while he moved his finger slowly in and out of her.

She whimpered, and her breasts swelled. Her sex grew damp as his finger pumped in her ass. Shayla felt every heated touch. Vance was gentle with her, but soon a second finger joined the first, and Shayla went a little wild at the intense invasion.

She moved up and down, fucking his fingers. When Vance's other hand massaged her clit, she climbed higher. Her climax came on so fast she couldn't catch her breath. She screamed his name as she flew apart.

Vance's rough voice just barely broke through the quagmire of her mind. "I want you, Shayla," he growled. Then he slid his fingers out of her and covered her body with his. "Look at me, beautiful."

She turned her head, already limp and sweating from her orgasm, but when she saw the intensity, the insane yearning etched into every plane and angle of his face, her body went from sated to famished all over again.

"I love you, Shayla Riggs," he whispered as he stared down at her.

"I'll never get tired of hearing you say that to me, Vance," she said, grinning from ear to ear.

His lips kicked up on one side. "Feel like saying them back to me, then?"

She took his face in her hands. "I love you, Vance Jennings."

He didn't say another word, but he didn't have to; the pleasure on his face was enough. When he sat back on his heels and squirted some of the lube down the length of his cock, Shayla's heart sped up. At the first touch against her ass, Shayla stiffened.

"Vance, I'm not sure about this," she said, worried it would hurt.

He leaned down and nipped her behind the ear. "I want all

of you, honey. From here on out, we trust each other completely," he whispered.

When he braced himself on his elbows beside her head and his entire body was surrounding her, Shayla's fears began to vanish, and her body hummed back to life. "Another of Vance's rules?"

"Hmm, think of it more like a promise. You trust me not to hurt you, and I promise to always love you with my whole heart." He stroked the length of her hair and situated himself until he sat between her thighs on his haunches. "What's it going to be, beautiful?"

"Yes, I do trust you, and I desperately want to give you everything," she murmured as she watched his face cloud with emotion.

"My heart belongs to you, Shay. Only you," he said in a low voice.

The sincerity of Vance's words in that tender moment would forever be branded on her mind. She wanted to speak, to tell him how much she loved him, but her mouth simply wouldn't cooperate.

"Put your legs over my shoulders," he softly ordered.

Shayla bit her lower lip, and her legs shook as she positioned them on either side of his head. When he started to slowly push his cock inside her ass, her inner muscles clutched each inch in a tight fist, and Shayla felt every little movement. It was like nothing she'd ever experienced. The forbidden nature of what they were doing sent a rush of excitement skittering through her.

Once he was seated deep, he began to move in and out. Each stroke drew a moan from deep inside her until soon Vance was pumping in and out. He reached between their bodies and danced his finger back and forth over her clit. The teasing sparked off another orgasm, and Shayla had to grip on to the short carpet threads to keep from flying into orbit. Vance pushed deep one last time and spilled his hot seed deep inside her ass.

A few minutes went by, neither of them moving or

speaking. Neither of them were able. Finally, he carefully pulled out of her, and Shayla let her legs drop to the floor on either side of his body. When the heavy weight of him came down on top of her, pressing her into the floor, Shayla's heart overflowed with emotion. It should've been uncomfortable to have Vance crushing her in such a way, but it felt so right, and all she wanted to do was savor every second of it. Besides, she was too exhausted to care about pesky things like rug burns. As he brushed her damp hair from her face and kissed her cheek, Shayla heard him whisper something that sounded suspiciously like the three little words again, but she couldn't be sure. She opened her eyes to find him staring down at her.

"I was a coward for not telling you sooner how I felt. This week sucked, and I only have myself to blame."

"I missed you so much after you left the other night," she said as she ran her hands through his thick hair.

He tweaked her nose and murmured, "We've talked every night, honey."

"It wasn't the same thing, though. I've barely been able to sleep, thanks to you." She smacked him lightly on the back of his head. "I hope you're happy."

Vance chuckled. "You came back to me, Shay," he whispered. "I'm the happiest man on earth."

Shayla teared up at the quiet statement. "And now you're stuck with me."

"Ditto, beautiful," he said as he kissed her once more.

Shayla knew in that moment that whatever her father had tried to destroy had only made them stronger. True love was like that, she supposed.

Breaking Brodix

Dedication

For Mari Carr. You're a terrific author, a wonderful friend and an incredible multi-tasker. Your energy makes my head spin!

Chapter One

Brodix ran the numbers again, even though he knew it was useless. The renovations on the Blackwater Bar and Grill were finished, and right on schedule too. It was Saturday, and the grand opening was scheduled for Friday. Six days away. Brodix groaned. "It had better be a frigging record-breaking night," he mumbled to himself. They needed the cash flow in a bad way. He'd crunched the numbers, done what he could to keep things on budget, but the bills were piling up. He sat back in his chair and pushed a hand through his hair. What were they going to do if the restaurant failed after all the money and time they'd put into rebuilding it?

He looked around at the work they'd done. The old diner was gone. His chest tightened at the thought even as pride shot through him at all the work they'd done. The bar top Vance had designed had a beautiful, dark wood finish, and the smooth swirl design down the sides of the bar was a work of art. The old, plain white walls had been replaced with more rustic, weathered barn siding. He and his brothers had even added on to allow room for a dance floor. They'd decided on live music for the busier weekend crowd, and it had become Reilly's job to find the right band for the job. They wanted someone with a Southern rock sound, but as of yet, Reilly hadn't settled on anyone. They'd taken out the ugly, harsh lights and installed recessed lighting, which created a cozier atmosphere.

The changes were all going to be good for business, and although the place no longer resembled the little diner it'd once been, Brodix could still picture his father, Chet Jennings, standing behind the counter with his apron tied around his waist and laughing with the customers, even as he worked himself to the bone to keep the place running. Letting the restaurant go now would be more than any of them could bear. It had to do well. There was no other choice. It was a part of their family, their father's legacy. None of them would let that go without fighting tooth and nail.

A high-pitched yelp tore Brodix out of his maudlin thoughts. He looked out the front window, but no one was there. Still, he could've sworn he'd heard a woman.

Reilly came striding out of the kitchen. White paint from the finishing touches he'd been putting on the trim in the kitchen splattered the black T-shirt and sweats he wore. Christ, he was a mess. His shaggy black hair needed a decent trim too, Brodix realized. Now that he was looking, Brodix noticed his little brother had somehow gained a few more muscles. When had that happened?

"Did you hear that?" Reilly said. "Sounded like a woman."

Brodix nodded and stood. "Yeah. Were you expecting anyone this early?" The depressing numbers he'd been working on all morning were forgotten as they both went to the front door.

"Nope."

Brodix flipped the lock and stepped outside into the cool springtime sun. He heard a string of curses and glanced down to see a woman sprawled out on the ground. A sexy, curvy woman. His blood heated instantly.

Brodix wanted to sink his fingers into the blonde curls flowing around her shoulders. Their gazes met, and for a moment, Brodix got caught in the pretty blue depths of the woman's almond-shaped eyes. But something wasn't right. The eyes, the hair, they were all too familiar, and not in a good way. She all but growled his name, and that was when it hit him. She was none other than Sarah Greer, a reporter for the local newspaper. And the one woman he'd been dodging for the last two weeks.

She squinted up at him. "Do you think one of you could possibly help me up, or is that simply too much to ask?"

Brodix forced himself to stop eyeballing her. "Are you all right?" He crouched in front of her to get a better look at the ankle she held in the palm of one hand as if she'd twisted it. "Does it hurt?"

She rolled her eyes. "Only my pride managed to get bruised, I assure you."

Brodix knew he shouldn't look past her face, but he didn't seem to have any control over his own body at the moment. When his gaze traveled her length, his heart sped up. She had curves, but they weren't overblown and in your face. They were subtle. As if a man had to get up close and personal before he could truly appreciate them.

Not a bad idea.

The fact that her black skirt had gotten pushed up around her thighs, showing a tantalizing glimpse of smooth, sexy skin, hadn't escaped his notice either. They were quite possibly the longest, prettiest legs he'd ever seen. When he took in the angry expression pinching her brows together, his lips twitched. Oh yeah, she was good and pissed.

He started to help her to her feet, but his brother was quicker. Sarah's face softened as she placed her hand in his palm. He grinned down at her. "Reilly Jennings. And you are?"

"It's a pleasure to meet you, Reilly. I'm Sarah Greer." The sweet smile spreading across her face turned her into a gentle beauty right before their eyes. She had the look of an innocent. A delicate flower in need of a man to keep her safe and secure. What a crock. Sarah was as ruthless as they came. Oh, Brodix didn't know her personally, but he'd seen her type a hundred times over. Had even dated a few, much to his dismay.

Sarah had a reputation for being ruthless when it came to getting a story. Brodix remembered the article she'd written last summer about Blackwater's mayor, Michael Coburn. She'd gotten her facts wrong when she'd accused the man of taking contributions from a controversial source. As a result of Sarah's erroneous information, Coburn's reputation had nearly been ruined. Hell, Brodix was surprised she was still a reporter after that fiasco.

Brodix stood and glared at Reilly, willing him to back off, but Reilly suddenly only had eyes for Sarah. That would change, he knew, as soon as Reilly found out why Sarah had shown up at the Blackwater Bar and Grill unannounced. What had she thought? That she could get around him with her baby blues and cute smile? It'd take a hell of a lot more than that. Brodix hid a grin and crossed his arms over his chest. He looked over at Sarah and waited while she brushed fresh grass clippings off her white blouse. When her gaze met his, the frown came right back.

Sarah released Reilly, and Brodix relaxed a fraction. For some ridiculous reason, he didn't much care for the smile Reilly was giving Sarah, as if he was a step away from asking her to dinner. Sarah looked down at the ground and lifted her right foot in the air, twisted it this way and that, then sighed and stood on both feet once again. "I've been attempting to get in touch with you, Mr. Jennings," she said as she pinned him with a hard glare. "You've been avoiding me." Her voice was as stern as a schoolteacher scolding a naughty child. "I've left several voice-mail messages on your cell phone and at your office. You haven't returned a single one of them."

Brodix grinned. "That should have clued you in right there, but yet here you are."

She let out a sigh. "Look, I don't see why you won't consider my proposal. Your backgrounds would make a fabulous human-interest piece, and the exposure would be good for business. From what I've learned about the Blackwater Restaurant, Mr. Jennings, you could use all the help you can get with the grand opening."

Reilly cleared his throat, and they both looked over at him. "Exposure? Someone care to catch me up here?"

Brodix quirked a brow and pointed to Sarah. "I can see how you might not recognize our little reporter here, considering the stains on her blouse and the blades of grass in her hair."

Reilly frowned. "Reporter?"

Sarah clearly wasn't daunted by the change in Reilly. He'd gone from flirtatious to cautious in a heartbeat. Sarah merely turned on the charm like a pro. Brodix tried not to let the sexiness of it affect him, but his dick was already standing at attention. Damn it all to hell.

"Yes," she answered as she held her hand out for Reilly to shake. "I'm here to interview the Jennings family for the front page of the *Gazette*." She jabbed a thumb at Brodix. "I've explained everything to your brother here, but it's clear he didn't bother to fill you in."

Brodix wasn't the least surprised when Reilly didn't move to shake Sarah's hand. In fact, he actually took two slow steps backward. Brodix glowered at him. Hell, he didn't much care for reporters either, but it didn't feel right for Reilly to snub Sarah in such an obvious way. Their mother had raised them better than that.

"You're a reporter?" Reilly asked as if attempting to swallow cotton.

Sarah seemed oblivious to his brother's mounting tension. "Yes," she said, "and I'm here to help you promote the grand opening of the Blackwater Bar and Grill. As I stated in my messages to your brother, the fact you and your four brothers were all adopted from foster care and raised by a local couple would make a fantastic story." She grinned as if she were imparting some fantastic news. "Unfortunately, your general manager here," she aimed a frown toward Brodix, "has been very difficult to pin down. So I decided to take my chances and come straight to the source."

"There will be no interviews," Reilly said as he took a step back. "Now or ever."

"But you haven't even—"

Reilly held up a hand. "You've wasted your time, Ms. Greer. None of the Jennings are interested in what you have to say."

Sarah opened her mouth, no doubt to continue arguing her case, but Brodix knew it would be a waste of time. Ever since their foster-care days, when one of his two younger brothers, River—Reilly's twin—had been sent to live with Mr. and Mrs. Larry Briggs, Reilly and River had hated reporters with a passion. Larry had been a reporter. He'd also been an abusive piece of shit. He'd treated River like garbage.

When River had once confided in a teacher about the

beatings, charges had been filed. But Larry knew how to manipulate people, and he'd worked the police like a pro. He'd twisted River's words so efficiently that by the time he was through, everyone thought River had made it all up. Was it any wonder that River and Reilly considered reporters to be the next best thing to the antichrist? As River's twin, Reilly still harbored a truckload of bad feelings for anyone who had anything to do with reporting the news.

When Sarah started to speak once more, Brodix could easily see things getting out of hand. He stepped between the two and clapped Reilly on the shoulder. "I've got this." Reilly hesitated a moment, but when Sarah went to step around Brodix, Reilly nodded and went back into the restaurant.

"Wow," Sarah said. "Okay, so I'm getting the feeling that you all don't care for reporters much."

"No, we don't." When he caught her favoring her right foot, he muttered, "You did get hurt."

"Not really." She winced when she tried to put weight on it. "It's just a little twinge, nothing more, I promise you."

Brodix closed the distance between them and took her elbow in his palm. He could feel the warmth of her skin through the flimsy material of her blouse, and it turned him on. To hell if he wanted to be turned on by the woman, though. She was nothing but trouble. The mess she'd made of Coburn's life was proof. "Come on, we'd better get some ice on it before it swells. We can...talk."

As if he'd just handed her a million dollars, her eyes grew wide. "You're going to do the interview?"

"No," he gritted out, dashing her hopes. "Interviews are out of the question. But maybe we can figure out something else. Something that will help you with your story and help the Jenningses drum up business for the restaurant."

She stared at him a few seconds, mulling over his words, then nodded and followed him into the restaurant. "Okay, but I warn you. I'm not letting up about the interviews."

He chuckled, despite the fact she was a complete pain in the ass. "I didn't really think you would."

"The thing is, Mr. Jennings—"

"Brodix," he corrected her. "Every time you call me mister, it reminds me of my father. He was a good man, but I'm a little raw about him just now." He paused, wishing he hadn't said so much. "So, please, call me Brodix."

"I'm sorry. He died a few years ago, didn't he?"

"Save the questions, little Miss Nosy." He patted a seat at the bar. "Here, stay out of trouble while I get some ice."

Brodix headed around the bar, but Sarah called out his name, and he turned. "Yeah?"

"I can make polite conversation, you know," she stated. "I'm more than a reporter."

The sadness dulling her bright blue eyes had a knot forming in Brodix's throat. Had he hurt her feelings? The way she suddenly found the bar top fascinating told him he had. The woman was an enigma. In that moment, Brodix decided the only way to have any peace of mind would be to learn more about her. Maybe while she was busy trying to learn all his dirty little secrets, he could learn some of hers.

Wait, what was he thinking? He must be insane to even consider spending time with a reporter. Ever since River had been forced to endure Larry's abuse, it'd been an unspoken agreement among the Jennings that reporters were right up there with lawyers, basically bloodsuckers and ambulance chasers and nothing more. But Brodix had a feeling Sarah was different. For one, she wasn't Larry. Even though Brodix had spent only a few minutes in her company, he could see he'd been letting his attitude about River's foster dad color his view of Sarah. Still, she'd dragged Coburn's name through the mud, hadn't she? It was clear the woman was no saint. Did that mean Sarah didn't deserve to be heard, though? What harm could it do?

The bigger question was, what would his brothers want? Reilly didn't want anything to do with an interview, which meant River most likely wouldn't either. But what of Vance and Sammy? If they knew how important it would be to the success of the grand opening, would they agree to do whatever was necessary? A nasty dose of guilt washed over him. Hell, just bringing her into the bar seemed like a betrayal to all River had been put through. Sarah had pegged it, though. They did need the publicity. They couldn't afford to turn up their noses based solely on what Larry had done. As for the disastrous article about the mayor, it was in the past. Like the horrors of River's childhood, it was over and done with. Time for all of them to move on. Besides, the free promotional opportunity wasn't something to scoff at, not this late in the game.

When he grabbed some ice out of the freezer and turned to get a towel, Reilly was standing there, glaring at him. Shit. "Might as well say it," Brodix muttered as he picked up a towel off the counter and wrapped it around the cubes of ice.

Reilly pointed to the door leading to the main room. "What the hell is she doing sitting at the bar? I thought you were going to get rid of her."

"I was until I saw her ankle." He held up the makeshift icepack he'd taken out of the freezer. "She's hurt and on our property. That's not good no matter how you slice it."

"So ice her ankle and send her on her way," he bit out. "We don't need her kind here."

Brodix didn't much care for his brother's attitude toward Sarah. She was a veritable stranger, but a sense of protectiveness shot through him all the same. "Look, I'm not any crazier about Sarah snooping around than you, but she's not Larry. I don't think it's fair to measure her by his misdeeds." Brodix left off the part about Sarah's own misdeeds. He didn't think Reilly needed more of a reason to hate the woman. Hell, if Reilly didn't remember the Coburn article, then Brodix sure as hell wasn't going to remind him.

"She's committed a few sins of her own, and you damn well know it," Reilly gritted out.

Brodix felt his face heat. "I was hoping you'd forgotten about that," he admitted.

"Not damn likely. Now she wants to interview us, Brodix," he said, his tone rising right along with his temper. "And we both know the questions she'd ask. 'What was it like growing up in foster care?' 'Where are your biological parents?' 'Why'd they give you up?' And if she gets even a tiny hint about River's lousy foster homes, she'd go for the jugular, and we both know it."

"Keep your voice down," Brodix warned as he leaned against the refrigerator. "I hear what you're saying, but before we dismiss her completely, let me talk to her."

"Is this because she's hot? Is that it? You're attracted to her, so you're willing to give her the benefit of the doubt?"

Brodix knew Reilly had it at least half right, but to hell if he was willing to admit it aloud. "Let's stick to the facts, shall we? First, this restaurant is teetering on the brink, and we need all the help we can get to bring it back into the black. Second, this is Dad's legacy, and it's close to disappearing in a puff of smoke. Third, the publicity she's offering could do us a world of good here. Do we agree so far?" When Reilly nodded, Brodix continued. "We need the grand opening to be a hit in a bad way. We need the exposure she's talking about giving us. Give me a chance to talk to her. That's all I'm asking."

Reilly shoved a hand through his hair. "Do you even know what her master plan is besides dissecting our entire life and plastering it on the front page for everyone in Blackwater to see?"

"No," he growled, his own temper flaring to the surface. "And until I hear her out, I don't think we should make any hasty decisions."

A few seconds of silence passed between them before Reilly finally let out a long sigh. "You need to bring the others in on this."

"We all agree or nothing," Brodix said, knowing Reilly was right. "I get it, believe me. First, I need to see if there's anything to vote on."

Without another word, Reilly went back to painting. Brodix wanted to say more, to reassure his brother, but he didn't know what he'd be reassuring him of. Sure, the fact they were all adopted was known around town, but the dirty details of their past weren't. The abuse and neglect, they'd managed to keep that shit hidden. On the other hand, Brodix was a businessman. He better than anyone knew that connecting their story of triumph over adversity with the diner would win the sympathies of the small-town residents. And that would surely be good for business.

Would it even be worth trying to balance exposing some of their painful secrets while attempting to keep the worst of it private, just to make people curious enough to check out the restaurant? Only one way to know.

When Brodix brought the ice out to Sarah, he found her sitting at the bar where he'd left her. She was hunched over and staring at her phone, her hair hanging on either side of her face like a shiny golden curtain. His body responded with a rush of heat to his groin. God, she was pretty. Yeah, Reilly had been right on the money. Brodix was attracted to little Miss Nosy, and mixing business with pleasure was something he'd always sworn never to do. Some things were worth breaking a few rules for, though.

Chapter Two

"Ice," a deep male voice said close to her ear. Sarah's heart jumped, and she looked up from her phone to see Brodix standing next to her stool, a small smile playing at the corners of his mouth. God, she'd been so freaked out by the text message she'd just received that she hadn't even heard the man enter the room.

She dropped her cell phone on the counter and held out her hand. "I really don't think it's necessary, but thanks all the same."

Brodix held the ice away and sat in the stool to her right. He patted his thigh and said, "Here, let me see your ankle."

No way was Sarah getting that close to temptation. She knew her limitations, and where the sexy, dark-haired Brodix was concerned, she had practically no sense of self-preservation. The crisp white dress shirt he wore seemed to barely contain the muscular chest it covered. And her gaze had already eaten up the way his black slacks molded to the man's sculpted legs and buns. He was a work of art. Lean and hard all over. His black hair was neatly trimmed, but he sported a five o'clock shadow. She wondered if he realized how incongruous the facial hair was in relation to the rest of him. He was Mr. Neat-and-Tidy, except for the dark stubble covering his chin. Sarah yearned to reach out and touch his jaw line with her index finger, simply to see if he felt as good as he looked. But to touch would be to drool. Not a good way to start off their professional relationship.

She restrained herself, barely, and cleared her throat before saying, "I think I can manage, really." Sarah kept her hand in the air, palm up, expecting him to give her the pack. When he reached down and cupped her ankle, then and brought it to his thigh, she let out a startled breath. "What are you doing?"

With more gentleness than she would've thought a man his size was capable of, Brodix placed the towel-wrapped ice on her ankle and said, "Do you want to talk to me or not?"

Sarah stiffened. "I want an interview."

"Then let me see to your pain, and maybe you'll get one," he replied, his voice lowering an octave until it seemed to skate over her skin like a tender caress.

Sarah shook the dreamy haze away and attempted to focus on business. With his hand wrapped around her calf, it wasn't easy. "Brodix is an unusual name," she said, needing a place to start. She ached to get to know him. To know all the Jennings brothers.

Frustration ate at Sarah that she'd practically had to hunt Brodix down, but what choice did she have? After that pivotal moment last year when she'd been steadily working her way up the chain from the reporters' pool, only to fall flat on her face, Sarah needed to prove herself again. She could be an outstanding reporter, if only she had the opportunity. She had Wendy Castle, the mayor's former assistant, to thank for this mess. The woman had given her bad information on Coburn, and all because she'd been pissed the mayor had fired her. God, Sarah had been so naïve, proudly writing the article about the mayor's sketchy campaign contribution, only to have it come back and bite her in the ass. Now Sarah was left with the odd jobs, like writing about a restaurant opening.

She desperately needed to prove to her boss that she was worthy of a second chance. With any luck, delving into the personal aspects behind the Blackwater restaurant, Brodix's parents and what they'd done for the boys and the history of the diner, would be her ticket back into the inner circle. If only Brodix would stop pushing her away.

He shrugged. "I didn't pick it, and before you ask, no, I don't know why my biological parents chose it."

"Have you ever looked it up?" she asked as he moved the ice-packed towel around in small circles, easing the pain with each gentle stroke. The chill went straight through her, but it didn't douse the fire slowly building inside her body. Nothing would cool that down, except maybe putting a few hundred feet between her and the man hovering over her.

Brodix quirked a brow. "My name?"

She cleared her throat and forced her gaze back to his face and away from his talented hands. "Yes."

"Why would I?"

"Curiosity, if nothing else," she replied, surprised by his complete lack of interest in his own name, which was decidedly unique. "I've never met another person with your name. And I've met a lot of people, so that's saying something."

"Me either," he said as he absently caressed the back of her leg with his thumb. "I guess I don't see the big deal. A name is a name."

Sarah's stomach did little cartwheels as his thumb moved higher. Was he aware of the gentle massage he was administering and the riot of sensations it created inside her? Somehow she thought very little got past Brodix. He seemed a very astute man. "I did an Internet search on it." His fingers went still, and his gaze caught on hers. "The closest I could find is the name of an engine part."

"You looked up my name?" She nodded, and he frowned. "What on earth for?"

Heat filled her cheeks. Sarah couldn't very well tell him the truth—that she'd been wildly curious about him and hadn't been able to keep herself from learning every little thing. Her interest in the man had started when he'd ignored her phone calls. Most people were at least a little flattered by the prospect of being interviewed by a reporter, but not Brodix. For all intents and purposes, he'd flat-out snubbed her. So she'd done a little digging, come up with practically nothing, and her interest had grown into a full-fledged fascination. He was a mystery and she aimed to unravel him. But Sarah couldn't very well tell Brodix that. He'd think she was a stalker, for crying out loud. "I always do research on the people I interview," she replied. Well, it was true, just not the whole truth.

"Huh, interesting. So, they named me after an engine part."

He shook his head and resumed his tender ministrations. "Real, uh, fascinating."

Sarah cocked her head to the side, wondering at the lack of emotion in his voice. "Doesn't it upset you?"

"Why should it?" he asked, not bothering to look up from her leg.

"I'd think at the very least you would wonder why they named you after something so...cold. I mean, a lot of times, parents name their children for emotional reasons. A loving grandparent who passed away, a special aunt or uncle, that sort of thing."

Brodix moved his hand away from her leg, then placed the rapidly melting icepack on the counter. "You're missing an important point here, Sarah."

"What's that?"

"My biological parents brought me into this world, and that's pretty much the extent of their involvement in my life. I never even knew my father. He was never in the picture at all. My mother was a drug addict. She cared about getting her next fix and not much else. My *real* parents, Wanda and Chet Jennings, they're the ones who gave me a home. Their love is what matters. The people you seem so intent on finding out more about matter to me about as much as a gnat to a dog." He patted her leg and said, "I think the ice has done all it can. If it's still sore, you should go to the hospital. Of course, the restaurant will pick up the tab."

Sarah dropped her leg from his thigh and immediately missed Brodix's warmth. She stood and tested her ankle by putting most of her weight on it. When no pain radiated through her foot, she smiled. "Apparently, you have the magic touch."

His eyes darkened as he caught and held her gaze. "No pain?"

"Nope," she said, then grabbed her purse off the counter. "The way I see it, I owe you. How about dinner?"

He chuckled and picked up her phone, then handed it to

her. "Still after that interview, huh?"

As she recalled the nasty text message she'd received earlier from her ex-husband, Sarah reluctantly took the cell from Brodix and willed it not to ring. "Like I said, the human-interest piece would be great publicity for the restaurant. It's my understanding that you went from one foster home to another. That doesn't sound like a picnic. Later you were all adopted by what appears to be two very special people. If you ask me, that's something this town would want to read about. Don't you think? I mean, I don't see what you have to lose."

"Let's see," he said as he stood, his taller, much larger frame dwarfing her. "There's the little matter of privacy, for one. You digging around in my past—in my brothers' pasts—poking at old wounds, that's not my idea of a good time." She started to protest, to make him see that she didn't intend to hurt his family, but he didn't give her a chance. "And while I might appear to be a gentle lamb, Sarah, I do have my limits."

She snorted at his description of himself. "No one would ever mistake you for a gentle lamb, least of all me." Sarah fished around in her purse and took out her business card. "If you change your mind about dinner, call me." She handed it to him, pleased when he took it and tucked it into the front pocket of his slacks.

"I—"

Sarah's cell phone rang, interrupting Brodix. She held it up and read the number on the screen, then cursed.

Brodix's entire body went rigid as if gearing up for a fight. "Not someone you want to talk to, I take it?"

"My ex-husband," she replied. "He's back in town and looking to get together for drinks." She rolled her eyes. "He's been calling me every half hour. It isn't just drinks he's after."

"And that's the last thing you want," Brodix surmised in a voice edged with steel. There was a hardness about him that hadn't been there mere seconds ago.

"I'd rather he do the world a favor and jump off a cliff," she admitted, "but I guess that's asking too much." She groaned when it rang again. Sarah hit Ignore.

"You know," Brodix said, staring at the phone in her hand, "I've changed my mind about dinner. How about we meet tonight at seven? Does that work for you?"

The sudden turnaround had Sarah suspicious. "Definitely, but why the change of heart?"

He stuck his hands in his front pockets and smiled. "It just occurred to me that we need each other."

Sarah stiffened. She didn't much like the idea of needing anyone, much less a man. "And why might that be?"

Brodix pointed to the phone clutched in Sarah's hand. "He's going to keep calling until he has a legitimate reason not to. And when he does, you can tell him that you already have a date. If he thinks you're unavailable, he'll leave you alone."

"How do you know I don't already have a boyfriend?" She paused, then added, "I don't, but you couldn't have known that."

"Just a guess, but it seems to me that if you had a boyfriend, then your ex wouldn't be bothering you so much. Your boyfriend would've put a stop to it."

The affront to her feminine pride was a little more than she could take. "I don't need a man to protect me."

"I don't imagine you do," he said, his voice ringing with honesty and a touch of respect, if she wasn't mistaken. "You're obviously a very capable woman, but any man worth his salt wouldn't allow his woman to be harassed the way your ex is harassing you."

"Okay, I see your point. So, basically, you're doing me a favor, is that it?"

"I'm doing us both a favor."

"What do you get out of it, then?" A thought struck, and she asked, "Or are you saying you've changed your mind about doing the interview?"

"I get the pleasure of your company," he murmured as he touched a finger to her cheek. "Not a bad deal, trust me. We'll talk about the interview over dinner."

Sarah's nerve endings fired to life with the barely there

touch. "Oh, okay," she said, her voice a little too breathless. She could all too easily imagine that stroke elsewhere. Brodix had the gentlest fingers. What would it be like to feel his caresses all over? When her phone chimed yet again, Sarah snapped back to reality. She glared at the small screen and this time hit Answer. "What do you want, Jack?"

When Jack's silky-smooth voice came over the line, she had to hold back a shiver. The overly charming tone brought back too many ugly memories for Sarah. The instant the invitation to meet him for drinks was out of his mouth, Sarah quickly shut him down. "I told you before, I'm busy." She thought of Brodix and added, "We're divorced, remember? Besides, I have a date tonight." His loud curse caused Sarah to yank the phone away from her ear to prevent rupturing her eardrum. Before she could hang up on him mid-tantrum, Brodix snatched the cell out of her hand.

"Hey, dumbass, get it through your head that she wants nothing to do with you," he gritted out. Sarah didn't know Brodix well, but even she knew the man meant business. She watched, dumbfounded, as Brodix listened to whatever tirade Jack had launched into this time. A few seconds went by before Brodix was afforded the opportunity to speak again. "Be smart, Jack, and leave Sarah alone." He hit a button and handed the phone over. "Your ex has a really foul mouth. How long were you married to the jerk?"

Sarah took the phone and stared down at it, then looked back up at Brodix. "A year and a half." She shook her head. "I can't believe you just did that." His high-handedness should've had Sarah spitting mad. Usually, she hated it when a man felt the need to protect and shelter the "little woman". But she was too stunned to be angry.

Brodix shrugged. "He was interrupting our conversation."

She shook her head. "Yes, but it wasn't your place to defend me," she finally managed to say—even though a secret part of her had thrilled at Brodix's protectiveness.

"My mom would never forgive me if I stood by and did nothing while a woman was being harassed."

Her lips twitched as she slid her phone into her purse. "You're afraid of your mother?"

Brodix winked. "Clearly you haven't met her, or you wouldn't be so quick to laugh."

"Maybe I'll get my chance on Friday," she tossed back, thinking once again how terrific the woman must be to take five boys from foster care and raise them as her own.

"Friday?" Brodix asked as he sat back down on the stool.

"The grand opening," she reminded him, then started backing her way toward the door. "She'll be here, right?"

He nodded and leaned against the counter. "She'll be here."

Brodix's relaxed position gave Sarah the perfect view of his body, from his powerful chest to the flat abs she was sure had to be a six-pack. Yum. When her gaze landed on his crotch, she bit back a moan. He filled out the slacks like nobody's business.

"I'll get to meet her, then," she replied, "because I'll be here too. I wouldn't miss it for the world." She took another step backward before adding, "And with any luck, it'll be a raging success, thanks to the story I'm going to run."

He laughed. "You don't miss a beat, do you?"

Sarah grinned. "No, usually I don't." She turned around to leave, but Brodix called her name. She looked over her shoulder. "What?"

"Tonight at seven?" he asked. Even from the distance, Sarah could see the heat in Brodix's gaze.

"Sounds wonderful," she managed around the sudden desire clogging her throat.

His lips curved upward. "I'm going to need your address, don't you think?"

"Right, sorry." She told him where she lived and hoped she wasn't blushing too badly.

"Ah," he said, "I know where that is."

"Good. I'll, uh, see you then."

"Count on it," he replied, his voice as soft and smooth as velvet.

When she reached her car, Sarah let out a long breath.

"Holy mother, what have I gotten myself into this time?"

She was having dinner with Brodix Jennings. She'd have the big, sexy man all to herself for the entire evening. Her heartbeat sped up as she became aware of how much her excitement had absolutely nothing to do with getting the story, and everything to do with getting her hands on Brodix.

"Whoa, hold up there, girlfriend," she mumbled to herself. "Get your head in the game."

Half the reason she'd screwed up with the Coburn story was because she'd been too quick to the finish line. This time around, she would need to make sure to do everything by the book. All her Ts crossed and facts triple-checked. If she had any hope at all of getting her career back on track, then she needed those interviews. The Jennings brothers had secrets in their past, she was sure of it. Sarah was determined to find out what they were.

Chapter Three

Two hours after Brodix had watched Sarah leave the Blackwater Bar and Grill, he found himself sitting across from his four brothers in his mom's kitchen. He'd called a meeting to discuss Sarah's proposal, but judging by Reilly's rigid expression, the discussion wasn't going to go well. "Should we wait on Mom to get back from the store? After all, she does have a bigger stake in the restaurant than the rest of us."

When Brodix had called his mom about getting together to talk about the business, his mom had said she was just heading out to get a few things from the grocer. She'd let him know they were welcome to use her house. They'd grown up in the large, brick, two-story, and even now, Brodix and his brothers still thought of it as home. While he had his own apartment a half hour away near Grant Enterprises, the financial consulting firm where he worked, it wasn't really home, sweet home and never had been. It was just the place he rested his head when he wasn't working.

"I don't think she'd mind if we got started," Sam said as he gave Brodix one of his patented big-brother stares. Brodix knew Sammy was attempting to figure out what was going on. "What did you want to talk about?"

"We had a visitor today at the restaurant," he said, deciding to get straight to it.

Sam sat back in his chair. "Oh yeah?"

"Sarah Greer. She's a reporter for the *Gazette*." Brodix tapped his foot on the floor beneath the table and waited for the protests to start. He wanted his brothers to agree to Sarah's proposal, he suddenly realized. His reaction to the woman was nuts, and he already felt like he was betraying his family to some degree. Worse yet, he wasn't sure if his reasons were strictly for the good of the business or because he was attracted to her. He suspected it was a little of both.

Vance's eyes widened in obvious shock, but no anger registered, from what Brodix could see. "Seriously? Isn't she that reporter who broke the story about the mayor's shady contributions, then later ended up with egg on her face?"

Brodix frowned. It'd been too much to hope that the Coburn debacle would be forgotten by the lot of them. "Yes, the same reporter," he said, then waited for the questions to start. Vance only rubbed his jaw and silently waited for him to continue. "What would a reporter want with us?" Sam asked as he sat up straighter, suddenly more alert.

"She wants to interview us," he replied, then braced for the fallout.

Brodix heard a curse, and the room fell silent as everyone looked toward River. His brother's pale green eyes were definitely shooting daggers at him now. Great. River, with his unkempt black hair and lean six-foot-four build, wasn't someone you wanted to piss off. "What the hell for?" his brother asked as he scowled across the table at him.

"It's for the front page of the paper. Sarah thinks that our life, specifically going from one foster home to another and later being adopted by two loving people, is something this town would want to read about."

"A feel-good sort of thing," Vance speculated as he rubbed his jaw. "I've read her news stories. Last week she wrote about that woman who had been kidnapped as a child only to escape years later. Anyone read about that?"

Sam nodded. "Julie read that to me. The woman went on to help other trauma victims."

"Yeah, I caught that story too. I didn't realize that was one of Sarah's, though." Brodix noticed Sam and Vance seemed to be open to the idea, so he went for broke. "I think that might be similar to what Sarah wants to do with us. We're having dinner tonight, and I plan to get all the details then."

"I'm not talking to a reporter," River bit out as he scooted his chair back and stood as if the matter was closed. "Especially one who has a bad habit of screwing with a man's life."

"Ditto," Reilly stated, getting to his feet, clearly intent on backing his twin.

Brodix wasn't surprised by their reaction, but he wasn't ready to give up the publicity the story would afford them either. So he came up with another idea, one he hoped would appeal to everyone. "Before you two decide, I have a plan that might suit everyone." He paused before asking, "What if Sarah only interviews me?" Brodix held out his hands, palm up. "Does anyone have any objections to that scenario?"

River's gaze narrowed. "Why are you so eager to talk to this woman?"

"Because the restaurant needs help," Brodix answered, giving him only part of the truth. He didn't think his brothers needed to know he was attracted to the woman. "I don't know if you're all aware, but the till is empty. The grand opening is only days away. If we want a full house, then we're going to need all the help we can get. Now, Sarah is talking about front page here. That'd be great for business."

"We don't need help from her kind. We have everything we need to open the restaurant. Supplies are bought, extra help has been hired, and the remodel is complete," Reilly said as he glared across the room at him. "Sarah isn't welcome around the restaurant, and she sure as hell isn't welcome around this family. Even if she is a sexy blonde with legs that go on for miles."

"Blonde?" Sam asked as he looked from Reilly to Brodix. "I sense there's more to this story. Brodix?"

Brodix could feel the heat creeping up the back of his neck as everyone's gazes landed on him. "Her looks have nothing to do with the fact we need help promoting the grand opening."

Sam cocked his head to the side and stared at him. No one said a word. As they'd done in the past, they all waited for Sam to make up his mind first. Since he was the oldest, that was usually the way it went.

"You really think the restaurant needs this?" Sam asked.

Brodix slumped in his seat. God, he was so tired of trying to manage the restaurant's finances along with his own career too. Burning the candle at both ends was getting to all of them. "I never would've brought it up if I didn't, Sammy. We might have everything we need to open, but without customers, we'll go under. It'll all be for nothing."

"Okay," Sammy said, his voice firm. "Assuming Sarah will agree to direct all her questions to Brodix, then I see no reason why we shouldn't take advantage of the opportunity."

"You're okay with this woman digging around where she doesn't belong?" River asked, his anger rising with each word. "Stirring up shit that's best left alone? Hell, look what she did to Mayor Coburn."

Sammy stood and faced his brother's angry glare. "I'm not overly comfortable with someone with her track record sniffing around either. But I'm also not going to turn my nose up at her offer simply because she made one mistake. We've all made mistakes, River." He paused, then added, "If Brodix says we need the publicity to give the restaurant a decent fresh start, then I believe him. No one knows finances like he does." When River started to speak, Sammy held up a hand. "And before you say anything else, I'd also like to say that I trust Brodix to keep Sarah in line." He quirked a brow. "Don't you?"

"I wouldn't let anyone hurt my family," Brodix stated as he looked each of his brothers square in the eye. "You should all know that by now."

Reilly was the first to look away. Neither he nor River spoke. Vance shrugged and leaned back in his chair. "I'm not real fond of reporters either, but I've read damn near all Sarah Greer's stories. From what I can see, she doesn't spew trash. Other than that one mess, she seems to be a professional, and I think she'd do the Blackwater Bar and Grill a world of good." He looked at Brodix. "I say go for it." He wagged his eyebrows and grinned. "And I've seen her picture too. She's a cutie."

Brodix chuckled. "Better not let Shayla hear you say that." As it happened, Shayla was Vance's high school sweetheart, but when she'd come back to town to rekindle what they'd once had, Vance had fallen for the petite redhead all over again. Brodix hadn't seen his brother so happy in years.

Sammy looked at the twins. "Guys? What's it going to be?"

Reilly and River exchanged a glance. Finally, River's gaze landed on him. "If she comes anywhere near me and starts hammering me about my past—"

Brodix held up a hand. "She won't. You have my word."

A muscle in River's jaw jumped, and he nodded. "That's good enough for me, then. She can have her front-page story."

Reilly shrugged. "If River is okay with it, then so am I."

"Good," Brodix said as he let himself breathe a little deeper. "I'll get the ball rolling tonight at dinner."

There was some commotion in the front room, and when Brodix heard his mom's voice, he smiled. "I nearly forgot that we need to bring Mom in on this."

Sammy laughed. "Are you kidding? Mom's going to love the idea of her boys being front-page news."

Vance snorted, and even River cracked a smile. Brodix didn't get a chance to respond because in that moment, his mom walked into the room, and she wasn't alone. Brodix frowned when he saw Sarah holding a bag of groceries in one hand and her cell phone in the other.

"Look who I ran into at the supermarket!" his mother exclaimed. "Sarah Greer from the *Gazette*. Can you believe it?" The way his mom stared at Sarah, one would think they were in the presence of a celebrity.

It was Brodix's bad luck that after spending the last several minutes convincing his brothers Sarah wouldn't be a nuisance, the woman showed up carrying his mom's groceries. Jesus H.

"I thought we agreed to meet at your place at seven, or was I mistaken?" he asked as he moved to take the bag from her. When he put it on the counter, he saw River moving closer to their mom. River took the grocery bag from her, but he never took his gaze from Sarah, as if she were a big bad wolf about to have lunch. Brodix wanted his brother to move past his reservations about reporters, to see that Sarah wasn't cut from the same cloth as Larry. But wanting something didn't necessarily mean it was going to happen. He was at least grateful that River hadn't picked her up and tossed her out onto the front lawn. Judging by Reilly's expression, the jury was still out on the possibility of that happening.

"Thank you," Sarah replied when Brodix pulled a chair out for her at the table. As she looked up at him, her cheeks turned rosy. God, she was cute when she blushed. "I hope I'm not intruding. I told Wanda I didn't really have to have a slice of her peach pie, but she insisted."

"I did sort of twist her arm, Brodix," his mom said, completely oblivious to the turmoil brewing in the room because of Sarah's presence. "When I spied her checking out the frozen dinners, I couldn't resist introducing myself." His mom looked at Sarah, a sparkle in her eyes. "I'm such a fan of your news stories, it's not even funny."

Sarah waved the words away. "Oh, please. I'm a small-town reporter. Most of what I write gets buried so deep that you'd have to have a magnifying glass to find it." She shrugged. "Every once in a while, I write something that people want to read."

Brodix stayed standing, not sure if he should usher her out of the house, or wait and see what she was up to. When Vance propped an elbow on the table and smiled at Sarah, Brodix was shocked to see Sarah smiling right back. He decided to hang back and watch the show unfold. If she thought charming her way into their lives would work, then she definitely hadn't done her research as thoroughly as she thought she had.

"I read your articles too," Vance said. "I like them."

"Thank you," she replied as she cocked her head to the side. "You're Vance, right?"

"Yep."

"Oh lordy," his mom muttered as she slapped a palm against her forehead. "I didn't even think to introduce you. Where are my manners?" She pointed to Sammy first and smiled. "That's Sam; he's my oldest. He recently found the love of his life, Julie." His mom winked at Sarah. "You'll meet her at the grand opening. She's a terrific woman. You two are going to get along great." His mom's words had Brodix smelling a setup. Was the woman attempting to play matchmaker with him and Sarah? Scary thought, considering how tenacious his mother could be when she set her sights on something. As she moved closer to Reilly and patted him on the shoulder, Brodix braced himself for battle. "As you can see, these are my twins. This is Reilly, and the quiet one there is River."

"We've met," Reilly bit out, clearly irritated.

"Yes, it's nice to see you again, Reilly," Sarah said, her smile a little stiffer than before. Brodix noticed the way she kept darting nervous glances at River, then back at Reilly. She definitely wasn't feeling the love, Brodix thought. Hell, the tension in the room was thick enough to cut.

Brodix stiffened when he saw Sarah slowly get to her feet, then scoot her chair in. "I think I'll take a rain check on the pie, Wanda." She made a point to check her watch before adding, "I really do need to be getting home."

That same protective instinct that he'd felt earlier came rushing to the surface again. Brodix moved up beside Sarah and smiled down at her. "You should stay for Mom's peach pie." He placed a hand at the small of her back and said, "You won't regret it, I promise." When he looked over her head, he noticed Reilly frowning at him. Brodix narrowed his eyes and kept his hand on Sarah. A silent battle ensued as they stared at each other, neither of them backing down. When Sarah took a step toward the doorway to leave, Brodix saw Reilly's lips curve upward, clearly satisfied.

"Maybe you can bring me a slice when you pick me up tonight," Sarah said, reminding him they'd be seeing each other in a few hours. His blood heated at the thought.

"Let me walk you out," he said as he caught up to her. "I forgot to give you my cell phone number anyway."

When they reached Sarah's little silver coupe, Brodix flattened a hand against the door to prevent her from leaving. "Why'd you really come here, Sarah?"

She sighed. "Your mom wasn't lying. She saw me at the

supermarket and invited me over." She flung her hands up in the air. "It's honestly as simple as that."

"So, you're totally innocent?"

Sarah looked away. She was pissed. Brodix could see it in the way she held herself, as if gearing up for a defensive maneuver. How often had she had to do that, he wondered. Blackwater was a small town with a big memory. He'd bet his last nickel that Sarah had been shunned more than once since the Coburn mess. While he knew it wasn't fair to automatically think the worst, Sarah had made it damn clear that she wanted to interview them, and she wasn't giving up without a fight. How far would she go?

Brodix took hold of her chin and forced her gaze back to his. Her skin was as soft as rose petals. He bit back the need to dip his head and taste her, and instead asked, "Tell me this had nothing to do with you attempting to get closer to my brothers, and I'll believe you."

She tucked a lock of hair behind her ear, a gesture Brodix found sexier than he should, and answered, "I seriously don't get the aversion to reporters that you and your brothers have. I'm sure you have your reasons, but truly, I'm not the devil you all seem to think I am. I want to do a piece about your life, yes. But not because I want to hear about all the horrible things you five went through. It's because...because I think it's pretty great that your mom took you all in the way she did.

"She's a special lady. That she and your dad gave you a home, love, and all the things that come with being a family, well, in my eyes that makes the both of them rather awesome. And if you ask me, there aren't nearly enough awesome people in the world. Wanda and Chet Jennings are rare, and I think it would be nice to show the world that good people still walk the earth. It sounds corny, probably, but that's the bottom line."

For the first time since he'd first heard Sarah's voice on his machine, Brodix knew he'd misjudged her. Badly. "I'm sorry."

Her eyes shot wide, affording Brodix a better view of the pretty blue pools. "What?"

"I can see how passionate you are about this." He released

her and stepped back, giving her some breathing room. Giving him the space required to keep his hands to himself. "I've had you pegged all wrong, Sarah, and for that I'm sorry."

"Thank you. It means a lot." She frowned as she looked past him toward the front of the house. "What about your brothers, though? I got the feeling Reilly and River would rather I go die in a hole. A deep one. What's that about?"

"That's only because they don't know you. Give them time, and they'll see you for who you really are."

"And who am I?"

Brodix grinned and leaned closer to her ear. "Right now, you're the woman setting me on fire."

He heard her gasp of surprise, and Brodix groaned. Damn, he wanted to hear that little hitch in her voice in bed, while he brought her to climax. He reached around her, took hold of the door handle and gave it a tug. "You should go while I still have enough sense to remain a gentleman."

"Yes, I-I think maybe you're right," she said, her voice low and soft.

As Sarah turned and got in the car, Brodix bent down and murmured, "This dinner isn't strictly business. Not for me anyway."

Sarah took hold of the steering wheel in a tight grip. "For me either."

The small admission had Brodix's cock thickening beneath his slacks. "Seven o'clock," he growled. At her nod, he shut the door and stepped back.

Brodix watched as she started the car and backed down the driveway. In a few hours, he'd have her all to himself. Anticipation hummed through him at the thought. He couldn't remember the last time he'd been this eager to spend time with a woman. He pulled out his phone and checked the display. Two hours and thirty-eight minutes. "And counting," he mumbled to himself.

Several seconds ticked by while he stood there, grinning like a damn fool. When he heard someone call his name, Brodix turned to find his mother in the doorway, a sneaky grin curving her lips. *Ah crap, Matchmaker Wanda strikes again.*

He'd be damned if he could muster up even an ounce of resentment, though.

Chapter Four

Brodix arrived at Sarah's apartment at seven sharp. Of course, he was on time. After all, he wasn't about to be late for this. When she opened the door to her apartment, he nearly swallowed his friggin' tongue. For their dinner date, she'd chosen a silky black dress that molded to her curves like a soft glove. The scoop neck showed off a delicate amount of cleavage. Just enough to lend to the beauty of her supple curves. Christ, she was perfect. Every man's fantasy. *His* fantasy. Sarah Greer fit his definition of temptation to a T.

The hell of it was, he couldn't remember another woman who'd ever made him feel so edgy. As if he were on the very verge of flying out of control at any moment. He'd been with women of all types—brunettes, redheads, blondes—but none compared to Sarah. She was turning out to be in a class all her own.

"You're gorgeous," he told her, giving her the raw truth. Brodix noticed she didn't invite him, though. Instead, she kept him in the doorway, her body partially blocking his view of the room beyond. He had a contrary urge to nudge his way around her so he could get a better look at Sarah's private sanctum.

"Thank you." Sarah looked down and smoothed a hand over the waistline of the dress. "I bought this little number for a convention one year. It was pricey, but I figured it'd be worth it at the time. Unfortunately, I never even had the chance to wear it, until now."

"So you saved it for me," he said, knowing he sounded cocky as hell but hoping to get a rise out of her because of it.

She chuckled. "Don't let it go to your head," she said as she reached behind the door. When she brought out a black leather purse and a set of keys, Brodix stepped back so she could move into the hallway.

"You didn't invite me in," he said, smiling down at her. "What's the matter, don't you trust me?"

As Sarah stepped into the hall with him and pulled the door shut, she locked it behind her. "It isn't that," she said, "although you are a virtual stranger. I just haven't been out on very many dates since my divorce. I'm somewhat cautious these days, I suppose."

He nodded. "That's smart, but why haven't you been out on many dates?" he asked, genuinely curious about her.

She shrugged. "Too busy with work. You know how it goes."

Yeah, he knew exactly how Sarah felt. Holding down his day job and working at the restaurant on nights and weekends over the past several months had pretty much screwed his personal life all to hell. He was past due for a night out.

As they headed toward the elevator, Brodix caught himself staring at her breasts. God, how he wanted to dip his head and taste her there. Just a sample to tide him over. He forced himself to look away. He didn't think getting a hard-on in the middle of her apartment building before their date even began would make a real great impression. He needed to cool off. Take his mind off the woman striding down the hall with enough confidence to rev his engine. "When was the divorce?"

They reached the elevator, and Brodix hit the Down button. "We've been divorced two years now," she answered. "Every so often, he gets it in his head that he wants me back. The truth is that Jack just wants sex. He's so transparent, and yet he thinks he's all charm and sophistication." She rolled her eyes. "Sadly, I bought into that load of crap at one time. Stupid."

"Falling in love isn't stupid," he said as the doors slid open. He waited for her to precede him. "You might have been a little blind, but who isn't when it comes to love?" After the doors closed them in and he hit the button for the lobby, Brodix allowed his gaze to travel the length of her. When he reached her long, lean legs, he had to stifle a groan. "He, on the other hand, must be an imbecile."

She pulled her purse onto her forearm and looked up at

him. "You haven't even met him. Maybe I was the imbecile."

"Don't forget the conversation I had with him on your cell."

Sarah winced. "Yeah, he didn't really start off on the right foot with you, did he?"

When the doors opened, Brodix placed his hand at the small of her back. The light contact sent fire licking through his veins. "Whatever," he replied. "All I know is that he let you go. That's enough proof right there that he's not firing on all cylinders." When she walked through the lobby, Brodix stole a glance at her legs once more. Damn, Reilly had been right. Sarah's legs did go on for miles. And he had a feeling they'd wrap around his hips nicely. Right now they were beautifully displayed in a pair of black pumps.

As they reached the parking lot, Sarah turned her head. Their gazes caught, held. "Thank you," she said in a voice so soft he had to strain to hear.

He quirked a brow. "For what?"

"For giving me a chance. And for taking me out tonight. It's been too long since I've let myself have any fun."

"You're welcome," he said, at a loss for words. Sarah's little confession fueled his need to have more than a meal with her. To strip her out of her sexy black dress and discover all her naughty secrets.

What would it be like to make love to her, slowly? The kind of loving that lasted clear into the night. He'd want to do it all over again when morning came. Only rougher. Brodix ached for no-holds-barred sex with Sarah. He had to have her soon. Simple as that.

His steps never faltered as he brought her to his black BMW. When he placed her in the passenger seat, he took a moment to look at her. With her oval face and honey-blonde hair, she looked like an angel. The shiny strands drifted down past her shoulders in loose, sexy curls.

When he caught on to the fact he was staring, he smiled. "Let the fun begin."

She grinned up at him, and Brodix's heart nearly stopped.

Christ, he was toast.

Breathe, woman, breathe. The reminder wasn't helping, not when the only thing separating her from Brodix was the center console. Just as the engine hummed to life and he drove out of the parking lot, Sarah thought to ask, "Where are we going?"

"I managed to get reservations at The Cozy Catch. It's up north. Ever been there?"

The mention of the upscale restaurant sent her heart fluttering. It was silly, she knew, but it seemed rather romantic that Brodix had taken the time to make reservations at one of the more expensive places in town. "I've been there a couple of times for work but never leisure. I love their baked cod." She quickly glanced down. "Now I'm really glad I wore this dress."

When his head turned, Sarah knew he was looking at her, but she couldn't make out his features in the dark confines of the car. "I am too," he murmured.

Sarah stifled a grin. Brodix liked to flirt. She'd noticed that little character trait already. While it wasn't the first time he'd complimented her—and she was probably naïve for thinking it meant anything—Sarah enjoyed hearing the words all the same. She took advantage of his attention to the road to get a longer look at him. Brodix wore a navy-blue suit and a white dress shirt. When he'd arrived at her apartment, she'd noticed how yummy the man looked in the fitted jacket. He filled it out in all the right ways. The shirt beneath showed off his chest to perfection. Oh yeah, definitely a hottie.

When they arrived at the restaurant, Brodix opened her door for her, which was something Jack had never done the entire time they'd been married. Without even knowing it, Brodix was racking up points left and right. He took her by the elbow and leaned close. Sarah heard him inhale and mumble something under his breath.

"What did you say?"

"I don't know what that perfume is you're wearing, but I like it. It's delicate and feminine, like you."

The compliment had her heart soaring. "Thank you. It's my one indulgence. I'm normally very careful to stay on a budget, but this particular perfume is my favorite." She thought of his deliciously masculine scent, and her pussy throbbed. Whenever the man was near, she had the urge to take several deep breaths.

"You should definitely indulge, then," he told her as he led the way to the front of the restaurant. He let go of her long enough to open the door for her, but once they were inside, his hand reached out and took possession of hers. Sarah liked the feel of him holding on to her. Brodix made her feel wanted. And wanted was definitely good. Sarah peeked over at him and caught him staring at her, a wicked smile on his face. Her stomach filled with butterflies. *This is supposed to be a working dinner.* She was supposed to be interviewing him for the story. She needed to get her reputation back. It was important, she reminded herself. The newspaper didn't matter right now though. The only thing on her mind was Brodix.

The Cozy Catch restaurant was an impressive establishment. The main dining area consisted of three levels. On the entry level was the bar and a door that led to the kitchen. An exit at the back of the restaurant led to a large garden. On the lower level was an area where a band could set up to play live music. A short flight of stairs led to a balcony that overlooked the ground level. The seating in the balcony was usually minimal, and reservations had to be made way in advance. A little thrill went up her spine as the hostess led them there. Once they were seated, the hostess left them to look over the menu.

"I don't know how you managed to get such a great table, but I'm impressed."

Brodix winked, his intense blue eyes focused on her as if she were the only person in the room. "I admit, I know the owner. Duke Wells and my dad go way back."

Sarah laughed. "That's cheating."

"A man will go to great lengths to impress a pretty lady," he said.

His voice was low and deep, and the sound fueled her imagination. Sarah immediately pictured them alone in a candlelit room. In her mind, Brodix was nude, and his strong, gentle hands were slowly undressing her. An image of him dragging her to the floor and making love to her sent her head spinning and her body temperature spiking.

Sarah pushed the erotic thoughts aside and forced herself to peruse the menu. After she settled on her usual, baked cod and steamed vegetables, Sarah put the menu aside and looked at Brodix. His gaze, so warm and tender, rested on her instead of the menu. She wondered what he was thinking.

"Did you decide what you want to eat?"

"I always get the same thing here. The filet mignon and baked sweet potato. You?"

"The cod," she answered without a second thought. "The fish here is amazing."

"So," he said, leaning forward, "when does the interview start?"

Heat crept into her cheeks as she became aware of just how little she cared about the interview. And a knot formed in her stomach as she thought of the little white lie she'd told him earlier at his mother's house. Oh, she did intend to write a piece honoring Wanda and Chet Jennings, but she'd left out a key ingredient. In order for the story to make it to the front page, there would have to be something juicier for the readers to sink their teeth into. Guilt assailed her as she looked across the table at him. He trusted her with his family. For the first time since becoming a reporter, Sarah wasn't sure she had the right stuff for the job.

She yanked herself out of her depressing thoughts and said, "Uh, we can start anytime you're comfortable."

Brodix held out his hands. "Fire away, then."

As if on cue, their waiter came over, and their conversation was temporarily put on hold as they ordered. After he hurried off, Sarah said, "Before we start, I wanted to ask you something, but I'm not sure how you're going to respond."

Brodix cocked his head to the side. "You can ask me anything, but some things might get you a 'no comment'. My family can be damn prickly about their privacy, and I'm no different."

"I understand, and if I ask you something you aren't comfortable answering, just say the word." At his nod, she continued. "It was made very clear to me earlier that Reilly and River are extremely bothered by my profession." She frowned when she thought of the twins and the tension they'd exhibited while in her presence. "Can you tell me why?"

Brodix hesitated a moment, a scowl marring his handsome face. "It's because of a man River had to live with once. It was while he was in foster care. He was abusive to River. It just so happens that the asshole was a reporter."

Ah, now it was all making more sense. "I remind River of that time in his life," Sarah surmised. All these years later and River still carried the pain with him. "It must have been pretty awful."

Brodix nodded. "Yeah, and that's not for public consumption, just so you know. The last thing my brother needs is to have those years splashed across the pages of the *Gazette*."

Sarah shook her head. "I would never do anything to hurt your family, Brodix." She only hoped that was true. "I know there are some in my business who would do anything to snag a headline, but I don't work that way."

"I know." He winked. "I just felt a reminder was in order."

She propped her chin on her fist. "What about you? What were your days in foster care like?"

"Nothing like what River went through." Brodix shoved a hand through his hair. "Some neglect, I suppose, but nothing life-changing."

"Why do I get the feeling you're oversimplifying?" she asked as she narrowed her eyes.

He chuckled. "Maybe, but the fact remains that nothing newsworthy happened during those early years."

Sarah cocked her head to the side. "And here I thought we'd established a measure of trust," she said, hoping to loosen his tongue a little. Brodix was holding something back; she could feel it in her bones.

He was quiet for a minute as he stared across the table at her. Finally, he shrugged. "You're right; it wasn't all roses and sunshine."

There was raw pain in the tone of his voice, and Sarah immediately wanted to stop the interview. *Quitting isn't an option.* Damn it, she knew that, but she didn't have to like it. "What happened?" she asked, hating herself for forcing Brodix to dredge up bad memories.

"I was seven at the time, and I'd been living with this couple, the Beattys. Mrs. Beatty was a nice lady, but sad. I remember her crying a lot. Her husband was a self-absorbed ass. He didn't care that his wife was in pain. All he wanted to do was go out drinking with his buddies."

"Real hero material, huh?"

Brodix rolled his eyes. "Not sure what she ever saw in him. Anyway, one day when I came home from school, I found Mrs. Beatty lying on the couch. I thought she was asleep at first, but when she wouldn't wake up, I got scared and went to a neighbor's house." He exhaled deeply. "As it turns out, she was dead. An overdose."

Sarah gasped. "Oh my God, she killed herself?"

"Yeah," he said, his voice quiet, as if he'd mentally stepped back in time. "I guess she finally reached her breaking point."

"Brodix, I'm so sorry." Sarah wished she could simply erase the last few minutes of conversation, for his sake. "How awful for you to see that."

He raked his hand through his hair, tousling the dark strands. "I got shipped off to another family pretty fast. It was years before I could get that image out of my head, though. Her lying there, eyes staring at nothing." A muscle in his jaw flexed. "Gave me nightmares, let me tell ya."

Sarah cringed. "I can only imagine." Something Brodix said

earlier struck her as odd. "Before, when we were discussing River, you said River's foster home but not yours? Are you saying the five of you were split up? Don't siblings usually go to the same foster home, though?"

"Yeah, but there aren't a lot of foster parents willing to take on five rowdy boys." He picked up his knife and twirled it around. "See, by the time the system got involved and took us away from our mother because of the drugs and neglect, we weren't all together again until Wanda came in and swooped us up."

"That must've been quite an adjustment for you all. What was it like to finally be together again?" she asked, hoping to get Brodix past the awful memory of finding his foster mom dead. She felt like the lowest of low for making him relive it. "What was it like to be a family?"

He stroked his thumb across the wooden handle of the steak knife, and Sarah suddenly wished Brodix was stroking her instead. "You'd think it'd be the greatest thing in the world, wouldn't you?" He snorted. "And it was, eventually. But at first it was tough. We weren't the easiest bunch of boys, for sure. We gave Mom and Dad a hell of a time."

"But they loved you enough to adopt the five of you?"

"Dad was a former Marine, so he didn't exactly wear his heart on his sleeve, but yeah, he loved us." A corner of Brodix's lips kicked upward. "He used to say that we always belonged to him, it just took God a little longer to bring us to him is all." He laughed. "And hell, you've met Mom. Does she strike you as the type to give up?"

Sarah laughed. "No, she doesn't. When I tried to decline her peach pie offer, she brushed my denial right off and practically dragged me out of the store."

Brodix set down the knife and took a drink of his ice water. "When Mom sees something she wants, something she's passionate about, she doesn't stop until she gets it. That's how she was with us. We gave her plenty of reasons to dump our asses too, believe me. But she never gave up, never let us forget that she was there for the long haul." He paused before adding,

"She was the first person to ever tell me she loved me."

Sarah's eyes widened. "Seriously?"

"Yep. I didn't buy it, though." A smile curved his lips. "I figured for sure she'd leave. They all did eventually."

Learning more about Brodix might have been part of her job, but at the moment, she could care less about the *Gazette*. She simply wanted to know everything about him because he fascinated her on a much more personal level. "And Chet Jennings, your father, sounds every bit as tenacious and loving. Together they must have been quite a pair."

"They were." It wasn't a question, but Brodix responded anyway. "Dad definitely had a different way of showing affection than Mom. He wasn't as gentle, but he loved with his whole heart."

There was a wealth of emotion in Brodix's voice. "What's your fondest memory of him?" she asked gently.

"The day I graduated from college," he answered, as if he didn't even have to think about it. "He looked at me in that cap and gown and teared right up. It was the only time I ever saw my dad cry." Brodix cleared his throat. "He told me he was proud of me."

Sarah's throat closed up. For the first time, she was at a loss for words. Without thinking, she reached across the table and placed her hand over his. Brodix went completely still; his intense gaze held her captive. "Sarah," he whispered. Her name was a caress on his lips. Sarah had to remind herself to breathe. She looked at their hands, mesmerized by the feel of his thumb stroking over her palm. Once more, Sarah wondered what it would be like to have him touching more than her hand. When Brodix's fingers drifted over the inside of her wrist, Sarah trembled.

As the waiter brought their food, the spell around them broke. They ate in relative silence, as if neither of them was willing to ruin the moment with idle chatter. When their check came, Sarah's heartbeat sped up. Soon they'd be back in his car, but would she be going back to her cold apartment to sleep in a lonely bed, or would Brodix want more from her than a quick peck on the cheek and a promise to call? When she found him staring at her, his warm brown eyes eating her up, Sarah knew the answer. He wanted her. The offer was written all over his face. The only question remaining was what did *she* want?

"Come home with me," Brodix said, putting her thoughts into words. "No expectations, just two people sharing a nightcap and great conversation."

Sarah's pulse went from a gallop to a sprint. "That's it?" she asked, needing it spelled out for her. The last thing she wanted was to get their signals crossed. "A nightcap?"

His gaze darted to her chest, and he licked his lips. Oh yeah, they were definitely on the same page. "Unless you want more," he murmured.

"I...I don't know," she said with total honesty. "We only just met today. And I don't make a habit of mixing business with pleasure."

"Sweetheart, we did that the moment I iced your ankle."

The endearment went straight to her heart and stayed there. "But—"

"Say yes, Sarah," he growled.

She should be turning him down. Sarah should do the professional thing here. A quick no and he'd leave her on her doorstep. Why wasn't she saying no? Because she was completely enthralled by the man. She yearned to taste his kiss and she desperately ached to feel his touch. Saying no simply wasn't an option.

"Yes," Sarah rushed out. His smile was predatory, and Sarah's insides turned to molten lava.

After he paid the bill, Brodix took her hand in his and led her out of the restaurant. A sudden bout of insecurity swept over her, and she quickly pulled him to a halt.

He quirked a brow. "What's wrong?"

"I don't know." She closed her eyes tight. "Oh crap, that's not true. I do know what's wrong. This." She waved a hand in the air between them. "Us going home together. I must be crazy."

Brodix's gaze darkened. "Believe me, I know what you mean. This morning, we didn't even know each other. We're moving pretty fast here. It's got your head all clouded with doubt, is that it?"

"Yes, I-I'm not the type to go home with a man on the first date. I'm really not." For some reason, she needed him to know that.

"No expectations, Sarah, remember?" he reminded her as he cupped her cheek in his palm. "We'll take baby steps, I promise."

"I know." Sarah felt ridiculous all of a sudden. She was a grown woman. Single. And it'd been way too long since she'd been in bed with anything more than a good book. Wasn't she due?

He turned his hand and stroked her cheek with the backs of his fingers, then whispered, "We won't do anything except talk if that's what you want. You can even grill me some more. I'm just not ready for this evening to end. Okay?"

"Me either." The words were out of Sarah's mouth before she could stop them. When Brodix opened the car door for her, Sarah slid inside. Tingles of excitement skittered up and down her spine.

But when she thought of her plan to get her position back at the paper and to recover her reputation as a reporter, she frowned. Hadn't she told herself that this time around she was going to keep her head in the game? Allowing Brodix more than a nightcap tonight would be unwise and incredibly irresponsible. Even so, she just knew if he touched her, she wasn't going to show him the door. Of course, the naughty vixen inside of her, the one she rarely let out to play, prayed he touched her. A lot.

Chapter Five

By the time they arrived at Brodix's apartment, Sarah was fairly buzzing with jittery excitement. When Brodix flicked on a light inside the front door, she got her first glimpse of his world outside the Blackwater Bar and Grill. Beyond the man she'd researched. The small lamp on an end table illuminated the room with a soft glow. A large black suede couch, matching loveseat and recliner took up a large part of the room. It looked cozy and inviting. As her gaze roamed, Sarah spied a corner bookshelf and an old comfortable chair sitting nearby. Perfect for a lazy Sunday morning of reading a good book and a hot cup of coffee, she thought. Overall it was a nice place, in a bachelor sort of way. She wondered how many women he'd brought here, then quickly squashed the thought. It wasn't any of her business, really.

"What would you like to drink?" Brodix asked as he took off his suit coat and laid it over the back of the couch. "I have a bottle of merlot, or if you prefer, I can make us a pot of coffee." He picked up a remote control, and gentle music suddenly filled the air. It relaxed her frayed nerves a measure.

"Coffee sounds good to me," she replied, knowing she'd need all her wits about her tonight. She didn't want her senses dulled by alcohol. She didn't want to take the chance of forgetting a single minute.

"I was hoping you'd say that," he said as he led the way into the kitchen. "The glass of wine I had at the restaurant is the most I ever drink in a single night." Sarah watched as Brodix moved to the coffeemaker and took out the glass pot.

"You're apartment is nice," she replied as she took a seat at the round oak table.

"In a manly sort of way, right?" He laughed when she

stayed silent. Heck, she didn't want to offend him. "It's okay; I'm not attached to this place. It's only where I hang my hat."

When he leaned over the sink to fill the pot with water, Sarah's gaze landed on his ass. God, a gal could have a lot of fun squeezing such a firm tush. "It's not home, sweet home, huh?" she asked absently, a little proud of herself for keeping to the conversation even as she gawked at him. Talk about multitasking.

"Nah, not really." He shrugged. "Mom's house has always been home to me." He measured out the coffee and started the pot brewing before he turned back toward her. "What about you?"

The question halted the runaway train of her libido. "Uh, what about me?"

"You've met my entire family, but I don't really know anything about you." He crossed the small room and pulled out a chair. After he sat down, he asked, "Do you have brothers and sisters? Parents?"

"I have one brother two years older than me. Paul and I aren't terribly close. While I was growing up, I spent a lot of time reading. Books were often my companions. That's when I became interested in writing, and later reporting." She thought of how close Brodix's family was, and somehow felt lacking. She and Paul were so distant, and nothing at all like the Jenningses' close-knit bunch. "He lives in California so we rarely see each other. And my mom moved to Florida a few years back. She and I talk every day, though."

"Your dad?"

"He died when I was two years old," she answered. Like so many times in the past, Sarah wished she could've known her father. "A car accident. Mom never remarried."

A small smile played at the corners of his lips, but there was a hint of sadness to it. "He was her one true love, huh?"

"That's the way she describes it. I don't remember him. Paul does, but he doesn't like to talk about Dad."

"It hurts him too much," Brodix said in a quiet tone. "I

know how he feels."

Sarah nodded. "Yeah." She thought of Brodix's father and asked, "Do you still miss your dad?"

"Every day," he said as their gazes connected. "Before the stroke took Dad from us, he was always so full of life, you know? The house feels sort of empty without him there."

The coffeepot beeped, and Brodix stood to get mugs out of the cupboard. "Cream? Sugar?"

"Neither. I prefer mine black, thanks." After Brodix handed her cup to her and took his seat, she asked, "So, you've told me a bit about your own foster days, as well as the difficulties River had during those early years, but there's still a lot left unsaid."

"Like?"

"What about your oldest brother Sam?"

He quirked a brow. "What about him?"

"Did he have it rough too?"

"If you're asking was there any abuse, no." He looked down at his cup. "River received the worst of it. For the rest of us, it was just a matter of not really having a permanent home. I mean, you always knew that it was temporary and so you understood that you couldn't form attachments to people or things. Changing schools wasn't any fun. Always having to live with a new family meant new rules as well."

"I can't imagine what that must have been like," she said, her heart breaking for all of them.

"It was tough on Sammy, since he was the oldest and all," Brodix replied. "He always felt somehow responsible for not keeping us together and for what River went through. It haunts him that he couldn't protect us."

"But that's crazy," Sarah replied, wishing she could do or say something to make it better for Brodix and his brothers. "Sam was just a kid himself at the time. He couldn't have controlled what happened any more than you can control the weather."

Brodix took a sip of his coffee, then pushed the cup aside. "True, but try telling Sammy that, would ya?"

"I would, but I've been warned not to talk to them, remember?"

When Brodix's head shot up and his gaze sought hers, Sarah let a smile slip across her face to show she was teasing. All at once, the mood in the room changed. Sarah no longer wanted to know about their past. She didn't think her heart could take it. Brodix seemed to feel the change too. He stood and pulled her to her feet. "How about we put this interview on hold?"

"Yes," she said, unsure what she was truly agreeing to in that moment.

When his large, skillful hands cupped her cheeks, and his head slowly descended, Sarah sucked in a breath.

"I've been dying to do this since the moment I met you," he whispered as his mouth crushed against hers, forcing her lips apart. Brodix quickly took possession of her in a way that had her swaying forward against his rock-hard body. Her arms wrapped around his neck as she gave in to the sweet taste and feel of him. For once in her life, Sarah didn't want to think. She didn't want to worry about work or deadlines or her demanding boss. She only wanted Brodix. Every gorgeous inch of him. Tonight.

When he sucked at her lower lip and probed her mouth with his insistent tongue, Sarah surrendered. He seemed to sense it and growled low in his throat, then deftly bent down and swept her high into his arms. Brodix carried her out of the kitchen and into the living room. He didn't stop until he reached his bedroom. Within seconds, Sarah found herself laid across Brodix's large bed. He flicked on a lamp, and the room flooded with soft light.

Sarah reached up and stroked the rough stubbles covering his jaw. "Make love to me, Brodix."

"Thought you'd never ask, sweetheart," he murmured as he kissed her and proceeded to set her on fire.

Brodix savored the taste of Sarah. "Your lips are as addicting and intoxicating as any drug," he whispered. Her only reply was the tightening of her arms around his shoulders. God, he was hungry for her sweet flavor. Brodix was moving too fast, and he knew it, but to hell with it. There was something between them, something he'd never experienced with any other woman.

He slid his hands down her body, touching and caressing every smooth inch of her through the silk of her dress. She felt so good beneath his palms, as if she belonged in his bed, belonged to him. Brodix moved his fingers downward and pushed under the hem of the black material. He encountered the soft skin of her inner thigh, and he bit back a groan of need. His blood heated and turned his lust into a sharp ache deep within his core. He had the craziest notion to possess Sarah. To watch as she surrendered completely to him. He wanted his scent on her so it was clear who she belonged to. He wanted other men to know without a doubt that she was off limits. But he had no rights to Sarah beyond this night. As much as he hated to admit it, she wasn't his to keep.

The knowledge didn't lessen the need to make her beg with pleasure, though.

"Do you want me here?" He cupped her hot little pussy through the satiny material of her panties. "Do you want to come all around my dick, Sarah?"

"Yes, Brodix, please," she moaned, widening her legs to give his hand more room to play. "I need you so badly right now."

"God, yeah," he said against her mouth as he demanded her lips to part for him. She opened on a sigh, and his tongue swept inside the welcoming heat. Her hands shook as they grasped the back of his head. Brodix could feel her slim fingers biting into his scalp, and he reveled in the knowledge that he could make her so wild.

"I don't have it in me to give you pretty words or slow, easy movements," he warned her as he pulled away a bare inch. "This first time is going to be hot and fast. Later we'll take our time, I promise."

Brodix waited for her to decide for them both. Decide to give herself to him completely, explicitly. It was frightening how much she'd seeped into his heart already, blocking out all rational thought.

"I don't care about easy," she admitted in a thready voice. "I just need you inside of me."

When Sarah slipped her hand between them and cupped his cock through his slacks, Brodix cursed. "Fuck, we have too many clothes on," he bit out.

Within minutes, he had them both stripped bare. He covered her with his body, pressing her into the mattress. "Touch me," Brodix urged her. Sarah slipped her hand between them and took his cock in her fingers, touching the tip and palming his hard length. "Harder," he growled.

When she squeezed, Brodix pulsed and throbbed under her ministrations. She positioned him at her entrance and wrapped her legs around him, drawing him down with her heels on his buttocks, pulling him in, and Brodix groaned.

"Easy," he warned her as he barely managed to regain control.

"You said fast." She pouted. "Now I want fast."

A frown marred her pretty face, but Brodix wouldn't be swayed. "You aren't ready yet, sweetheart," he murmured, but as his fingers caressed her clit, he could feel just how wet she was for him.

"I was wet with the first touch of your lips," she told him, her honesty laying him bare.

"God, Sarah," Brodix groaned as he fingered her pussy. "I don't think I could ever get enough of you."

"Good, we'd be even, then," she said as she pulled him down for a brief kiss.

Brodix caved. Hell, he was only human. He drifted his fingers over her stomach, smoothing their way over her ribs to her breasts. As he cupped one small orb in his palm and stroked his thumb over her nipple, he felt her quiver beneath him. His fingers squeezed and pinched, and she seemed to go from lust-filled to ravenous. Her lips covered his and their tongues met and played. Her sweet flavor did him in. He positioned his cock at her entrance once more and slipped inside her heat an inch, then stilled. "Condom," he breathed against her mouth. Damn, he couldn't believe he'd forgotten. The woman went to his head quicker than whiskey.

"I'm on the pill, and I had a clean bill of health just last month."

"I'm clean too, but are you certain?"

"Brodix, please!" she pleaded, as if flinging away all pride.

That was all the encouragement he needed. "Please what, Sarah?" His voice was low and rough from the passion speeding through him. Brodix wanted her to ask him. He ached to hear her say exactly what it was she wanted. That she wanted him and no one else.

"Please make love to me."

Her sultry plea whispered over his spine, and though it was a small thing, he clung to her words. That she wanted him to make love to her and not just sate her lust gave him hope. Until that moment, Brodix hadn't realized how much he needed more than sex from Sarah.

"This time and a hundred times after," he told her. Words were no longer necessary after that, because their bodies took over. He pushed his cock inside her tight, hot pussy. Her inner muscles stretched to accommodate him, welcoming him. "Fuck, making love to you is the sweetest damn thing I've ever felt." All others paled to Sarah. Every other woman was forgotten the moment he'd set his gaze on her.

"Yes," she moaned as she lay beautifully pliant beneath him, totally trusting. It humbled him as much as it swelled his chest with pride.

Their gazes connected as Brodix bent his head and kissed her waiting mouth. He felt the quiver of anticipation cruise through her body, tasted the heat of eager breaths as his tongue tangled with hers. He wanted to stroke her to a fever pitch, send her over the edge of madness with anxious desire. Tap into the passion that burst through her.

His mouth went on a journey over her cheeks and down

her chin, until he reached the smooth column of her neck. His fingers delved into the patch of glistening wet curls protecting her pussy. When he encountered the swollen nub of her clit, Brodix began stroking and flicking, teasing little sounds from Sarah. When he nibbled on her neck, licking and creating a light bruise, she pushed her hips upward, imbedding his cock deep. He cursed at the silky clutch of her pussy. When he caressed her clitoris, Sarah cried out as an orgasm swept over her. She slammed her lower body against his, her legs hugging him tight.

"Christ, yeah. Fuck it, sweetheart," he softly demanded as he took small, nibbling bites of her nipples. He began pumping into her, ready to take his own pleasure now that she'd burst all around him so beautifully. Sarah's body surrounding his cock, milking him into oblivion. Her blonde hair fanned out around her head. "So pretty and seductive. A sexy little witch weaving her spell," he whispered against the swell of her breast.

Brodix braced himself on his elbows and pushed into her hard. Fast. Fucking her soft, wet pussy. His name on her lips sent Brodix over the edge. He bent his head and tasted the tip of one soft tit, his teeth gently scraping over her sensitized nipple. When Brodix sucked one turgid peak into his mouth and his hips thrust against her once more, driving his cock ever deeper, Sarah whimpered. The breathless sound drove Brodix wild. His arms tightened to steely bands, holding her in place. When Brodix's mouth covered her other breast, drawing her nipple between his lips, Sarah burst wide as another climax took hold of her. His thrusts turned more forceful as he drove into her; his appetite for her seemed unquenchable. He pushed against her hips one last time, then spilled his come deep, filling her.

He stayed inside her when he collapsed on top of her, careful to keep most of his weight on his elbows on either side of her body. Sarah closed her eyes, a dreamy look on her face. He brushed damp strands of her golden hair from her cheeks and kissed her forehead. "You've killed me, sweetheart."

She let out a languid sigh and murmured, "Yeah, I know

the feeling. I don't want to move, ever again."

He chuckled. "That could get awkward after a while, though, I'm thinking." Brodix slipped free of her warm body and lay down beside her. He pulled her in close and cradled her body to his, then stared down at her. His heart tore when he saw the flesh of her breast, reddened from the rough stubble on his face. The hickey forming on her neck should've made him feel a touch guilty, but it didn't. "You have marks all over you."

Her hand went to her neck, covering the purplish mark. "I know, and I like it."

"Me too," he admitted as he kissed her forehead. "As a matter of fact, I'm going to see to it that it never fades."

Her head swiveled around, and their gazes caught. "And how do you plan to do that?"

He tapped her nose, unaccountably mesmerized by her. "I'll give you a new one each week as a precaution."

She laughed. "You're a little crazy, you know that?"

He wagged his eyebrows and wrapped an arm around her middle. "You like me just the way I am, though."

She cupped his cheek in her palm, and her softness stirred his appetite all over again. "Yes, I do. Very much."

She sounded far too serious for his peace of mind. "Do you have to work tomorrow?"

She shook her head. "It's Sunday. I'm off."

Brodix wasn't sure what was happening between them, and until he had time to think about it, he aimed to keep her close and off balance. "Stay the night, then," he softly demanded, then swept his mouth over hers.

"Yes," she breathed out as she returned the kiss. Soon their bodies were doing all the communicating, and words were no longer necessary.

Chapter Six

The next morning, Sarah woke to the smell of food cooking. *Is that bacon?* She pried her tired eyes open and looked around the room. "Brodix," she mumbled, her voice hoarse from all the screaming and moaning she'd done throughout the night. The naughty thought brought a smile to her lips. "I spent the night with Brodix Jennings," she breathed out. "Oh wow." Sarah should feel at least a modicum of regret for sleeping with him on the first date. Add in the fact she was supposed to be writing up a piece for the *Gazette*, his family as the star attraction, and you had a quite a fine mess. But it'd been too fantastic, and she refused to beat herself up over it.

Sarah got out of bed and looked around for something to wear. She recognized the black heap on the floor. "My dress. Lovely." She groaned as she held it up and took in all the wrinkles. The blasted thing was ruined. After laying it on the end of the bed, she noticed a gray T-shirt tossed over a chair. She went to it and picked it up. When she brought it to her nose, she could smell Brodix's masculine scent all over it, and butterflies took flight inside her stomach. She slipped the T-shirt on, and it fell nearly to her knees.

She spied a bathroom and moved to clean herself up lest she scare the man half to death with her wrecked hair. As she glanced at her face in the mirror above the sink, Sarah groaned. Smeared mascara, ew. And her cheeks were red, scraped raw from Brodix's whiskers. Sarah's nipples hardened as she thought of the way he'd kissed every inch of her face with his sexy mouth. God, those lips were talented. She wanted more, glutton that she was.

Yeah, okay, so sleeping with a guy on the first date wasn't the smartest thing she'd ever done. In fact, it ranked right up there as certifiable. But Brodix had been so gentle and attentive. He'd teased and enticed her body to new heights of passion. She didn't even know it was possible to feel so much edgy excitement. Her nerve endings hummed to life as she recalled every detail. But that didn't mean it was smart. How could she possibly move forward with her plans to reveal intimate details about the Jennings brothers past if she became romantically involved with Brodix?

Her head knew she'd made a horrible mistake, but her body didn't much care. Besides, wasn't a woman allowed one outrageously spontaneous act in her life? Excuses, that was what she was making. One excuse after another for messing around when she should've been hard at work.

As she washed her face and finished repairing the damage, Sarah's stomach rumbled. Without further thought, she headed in the direction of the delicious smells filling the air.

When she found Brodix hovering over the stove with his back to her, she took a moment to drink him in. He wore a pair of black flannel pajama pants and a loose-fitting white T-shirt. She came close to drooling over his yummy athletic build and rumpled morning hair.

"Good morning," she said as she stepped farther into the room.

As he turned around, Sarah noticed a phone pressed to his ear. He smiled at her, his gaze heating as he looked her over. He motioned for her to have a seat at the table, and Sarah obliged by pulling out the chair nearest to her. When Brodix said something about a cookout later today to whomever was on the other end of the phone, Sarah frowned. She'd hoped they could spend the day together, but that idea was apparently off the table. Darn it.

After a few more minutes of conversation, Brodix hung up and put the phone on the counter. He crossed the room in two strides, his eyes dark with arousal. Sarah's breath caught in her throat when he bent close and murmured, "Good morning," a second before he kissed her in the most passionate way possible. Sarah flung her arms around his neck and sank into him. As if he hadn't just made love to her mere hours ago, the juncture between Sarah's legs moistened and throbbed.

Brodix's hands cupped her cheeks, holding her still for a deeper taste; then he teased her mouth open and slipped his tongue inside. Just as she was about to urge him to take her right there in the kitchen, a loud alarm began blaring.

Brodix jumped back. "Damn," he grumbled as he hurried to the stove. "Forgot about the bacon," he explained when he picked up a potholder and took the frying pan off the stove. He put it on a hot plate and turned to her. "How do you feel about burned bacon?"

Sarah laughed. "I'll pass, thanks."

He grabbed a bag of something to his left and held it up. "A bagel instead?"

"Perfect," she replied as she watched him move about the kitchen. "Who was on the phone earlier?" she asked, too curious for her own good. "I thought I heard you say something about a cookout."

He nodded. "My mom called. She's having everyone over for a barbeque later today." He looked over his shoulder at her, a smile kicking up one corner of his mouth. "And you're invited."

That surprised her. "I am?"

"Yep. She, uh, heard you tell me good morning just now."

Red-hot embarrassment lanced a path clear to her face and lodged there. "Oh my God, she knows I slept with you?"

He shrugged as if it didn't matter either way. Well, it sure as heck mattered to Sarah! "I think she was trying to fix us up anyway, so I don't suppose she's too bothered by the turn of events."

"She was?" This day was getting stranger and stranger. "Wait, I hadn't even exchanged two words with you before yesterday."

"My guess is she saw you in the frozen foods, knew you were a reporter for the *Gazette*, and her wicked mind did the rest." He chuckled as he turned and placed a plate on the table in front of her, the smell of the toasted bagel causing her mouth to water. "She's something of a matchmaker, my mom."

Sarah couldn't take it all in. A cookout at the Jennings' home and she was welcome to attend. "You know, your brothers won't like it if I showed up a second time at your mom's house. Especially Reilly and River."

As Brodix handed her a tub of cream cheese and a knife, he sat across from her and picked up his own bagel. "They'll live," he said as he began to spread the cream cheese. "Besides, Sammy and Vance liked you just fine."

"*Like* is a strong word. More accurately they were merely being polite." Brodix started to say something else, but Sarah wasn't through yet. "How can I possibly face your mom? She knows we slept together, Brodix. Talk about awkward!" Suddenly, Sarah wasn't even the slightest bit hungry.

After a few bites of his breakfast, Brodix pushed his own plate to the side and reached across the table to take her hand in his. "She's going to take one look at you and know the truth."

She squinted, not quite following him. "The truth? And what's that exactly?"

"Mom will see you as a beautiful woman who has managed to enrapture her son."

"But—"

Brodix cut her off with a finger to her lips. "Stop worrying, sweetheart. You don't need to do anything special or be something you're not just to please my family."

Were her insecurities so easy to read? How was it possible that Brodix could see her so clearly, while she'd been married to Jack for over a year and he'd never once taken the time to truly know her? "It's embarrassing, that's all," She said, entwining her fingers with Brodix's. "This is your mom, after all. She'll think I'm some sort of floozy."

Sarah watched with fascination as Brodix's sexy mouth tilted sideways. "You're not a floozy, and my mom is smart enough to know that. Trust me."

Still hesitant but willing to give Brodix the benefit of the doubt, she said, "Okay."

She looked at her uneaten bagel and said, "That looks delicious, but I'm not very hungry."

Brodix leaned toward her until Sarah could smell his woodsy scent. She had to force herself not to close the remaining few inches and inhale deep. If she were bolder, she'd do more than breathe in his masculine heat, she'd take a taste of his lips while she was at it. A good long taste.

"And do you also find me delicious, sweetheart?"

God, the man was a mind reader now. Sarah's cheeks heated. "Brodix..." Desire hindered her ability to speak all of a sudden.

When his hot breath caressed her ear, Sarah wanted to crawl onto his lap and purr. "Answer my question, Sarah."

The soft demand had her heart speeding up. He was so close, yet too far away. "Yes," she breathed out, uncaring if she sounded desperate and needy. "As yummy as hot fudge, to be totally honest."

"Mm." Brodix angled his head and licked her earlobe, then gently nibbled at the delicate skin. "And I think you're exactly the flavor I've been missing all these years."

He drew little circles with his tongue, then teased his way down her neck and sucked at her pulse. Suddenly Sarah was surrounded by his large, powerful body. He effectively blocked out her worries. Everything vanished as Brodix's tongue made a journey over her too sensitive skin. When he pulled back an inch, Sarah whimpered, wanting more. Wanting everything.

"Give yourself to me," he murmured.

As Brodix began smoothing a palm over her back, Sarah knew there was only one answer she could possibly give him at that moment. "Yes."

Brodix so easily turned her body to fire and robbed her of the ability to think clearly. But for once she didn't care. Didn't want to think.

His answering grin was predatory. Liquid heat dampened Sarah's panties. Brodix looked like temptation in the flesh with his sinfully gorgeous black hair, and intense eyes. Eyes a woman could drown in. Last night, those eyes had been focused on her as if she'd been the only woman in the universe.

Feeling a little more brave, Sarah reached beneath the table and grasped the length of Brodix cock beneath his pajama pants. He was hard as a rock, and Sarah's mouth watered for a lick of the bulbous head. Their gazes clashed. He thrust against her palm and cursed. "You like playing, don't you?"

"With you, yes," she admitted, her voice husky with unspent passion.

When Brodix suddenly stood, Sarah went completely still. As he reached out a hand for her, Sarah stared at it, then slowly took it. He pulled her to her feet and murmured, "Sure you aren't hungry?"

"Not anymore." The only thing that could satisfy her now was a large helping of Brodix.

He wrapped his arms around her and brought her up against his body. "I've missed you, sweetheart. Maybe we should finish this in the bedroom."

It hadn't been that long since he'd made love to her, but Sarah didn't bother to remind him of that. She bit her lip and looked at the clock. It was only nine in the morning. "Do we have time?"

"The cookout isn't until four this afternoon," he said. "Plenty of time." When she didn't respond right away, Brodix swatted her bottom.

She cried out. "Ow!"

He rubbed her ass and groaned. "Bedroom, sweetheart," he growled.

This time, Sarah didn't hesitate. The instant she walked into his room, Brodix was stripping her out of the T-shirt she'd pulled on earlier. Within seconds, he had them both naked. "Mm, that's better. I like seeing these pretty pink nipples."

Brodix's right hand moved, and then the left, until he was cupping and massaging both of her breasts. He flicked his thumbs over the hardened buds, then pulled them upward for a long, lazy lick. His tongue swept back and forth over one tight nipple while his fingers played with the other. When he pulled back, she watched through half-opened eyes as he bent to lick and tease her belly button. He muttered something unintelligible; then he wrapped his arms around her middle and whispered her name. Sarah thrust against him, so incredibly hot and ready for him to make love to her.

"That feels so good," she whispered, grasping his head and holding on tight.

"I'll give you more, much more," he promised as he lifted up. "First, I want you on your knees."

Her pussy throbbed at the mental image. "I've been dying to taste you," she admitted and started to lower herself to the floor.

"Wait," he whispered. He wrapped a hand around her upper arm. "Have you ever had your wrists bound?"

Her face flamed as she imagined Brodix tying her up. "Uh, no. Why?"

"Are you willing?" Brodix asked, giving her the option to say no. Did she trust him enough to be completely at his mercy? When Brodix moved away from her and looked around the room, she knew the answer was yes. She did trust Brodix. More than any other man before him. His gaze stopped on something lying over the back of the chair. When he walked toward her bed and picked up a long black cloth belt, her pussy dampened in anticipation of what he was about to do to her.

When he walked back over to her, Brodix moved behind her and clasped one wrist in his strong hand. He wrapped the black cotton material around it, then grabbed the other wrist and did the same. Her hands securely tied behind her back, Sarah was now completely at his mercy.

"Mm, I like you this way. You're mine now, Sarah."

The notion stirred emotions in her that were a little scary. She liked the idea of belonging to the yummy man, but she wasn't sure she was ready for her feelings to get all tangled up. And she had a sneaking suspicion that a relationship with Brodix would be a roller-coaster ride of ups and downs. After the divorce, after having her love thrown in the trash by Jack,

Sarah had vowed to protect her heart. So, why was excitement skittering along her spine at Brodix's words? She didn't know, and she simply wasn't coherent enough to explore the whys of it just then.

Brodix moved around the front of her and looked into her eyes. "Do you like the idea of being mine, sweetheart?"

"Yes," she said, unable to say more without betraying the riot of feelings flowing through her.

"Good, because I do too." He cupped her chin in his palm and kissed her. She tasted a hint of coffee, but mostly it was Brodix's delicious flavor she savored. "Will you go down on your knees for me?" He wrapped a hand around his cock and stroked. "Do you want to taste me on your tongue?"

Sarah didn't speak, merely started to lower herself. With her hands tied, Brodix had to help her, though, and she felt awkward. He lifted her face until their gazes locked. "You look so damn sexy like this," he groaned, the sexual hunger written all over his face. He touched her breast, then flicked her nipple. "Open your mouth, sweetheart," he gently ordered.

Sarah nearly whimpered with her need to have his cock in her mouth and lick up the sticky droplets of his precome. The thought caused her pussy to drip with need. Sarah's gaze took in the perfection of him. His cock was hard and pulsing with life, the bulbous head darkly engorged. Unable to wait another second, Sarah leaned closer and opened her mouth. She slipped her tongue out and tasted his sensitive tip. She licked the small bead of moisture that appeared, then let her tongue roam freely over and under his entire length.

"Fuck, yes, lick it good," he bit out.

Hearing how turned on he was sent Sarah's inhibitions into hiding. She swiped her tongue back and forth, then teased the softer skin of his balls. She sucked on them before moving back to his dick, licking and playing.

"Stop, I'm too close," he whispered as he tugged on a lock of her hair. Sarah eased back on her heels and looked up at him. Brodix appeared ready to explode, as if it was taking all his strength to keep from tossing her on the bed and fucking her into oblivion.

"At times, you tempt me beyond reason," he admitted as if reading her mind. When he dipped down and swung her into his arms, Sarah yelped.

"It's so strange to not be able to use my hands," she explained at his puzzled expression.

"In about a minute, you won't care about your hands," he promised as he carried her to the bed and carefully placed her in the center of it.

Sarah adjusted to get more comfortable but went utterly still when he placed one knee on the bed and crawled toward her. God, he was just too good-looking for her peace of mind. The unkempt mass of black hair and morning stubble only enhanced his rugged masculinity.

"Now it's my turn," he whispered. He pushed her legs wide and descended between them, then proceeded to kiss her clit. She arched upward and tried to get him closer, to get his tongue inside her, where she needed him so badly, but he seemed in no hurry.

"Brodix, please don't tease," she pleaded.

He chuckled. "But it's so much fun."

She glared down at him. "I'm beginning to regret letting you tie me up."

"Ah, but soon you'll change your mind, I guarantee it," Brodix whispered, the heat of his breath stroking her clit causing her femininity to throb to life.

"So confident of your abilities, huh?" Sarah struggled to say the words coherently, she was so turned on.

"No," he said, "so confident of you." As his tongue delved deep between her pussy lips, Sarah's thoughts scattered.

Chapter Seven

As Brodix tasted and teased Sarah, feeling the quiver of her supple legs on either side of his head, he knew that no man could ever touch her like this. She belonged to him. He would be the only one to witness her desire. Christ, just the thought of another man using his tongue on her sweet, hot pussy drove him crazy with jealousy.

He lifted his head and looked up the length of her nude body. Her eyes were closed, her hands tied securely behind her back. She took his breath away. She was so damn hot Brodix felt singed. Using his thumbs to part her delicate folds, Brodix exposed her swollen clit. He dipped his head once more and sucked the tiny bit of flesh into his mouth, flicking back and forth with his tongue.

Sarah came undone, screaming his name and arching high off the bed, but he held her firm as he swallowed every last drop of her tangy flow.

This time when he lifted his head, she was staring at him through half-raised lashes, a sexy hint of a smile on her pretty face. When he slipped his hands beneath her hips and cupped her ass cheeks in his palms, he felt her clenching up on him. "Have you ever had a man's cock in your tight ass, Sarah?"

Her eyes widened with shock, and her mouth dropped open.

"I take that as a no," he mused aloud, massaging the soft skin of her buttocks in an attempt to calm her. "Would you like to feel me there?"

"I-I don't know," she answered as she shifted restlessly on the bed.

"Shh," Brodix whispered, but he could tell she was far from

relaxed. "What's wrong, sweetheart?"

"It's just that this is such unfamiliar territory for me."

He smoothed a palm over her belly and murmured, "You trust me with your body. I know you do. I would never hurt you."

Several tense seconds passed. Finally, she said, "I'm willing to try, I guess. But if I don't like it—"

"We'll stop, I swear it," Brodix whispered as he moved over on top of her and kissed her. A little moan escaped from between her lips, and Brodix thought it was the sweetest sound he'd ever heard.

He moved away and said, "Hold that thought." As carefully as possible, Brodix slid his hands beneath her and turned her to her belly. He arranged her legs, spreading them open until he could see the wet softness of her pussy. Next, he quickly untied her hands and brought them above her head, then wrapped the soft belt around her wrists once more. His cock thickened at the lovely sight of having her all stretched out before him. "Are your arms okay? Not too tight?"

"No, it's fine."

Brodix looked at her lying in the center of the rumpled bed, the soft morning sun filtering in from the sheer curtains, her luscious body and plump bottom mere inches away from his eager fingers and cock. He grabbed a pillow and slid it beneath her until her ass was raised in the air. "You're fucking gorgeous, Sarah."

She turned her head. "Thanks, but I feel very...exposed right now."

He pushed her hair off her face and kissed her cheek. "I like it," he said as he moved off the bed. "Stay put. I'll be right back."

"Please hurry," she said, a hint of desperation in her tone. "I'm losing my nerve fast here."

He touched the cleft of her ass and stroked her intimately. "I'm going to make you feel so damn good." He strode from the room and quickly retrieved a bottle of oil from his bathroom cabinet. Without wasting another second, Brodix left the bathroom and resumed his position between Sarah's silky thighs. When he popped the top of the bottle, he watched her expression for signs of fear. After he poured a small amount into his palm, Brodix smoothed his hands together to warm the slippery liquid. Sarah's breathing increased, and she stiffened. He touched her shoulders, moving his hands in little circles, massaging and soothing her. When he spotted her neck, Brodix rubbed the elegant column. "Feel good?"

"God, yes," she moaned. "Heavenly."

"Good. Just relax for me, sweetheart." As he skated his palms upward to her arms, then over her bound wrists, he could feel the quickened hum of her pulse beating out a rapid tattoo. He massaged the oil into the delicate skin there, easing the restraint a little so her arms weren't pulled quite so tight. Once Brodix was satisfied he'd made her as comfortable as possible, he poured more oil into his palms and touched her spine. He took the utmost care in massaging each vertebra, feeling her muscles relax beneath his touch. He leaned down and kissed a spot he'd already massaged.

"Sexy," he murmured. "And all mine."

"Brodix," she mumbled as if half asleep.

When he trailed his fingers over her lower back to the small indentations above her ass, he said, "This ass needs fucked, Sarah." His slick fingers slid between her ass cheeks then. He circled the tight hole, over and over again, making certain she was completely slick with the oil before he slipped his index finger into her a single inch. Her body, once so pliant, was now strung as tight as a bow.

"Oh God, that feels..."

She didn't finish the sentence, but Brodix didn't need her to. "It feels forbidden," he answered for her. She mumbled something he couldn't quite make out. Brodix leaned over her and whispered, "Every inch of my cock, Sarah. I'm going to love you so damn good. And when I come inside you, right here," he wiggled his finger for emphasis, "in this tight little ass where no man has ever touched you, it's going to be paradise."

"You make me crazy. I need you so much, please don't make me wait any longer," she cried out, her passion equaling his.

"Two fingers, sweetheart," he explained. "You need to be ready." Brodix slid two fingers in, and Sarah moaned. She spread her legs a little more and pushed back against his fingers, forcing them in clear to the knuckle.

"Ah, that's my girl," he ground out. Brodix's body was on fire, and his dick ached for release. He couldn't wait another second to be inside Sarah.

He reached for the bottle of oil once more and slicked some over his throbbing shaft, already swollen and dripping with precome at the thought of being buried deep. Gently, Brodix separated the round globes of Sarah's backside and touched the head of his cock to her entrance, then slowly moved a mere inch inside. The snug fit was the sweetest torture. It took all his control to keep from thrusting deep and fucking her hard and fast.

"Oh, B-Brodix."

The tremor in her voice chipped away at another layer of his restraint. He slipped inside her ass a few more inches, and suddenly, Sarah wiggled her hips. Brodix gritted his teeth against the need to come. He clutched her waist in a tight grip to keep her from moving too fast. "Gently, sweetheart," he whispered. "You're new to this, and we need to go slow."

His primal instincts kept battering at him to fill her completely, but Brodix refused to take the chance of hurting her. Holding her hips firmly, Brodix heard Sarah let loose a needy little whimper. The pleading sound turned his heart to putty, and he gave her another thick, hard inch of his dick. He couldn't deny her, because in that instant, they wanted the same thing. He toyed with the delicate bud of her clitoris, turned on beyond measure when she moaned his name. She pushed against him as her orgasm took hold. She came, screaming his name.

"Now," he gritted out. "All of me."

"Yes," she said in a voice barely above a whisper. "Please,

fuck me."

A rumbling growl escaped him at her feral response. He pushed himself the rest of the way inside her ass, and her muscles sucked him in. Brodix cursed at the sweet torment.

"Sarah," he groaned as he reached up and tore the belt away from her wrists. Sarah immediately grabbed on to the blanket on either side of her body. "Do you like my cock filling you like this? Fucking your ass?"

"Y-yes, please don't stop."

"No way in hell," he promised as he stroked her sweat-soaked hair away from her face, then covered her body with his, folding himself around her protectively. He kissed her upturned cheek and felt her muscles relax a little more. "Yeah, that's it," he praised her. He dipped his head and gently bit the smooth line of her neck. Sarah's eager response was all the encouragement he needed. Brodix licked and suckled at her soft skin before he began slowly pushing in and out of her ass. He built the pace, little by little, until he filled her balls-deep.

"You belong to me," he whispered against the shell of her ear.

Sarah didn't respond with words. Instead, she pushed against his hips, joining in the rhythm of their erotic dance. Soon, his cock swelled and his balls drew up tight. One more thrust and he was flying over the cliff as his cock erupted inside of her, spurts of hot come filling her and robbing him of the last shred of his control. When she shouted his name, joining him with another orgasm, Brodix knew the moment would be tattooed on his heart forever.

"You've killed me," she said, her voice nearly gone from her pleasure-filled screams.

"A damn nice way to die, though," he murmured. A few moments passed before Brodix pulled out of her. He removed the pillow and tossed it aside, then helped Sarah roll to her back. He didn't move to the side, and he wasn't quite ready to release her bound wrists either. Not quite yet. A primitive side of him, one he didn't even know he possessed, wished like hell he could keep Sarah tied and naked in his bed forever.

As his lips caressed her cheek and forehead, Brodix tasted her perspiration. Beneath that he recognized her subtly enticing flavor. He suspected he would always crave her. Would never get enough of her. What that meant exactly, Brodix wasn't sure. All he knew for a fact was that he wasn't giving her up. One way or the other, his family would simply have to get it through their collective heads that Sarah was in his life to stay.

Chapter Eight

On the way to the cookout, Sarah had managed to wiggle in a few more interview questions. She didn't pry, but Brodix no longer felt the need to keep secrets from her either. He trusted Sarah. Apparently, he had good instincts, because they'd been at the cookout less than an hour before Sammy gave Brodix a look that said he approved of her. Vance hadn't been far behind. His mom was so taken with Sarah that Brodix was having a hell of a time getting any alone time with her. If he could only get Reilly and River to stop glaring, he'd be in business.

That was the least of his problems though. At the moment, Sarah was his problem. She was killing him. He leaned across the picnic table and muttered, "One more lick and I'm dragging you out of here. To hell with the cookout."

Sarah went utterly still, and her face flamed. "Behave," she muttered.

Brodix cursed as she took another lick of the pralines and cream. "I can't believe I'm going to say this, but I think I'm jealous of that damn cone."

She laughed. "It's just an ice-cream cone. Everyone here has one." She took another lick of the sweet cream, and Brodix was forced to watch her pink tongue dart out to nab a nut. It sent him over the edge. "I'm not a damn saint, woman," he growled as he stood and moved around the table.

Sarah's eyes widened when he reached her side. Her gaze darted to the fly of his jeans, and she bit her lip. "Uh, you're..."

Brodix grinned. "Yeah, I am." He took her by the arm and helped her to her feet. He looked her over and cursed. They'd stopped off at her apartment so she could change and freshen up. The outfit she'd chosen was a pretty yellow sundress with daisies all over it. It reached just above the knees. "It's not my fault that you're sexy as hell."

She gave him a wicked smile and whispered, "So, watching me is turning you on, huh? I'll have to make a note to get cones and ice cream the next time I go grocery shopping."

The little tease. "That's it. We're leaving."

"But I'm not done with my ice cream."

"Take it with you," he replied. After they said their good-byes, Brodix headed to his car.

"Slow down, for crying out loud," she muttered as she finished off the last of the cone.

Brodix heard her giggle, and it turned him on even more. When he reached the BMW, he pushed her up against the passenger door and caged her in. He thrust his hips into hers, letting her feel the evidence of his arousal. His mouth covered hers in a quick, firm kiss. He inhaled, breathing in her mysterious scent, and ground his pelvis into her soft womanly curves.

"Do you feel what you do to me, sweetheart? I need to be buried deep inside of your tight body right now."

She wrapped her arms around his neck and pressed against him. "That could get us arrested," she murmured against his lips.

"Let's take this party back to your place, then." He stepped back and opened her door for her. Once she was safely inside, he slammed the door shut and jogged around to the driver's side.

After they were on the road, Brodix let himself breathe a little easier. Christ, what was wrong with him? He'd all but dragged her out of his mom's house. It hit him then like a load of lumber. Love. That's what it was. It was so damn obvious now that he recognized the signs. He'd never been in love before Sarah, though. Oh sure, he'd lusted after women. There'd even been a few he'd cared about. But Brodix had never gone so far as to fall in love. What was he supposed to do now? It was too soon; even he knew that. She'd run screaming if he dropped that particular bomb on her now. He needed time to think. To figure out a plan. Brodix always had a plan.

Sarah knew now what the term "weak in the knees" meant. She was glad Brodix had taken the initiative by putting her in the car. She definitely would have fallen if she'd attempted to climb in without his help. Her legs felt as if they were made of rubber. She didn't have a clue what to say to his erotic words. She opted to talk about something less...volatile instead.

"So is everything in order for the grand opening?" It was inane, but her circuits were fried from his electrifying kiss.

"Yep," he said as he maneuvered the car through traffic. "So, take my mind off my raging hard-on and tell me more about your ex. You were married for a year and a half. Why are you divorced?" he asked in a deep rumble.

Shoot, she was beginning to think he wasn't going to inquire about Jack. She supposed it was too much to hope for, though. After all, Brodix wasn't the type of man to let matters like that go unexplained. She prepared herself to tell him everything. He'd been completely open with her about his family, his past, and Sarah could do no less with him.

"Want me to start at the beginning?" she hedged. "It's sort of a messy story."

"I want to know everything about you, sweetheart." He paused, then added, "But if it makes you feel any better, we've all made mistakes. I was never married, but I've made mistakes in love." He smiled at her a second before turning his attention back to the road. "I'm all ears."

"One thing for sure, Jack was definitely a mistake. He made me feel special at first. I sort of fell for his act."

"We've all been there," he said as he reached over and took her hand.

"Jack was all charm. The charm wore off after we got married. That's when I found out he had commitment issues."

His gaze darted to hers. "Damn, he cheated on you?"

She shrugged and looked out the windshield. "Yeah. As it

turns out, Jack was committed only to himself. It was all about his wants, his needs. He paid no attention to the people he hurt, namely me."

"So far, he sounds like a real prick," Brodix gritted out.

"Things sort of came to a crashing end when I came home and found him having sex with one of his coworkers on our living room couch." She cringed, thinking about how naïve she'd been. "Get this, I'd gotten off work early that day, and I had plans to surprise him. I bought some sexy lingerie and walked smack dab into him getting busy."

Brodix cursed, his hand tightening around hers. "I'm sorry, sweetheart."

"I should've known Jack wasn't the type of man to be content with just one woman, though. I guess I didn't want to face reality."

"What did you do?"

"I called my friend Lucy, and she let me crash on her couch until I got an apartment of my own."

"You should've kicked his ass out, if you ask me," Brodix said, clearly angry on her behalf.

She shook her head. "No, I didn't want to live there. I would've been forced to always think about him and that woman. I wanted a fresh start."

He nodded. "Makes sense."

When they arrived at her apartment, the conversation was put on hold until they were both seated on the couch.

Brodix maneuvered them until she was snuggled up against his side. "If he cheated on someone as sweet you, he must be a few bricks shy of a load." He shrugged. "Just saying."

She laughed. "Either way, good riddance."

"I'm sorry, sweetheart," he murmured into her hair. "I just hate that he hurt you like that."

Sarah knew Brodix would never treat a woman the way Jack had treated her. He was too honorable to do something so despicable. Too decent. Her heart filled to bursting as she realized she was falling in love with Brodix. As crazy as it seemed, considering they'd only just met, it felt as if she'd been waiting her entire life for him. Love at first sight—wasn't that what they called it?

He tapped her nose to gain her attention. Sarah looked up. "Yeah?"

"Finish telling me what happened." When she didn't say anything, Brodix frowned. "I know there's more to it. I want to know everything, so don't even consider holding back on me, because I will know if you are."

"Isn't that enough? He cheated on me, end of story. I divorced him and moved on with my life." She was desperate for the conversation to come to an end. She didn't want to get into the rest of it. It was too depressing.

"Spill it, woman," he softly demanded.

"Fine. I learned the hard way that Jack wasn't a very nice drunk."

Brodix stiffened. "How so?"

"On a couple of occasions when he'd had a few too many at the bar after work, he got...physical with me."

"What the hell?"

"Don't get all crazy. It's in the past. Over and done with."

"That son of a bitch. I'll kill him."

Sarah sat up and looked at Brodix. "No, you won't. It's in the past, and I don't want him smack dab in the middle of our relationship. Leave it alone. Please, Brodix," she pleaded. She drifted her hands down his nape to his shoulders, then his pecs and ripped abs. He was so hard and muscular all over it nearly melted her every time she touched him. Feeling wild and impetuous, Sarah slid her palm over the bulge in his faded jeans, cupping his rigid length. She was way too happy to note he was as turned on as she. "I'm done talking about Jack."

"To hell with him," Brodix growled as he slid his free hand up her thigh and beneath her dress. He caressed his way higher until he cupped her mound. Sarah's clit swelled and throbbed at the feel of him there. His mouth moved to her neck, and he began to nibble and lick.

"Oh God, that feels so good."

Brodix moved to her ear and whispered, "I've only just begun." He pulled away and patted his thigh. "Up we go," he murmured. In a flash, Brodix picked her up around the waist and plopped her down on top of his lap so that she straddled him. When he went back to kissing her, his talented mouth pressed against hers, Sarah forgot about her troubling thoughts of love. She would worry about Brodix breaking her heart later.

She opened her mouth and danced her tongue over his lips. At his rumble of approval, Brodix opened up and took her in. Their tongues mated, and Sarah clutched on to Brodix's biceps, excited and scared. Her body was on fire. She wanted him. Inside of her. Around her. Drinking her in, filling her up. He was a craving in her blood, one she could no more deny than she could her own name.

Sarah trailed her fingers over his muscular arms, and she drew in a breath when they came around her waist and pulled her in tight. A moan escaped. He was so strong, so virile. She felt safe and secure with him.

"I want this pussy. It's mine. Will always be mine. Say you want me. Deep. Here and now."

"Yes," she said. "Desperately."

He grinned and slipped his hands beneath her dress, pushed her panties aside, then commanded, "Unzip me."

Sarah quickly obeyed. Her fingers fumbled over the button in his jeans. As she opened his fly and glimpsed his black boxer briefs, her desire increased by a million. She licked her lips and gently drew him out. The head of his cock tempted her to taste, but in their awkward position, there was no way she'd be able to get him into her mouth. She started to move off his lap, but Brodix stopped her.

He stroked the length of her hair and murmured, "Later for that. Right now, I'm too hungry to feel that tight pussy."

She needed him there just as much. "Yes."

"Guide me in," he instructed. "Show me how much you want my cock. Take us both there, sweetheart."

His erotic words had her heart pounding harder and her body quaking with need. "My pussy is dripping for you," she admitted in a breathless voice; then she took his heavy cock in her hand and slid him inside. Her body closed around him, tight and hot. She shuddered, flung her head back and rode him.

"That's my girl. Fuck it sweetly, Sarah," Brodix urged as he clutched her hair in his fist and lowered his head, feasting on her breasts through her dress.

The heat of his mouth seeped through the thin material, sucking the breath out of her and driving her into another world. When his fingers found their way over her swollen clit, expertly flicking it just the way she liked, Sarah's body seized. Her muscles clenched as she rode him faster, harder, their bodies slapping together, melting into each other until there was no separating them.

Soon she was there, spiraling out of control. Sarah's hot pussy bathed Brodix's cock with her come. He sank his mouth over hers and captured her shouts. Once the desire began to ebb, Brodix clutched her hips and pushed into her once, twice; then he arched his neck and moaned her name as he emptied his seed deep.

Sarah's breath came in short pants, her body sweaty, the dress clinging. Her legs shook from exertion as she collapsed against Brodix's heaving chest. No way could she ever move again. Brodix's arms came around her shoulders, holding her tight against him, as if unable to release her.

She wiggled, gaining his attention. As his eyes came to hers, she saw raw hunger in their passionate depths. If he hadn't just spent himself inside her, she would have thought he was ready to go again.

"I think I'm going to be a bit sticky," she teased, trying to inject some casualness into the intensity that surrounded them. It didn't work.

"I could fuck you twenty-four hours a day, seven days a week, and it still wouldn't be enough. Not nearly."

She had no words for such a bold statement. Good thing he

didn't seem to expect any. He merely slipped out of her and replaced her panties. When his heavy length was once again confined, he slid both his palms up her thighs, then cupped her mound possessively. "You—"

A loud knock on her front door interrupted whatever Brodix was about to say. Sarah frowned as she looked at the clock on her cable box. "Who in the world is at my door at nine o'clock at night on a Sunday?"

"Good question," Brodix bit out as he lifted her off his lap and placed her on the couch beside him. He stood and crossed the room, then pulled the door wide.

Sarah couldn't see around Brodix's big body to see who it was, but when she heard a male voice, she had a pretty good idea. Uh-oh, this could be bad. Real bad. Before she could intervene, the room erupted into chaos as Brodix yanked Jack inside her apartment, his hand clutching the front of Jack's white T-shirt as he pinned him to the wall. For crying out loud, talk about stranger than fiction!

"Brodix, stop!" Sarah yelled when she heard Jack spit out a few not so nice words. "This is ridiculous!"

He turned his head in her direction, his hand still firmly holding Jack in place, raw fury in his eyes. She needed to do something fast. "Let him go, Brodix," she explained in a calm voice as she placed her hand over Brodix's forearm and squeezed. "He's not worth the trouble."

Brodix narrowed his eyes, then turned back to Jack, who was now flailing his arms about like a windmill. Brodix outweighed Jack by at least fifty pounds of solid muscle. Finally, Brodix dropped his hands, and Jack fell to the floor, cursing a blue streak.

Then Brodix turned on her. "You just finished telling me that he cheated on you *and* knocked you around. Want to tell me why I shouldn't beat the shit out of him right now?"

Sarah recognized Brodix's anger for what it was. He was suffering from a heaping helping of protectiveness. She knew it rankled Brodix that he couldn't give Jack a taste of his own medicine. Her heart did a little cartwheel. Did Brodix want her for more than sex, then? She shook her head, too tired to see about making any sense of things at the moment.

"Mostly because I don't like the sight of blood," Sarah answered as she reached down and helped Jack to his feet.

Now that she wasn't trying to diffuse a bomb, Sarah saw that Jack had put on a few pounds around the middle. A beer belly, she'd bet money on it. Jack had always been way too fond of alcohol. She caught a hint of silver and noticed an earring flashing in his left lobe. That was new. When Jack moved closer to her, Brodix let out a low rumble. She swung her gaze toward his, her own anger rising up. "Seriously? I'm getting a headache here." She sighed at the tight expression on his face and said, "I did not invite Jack here, Brodix."

Brodix went so quiet it made her jittery. He stood absolutely rigid as he looked from her to Jack. "Do the smart thing, Jack. Go away," he said, his voice low, deadly.

For Brodix's sake, Sarah put a few feet of carpet between herself and her ex. Jack's lips thinned as he pointed a pudgy finger at Brodix. "Who the hell is this?" he asked. When Jack stood a little straighter and puffed out his chest, Sarah had to hide a grin. The drinking must have killed off a few too many brain cells if he thought he could intimidate Brodix.

"None of your business," Sarah shot right back. She pointed toward the door. "Now go, before I call the police."

"He damn near attacked me," Jack whined as he smoothed a hand down the front of his wrinkled shirt. "Go ahead and call the police. They'll arrest him for assault!"

Sarah snorted. "Seems to me it could've been much worse." Jack's cheeks reddened. Sarah had to count to ten before she had her anger under control. "What are you doing here so late on a Sunday? For that matter, why are you here at all?"

Jack crossed his arms over his chest. "Before this asshole came at me, I was trying to explain all that."

"Explain now," she said, trying to remain civil and failing miserably.

"Fine, but I don't see why he needs to be here." Jack

glanced over at Brodix.

Brodix only stood there, his face devoid of emotion, and silently waited.

Jack rolled his eyes. "Whatever. Look, Sarah, I came here because I wanted to apologize."

"Wow, that'd be a first," she mocked.

Jack took her hand in his and moved closer. Sarah could smell the alcohol on his breath, and her stomach rolled. Out of the corner of her eye, she noticed Brodix shift restlessly. He didn't like Jack touching her, she realized. Not even to hold her hand. Surely that meant something. She was too tired to try to figure out what, though.

"I made a mistake letting you go, Sarah. I know we left it on bad terms, but I want you to give me another chance. Give us another chance."

Sarah couldn't believe her ears. "Bad terms?" She pulled her hand away from his grasp. "Are you kidding me with that?"

Jack had the gall to look affronted. "I had hoped you'd be a little more forgiving. What happened before, it's all in the past, baby. I still care about you."

Ah, now that was the idiot she remembered so well. "No."

His head jerked backward as if she'd slapped him. "What?"

"You heard me. No way in hell will I ever give you another chance."

Jack's eyes went round. "You don't mean that. It's late, and you're tired." He stepped closer to the door. "I'll come back tomorrow, and we can talk more."

"No need; we're done."

He stared another few seconds before he finally let out a breath and turned toward the door. No more words were exchanged between them. He mumbled something about calling her in a few days, after she had a chance to calm down, but Sarah was beyond listening to anything Jack had to say.

"Asshole," Brodix gritted out as he slammed the door behind Jack.

Sarah took hold of the knob and opened it right back up

again. "You too. I have to work tomorrow, and if you stay, I'll never get any sleep."

Brodix smiled, and Sarah's heart fluttered. "I like the way you took care of Jack, sweetheart." He pulled her into his arms and held her tight. She instantly sank against his warmth. Okay, so she was putty in the man's hands. Whatever.

He leaned down and kissed her forehead, and Sarah's body vibrated to life. "You do realize that no other man can ever do for you what I do for you, right? And you're the only woman for me. No other can hold a candle to you."

Boy, he played dirty. "Brodix," she whispered.

"And you can be sure that I'll never be quite so easy to get rid of," he murmured. "Jack's a damned fool. I'd fight like hell for you, Sarah."

After a fleeting kiss to her lips, Brodix gently set her away from him and walked out of her apartment, softly closing the door behind him. Sarah was proud of herself. She gave it a full ten seconds before bursting into tears. She was in love. What on earth was she supposed to do with that?

Chapter Nine

Sarah hadn't seen Brodix since she'd pushed him out of her apartment on Sunday. They'd talked every morning and every evening. In the middle of the day, Brodix often sent her naughty text messages. He told her he missed her, but work had kept him busy and he hadn't been able to get away. She'd emailed the rest of her interview questions, and she'd been pleased when he'd replied to all of them. The article was written and turned in. She'd written an incredible piece, but she wasn't sure Brodix would see it that way. Her stomach churned when she thought of him reading the article, or more specifically the part about how he'd found his foster mom dead. She'd waffled back and forth about whether or not to put it in there, but in the end, she'd left it. It was a better story for it and would grab readers' attention. It would be great for the grand opening, she just knew it. But would Brodix see it that way, or would he think she'd betrayed him? Used him to get what she wanted, a great front page story?

Yeah, she'd gotten what she wanted. He'd gotten what he'd wanted too, hadn't he? And even though she knew he was working—practically around the clock, thanks to the day job and trying to get ready for the grand opening of the restaurant—she worried maybe he didn't really want to see her anymore. That maybe he was making excuses. Was he done with her? Half of her knew Brodix would never be so despicable as to dump her without an explanation, but part of her, the part that had been hurt by Jack's infidelity, wondered.

Now it was Friday evening, and the grand opening of the restaurant would be fully underway. She was curious how it was going but was too chicken to call Brodix and find out. She was afraid of what he and the rest of the Jenningses thought of the article. Her editor had loved the piece. It hadn't been the headliner, but close enough that it should've helped bring in customers. And her career was finally beginning to get back on track. All great stuff. So why was she down in the dumps? Easy—because of Brodix. Her heart squeezed tight as she imagined his face when he read the paper. Would he hate her for what she'd had to say about him and his family?

She looked at the clock and groaned. Brodix was expecting her at the restaurant at seven o'clock, but she wasn't sure she wanted to go. She was afraid. Afraid Brodix would never share the same feelings for her that she felt for him Afraid he hated her now.

"God, loving a man isn't supposed to be this difficult," she muttered.

When her doorbell rang, Sarah's heartbeat sped up. Had he changed his mind about meeting at the restaurant and decided to pick her up instead?

Excitement skittered through her as she jogged across the room and yanked the door open. "Lucy," she said when she saw her coworker and best friend standing in the hall, a garment bag slung over one arm.

"Wow, don't sound so thrilled," she said, pushing her way inside the apartment. She'd pulled her long, straight dark hair into a high ponytail, and she wore a pair of old jeans with holes in the knees. With the tight, long-sleeved red V-neck T-shirt, Lucy appeared all of eighteen. Young and cute, that was Lucy. A burlap sack couldn't hide her friend's beauty. The garment bag Lucy carried in one hand caught Sarah's attention and she frowned, curious what was in it.

Sarah closed the door behind her. "I'm always happy to see you, of course, but I was expecting someone else."

"That hottie you told me about?" She tossed her load over the back of a chair and wagged her eyebrows. "The one in the article?"

Momentarily forgetting about the bag, Sarah plopped onto the couch, feeling ridiculously weepy. "Yeah, that one. We're meeting at the restaurant later."

"Then why the long face?"

"I'm not sure I'm going," she admitted.

"And why the hell not? He's gorgeous, and he's into you. As an added bonus, he owns the Blackwater Bar and Grill, which just happens to be the talk of the town. The place is a huge hit, babes." She sat next to her and patted Sarah's thigh. "Thanks to your article."

Sarah covered her eyes and let out a miserable groan. "I haven't been able to ask him what he thought of the article. I'm terrified he hated it. Scared because I revealed something personal."

"It'll be fine. He'll understand. Plus, you love him. So, there's that."

Sarah's head shot up, and she stared at Lucy. "Huh?"

"You're in love with him, but you don't know if he feels the same way. Am I close?"

"Dead on, but what gave me away?"

"If you could see yourself right now, you wouldn't have to ask. It's clear you haven't showered, and I'm betting you haven't eaten. You're lovesick."

"Great, so do you have a cure or what?"

"Yeah." She pointed to the black, zippered bag. "There's a dress in there with your name on it. We're going to that restaurant, and you're going to look hot as hell. He won't know what hit him. Then, while he's down for the count, you spring it on him. Tell him how you feel."

"And if it's not...reciprocal? If he hates me because I shared his personal tragedies with the entire county?"

"Kick him in the teeth," she helpfully supplied.

For the first time all day, Sarah laughed. "Wow, you're nuts, but I love you."

"Awesome. Now go shower." She wrinkled her nose. "Seriously."

An hour and a half later, Sarah found herself standing with

Lucy inside the Blackwater Bar and Grill. Several heads turned their way, and Sarah's face heated. "What was I even thinking wearing this thing," she grumbled. "I feel like I'm wearing two Band-Aids, for Christ's sake."

Lucy winked and looked her over from head to toe. "Yeah, but you look really hot. He'll have to drag his tongue off the floor once he gets a load of you. You'll see."

Sarah groaned, suddenly not so sure about anything. "And what about you, huh? I didn't even know you owned dresses like these."

She shrugged. "David used to want me to dress like a soccer mom. So of course, as soon as I kicked his mooching ass out, I bought several outfits that no soccer mom would ever be caught dead wearing."

Sarah looked at Lucy again. The dress she wore was black, strapless, and had triangle-shaped cutouts down the front, stopping just below her navel. She could see Lucy's cleavage through the little triangles. It was weird, but she hadn't realized Lucy even had cleavage. She looked sexy and wild. The purple streak down the left side of her long black hair seemed to shimmer in the low lighting. Sarah thought she looked exotic. With Lucy's large, almond-shaped blue eyes and full, unpainted lips, she could have passed for a runway model. She was a mysterious gypsy, and every man in the room would want a taste of her. Sarah hadn't realized Lucy could look so incredible.

Not that what Sarah wore was anything less than devastating. The figure-hugging, cream-colored silk dress had narrow strips of butter-soft cloth that wrapped around her breasts and hips. Falling well above her knees, it was the most lethal thing she'd ever worn. It left her midriff exposed, and Sarah had the urge to wrap her arms around her middle to hide the expanse of skin.

They'd been there for a while, making the rounds in the bar. Sarah had looked around for Brodix but came up empty. "Come on, I need a drink. Preferably something strong."

"Now you're talking," Lucy said with a grin.

Side by side, Lucy and Sarah strode up to the bar and

grabbed a couple of stools. The bartender came over straightaway. "What can I get you lovely ladies?"

"A cosmopolitan for me, thanks," Sarah said as she surreptitiously looked for Brodix.

"The same," Lucy answered, giving the man a beaming smile.

The bartender's eyes lit with warmth and lingered on Lucy's triangles as he murmured, "My pleasure, ma'am." As he went off to mix their drinks, Lucy leaned close and asked, "So, I heard they're looking for live music here, but they haven't found anyone that fits the bill. Has Brodix said anything?"

"No, I didn't know they were considering hiring a band." Her mind stuttered to a halt as she realized Lucy's intentions. "You want to audition." She stared at her friend. Lucy had the voice of an angel. "Oh wow, I don't know why I didn't think of it before. They're going to eat you up."

To Sarah's utter shock, Lucy blushed. An honest-to-goodness blush. She hadn't seen her friend blush once since they'd met five years ago. "I don't know about that, but I'm going to try." She slumped and looked down at the bar top. "Working at the *Gazette* as a copy editor pays the bills, but it's boring as snot. I need some excitement in my life, you know?"

"Just look at you. You're gorgeous, and every man in this place is staring. Heck, I wouldn't be surprised if our drinks were free with the way that bartender looked at you. Add in the fact you sing like a goddess and you're smart as hell, and they'd be crazy *not* to hire you."

"Yeah, well, we'll see. I'm not getting my hopes up, though."

When the bartender came back with their drinks—free, as Sarah had predicted—she watched on as Lucy graced the older man with a grin. The bartender began to stammer and turn red. Sarah bit back a smile. "I'm pretty sure he's old enough to be your dad," she whispered.

As she brought the drink to her lips, she saw a familiar face out of the corner of her eye. Sarah turned her head and saw Reilly walking through the kitchen door. His gaze zeroed in on her. She braced herself for his anger, and it hit her like a Mack truck. Okay, so at least one of the Jenningses hated the article after all. When his gaze landed on Lucy, though, the frown fell away to be replaced by a scorching amount of heat. Whoa.

Sarah nudged Lucy. "You have an admirer," she whispered in her ear.

Lucy followed her line of vision, and Sarah could swear her friend stopped breathing. The chemistry arcing back and forth between the two was something for the record books. When Reilly started toward them, Lucy stiffened.

"Hello, Sarah," Reilly said. "I read the article."

Sarah braced herself. "Oh?"

"I wasn't real thrilled about it at first. You had no call to share that bit about Brodix's foster mom," he said. "Brodix won't thank you, believe me."

Her hopes sank clear to the hardwood floor. "I'm sorry. I tried to skate over it as best I could, but without at least some personal information, the article never would've made it to the front page."

Reilly nodded, and his lips curved upward as if attempting to smile. "I know, and the grand opening is a hit, thanks to you."

"Oh, uh, thank you. I'm glad it helped." Sarah was surprised she could speak past the shock riding her body in that moment.

"Well, uh," he said, shifting from foot to foot, clearly uncomfortable. "River and I sort of owe you an apology," he said. "We misjudged you." His stiff voice had her hiding a grin. Sarah got the distinct impression that he rarely apologized.

She smiled and let him off the hook. "It's all water under the bridge."

He nodded; then his gaze darted toward Lucy once more. "Care to introduce me to your companion?"

"Lucy Rice," Sarah said, "this is Reilly Jennings. He's Brodix's younger brother."

Reilly took Lucy's hand in his, a gleam of arousal in his eyes. "It's a pleasure to meet you, Lucy."

"Likewise," Lucy said in a sultry, bedroom voice. Sarah suddenly felt like a third wheel.

Reilly's gaze came back to hers. "I would assume you're here for Brodix?"

"He said he'd meet me here at seven." Of course, that was nearly thirty minutes ago, not that she was watching the clock or anything. God, she was lame.

"I see," Reilly said, as his gaze swung back to Lucy. He stared at her as if she were the all-you-can-eat buffet. When he looked down at his watch, his brows furrowed. "He's not usually late. I'm not sure what's keeping him." Reilly nodded to the far corner of the room. "How about we grab a table until he gets here?"

"Sounds wonderful," Lucy quickly agreed.

"Ladies," Reilly said as he held out both arms. Sarah looked around one more time for Brodix, but when she came up empty, she sighed and took the arm Reilly held out for her.

He led them to a round table and held a chair for Lucy, then Sarah. As he sat in the chair closest to Lucy, he said, "You two look amazing, by the way." His gaze fairly devoured Lucy. When someone tapped Sarah on the shoulder, her heart caught in her throat. She turned her head, and her hopes plummeted. The handsome, tanned blond was most definitely not Brodix.

"You here alone, darlin'?" he asked her.

"I'm not sure," Sarah answered. It was nothing short of the truth, considering Brodix still hadn't shown up.

The man grinned and held out a hand. "In that case, care to dance with me until you figure it out?"

Unaccountably charmed, Sarah said, "Sure." She started to get up, but Reilly quickly stopped her with a large hand on her shoulder. "What?"

"You should wait for Brodix," he replied as he glared at the stranger.

"In case it escaped your notice, I've been waiting for Brodix for the last half hour now," she told him, more than a little miffed that Brodix had apparently stood her up. With her head high, Sarah turned to the man and smiled.

"Sarah," Reilly warned, the deep timbre of his voice nearly causing her to pause. Lucy leaned close to his ear, distracting him. Whatever she'd said caused Reilly to completely lose interest in Sarah.

The blond guy gave her his arm and leaned close to her ear to be heard over the music. "Name's Josh."

"Sarah," she replied as he led her out to the small dance floor.

Once there, Sarah became acutely aware the song they were about to dance to was a slow country tune. When Josh pulled her into his arms and began moving to the beat of the music, Sarah had to hold back tears. He wasn't Brodix. No man could compare to him. She couldn't shake the feeling that dancing with Josh felt like a betrayal to Brodix. *You belong to me,* he'd stated. Did she? And if so, then where was he? Her heart sank when she realized he might not show up at all.

"So, Sarah, what's a beautiful woman like you doing here alone?" Josh asked, his voice close enough that she could smell his minty breath.

"What's a handsome man like you doing alone?" she countered, wishing she hadn't noticed how strange Josh's arms felt around her waist. His firm build was nice, but it wasn't Brodix's firm build. The knowledge made her want to scream.

"I aim to change that," he drawled in a sexy Texas accent Sarah knew the women probably loved.

When he tugged her in tight, Sarah went stiff as a board. He was big and muscular, handsome and polite. His deep voice was as soft as crushed velvet. Nope, not a single thing wrong with Josh. Still, there was only one man she wanted pressed up close to her body. One man who could make her insides hum with desire in ten seconds flat. And she was just so damn pissed he wasn't the one holding her now.

"Relax, darlin'," he urged her, "I don't bite unless asked."

Sarah shook her head. "You're a nice guy, Josh, but your timing is a bit off."

Josh pulled back and looked into her eyes. Several seconds passed before he glanced back over to where Lucy and Reilly sat. "I know you aren't with that big dark-haired fella, because he's all over your girlfriend. So, who is it that's keeping me from having a snowball's chance tonight?"

Sarah tried not to feel the kick in her gut as she thought of Brodix. She looked away from Josh's suddenly serious brown eyes. "The big fella's brother. Although I'm not entirely sure he's still interested in me."

"Ah, so it's like that," Josh replied as he pulled her back into his embrace. This time, he didn't try to get so close. As a matter of fact, it seemed as if the intensity that had been there a moment ago was gone. He'd obviously admitted defeat with remarkable aplomb. "Don't look now, darlin', but I think the brother just walked in the door. Judging by the look on his face, he's none too happy with me either."

Sarah started to swivel her head around to see Brodix. It'd been too long, and she missed him terribly. Josh stopped her before she could, and she frowned up at him. "What are you doing?"

"You want him to come after you, don't you?" How had he guessed? Josh chuckled. "It's as plain as the nose on your pretty face."

"I'm hopeless, aren't I?"

"Nah, just in love."

"He probably couldn't care less if I'm dancing with another man. This whole thing is stupid," Sarah ground out, feeling more and more like a fool.

He bent low and whispered, "Don't bet on it. It's eating him up watching me tell you all my dirty little fantasies right now, trust me."

Hope took root. "It is?"

"Hell, he never even made it past the front door," he said, a hint of mischief in his tone. "He's just standing there, looking for all the world like a raging bull ready to charge."

A little thrill went through her. Brodix did care? "So you

think if I do this," she asked, getting close to his ear, "then he'll maybe get the lead out?"

He chuckled. "Oh, I guarantee it."

Sarah laughed as she swatted Josh's arm. "You're pure trouble, aren't you?"

"Damn straight, darlin'." Josh straightened, and he appeared more alert. "Ah hell, here he comes." He kept his arms around her and whistled low. "You might've mentioned the fact he was bigger than the other one."

"Sarah."

The deep, dark voice was barely recognizable it was so cold and remote. Where was the warm, cajoling tone she remembered? She turned her head and tried to pretend she wasn't dying inside. "Brodix, I didn't realize you were here."

"I can see that," he ground out and pinned Josh with a steely look. "Mind if I cut in?"

Sarah looked back at Josh and saw the mischievous glint in his eyes. She willed him to say no. Bloodshed would be mega-bad for the grand opening. When he dropped his arms and stepped back, Sarah breathed a sigh of relief. As Brodix took her into his arms, Sarah gave up on holding back the tears.

He frowned and touched her cheek with the pad of his thumb. "Why are you crying? Did he hurt you?"

"N-no," she stammered. "Not him," she said as she buried her face in his shirt, giving her tears free rein.

Chapter Ten

Brodix had been ready to spit nails when he'd seen Sarah in the arms of another man. Anger had rolled through him like a runaway freight train. Only seeing Sarah's tears could dry his rage as quickly as it had. Damn it, he needed to get to the bottom of this, but that sure as hell wasn't going to happen if they stayed on the crowded dance floor. "Come on," he urged, then tugged her in the direction of the kitchen.

She wiped her face with the back of her hand, as if attempting to gain control. "Where?"

"We need some privacy," he explained. He took her to the back office. When he opened the door, he found Julie there, working on the computer.

She looked up, saw Sarah pressed to his side, and frowned. "Brodix?"

He shook his head. "Could you give us a minute?"

"Of course." She got to her feet and moved around the desk. When she drew closer to Sarah, Julie's eyes rounded. "Oh, I recognize you from the newspaper. The article you wrote about the Jennings family was wonderful." She laughed. "You made Wanda a popular lady down at the beauty salon." She held out a hand. "I'm Julie, Sam's better half. I'm sorry I missed you at the picnic. I got caught up working on a paper for one of my classes. By the time I arrived, you and Brodix had already left."

Sarah smiled, but Brodix could tell it was forced. "We left a bit early, I'm afraid," she said, her voice still a little wobbly. She shook Julie's hand. "It's nice to finally meet you, Julie."

"Likewise." Julie looked over at Brodix and winked. "I'll just leave you two to talk."

"Thanks," he said, grateful that she seemed to understand they needed privacy. After she was gone, Brodix turned to Sarah. "You were crying," he murmured and cupped her face in his palms. "The first time I've seen you since Sunday night, and you're in the arms of another man and you're crying. What's going on, sweetheart?"

She shook her head. "The dance didn't mean anything. He asked, and I said yes. It wasn't anything more than that." She slumped and squeezed her eyes closed tight. "I was just frustrated because I thought you had stood me up."

"We'll talk about you dancing with other men in a minute. First, why would I stand you up? And what's with the tears?"

Sarah tried to pull away, but Brodix wasn't having it. She gave up finally and muttered, "I'm afraid."

Brodix scowled. "Afraid? Of What?" Then a nasty thought struck, and he asked, "Did Jack come around again? Is he harassing you?"

She snorted. "No, nothing like that. That would require effort on his part, something he's not real big on."

"Then I'm lost," he said, as he dropped his hands to his sides. "Help me out here."

"I love you, okay?" She smacked his chest, her voice rising with each syllable. "I'm crazy in love with you, you big dork!"

Brodix felt like he'd fallen down the rabbit hole. "Wait, you were crying because you love me?"

"No," she bit out. "I'm crying because I'm afraid that *you* don't love *me*. That you might never love me."

He released her hand and stepped away from her, shutting down as he recalled the front page of the *Gazette*. "Is that why you put Mrs. Beatty's suicide in the article?" His gaze hardened. "Because you love me?"

Sarah's face paled as if he'd slapped her. Hell, she looked shattered. Brodix wanted to fix it, but he needed to know her reasons behind the article first. "I'm sorry, but you did know I was writing a human-interest piece. Did you think I could do that without putting at least something *interesting* in there?"

"You knew that was private," he bit out. "If I'd wanted it shared with the world, I would've done so myself."

"If you read the article, then you know I tried my best to gloss over that part to some degree." She blushed, and God help him, it turned Brodix on. "But the article never would've made the front page if I'd treated the story with kid gloves."

He stood there for a moment, absorbing her words. "I know, but what I don't understand is why you did it. Was it for us? For the restaurant? Or was it merely to salvage your reputation?"

Sarah looked down away. "At first I only wanted to gain back my credibility, but that changed."

"When did it change?"

"When I fell in love with you," she softly admitted. "I don't care about my position at the paper. I only care about you."

A tear trickled down Sarah's cheek, and Brodix knew she was telling the truth. His heart swelled at the confession, and emotion slammed through him. "The restaurant hasn't seen so many customers the whole of last year," he replied. "I think folks around had forgotten about the diner, but because of what you put in the article, it reminded everyone what our family went through. Living in Blackwater is part of what healed us. We're a hit. If Dad were alive today he'd be damn proud."

Sarah blinked several times as if unable to believe her own ears. "Does this mean you don't hate me?"

"I'm not as naïve as you might think, sweetheart. I had a feeling you might use a little of what I shared with you in the article." Now, Brodix decided, would be the perfect time to show her the gift he'd bought her. He reached into his jacket pocket and brought out the small black velvet jewelry box he'd tucked in there earlier. "And I was late because I stopped off to buy this," he murmured as he opened the lid.

Sarah gasped. "Oh, Brodix, it's exquisite!"

The gold necklace with the single pearl drop in the center lay in a bed of white satin. "I wanted to get you something special." He shrugged. "Something to show you I care."

She quirked a brow as she touched the pearl with a single finger. "And maybe that you love me?"

He chuckled. "Determined to hear me say it, huh?"

She shrugged. "If you don't mind, I really need to hear it. Please?"

"I love you," he whispered. "I'm not sure I've ever been in love, so I might screw up a time or two." One corner of his lips kicked upward. "Fair warning."

"Screwing up I can handle," she said, her voice quivering as she closed the gap between them and wrapped her arms around his waist, hugging him tight. "But letting you go would kill me."

"I told you before, sweetheart, I'd fight like hell to keep you." He slid his hand in her hair and tugged, forcing her to look at him. When he was staring into her pretty blue gaze, Brodix growled, "I meant it." He pressed his lips to hers and kissed her with all the passion and love coursing through him. His mouth was rough and demanding as he ravaged her mouth. "Open," he softly ordered against her lips. When she gave him access to the sweet warmth of her mouth, Brodix swooped in, drinking in her moans of pleasure. When he lifted his head, they were both panting and turned on, but there was one other little matter to settle.

"Now, about that dance," he muttered.

She shook her head vehemently. "I told you, it was nothing."

"Hmm, remember that little swat I gave you before?" Her cheeks turned a delicate shade of red as she nodded. "Well, you can look forward to several more of those later tonight."

Her eyes darkened with arousal. "How much later?" she asked.

He cursed and took hold of her hand. "Come on. We're out of here."

She didn't budge. "But don't you need to stay? It's the grand opening."

"The others can handle it, believe me."

"You're sure you don't hate me because of the article?" she

asked in a small voice, betraying a touch of vulnerability. "I didn't want to disappoint you."

He stroked her bottom lip with his thumb, loving the soft feel of her. "I'll only be disappointed if you don't move those sexy heels you're wearing and come home with me," he replied, his voice rough with need. "I'm dying to hold you in my arms, sweetheart. I've missed you like hell."

"God, I've missed you too," she moaned. She took hold of his wrist and kissed the pad of his thumb. "So much it hurts."

"I'm sorry I've been so busy, sweetheart," he murmured. "Although, I'm betting you're going to love what I have to tell you next."

"What's that?"

"I've quit the day job. I'm devoting all my time to running the restaurant."

Her gaze widened. "Wow, seriously?"

Brodix grinned, feeling better than he had in months. "Yep. With everyone working two jobs, we decided that the restaurant needed at least one of us here full-time." He shrugged. "I'm done with working around the clock. From now on, I aim to have plenty of spare time to do this..."

Then, in a wild show of possession, Brodix took her mouth. Sarah's arms wound around his neck, and she sank into his kiss. She could scarcely hold back a shudder of need as he ran his tongue along the seam of her lips, and she obliged him by parting them. Her heart began a rapid staccato at the now familiar taste of him. Brodix hummed his approval and teased her tongue with his. When he finally pulled away, she was panting, and her lips were wet and kiss-swollen.

"Let's go home," he whispered.

"Yes," she breathed out, a smile curving her lips. "Let's go home."

About the Author

Anne grew up in a small town in central Ohio the only girl with three rowdy, older brothers. When she wasn't playing tackle football with them she could be found tucked away in her mother's book room getting lost in mysterious worlds created by authors such as Martha Grimes and Andrew M. Greeley. She's had a variety of odd jobs including Chiropractic Assistant, Frame Stylist, Restaurant Hostess, and Nail Technician.

Anne now lives with her fabulous husband, two gorgeous teenage daughters, two ornery dogs, three snooty cats and a snake named Salizar. When Anne's not dressing, feeding, cleaning or spending time with them, she can be found at the computer writing stories hot enough to make your toes curl!

Anne loves to hear from her readers. You can find her on Facebook at www.facebook.com/pages/Anne-Rainey-Fan-Page/121274891238824 or email her directly at annerainey11@gmail.com. Join her newsletter for updates on new releases, signings and contests for a chance to win books. The link to join is on the front of her webpage at www.annerainey.com.

Taking turns was never their strong suit…

What She Needs
© 2011 Anne Rainey
Cape May, Book 3

Devon Mason and Con Walker are sexy, honorable, loving, and completely devoted. In other words, everything Tory looks for in a relationship. But what's she supposed to buy her two lovers on V Day? Chocolate? How average is that? Their little love triangle is anything but average!

When Con surprises her with a weekend in Cancun, just the three of them, Tory is all over it—until she realizes Con forgot to include Devon in the package. Now their little love triangle is suffering, thanks to a couple of hard-headed men who both want to be numero uno.

Con was content to let Devon take control at Christmas, but now it's his turn. A weekend in Cancun seems the perfect place for a romantic getaway—then Devon says he's planning to surprise Tory with a trip to Aruba, and Con's possessive instincts kick in. He'd always been happy to share Tory with the guy he cares for like a brother. But the deeper Con falls in love, the harder it is to keep from ripping Tory away from Devon.

Sooner or later something—or someone—is going to give.

Warning: This title contains lots of steamy, explicit sex. Hot, jealous men in need of a strong, intelligent woman. And a warm, loving ménage a trois relationship.

Available now in ebook from Samhain Publishing.

One spark could burn her world down.

Keeping Pace
© 2011 Dee Carney

Six years after her husband's death, Regina Pace is still just going through the motions, her only pleasure a nightly glass (or three) of wine to dull the ache. Tonight is no exception—until a sensual outdoor encounter with her neighbor's son, freshly home from college. He's older, wiser, more devastatingly handsome than she remembered. He's also fifteen years her junior.

Despite her misgivings, it isn't long before her nightly ritual includes a long, deep drink of Josh Smith. Ogling leads to touching, then the sparks flare into an erotic encounter that feels wickedly right—and deliciously forbidden.

Yet the intense heat can't burn away the doubt pestering the back of her mind. That the gap between their ages is too large, even for the most determined leap of faith…

Warning: Features a boy-next-door who won't take no for an answer, more than one sexual fantasy (including some outdoor self-loving!), and a burning romance that proves age is just a number.

Available now in ebook from Samhain Publishing.

SAMHAIN
PUBLISHING

It's all about the story...

Romance

HORROR

Retro ROMANCE

www.samhainpublishing.com

CPSIA information can be obtained at www.ICGtesting.com
Printed in the USA
BVOW08s1811220615

405627BV00002B/18/P

9 781619 223363